Judy Mays

Celestial Passions : Sheala

ELLORA'S CAVE
ROMANTICA PUBLISHING

What the critics are saying...

&

"The second in Judy Mays' *Celestial Passions* series is just as full of sex, action, sex, intrigue, sex, nefarious deeds and (did I mention) sex! [...] With the cast of characters from the previous story as well as a few new ones, Ms. Mays has developed and breathed life into a new universe for her readers to become so engrossed in that I wouldn't have been surprised if I saw a Gattan male walking down the street!" ~ *A Romance Review*

"With this offering, Ms. Mays is certainly rocketed to being one of my favorite authors complete with the honor of prominent positioning on my bedside table." ~ *ECataRomance Reviews*

"I adore Ms. Mays' werewolf books but her science fiction romance books are my favorite. Ms. Mays has created an interesting, diverse world and I love her characters—they seem like old friends." ~ *Paranormal Romance Reviews*

"Hurry over to Ellora's Cave to get your copy of SHEALA and enjoy a satisfying romance that'll keep you warm all over." ~ *Romance Review Today*

"I loved this book! [...] Ms. Mays pens a wonderful futuristic love story that is sure to be the favorite of readers for many years to come. Celestial Passions: Sheala can be read as a stand alone novel but for the sake of consistency I recommend reading both books in this fabulous series of love on other worlds." ~ *Coffee Time Romance*

"Wow, this was a wonderful book. The worlds that **Judy Mays** has created were so well described that it was possible to 'see' everything that was happening." ~ *Fallen Angel Review*

An Ellora's Cave Romantica Publication

www.ellorascave.com

Sheala

ISBN 9781419955891
ALL RIGHTS RESERVED.
Sheala Copyright © 2006 Judy Mays
Edited by Raelene Gorlinsky and Nicholas Conrad.
Cover art by Syneca.

This book printed in the U.S.A. by Jasmine–Jade Enterprises, LLC

Electronic book Publication January 2006
Trade paperback Publication July 2007

Also by Judy Mays

&

About the Author

∽

Foxier than a Hollywood starlette! More buxom than a Vegas show girl! Able to undangle participles with a single key stroke!

Look! At the computer!

It's a programer!

It's a computer nerd!

No! It's—Judy Mays!

Yes, Judy Mays—romantica writer extraordinaire who came to Earth with powers and ablilities far beyond those of mortal writers. Judy Mays! Who can write wild, wanton werewolves, assertive, alluring aliens and vexing, vivacious vamps. Who, desguised as a mild-mannered English teacher in a small Pennsylvania high school, fights a never ending battle for Heroic Hunks, Hot Heroines, and Sexy Sensuality!

Judy welcomes comments from readers. You can find her website and email address on her author bio page at www.ellorascave.com.

Tell Us What You Think
We appreciate hearing reader opinions about our books. You can email us at Comments@EllorasCave.com.

SHEALA
Celestial Passions

ഌ

Prologue

ૹ

"Brianna, I'd like you to meet my sex instructor, Bogarton don al' Chevin."

Immediately, Sheala slapped her hand to her mouth to cover her giggle as her sister-in-law halted in mid-waddle—she was so very pregnant—and gaped at her for a full thirty seconds before snapping her mouth shut.

"Your what!"

Sheala grinned. Brianna's reactions to the relaxed attitude about sex here on Drakan were priceless. "My sex instructor."

Brianna blinked then slowly lifted her hand to the…man—he was actually a hermaphrodite—at Sheala's side.

Chevin slid his knuckles under her fingertips and lifted her hand to his lips. "I'm honored to make your acquaintance, Alalakan dem al' Brianna. Sheala told me you were beautiful but her words pale next to the reality of your breathtaking personage. Are you, perhaps, interested in instruction of various Drakian sexual techniques?"

Another hand appeared and lifted Brianna's from Chevin's. "I'm quite capable of providing all the instruction my wife needs," Char said in an amused tone as he pulled Brianna to his side.

The older man smiled and nodded his head. "I understand completely." Turning, he held his arm out for Sheala. "Walk me to my transport, Sheala. I want to discuss how you used your tongue on my penis."

Char's laughter at his wife's bright red complexion followed his sister and her companion down the hallway.

"I can't believe you hired a man to teach Sheala how to have sex!" Brianna exclaimed as Char guided her into his study. "She's only seventeen!"

Still grinning broadly, Char kissed the top of his wife's fiery head. "Sheala will be eighteen soon, and we want her to be prepared and educated when she finally has sex. I warned you about our ways. Sex is very important to Drakians."

"Important my ass. You people are fixated on it."

"On your ass?" Char asked with an even wider grin. "I admit to my guilt. You have such a lovely ass."

Huffing with exasperation, Brianna settled into a comfortable chair next to a small table and shuffled some papers.

Char sauntered to his wife's side and looked down. "What are you working on now? You've managed to align Drakan's alphabet with Earth's."

Brianna glanced up.

His gaze was fixed on her breasts, not on the papers in her hands.

"You have a one-track mind."

His grin became lascivious. "You have beautiful breasts."

She smiled slowly. "My ass or my breasts. Make up your mind."

He bent and kissed the exact spot where her neck and shoulder met. "All of you."

Shivering, Brianna stared unseeing as he cupped her right breast and squeezed.

Then she blinked—and blinked again. Leaning forward, she stared at the numbers on the paper in front of her. "Drakan takes four hundred and twelve days to go around your sun."

"So?" Char kissed the other side of her neck.

"Earth only takes three hundred and sixty-five days to go around our sun."

"So?" He cupped both breasts.

"In Earth years, Sheala's over twenty."

Char lifted his head and looked into his wife's face. "This matters to you?"

She shrugged. "Seventeen just seemed so young..."

"To have a sex instructor?" Char grinned. "I thought you were losing your prudish ways."

She elbowed his hard stomach. "I'm not a prude."

He chuckled and pulled her to her feet. "No, you aren't—only some of your ideas are."

"My ideas are—"

He silenced her with long, hard kiss then lifted his head. "We're alone."

Brianna looked down at her stomach. "No, we aren't."

Char spread his hand over her swollen abdomen, smiling as a small foot kicked it. How had he gotten so lucky?

Chapter One

ഇ

"I do *not* like this plan!" Crossing his arms over his chest, Marljas scowled at his older brother.

Leaning back in his chair, Wendjas raked his hair back behind his tufted ears. "Mother and the matriarchs have decided trade is better than war. We have no choice."

"Why our family and not another? Why not the ambassador on Drakan?"

Wendjas looked up into his brother's face. "Because we've had contact with the Alalakans."

Marljas snorted. "If you can call a blood challenge contact."

The corners of Wendjas' mouth twitched. "A challenge met, fought and settled with honor."

Marljas continued to stare at his brother. "The *Leonine* are only one tribe. What of the others? Except for the ambassador on Drakan and a few others, the *Tigre* will choose war."

Extending the claw from his index finger, Wendjas gouged a thin line across the top of the battered table that stood between them. "The Queen sides with us."

Dropping his arms to his sides, Marljas didn't bother to hide his astonishment. "The Queen goes against her own tribe?"

Wendjas nodded. "In the months you've been gone, she and Deni have been in close contact. She agrees that we can't defeat the combined might of Drakan and Mediria. They're too powerful and too closely allied. That's not even taking into account those damned Medirian assassins. Any war with them would be long and bitter. And—Gattan would lose."

Snarling, Marljas turned away. "I know. I've spent enough time on those two planets in the last two years to know that. But this fighting with words goes against everything I am, everything a Gattan is. The sweat and blood of combat is far more satisfying than spitting words across a table. What's a man to do if he can't fight?"

Wendjas smiled. "Mother only needs to find you the right wife if you want to fight."

Marljas smiled back and glanced towards his brother's heavy biceps and thick neck. "I thought I noticed a few new scars."

His smile exploding into a full-fledged grin, Wendjas nodded. "Denieen isn't afraid to use her claws. A man couldn't have a better wife."

Smile fading, Marljas stared into his brother's face. "You can't make her stay home with your sons?"

"Make Denieen stay home? How?"

Marljas jerked his gaze away from his brother's face. That was a truly stupid question. No Gattan could make his wife do what she didn't want to do.

Wendjas' chuckle pulled Marljas' attention back. "The matriarchs insist on a representative. She's the best choice."

"Why take your sons, Wendjas?"

"With my wife and sons along, the Drakians won't be suspicious of ulterior motives."

"But we don't have any ulterior motives!"

Shoving his chair away from the table, Wendjas rose and began to pace. "I know. But neither Mother nor Denieen will be swayed from their plan."

Marljas' snarl echoed around the room. "Brother, we go undefended. What if you're wrong about this Drakian? You practically gutted him. He may seek revenge. A Gattan *would* seek revenge."

Wendjas shook his head. "He is Drakian, not Gattan, and

we've learned he has married."

"Women on other planets are not like ours."

Wendjas chuckled again. "Brother, you have a great deal to learn about women. Besides, the Alalakans have always been far more interested in trade rather than war. More of our people should be so inclined."

Marljas snorted. "Conquest is far more satisfying."

The table shook when Wendjas slapped both palms against it. "By all the levels of hell, we've been over and over this. We *cannot* win that war."

Stepping back, Marljas blew out a deep breath and held up both hands. "I know, I know. I've agreed to Mother's plan. But your sons, at least, should stay here."

A very sharp claw was pressed against his throat.

"Do you doubt my ability to protect my children, brother of my husband?"

Very carefully, Marljas swallowed both the harsh words that threatened to leap from his mouth and the temper that demanded he defend himself. A scar placed on his neck or throat by any woman other than his wife was a mark of shame rather than honor. But this was his brother's wife, his mother's daughter-by-marriage. At least there wasn't anyone here but his brother to see his humiliation. Besides, his slightest move towards Denieen would have his brother leaping to his wife's defense. The last time he sparred with Wendjas, it had taken a month for his cuts and bruises to heal.

He let out another deep breath. "I don't doubt your ability, Deni, but you can't keep them by your side at all times. What of treachery?"

The claw disappeared from his neck, and Deni crossed the room to stand next to her husband. "There's more treachery on Gattan at the Queen's court. And they're looking forward to their adventure. I wouldn't want to disappoint them."

Marljas dipped his head to hide the frustration he knew

was in his eyes. Any argument with Deni was one he would lose. Better to let Wendjas handle his headstrong wife. "I bow to your superior knowledge."

Sighing with exasperation, Denieen shook her head. "It's past time you were married, Marljas. You need a wife to guide you." Then her voice softened. "Is everything arranged?"

Marljas nodded. "The *Scrathe* is ready. How you managed to get the queen to agree to this..." He paused. His voice became troubled. "Deni, are you sure? Must you take your sons? No Gattan children have ever left our planet. They could be used as hostages. You know both your parents and mine would give anything to get them back. How do we know this Drakian can be trusted?"

Laughing, Denieen turned to her husband.

Wendjas smiled at her and she smiled back. At least one man in this household trusted her completely. Denieen glanced back to Marljas. She understood his misgivings. But the Alalakan clan of Drakan was as honorable as any Gattan tribe. "Hostages? Alalakan don al' Chardadon take children as hostages? He would sooner cut his own throat first."

* * * * *

"Are my breasts too big?"

Arms flailing as she tried to stop in mid-dive, Vani did a spectacular belly flop into the pool. She came up sputtering. "What are you talking about?"

Sheala cupped her full, bare breasts and jiggled them. "Are they too big? Crystas said they were."

Wiping water from her eyes, Vani splashed over to Sheala's side. "When are you going to stop believing everything Crystas told you? She's gone. Stop thinking about what she said."

Dropping her hands to her sides, Sheala shrugged. "But men, a lot of men, think she's beautiful."

17

Vani wiped water out of her face. "That's what she *told* you. She was jealous because you're far more attractive. Almost everything she said was a lie!"

Sheala jiggled again. "But they are bigger than any of my Drakian friends' breasts."

Snorting with frustration, Vani cupped her own. "Are mine too big?"

Sheala shook her head. "Of course not, but you're Medirian. I'm not."

Vani splashed Sheala. "You're part Medirian, and the Medirian blood makes you more exotic. There's something different about you, and you know how Drakians love what's different."

Sheala smiled. "That's true." She slid off the side of the pool and into the water. "I can't wait for my birthday. I'll finally be able to take a lover."

Vani slicked her dark green hair back over her forehead. "Talk about switching the subject of a conversation."

Reaching above her head, Sheala stretched. "Maybe if Mother and Father hadn't gotten me an instructor on sexual satisfaction it wouldn't be so bad. But..." She shivered. "The things he did to my body and I did to his! And always stopping before he penetrated me." Sheala stared at her friend. "There were times I thought I'd die of frustration!"

Vani cocked an eyebrow. "He didn't teach you how to satisfy yourself?"

Sheala flicked some water into her friend's face. "Of course. That was the first thing he taught me. But it's not enough, not anymore. I want more. I need to feel a man inside of me."

Vani splashed her again. "Quit complaining. You're the one who had to be dramatic and announce you were going to remain a virgin."

Sheala splashed back. "And look at the prestige it's brought to the clan. It's been three generations since an

Alalakan retained his or her virginity until reaching majority. And I get to wear this cool nose stud."

Vani stopped splashing. "Cool?"

Sheala slapped a sheet of water towards her friend. "One of Brianna's Earth words. It means really wonderful or something like that." Sheala shivered and rubbed her arms.

Water dripped from her pebbled nipples.

"I want a man."

Vani shook her head. "You can't have it both ways, Shea. Either you stay a virgin three more weeks or you find a man and satisfy your cravings." With those words, Vani dove beneath the water, grabbed her friend's ankles, and pulled her under.

When she let go, Sheala exploded to the surface.

Vani sank to the bottom in the deepest part of the pool.

"Not fair!" Sheala yelled as she slapped the water. "I don't have gills!"

Vani's sister Jami exploded through the hedges and skidded to a stop next to the pool. "Shea! Vani! Come quick. A Gattan warbird has landed on the estate!"

Sheala gaped at Jami then snapped her mouth shut. "A Gattan warbird? Are you sure? Gattans never stay anywhere but at their embassy. Why would they come here?"

"What if they came for Ban?" Vani asked as she surged upward out of the pool. "I heard the Gattan ambassador tell Mother and Father that a girl Ban had been with on Gattan had disappeared, and her family thinks she left Gattan with him."

Jami grabbed Sheala's hand and pulled her out of the pool. "I don't know. Gattans never do anything without a reason, and coming here to your estate is unprecedented. But it must be safe. Char took Brianna with him to greet them, and you know your brother would never put his wife in any danger."

Shrugging into their robes, Sheala and Vani followed Jami

back to the house at a dead run.

* * * * *

Skidding to a halt a few feet before she reached the door to the study, Sheala shot a warning glance to her friends, took a deep breath and gathered her composure. If there were Gattans here, her parents wouldn't appreciate her running into the room like an undisciplined child. And judging from all the voices, the entire family plus some of the guests were in the room with her parents. After another deep breath, she motioned her friends forward into the crowded room.

Once inside, a cacophony of voices surrounded them. She'd been right. Everybody was there. As a matter of fact, there were so many people in the room, she couldn't see any strangers.

Her gaze swept the room once, twice…

…and jerked to a halt on an especially tall, golden-haired, half-naked Gattan whose back was turned to her. The noisy conversation faded to a dull murmur as Sheala stared at him.

She swallowed, then swallowed again as her gaze slid up and down his muscular body. His shoulders were broad, his waist was trim. Thick, golden hair, combed behind his tufted, pointed ears, cascaded in thick waves down to the middle of his back. The soft leather pants he wore clung to his behind…

Sheala shivered. Damn but he had a great backside.

She stared closer. Like her, he had a tail, though his didn't look nearly as supple and had a tuft of golden hair at the end.

It jerked once, twice, then stilled.

Why? Was he annoyed?

The redheaded Gattan woman standing next to him nudged his arm, and he turned around.

Sheala's stomach tightened then rolled.

He was the most compelling man she'd ever seen.

Though he was clean-shaven, she was sure he would

sport a full golden beard if he so chose. His nose was somewhat flatter and wider than she was used to but was by no means unattractive. Thick honey-colored eyebrows rode over piercing golden eyes that moved constantly about the room as if he were searching for—what?

Sheala mentally shrugged. He was probably nervous considering he was surrounded by strangers. She let her gaze drifted down over his strong chin and wide shoulders to his bare chest. Besides the three obviously fresh cuts visible above his right pectoral, numerous other white scars shone against the dark golden-brown skin of his muscular chest. Her stomach rolled again. No Drakian or Medirian had a chest so broad! Only the Aradab were more muscular. She turned her attention to his muscular arms. His upper arms were bare, except for more white scars, but he wore sheaths with red-diamond-tipped daggers on both wrists.

So many scars! How did he get them all? Fighting?

Sheala shivered.

Upon his return from a journey to Gattan, her brother Char had told them about Gattan bloodfeuds, but she'd thought he'd been exaggerating to make his stories more exciting. She stared at the scars. Maybe he'd been telling the truth.

Dragging her gaze away from his arms, she admired the thick belt of the red gold native to his planet. Embedded in its elaborately carved buckle was a large red diamond.

She shook her head. She'd never seen a man wear so many jewels and precious metals that looked so deadly, but then, the man wearing them was far more interesting.

Her perusal dipped lower. The dark leather pants he wore hugged his body, revealing powerful thighs. Boots of the same type of soft brown leather reached to his knees. A boot sheath held a dagger with another red diamond on its hilt.

Sheala trailed her gaze back up his calves and thighs, stopped at the bulge between his legs. A shiver danced up her spine. *Wow! I'd love to see him naked.*

A picture of him nude and looming over her appeared in her mind. She closed her eyes as she imagined his big, strong hands cupping her breasts.

"What's going on? I can't see."

Vani's voice wrenched Sheala from her fantasy, and she forced herself back to the present.

"Brianna's become a bloodsister or something like that to Marljas, the Gattan with his vest off. That's how he got those fresh cuts on his chest. The others are Marljas' brother Wendjas, Wendjas' wife Denieen, and their twin sons. Now, be quiet. I'll tell you everything later," Vani's oldest sister Meri hissed.

Sheala returned her stare to the bare-chested Gattan. Marljas, a strong, interesting name.

And that beautiful Gattan woman was his sister-in-law — not his wife...

Stomach rolling, sweat trickling down his back, Marljas fought the urge to unsheathe his claws. Things had already gotten out of control. He hadn't even been on Drakan half an hour and already he'd acquired a new — alien — bloodsister. Why had Alalakan don al' Chardadon's wife dragged her hand across his claws like that? Had she known the consequences of her actions? She'd seemed shocked when Denieen had explained what she had done. Worse, Denieen had then further compounded the awkwardness of the situation by demanding he complete the blood rite and take this woman as a bloodsister.

What's more, his sister-by-marriage had then confirmed that Gattan was ruled by the queen rather than the king, that their society was matriarchal. Why? The Varcians especially would view the Gattan as weak because their women had so much power.

And now, the two women, Deni and this Brianna, had

decided he had to have an Alalakan clan tattoo. He was Gattan, not Drakian! The only marks on him should be challenge and battle scars!

What was Deni doing? She was discarding traditions left and right!

Only half listening to the chatter going on around him, Marljas shifted his weight. The cuts he'd clawed on his chest to complete the blood ritual with Brianna burned but the pain was nothing. He'd experienced much worse in duels. Still, he couldn't relax. His tail bumped against something or someone, and he forced himself to hold it still, except for the tip which continued to twitch. There were too many people here, too many strangers, too many people from other planets. This Brianna was from Earth, a planet no one else in their galaxy had known existed, and at least half a dozen Medirians were spaced around the room. He glanced at a dark green, muscular man standing with his arms crossed. A Medirian Aradab. Everyone knew the Aradab race of Medirians were all assassins. Why had he ever agreed to bring his brother's family here? He flexed his claws. He'd fight to the death to protect them if he had to.

He flared his nostrils at a burst of female laughter. Denieen was certainly making herself at home, chatting away as if she'd known the other women in the room for years. Why? How could she trust them so easily?

Unease slid through his body. There was danger here, he just knew it. He stiffened; he was being watched. Slowly, he turned and causally glanced at everyone in the room, not hesitating to frown when his gaze collided with Bandalardrac Hardan's, one of the few people in the room he already knew.

Worthless Drakian–Medirian bastard! How the king of Mediria could tolerate his nephew's womanizing Marljas couldn't understand. And the Alalakans? Even if the half-breed was cousin to Chardadon, why have him here? All he'd do was cause trouble with the female servants. And no matter what anyone said, Marljas still believed the half-breed had kidnapped the Gattan girl who'd disappeared last year. Sosha was young. She had been out of her depth with a depraved rake like him. Even if she had gone with him willingly, she'd still been kidnapped as far as Marljas was concerned.

The other man crossed his arms over his chest and grinned at him.

Fop! Marljas snarled to himself as Ban turned his attention to the man at his side. The half-breed would pay for Sosha's disappearance.

Snarling silently, Marljas jerked his attention away from Ban. Someone else was watching him — closely. Sliding his gaze left, Marljas continued to peruse the room — and stopped on a young woman wrapped in a silky green robe standing against the far wall. His senses tingled. It was her. She was the one who was staring at him with such intensity that he'd sensed it, and now her stare was concentrated below his waist.

Marljas stared at her face. She was pretty, for a woman who wasn't Gattan. She was also, judging by the resemblance to Alalakan dem al' Xdana, his hostess, a close relative, probably a daughter.

He shook his head mentally. Even if she was interested in him, a smart Gattan didn't become involved in any way with his hostess's daughter. His mother would never forgive him such an appalling breach of etiquette! Besides, the last thing he needed was a Drakian female chasing after him.

One of her friends whispered something into the girl's ear, and she pulled her gaze from his crotch to glance back over her shoulder. She nodded and looked back. This time he caught her gaze with his. Extending the claw on his index finger, he crossed his arms, purposely scratching himself on his left biceps. A small drop of blood trickled down over his arm.

Momentarily, her eyes widened. Then she jerked her gaze away.

Placing his finger over the scrape, Marljas applied

pressure to stop the bleeding and looked away. Smiling to himself, he returned his attention to the conversation at hand. Claws and blood. It worked every time to scare away unwanted attention from non-Gattan females.

"Sheala," his hostess said, "you, Jami and Vani should go get ready for dinner."

Marljas glanced back towards the girls as they turned and left the room. Sheala. An interesting name.

Bandalardrac leaned against the wall and unobtrusively watched Marljas. The young Gattan's gaze had drifted more than once to the door where Sheala had disappeared. Nor had he missed that little display of claws and blood, and he was going to find out exactly what it meant, especially if it was some kind of weird Gattan mating signal.

Ban glanced around the room again. The others may not have realized exactly where Sheala's gaze had been centered before she left, but he had — Marljas' cock.

The mask of a smile on his face, Ban leaned back against the wall. Why were these Gattan really here? Gattans had never shown much interest in trade. They were far more interested in war. Yet, Wendjas Drefeson had brought his wife and children to Drakan. No honorable Gattan would put his family in such a position if he had treachery planned. Maybe what he said was true, and they were here to negotiate a trade contract.

Ban locked his gaze with Marljas'.

The other man was glaring at him.

Grinning, Ban nodded his head then shifted his weight. Gattans were here. That didn't mean he had to trust them.

Everyone else laughed, and Ban joined in though he had no idea what they were laughing about. He smiled at one comment and nodded in agreement with another. And even though he never again looked directly at Marljas, he noted exactly how many times the Gattan shifted his weight or glanced at the door. In a few weeks, Sheala would reach her majority and be free to take as many lovers as she wanted, when she wanted. That didn't mean, however, that the family would let just anybody jump into her bed. He'd make sure of it.

Chapter Two

ℰℴ

Vani slipped her arm through Sheala's as they hurried to their rooms. "Gattans here! Can you believe it? And Brianna actually cut herself!"

Sheala gaped, stared at her friend, then snapped her mouth shut only to open it again to ask, "Cut? What cut?"

Vani stopped, wrenching Sheala to a halt. "On Brianna's hand. Weren't you listening in there?"

From behind them, Jami giggled. "Sheala was too busy staring at the one named Marljas to pay attention to what anybody was saying. Did you see all the muscles he had? And when he took his vest off! I swear the temperature in the room went up twenty degrees! And he's going to get an Alalakan tattoo!"

Sheala blinked and swallowed the exclamation that almost burst free. *A dragon tattoo? How had she missed that comment?* A quick picture of the Gattan shirtless appeared in her mind. *Oh yeah, that was how.* She'd been paying more attention to his ass and chest than she had to the conversation. Sniffing, Sheala yanked her arm free and glared over her shoulder at Jami. "I was *not* staring at anybody. It was just too crowded in there, and so many people were talking that I didn't hear everything that was said."

"Yeah, and if we believe that, you have a bridge in Brooklyn to sell us."

Sheala blinked. "What?"

Jami shrugged as Vani grinned. "Another one of Brianna's Earth sayings. It means we don't believe you."

After another sniff, Sheala started back down the hall. "I

27

don't care what you believe. Mother told us to get dressed for dinner, and that's what I'm going to do."

Vani grinned at her sister as Sheala stomped away. "She couldn't take her eyes off that Gattan."

Jami nodded. "I noticed. He is handsome, in an alien way. And he has a great body. Do you think he could be tamed? Gattan are supposed to be awfully bloodthirsty, you know."

Giggling, Vani hooked her arm through her sister's. "I don't know, but I bet if anybody could tame a Gattan, it would be Sheala. Let's get dressed. Dinner should be pretty entertaining tonight. Do you think he could be as interested in Sheala as she is in him?"

* * * * *

Leaping down the last two steps, Sheala skidded around the corner and slammed into a solid wall of muscle.

"Oooof." She stumbled back.

Only the hands that grabbed her upper arms kept her from falling onto her behind.

"Excuse me."

His voice was deep.

Placing her hands flat against his chest, Sheala looked up into Marljas' golden eyes. Damn, but he was handsome. She smiled. "I'm sorry. I should've been watching where I was going."

He nodded once. "Yes, you should have been."

A tendril of honey-colored hair fell over his shoulder.

Then his words sank in.

Sheala stiffened. "What?"

He stared into her face. "You have many guests in your home far more infirm than I. You could have knocked one of them over."

Knocked one of them over! Sucking in a breath, Sheala glared at him. "I *beg* your pardon. I wasn't aware that Gattans were such—nitpicks—about decorum."

His eyes became even more golden. "There are many things you don't know about the Gattan."

Sheala tried to wrench her arms free.

He didn't release her.

Thrusting out her chin, she glared at him. "Let me go. I said I was sorry. It's not like I hurt you."

His lips twitched. "You didn't hurt me."

Groaning to herself, Sheala closed her eyes. Struggling wouldn't get her anywhere. He was as strong as an Aradab.

She sucked in a breath.

His musky scent came with it.

Hmmmmmmm, but he smelled good. Did he use a cologne? Or was that his natural scent?

Opening her eyes, she looked back up into his face. He was grinning.

"What's so funny?"

His white teeth flashed. "You're pouting like a child denied a sweet."

Pouting! Child! She'd show him how much of a child she was.

Stepping closer until her body was only inches from his, she slipped her fingers under the edges of the vest and began swirling them in circles in the silky hairs that grew there.

His skin was firm and warm, and the fine, golden hairs on his chest caressed the sensitive pads of her fingers. She stepped closer and pressed her hips against the tops of his thighs—and chuckled as the smile disappeared from his lips. "Am I so much like a child, then?"

His eyes darkened. Releasing her arms, he stepped back.

She stepped with him and smiled up into his face. "Tell

me, Marljas Drefeson, am I still a child?" Still tracing lazy circles on his muscular chest, she brushed a taut nipple.

A gurgle slipped from his throat.

His tail jerked, slapping against a small table the scraped across the floor. Water sloshed from the vase of flowers it held as the beautifully cut glass rocked a bit, then settled.

She chuckled again and slipped her hands down the bare skin of his chest, over the hard muscles of his abdomen, then around his torso to his back. She pressed her breasts against his chest. Slipping her tail between her legs, she wrapped it around his leather-clad leg—and stroked the inside of his thigh with the tip.

Muscles tightened and quivered under her palms. Sweat beaded on his brow. Shifting his hips away from her, he mumbled a curse.

When she stepped closer, his long, hard cock pressed through his pants against her stomach.

Oh my! Hoping he didn't hear her slight gasp, Sheala smiled up at him. She kept her voice low. "Am I a child, Marljas?"

Nostrils flaring, he stared down at her. He grabbed her arms again, his fingers tighter than they had been before.

Golden fire danced in his eyes. Slowly, he lowered his head until his face was only inches from hers. His thumbs caressed the undersides of her arms. Her breath caught in her throat. The thin material of her shirt tantalized her tightening nipples. His gaze drifted from her face to her chest. His eyes narrowed.

Excitement tingled its way through her body. A kiss. Just one kiss.

Momentarily his hands tightened even more. After sucking in a deep breath, he blinked then pushed her away. The knob in his throat bobbed as he swallowed—twice. "No, Alalakan dem al' Sheala, daughter of my hostess, you are not a child." Still looking at her chest, he pushed her down onto a padded bench then turned and retreated up the hallway.

Letting out the breath she was holding—and uncurling her toes, Sheala shivered and stared at the door through which he'd disappeared. Slowly, she lifted her hand and touched the tiny jewel at the side of her nose. Her mother and grandmother had been suggesting possible first-time lovers for the last two months, but none of the men—or women—they'd suggested had appealed to her. So far, this tall, golden-eyed Gattan was more appealing than any other man she'd ever met.

Sliding the latch to lock the library door behind him, Marljas raked his hair back off his forehead and leaned back against the wall. How had he lost control of that encounter with Sheala? All he'd done was reprimand her—gently—about watching where she was going, and the next thing he knew, she was caressing his chest, practically inviting him into her bed.

Closing his eyes, he wiped his face with his hands. Over the last week and a half, his brother had been very happy with how his trade negotiations were going with the Alalakans, and the Drakians had made their entire family welcome. His own relationship with his new bloodsister was flourishing, and he was now sure there was no danger for his family here on Drakan. He, however, faced a personal danger—Sheala.

Lowering his hands, he leaned back against the door and stared at the opposite wall. Sheala. No matter what he did, he couldn't push her from his mind. She was like no other woman he'd ever met. Her skin wasn't tan or brown or black with spots or stripes like most women on Gattan but rather the color of rich, ancient ivory. And it was soft, far softer than he'd expected. The dark brown hair that had tumbled about her shoulders was finer and silkier than a Gattan's. Her face was oval rather than round, her nose was smaller, and her lips were thinner. And just now, when her face had been so close to his, he'd been able to see that her almond-shaped eyes weren't black but rather a deep, rich brown that had darkened as her passion rose. He shuddered. He could lose himself in those eyes. He'd almost accepted that unspoken challenge, almost kissed her, lifted her into his arms, and carried her to the first bed he could find. Only the sparkle from the jewel at the side of her nose had stopped him. It had taken all his will to pull away, to not kiss her.

Then he'd made the mistake of looking at her breasts. Her nipples had been straining against the soft material of her shirt, aching to be touched, kissed.

He shuddered again.

Why? Why was he reacting to her like this? His control of his body had always been absolute. She was only a woman—a Drakian woman. What was so special, so compelling about her?

* * * * *

"Damn it!" Sheala threw the book she was attempting to read across her room. "Damn you, Marljas Drefeson. Get out of my mind."

Sheala stared at the wall. The Gattans had been here for a week and a half, and no matter where on the estate she went or what she did, she couldn't stop thinking about him. Why? What was so special about him? Even here in her own rooms, he haunted her.

She snorted and gazed at her reflection in the mirror.

Her reflection smirked back at her. *He's sexier than any man you've ever seen. That's why you can't get him out of your mind.*

Rolling off her bed, Sheala stepped to her mirror and pulled her shirt over her head. Cupping her breasts, she flicked her nipples with her thumbs. A shiver danced up her spine, but she ignored it. She had to think, and masturbating didn't help her thought processes.

Frowning, she jiggled them. Were Jami and Vani right? Would men like her breasts? Her sex instructor hadn't seemed too interested in them. He'd spent much more time teaching her how to use her mouth and tail on him. Sure, he'd fondled her breasts and suckled her nipples the first few lessons so she'd know what to expect from a sexual partner, but he'd spent most of her lessons below her waist. "He was a hermaphrodite and had breasts of his own. That's why he didn't pay so much attention to yours," her reflection seemed to state, "and Brianna and Meri have bigger breasts than you do. Char and Ademis seem to be pretty happy with their wives' breasts."

Letting go of her breasts, she finger-combed her hair back over her forehead. "Oh, damn it to all the hells, I shouldn't have vowed to remain a virgin!"

For a moment she frowned at herself. Then she sighed and fingered the tiny sapphire stud on the side of her nose. Char had given her this Deslossian sapphire, one of only twelve that ever left that planet, for her nose stud soon after she had made her declaration. The entire family had been proud of her decision. How could she let them down now? With so little time left?

Who cared what her arrogant ex-sister-in-law Crystas thought. She wasn't even a member of the family anymore.

Sheala smiled. She'd made good use of the sexual tutor Crystas had suggested, only stopping short of full penetration. Bogarton don al' Chevin had been a competent teacher who taught her everything she needed to know about sexual intercourse while still honoring her vow to retain her virginity. He'd gone so far as to tell Sheala that he was honored to teach a young woman who had chosen to remain a virgin because so few young people were willing to do so anymore.

After jiggling her breasts once more, Sheala slid out of the short pants she was wearing. Turning, she stared at the reflection of her ass. It wasn't flat like Crystas' had been, but then Sheala always had thought that Crystas looked like a board from behind. Turning, Sheala stared at her crotch. She had only a small tuft of pubic hair in the center of her pubis —

because she shaved most of it away. When she didn't, rich brown curls would grow into a triangle. She kept her pubis shaved because she didn't want to be different from her Drakian friends. None of them had much hair.

She stroked the small tuft of hair. Maybe she should let her hair grow in. Maybe Vani was right. Maybe being different wasn't so bad. Jami and Vani both had triangles of thick curls between their legs. Granted, the hair was dark green since they were Medirian and all Medirians were one shade of green or anther, but color didn't matter. And with all that red hair Brianna had on her head, Sheala just bet there were nice, thick curls between her legs too.

As Sheala turned away from the mirror and picked up her shirt, the door burst open, and Jami and Vani practically tumbled into the room.

"Happy birthday, Shea!"

Sheala stared at the package Jami held. "But it's not my birthday yet!"

"You've had gifts arriving for the last week," Vani answered. "If we don't give you ours now, it will just get lost among all the others."

Jami nodded. "This is only from Vani and me, Shea. Mother and Father sent something more elaborate with Meri. Hurry up, open it!"

The package wasn't large, and Sheala made short work of the wrapping. Removing the top, Sheala searched amongst the tissue paper and finally held up a tiny scrap of red material. Stretching it between her hands, she quickly deduced what it was.

"A Nissian bathing thong! Thank you!"

Both princesses grinned as Sheala slipped it on. The Drakian habit of roaming around nude made trying on new clothing very easy.

Sheala stood before her friends and modeled her newest acquisition. To say it left little to the imagination was an understatement. The leg straps rode high over her hips and dipped well below her navel to a small scrap of cloth that barely covered her. *Good thing I do shave. The hairs would stick out otherwise.*

A single strap ran between her buttocks to meet the hip straps just above her tail. A special sleeve, which supported the first inch of her tail, had been incorporated into the thong.

"Let me get my things, and we'll go to the pool right now. Thanks ever so much, Jami, Vani. I love you both!" After hugging both of her friends, she disappeared into the bathroom.

The sisters exchanged conspiratorial glances.

"Are you sure he's going to be there today?" Jami whispered.

Vani nodded. "I heard him tell Denieen that he'd take her twins swimming this afternoon so she could spend some time with Shea's mother and grandmother."

"Good. All Shea does is stare at Marljas when she thinks no one's watching. And he stares at her too, but every time she tries to talk to him, he finds somewhere to go, unless they get into an argument. Then one or the other always stomps off angry. If seeing her in this bathing thong doesn't get a reaction from him, nothing will."

"Come on," Sheala said as she left the bathroom wearing her green robe and carrying a fluffy towel.

* * * * *

When they arrived at the pool, her cousin Ban was floating lazily on top of the water. As soon as he saw them, he waved, pulled himself up out of the water onto the side of the pool and waited for them to join him.

Raking his hair back off his forehead, he grinned at them. Slowing, Sheala stared at him. He'd been handsome when he'd left Drakan five years ago, and maturity had only heightened his appeal. Bandalardrac lacked an inch to equal her brother Char's height of six foot nine and had features combining the best of his Medirian mother and Drakian father. Black eyebrows rode above vibrant, dark eyes that were rounder than a Drakian's. A hawk-like nose sat above full, expressive lips. Rather than being heavily muscular, though, as were some Merdirians, his body was slim and athletic. Like his mother, he had gills and no tail. His skin tone, however, was neither ivory-colored like most Drakians nor green like a Medirian but a pleasant mixture of the two, a warm tan with a subtle olive undertone. Riding Ban's right shoulder was his Alalakan dragon, a graceful, bluish-green beast, massive wings straining, rising from a turbulent ocean. All in all he was a very attractive man, a man to turn any woman's head.

Sheala let her gaze travel down his body. His own bathing suit was brief, though his entire backside was covered. The brevity of the suit, however, left little doubt about his manhood. Yes, Ban was a very handsome man. She could see why women on all the known planets wanted him in their beds.

She smiled. As handsome as Ban was, she felt absolutely no sexual attraction towards him. Besides being her cousin, he was too — Ban. She shook her head. Any woman who fell in love with him would spend much of her life fighting other women off.

When the girls removed their robes, Ban's rakish grin grew wider. He certainly wasn't interested in Shea, Jami, or Vani sexually, but that didn't mean he couldn't appreciate their beauty. After a quick perusal of Jami and Vani, his gaze lingered on Sheala.

During his years away from Drakan, she'd developed into a beautiful young woman, her body filling out in all the right places. Thank goodness for her Medirian blood which gave her more curves than the average Drakian woman.

Ban's gaze drifted to her face. To someone who knew her parentage, Sheala's Medirian blood was evident. But to the average Drakian, she looked much like every other Drakian woman—yet somehow different. Her hair was thicker and longer. Her lips were fuller, redder, lusher, her dark brown eyes slightly less slanted. Her skin was the same ivory hue as all other Drakians, her cheekbones were high and her ears were pointed. Granted, she was short, barely over six feet tall, but there were other Drakians as short as she.

All three dropped their robes and stood before him.

"What do you think of my new bathing thong, Ban?" Sheala asked as she turned slowly.

The last thing those three need are compliments on their looks, Ban thought as they preened before him. Leaping forward and upward, he grabbed Sheala around the waist and threw her into the pool.

"This!"

He tossed Jami and Vani in after her.

All three girls screamed with delight.

Ban dove in after them. The battle that ensued had him exactly where he wanted to be—the center of attention of three beautiful women, even if they were his cousins.

Ten minutes later, as he managed to dunk all three girls at once, Ban saw a chuckling Brianna settle her heavily pregnant body into a lounge chair with the ever-watchful Aradab Kahn close by.

Then two tan streaks flashed by. With identical yells, Denieen's twin sons, Hendjas and Charjas, tumbled into the pool and attacked all of them.

A pained expression on his face, Marljas appeared from between two hedges and stopped behind Brianna's chair where he remained standing.

Laughing, Ban pushed the girls out of the way and captured the two young Gattans. He'd spent the last weeks watching the three adult Gattans and come to the conclusion that they were exactly what they claimed to be, a family interested in negotiating a trading contract. So, he relaxed his vigilance—somewhat—and he spent as much time in their company as he could. Wendjas and Denieen were friendly. Marljas, however, was not. Though he obviously supported his brother and sister-in-law, he didn't make any friendly overtures to anyone except Brianna, and with her only because of their new bloodbond.

And though Marljas spoke to Sheala only when propriety and good manners demanded, he still watched her when he didn't think anyone was watching him.

So, Ban watched him.

Hendjas and Charjas attacked him simultaneously.

Sinking to the bottom of the pool, Ban attacked from below. Tucking a struggling boy under each arm, he climbed out of the pool. Their shrieks echoed joyfully as he heaved each one back into the water where the three girls converged them. Wiping water out of his eyes, he sat down next to Brianna.

"Must you drip water all over me?" she jested. "With all the splashing that's going on, I may as well be in the pool."

Ban grinned at her. "Coz, if that belly of yours weren't so huge, you'd have been tossed in long ago."

He ignored the low growl that rumbled from Marljas' chest. He didn't give a damn what that particular Gattan thought.

Chapter Three

ஐ

Behind them, Marljas flexed his claws and snarled to himself as he stared at Ban. Why did that arrogant womanizer have to be cousin to Brianna? He couldn't challenge a relative of his new bloodsister unless he was provoked, something he was sure a coward like Bandalardrac Hardan wouldn't do. The half-breed Medirian prince was only interested in how many women he could lure into his bed.

His nephews' joyful laughter drew his attention just as Sheala surged up out of the water to stand on the side of the pool. Leaping upwards, she twisted and caught the missile-shaped object Hendjas had just thrown at her. For a brief second, her gaze locked with Marljas'. She smiled as water rolled down her lithe body. Her full breasts jiggled as multicolored drops tumbled from warm, brown nipples to splash at her feet.

Then, turning, she dove back into the pool.

Marljas remembered to breathe a minute later. Since she was wearing nothing but a tiny strip of material that barely covered her crotch, there was little of her firm body left to his imagination.

He shuddered.

She may as well have been naked.

And by all the seven hells, he wanted her naked, wanted her legs wrapped around his waist while he plunged his cock into her over and over and over until neither of them could stand the sensation any longer. And that tail! What would she do to him with that tail?

Marljas closed his eyes and her almost naked image appeared immediately in his mind's eye. No Gattan maiden would allow so much of her body to be seen in public, but then, Sheala was not a Gattan maiden.

He shifted his feet to accommodate his growing erection. Ever since the afternoon when she'd run into him, her lithe figure had never left his mind. Now, though, standing practically naked before him, he had seen what he'd previously only been able to imagine.

More laughter drew his attention, and he opened his eyes.

Again, Sheala rose from the water before him and perched on the edge of the pool.

Gritting his teeth, Marljas let his breath out slowly as he stared first at her slender back then allowed his gaze to slide lower.

Her behind was perfectly rounded, not flat like so many Drakian women's. Just the right shape for a man's hands as he cupped her cheeks and drove his cock between her legs whether from in front or behind.

Raising her hands above her head, she dove back into the water.

Shifting uncomfortably from one foot to the other, Marljas continued to watch Sheala. His erection grew harder and more painful every time his gaze rested on her bouncing breasts.

Brianna's merry laughter finally wrenched his attention away from Sheala.

"You'll never see me wearing anything so skimpy, Bandalardrac."

"A man can dream, can't he, sweet Coz?"

Before she could answer him, the Aradab Beti appeared from between the hedges on the other side of the pool, walked to the edge, and called to Sheala in a quiet voice.

Sheala groaned, but she nodded, hoisted herself up and out of the pool and wrapped a thick towel around her almost-naked body. Then she followed Beti back through the hedges.

"Time for her lesson, I imagine," Ban commented as he

lay back on the lounge next to Brianna.

Marljas pulled his attention away from the disappearing Sheala and concentrated on what Ban was saying.

"Lessons?" his bloodsister asked curiously.

Ban closed his eyes and laced his fingers behind his head. "Hmmm. Beti, one of the Aradabs, has been teaching her Aradab hand fighting."

Marljas swallowed. Sheala was learning to fight. A picture of her supple body twisting and gyrating burst into Marljas' brain, twisting and gyrating as she fought hand-to-hand — with him — naked.

His erection began to throb.

His tail jerked. How was he supposed to survive this stay on Drakan with his cock aching all the time? He shifted again, trying to ease the ache between his thighs.

Again Ban laughed at something Brianna said.

Marljas' frustration slipped towards anger. Why should that bastard be so relaxed and comfortable around all these half-naked women! He, not Marljas, was the womanizer!

Then a sheet of water erupted from the pool to soak not only Brianna and Ban but also Marljas. The Medirian princesses tried to dunk his nephews and they splashed back.

Enough was enough! Snarling, Marljas strode to the edge of the pool. "Both of you, out now!"

Thoroughly dejected, both boys crawled from the pool.

Grabbing hold of their upper arms, Marljas turned towards Brianna and Ban. "Undisciplined and ill-mannered. It's bad enough that these two five-year-olds lack proper decorum. One can excuse them because of their youth," he snapped. Then he glared back over his shoulder. "What reasons can two Medirian princesses offer, however?"

Brianna tried to push her bulky body up. "Marljas!"

"And tell them to cover themselves. No decent woman displays her wares so blatantly!"

Instantly furious, Ban flew from his chair. Before he could get his hands on Marljas, though, Kahn wrapped both arms around him. Trying to move the Aradab was like trying to move a mountain. Still, Ban struggled against his hold.

Kahn's muscles bulged as he held Ban, who almost slipped free.

Then he stopped struggling. "I'll take whatever insults you throw at me, Gattan, but I won't take slurs against my family. Consider the feud renewed."

"My pleasure, half-blood," Marljas growled in answer as he released his nephews, who immediately sprinted towards the house.

Claws extended, Marljas glared at Ban. He ached to attack, but as long as Kahn held Ban, Gattan honor would not allow it.

Finally up from her chair, Brianna opened her mouth, but Kahn's flat voice stopped whatever she was going to say. "They must test each other. Neither will be content until they discover who is dominant."

Marljas felt a smile slide onto his lips. Yes, let him "test" Bandalardrac. A few deep cuts on that pretty face might make women think twice about falling into bed with him. An apt revenge for spiriting Sosha away from Gattan.

While Kahn held Ban, Brianna walked over and put her hand on Marljas' arm. Her voice dripped ice. "Very well, *Brother*. If you wish to fight my cousin, who is as dear to me as a brother, you will do so following my rules!"

"No," Kahn rumbled in his gravelly voice. "You know nothing of challenges such as this, therefore, I will enforce the rules. This fight will not be to the death, there will be no weapons, and I will stop it when I feel there is a winner. Do you both agree?"

Marljas' answer was delivered with an affirmative snarl. He wouldn't kill Bandalardrac. To do so would be a gross insult. But the bastard had challenged him. Gattan tradition demanded that he defend his honor, even if the man who challenged him was a family member of his hostess.

Ban's yes was just as surly.

"Good," Kahn grunted, "we go to the ring, now."

With those words he released Ban and motioned him to proceed. "Take the Gattan's arm," Kahn directed Brianna with a nod in Marljas' direction. "Prince Bandalardrac is already sure of your affection."

With those words he followed Ban away from the pool.

As Marljas began to step after his adversary, Brianna cleared her throat. "We go nowhere until you apologize to Jami and Vani."

With Ban's infuriating presence gone, Marljas' mind cleared. Glancing over his shoulder, his gaze was met by two icy stares. Swallowing nervously, he realized that he had insulted the daughters of the Medirian king in such a way that he could totally ruin his brother's future trade negotiations.

Shoulders hunched, he dropped his gaze and mumbled an apology.

Vani's angry retort cut like a knife. "I sincerely hope that Ban pummels some sense into that narrow-minded head of yours, Gattan. If you were on Mediria, you'd have been dragged before my father immediately. Whatever he did to you, I strongly believe that your brother would approve."

Marljas winced at the truth of her words.

Brianna's tone was no less disgusted. "Hotheaded, idiot ass! Come on! Let's get this over with."

With those words, she wrapped her fingers around his thick wrist and tugged him after her.

* * * * *

As first Ban and Kahn and then Brianna and Marljas strode into the training facility, Sheala stopped her exercises and rested the tips of both swords she carried on the ground.

"What's going on?" she asked as Brianna and Kahn came to stand next to them.

Kahn bowed. "Prince Bandalardrac and the Gattan Marljas Drefeson are finally no longer able to tolerate each other. They must fight to see who is dominant."

Sheala stared. Ban and Marljas fight? Were they fighting about that girl Ban was supposed to have taken from Gattan? "Don't you think we should stop them?"

Kahn shook his head. "No. They will fight sooner or later. Sooner is better. Hate has less time to fester."

"Men," Sheala muttered. "Why are they so obstinate? Char told Marljas Ban didn't take that girl from Gattan. Why won't Marljas believe him?"

Beti snorted. "Men are not known for logical thinking."

Kahn glared at her but said nothing.

With a curse and a snarl, Bandalardrac and Marljas flew at each other.

Marljas' claws flashed, and Sheala began to chew her lip.

"I thought you said no weapons!" Brianna hissed to Kahn. "Marljas' claws must be at least three inches long!"

"A Gattan's claws are part of him, and he will rely on them too much," was Kahn's noncommittal answer. "I myself have taught Prince Bandalardrac every skill I know. He will not fail me."

Sheala shifted her weight. *Was* Ban in danger? She shook her head. No. He couldn't be. She'd seen him spar with Kahn. Marljas' claws weren't as much of a danger to Ban as the Gattan thought they were. "You should probably worry more about Marljas. He is relying on those claws too much. Even I can see that, and I'm no expert."

Brianna snorted. "You better be right. If either one of them gets hurt, I'll make them sorry they lived."

Sheala chuckled to herself as she looked back to the fighting men. She'd heard the story of how Brianna had sewn up a cut on Ban's shoulder after he'd rescued her from her kidnappers. Brianna had *stabbed* the needle through his skin twelve times. Ban was probably in less danger from Marljas' claws than he would be from Brianna's needle.

Marljas dropped and rolled as Ban leaped and kicked. In turn, he twisted left and jumped when Marljas stabbed at him with his lethal claws. Attack, feint. Feint, attack.

Leaping high in the air, Ban kicked at Marljas' head. The Gattan countered by sliding to the left and swiping at Ban's groin with his claws. Ban jackknifed in midair, hit the ground rolling, and spun to counter Marljas' backhand when he reached his feet. Marljas spun away from Ban's punch. Back and forth, parry left and bluff right. Neither man could gain an advantage.

After thirty minutes, even though both men were in superb condition, it was obvious to Sheala that both were tiring. Perhaps it was this growing fatigue that caused Ban to misjudge Marljas' reach or perhaps he slipped. With one quick slash, Marljas opened a deep cut on Ban's shoulder.

Gasping, Brianna stepped forward.

Sheala grabbed her arm. "Wait. Watch Ban. He hasn't been fighting as well as he could. That cut will wake him up."

Sheala was right. After a series of swift feints that had the Gattan spinning in circles, Ban found an opening and planted a solid kick onto Marljas' rib cage.

Snarling, the Gattan lowered his arm to protect his chest and stepped back.

Sheala tsked. "He left his right side wide open. I bet Ban cracked a rib or two with that kick."

At her side, Brianna crossed her arms over her chest and glared at Kahn. "That's enough. Their honor must be satisfied by now. If Marljas has a broken rib, I don't want it piercing his lung."

Kahn grunted, but Sheala chuckled and leaped into action. "I'll stop them for you, Bri. They're both exhausted."

Sprinting across the floor, her specially designed swords whirling in her hands, Sheala flipped then rolled. Rising quickly, she stood between the two combatants with the tip of a very sharp sword pointed at each man's throat. "Where would you like them, Bri?"

Ban had seen Sheala practicing with her swords on more than one occasion and stood perfectly still.

Marljas, on the other hand, attempted to avoid her.

Misjudging his quick reflexes, she nicked his throat.

As soon as Marljas felt the blood on his throat, he froze. For a few brief seconds, his surprised glance locked with hers.

When Marljas' intense gaze met Sheala's, everything and everyone else around her faded into a gray background. Shivers of desire danced up and down her backbone, sending darts of warmth to her groin and nipples. In what seemed like slow motion, she watched him touch the cut she'd given him, wipe some blood on his fingers, then lift them to his lips.

Her breath caught in her throat when he slowly licked the blood away. A picture of him standing behind her, his lips and tongue on the side of her neck flashed into her mind.

"I hope you're both satisfied with yourselves." Brianna's voice penetrated her reverie, yanking her back from her fantasy.

Wrenching her gaze away from his, Sheala gathered her scattered wits, concentrating on her misjudgment of his speed. Marljas was faster than she'd thought. She wouldn't make that mistake again.

With Kahn at her side, Brianna stepped between the two men and began lecturing them.

Shaking her head slightly, Sheala lowered her swords and stepped back.

Amusement now coloring her thoughts, Sheala chuckled. Brianna could lecture better than anyone she knew—all those

Earth phrases that no one had ever heard before. Sheala cocked her head to the side. "Pigheaded jackasses" sounded interesting. She'd have to remember that one.

She glanced at Ban. Blood flowed freely from his shoulder. That cut would have to be stitched.

Then she looked at Marljas again.

He held himself rigidly upright, his arm tucked against his ribs, obviously in pain. Ban's kick definitely cracked some ribs.

Her stare drifted from his side to his muscular torso. She remembered the afternoon she'd stroked his warm chest. Those golden hairs were as soft as they looked. What would he do if she threaded her fingers through them right now and caressed the muscles of his chest? Traced the line of that white scar that trailed down over his flat abdomen to disappear beneath the waistband of his pants?

Or, if she caressed his dragon?

Sheala stared at his tattoo. She'd caught glimpses, but everyone had decided it best that a Gattan wearing an Alalakan clan totem wasn't a widely known fact at this time. Now, however, Marljas had his shirt off, and she was able to see it clearly for the first time.

Seemingly flying straight towards her off Marljas' right shoulder was a fully rampant, red-gold dragon with wings outstretched and flames shooting from its mouth. Beneath it leaped the animal Brianna called a lion, mouth gaping wide, a snarl on its face. The resemblance between it and Marljas was uncanny.

Beneath the tattoo was a very muscular pectoral muscle with the three parallel cuts he'd put there when Brianna had become his bloodsister. Already, they were healing, the redness faded to a pale pink, the edges white.

Instead of being appalled or disgusted by them, those cuts excited her.

Swallowing, Sheala shifted and squeezed her legs

together. Damn, but she was getting wet just thinking about touching him.

Silence pulled her attention back to Brianna.

The glare her sister-in-law had leveled at Ban was scathing. "Well?"

He acknowledged it with one of his swift grins. "As long as the Gattan is satisfied."

Brianna turned to Marljas, her voice still rippling with anger. "Is your Gattan honor satisfied?"

Marljas glared first at Ban then turned that intense, golden gaze on Brianna.

To Sheala, he didn't look in the least bit contrite or satisfied.

Brianna didn't look the least bit intimidated.

Sheala sucked in a breath. Just how stubborn was this Gattan? Shivers raced up her spine. If only Marljas stared at her with the same intensity! She felt her nipples pucker even more tightly.

She sucked in a breath and gripped her swords as Brianna stepped closer to Marljas and poked her finger against his chest. Her voice was very low.

"Are—" poke "—you—" poke "—satisfied?"

Marljas glowered a bit more and muttered something under his breath. Closing his eyes, he dropped his chin to his chest, obviously struggling with himself mentally. Finally, he opened his eyes, looked at Brianna, and nodded his head. "So be it. The fates have spoken. Honor has been satisfied, bloodsister. I will seek blooddebt against Bandalardrac no longer."

Turning to Ban, his expression underwent an amazing transformation. Smiling, he unsheathed a claw on his left hand and drew it quickly across his right shoulder. Smearing blood on his palm, he stepped forward and extended his bloodstained hand. "There's more to you than is apparent,

Half-blood. You're a worthy opponent."

At first, Ban just stared at Marljas' outstretched hand. After a moment, his usual lopsided grin appeared on his face. Smearing his hand with blood from his own shoulder, he clasped Marljas'. "Welcome to the family."

The intense look returned to Marljas' eyes as he stared into Ban's face. "To the family. Yes. I'm now an Alalakan by blood rites." An enigmatic smile appeared on his face as he fingered the cut on his neck. "More than you realize, Alalakan don al' Bandalardrac, Prince Hardan."

Sheala frowned. Blood rites? Wasn't Brianna becoming his sister the only blood rite that had been performed? Or did Ban and Marljas smearing their blood on each other's hands count? She was going to have to talk to Deni.

Marljas turned to her. "You fight well, Sheala. Few Gattan women would have dared attempt what you did today."

Sheala stared into his golden eyes. What did that mean? Again, shivers danced up and down her spine. She swallowed and inhaled.

His scent was hot, spicy, male. She almost stepped forward.

Ban coughed.

She glanced at her cousin. He was staring at her with a knowing look in his eye.

She jerked her gaze from his, conscious of the others standing around them. She gathered her composure, looked back at Marljas, and shrugged. "Beti taught me how to meld Aradab weaponless fighting with Drakian fencing techniques. It's nothing."

With those words, she flashed Brianna a warm smile and walked away with Beti who immediately began to critique her performance.

Marljas' hand strayed to the cut at his neck as Sheala

sauntered away from him. Since he'd been here, she'd placed herself in his arms, displayed her almost nude body to him. Now, she'd blooded him—on his neck. She'd made her intentions clear.

Saying something about willing nurses, Ban clapped him on the shoulder. Brianna ordered him to the estate infirmary to have his ribs bound.

Marljas looked one last time to where Sheala had resumed her practice with Beti.

Her movements were fluid as water as she parried a blow from the Aradab and then attacked.

Smiling, Marljas turned and followed Ban. Sheala had blooded him. She was his. And he was going to take her.

Chapter Four

ℬ

Grimacing at the sharp twinge in his tightly bound ribs, Marljas shifted his weight and touched the scab that had already formed over the small cut Sheala had given him.

A Gattan woman didn't cut a man's neck unless she was insulting him—or interested in him as a mate. Sheala had already shown her interest in him, stroking him that day in the hallway, displaying her almost nude body to him. This cut was no insult. She was his to take—when he caught her. So what if she wasn't Gattan. He was.

He smiled. How hard would she make him chase her?

The sound of a soft step caught his attention. She was coming.

He remained quiet, almost invisible amongst the bushes he'd chosen for his cover until she was before him. He reached out, grasped her arm, pulled her into the bushes—and found a very sharp sword at his throat for the second time that day.

He released her immediately and stepped back, holding his palms up. "I mean you no harm."

The sword disappeared from his throat. "Oh, it's you." She sheathed her sword. "Do you want something?"

Nostrils flaring, Marljas crossed his arms over his chest.

She stood before him, dark hair mussed, perspiration glowing on her face and on the bare skin he could see in the vee of her shirt. That day in the hallway, she'd smelled sweet and flowery, fresh from her bath. At the pool, her scent had been fresh and clean. Today, she smelled of hard work and woman's sweat—a heady, tantalizing mixture.

"You blooded me."

51

Finger-combing some stray tendrils of hair back off her forehead, she shrugged. "I didn't mean to. You moved faster than I expected. I'm sorry."

Again, he inhaled deeply. Her scent was hot, intoxicating. He smiled down into her face and shook his head. "You aren't sorry. I saw it in your eyes. Satisfaction appeared when you nicked me. You wanted to blood me."

Obviously nonplused, she stepped back and shook her head. "No! I didn't mean to cut you. You're a guest. I'd never intentionally hurt a guest."

He dropped his arms to his sides. His voice deepened as his desire for her rose. "You didn't hurt me, Sheala. You excited me. But then, I think you know that."

Surprise flashed in her eyes. "Excited you? Arrogant Gattan! Who do you think you are?"

He clasped his hands behind his back and smiled at her. "Your betrothed."

When her mouth dropped open, Marljas grinned. Now there was shock in her eyes—and anticipation, anticipation she quickly masked.

Stepping forward, she glared up into his face and snapped. "Are you crazy?"

His nostrils flared as he looked down at her. Another scent was drifting from her—desire. He shifted, spreading his legs as his cock rose. "On Gattan, a woman bloods a man's neck when she wishes to mate him."

She jerked her gaze from his and stared at his chest.

Marljas smiled down at the top of her head.

She didn't turn away.

Unclasping his hands, he reached forward and trailed his thumb down her bare arm.

She sucked in a sharp breath. "Mate?"

He slipped his knuckle under her chin and lifted her face to his. "You want me as much as I want you. I've seen the way you watch me. And today, at the pool, when you rose from the water and displayed your body. It was for me."

Again, she sucked in a quick breath. "I…"

He lowered his head until their breaths mixed. "Don't talk." Capturing her mouth with his, he kissed her, his lips moving slowly over hers.

When she flattened her palms against him, he lifted his head. "I want you, Alalakan dem al' Sheala." Lifting his hand, he cupped her cheek, brushing his thumb against the stud at the side of her nose. "But you are the daughter of my hostess. And even though you blooded me, to court you without her permission is grounds for a declaration of bloodfeud, on Gattan."

A slow smile slid onto her lips—a slow, seductive smile. Mischief danced with the desire in her dark eyes.

Marljas' cock hardened even more.

Her chuckle was low. "We're not on Gattan, and I've had one of the best sexual instructors on Drakan."

Marljas didn't try to hide the shock he felt. "Sexual instructor?"

She didn't answer. Instead, she cupped her hand between his legs, then danced her fingers up his erection. "No wonder you Gattan wear these tunics. They hide—a lot." Tugging open the seam in the front of his pants, she freed his aching cock and wrapped her fingers around it.

A long shudder raced up his body. "What are you…"

"Shhhhh. Let me show you what I desire." Bending, she slipped her head under the bottom of his tunic and sucked him into her mouth.

Desire such as he'd never felt before slammed its fist into the pit of his stomach as she sucked his cock into her warm, moist mouth. Her supple tongue slid around him. "Sheala. Stop. You…"

Her voice was muffled. "Just be quiet and enjoy yourself.

You aren't on Gattan." She tongued him.

Sucking in a huge breath that made his cracked ribs ache, Marljas spread his legs and leaned back against the wall. He *wasn't* on Gattan. He was on Drakan, the most hedonistic planet in the galaxy. And his betrothed, the woman he desired more than any other, was sucking on his cock. Who was he to question fate?

Ignoring another stab of pain from his cracked ribs, Marljas pulled his tunic over his head and dropped it to the ground. He didn't want Sheala hidden underneath a piece of cloth. He wanted to watch her every move. Sighing, he buried his fingers in her hair.

"Mmmmmmmm, you taste good," she whispered against his cock.

He answered with a grunt. When she sucked him into her mouth again, he thrust his hips forward, shuddering when she was able to take his entire length.

Her tongue danced and caressed. She sucked harder. Her hands stroked his thighs.

Groaning, he pulled his cock out of her mouth.

She fell to her knees, slid her hands into the crotch of his pants, cupped his balls, and began to roll them around in the palm of her hand. Her right hand she braced against the bare skin of his thigh, her fingers tracing small circles amongst his leg hairs. She kissed the head of his cock, licked it, suckled it. Then she raised her head and looked into his face. Her smile was the most seductive he'd ever seen. "How long can you hold back? How long shall I allow you to hold back?" Bending her head, she trailed small nibbles down one side of his erection then up the other. She released his balls and began to massage the base of his cock.

He threw back his head and closed his eyes, concentrating only on how her hot mouth felt. "By all the seven hells, Sheala, you're torturing me."

He was answered with an enticing chuckle.

He heard the rustle of cloth. Her mouth was replaced with supple fingers that teased and caressed.

"Open your eyes."

Obeying her, he looked down.

Her shirt hung open and she was rubbing his cock between her full breasts. She brushed it against her left nipple.

"Mother of all the fates," he muttered and thrust his hips forward.

She pumped him. "I want you to come on my breasts."

His stomach muscles quivered. "Yessssssssss."

She bent and licked his cock, pumped him more. With her other hand, she pinched her own nipple, which was a tight, hard nub.

Marljas licked his lips. He wanted to taste those nipples — but the sight of his brown cock against her ivory skin…

"Are you ready to come? Do you want to wait?"

Grasping her shoulders, he thrust his hips forward. She leaned back as his cock slid up between her breasts. His voice was a shuddering growl he didn't recognize. "No waiting. Now!"

Another low laugh escaped her. Tilting her head back, she smiled up into his face. "Very well." She slid her fingers down his cock to his balls and rolled them in her left hand as she squeezed and pumped him with her right.

Marljas shuddered. Her hands were pure magic. "Your mouth. I want your mouth!"

"And I want you to come. Now." She released his balls, slid her hand under his tail, and pressed a finger into his anus.

Fire exploded in his balls and rushed up through his cock. His hips thrust forward involuntarily. As he watched, his cum squirted onto her breasts.

She pushed her finger farther into his anus.

More fire, more cum.

Marljas felt his knees begin to buckle as she pulled her finger free and rose to her feet. Before he could say a word, she grabbed his hand and pushed it down the front of her loose pants.

She was slick and damp. Moisture coated his fingers as she moaned and pushed herself against them.

Her voice was a breathy whisper. "Help me. I need..."

Gathering his scattered wits as best he could, Marljas slid his fingers between her lips and rubbed the hard nub she pressed against his fingers. In a matter of seconds, more moisture coated his fingers, and she grabbed hold of his arms as she shuddered with her own orgasm.

When she rested her forehead against his chest, he wrapped his arms around her and held her tight. Long minutes passed before their breathing and heart rates returned to normal.

Slipping his finger under her chin, Marljas tilted her head back. "Sheala..."

Voices coming up the path interrupted him.

She pressed her hand to his lips, smiled and stepped back. Pulling her shirt closed, she spun around and disappeared in the direction of the house.

After a moment, Marljas shoved his now flaccid cock back inside his pants and raked his hair back off his face. He snatched up his tunic and pulled it over his head. Midsummer. Less than a week. He could wait that long to have her.

And he *would* have her. She *would* be his mate. No other man would ever touch her again. He'd kill anyone who tried.

* * * * *

Naked, Sheala lay stretched across her bed watching while her grandmother and sister-in-law Fionilina put the finishing touches on the dress she would wear on Solstice. Her family had told her over and over again that being born on

Solstice was extremely lucky, but she'd never believed it before this year. Brianna's arrival and Fionilina's marriage to her oldest brother Rodane had had a dramatic impact on the Alalakan household. And then the Gattans — and Marljas — had come.

She shivered. Marljas. Two days ago they'd practically made love. He'd avoided her ever since. Why? She shivered again. His cock had been delicious. To have it between her legs, buried deep!

"Are you cold?"

She blinked. "What?"

"I asked if you were cold," her grandmother asked again.

"A little maybe."

"Here, then. Try this on."

Pushing herself up, she stepped onto a stool and her grandmother dropped her dress over her head. A shimmery midnight blue, the dress clung to her like a second skin and outlined the smallest details of her body, from the pert nipples on her breasts to the springy pubic hair that grew between her thighs.

"Do you want your tail in or out, Shea?" Fionilina asked.

"I don't know. What do you think, Grandmother?"

"How do your friends wear theirs?"

"Out."

"Well, then you must wear yours in, of course," Jenneta answered. "One should always strive for individuality."

Sheala swiveled her head to look at herself in the mirror. "That's why you like Brianna so much, isn't it, Grandmother?"

Jenneta nodded. "That's one of the reasons, my love. She's also very self-assured and quite comfortable with herself."

Fionilina grinned. "And not afraid to let others know exactly how she feels."

"I don't understand, Grandmother," Sheala said as

Jenneta added a few more pins to the hem of the dress. "You've always told me to be polite and not push my opinions on other people."

Her grandmother chuckled. "I hadn't realized just how much the Alalakans had begun to stagnate in our behavior. Brianna's arrival and, to a lesser extent, Ban's return have revitalized our family. There has been more laughter in this house since Brianna returned with Char and Ban rejoined the family than there has been in years."

"Not to mention Charjas and Hendjas running about the house. If Meri's Celene were old enough to follow, we would be outnumbered," Fionilina added with a grin.

Sheala noted how Jenneta smiled gently herself.

"I'd forgotten how much joy children bring to a house. The Gattans' visit has been a blessing," the older woman said.

Sheala agreed completely with her grandmother's last statement but said nothing as her dress was pulled over her head. Jenneta's and Fionilina's discussion of the Gattans brought forth a mental picture of Marljas as he had stood over her while she suckled his cock. Desire flared in her belly and she quickly swallowed a moan.

"Sheala, are you listening to me?" asked her grandmother good-naturedly.

"What?"

"I said you can get dressed now."

"Oh."

Fionilina smiled. "Perhaps Sheala is deciding on her first man."

Jenneta chuckled. "It's a good subject to think on."

"Why?" Sheala asked a little too quickly as she pulled on comfortable clothing. "One man is much like another, is he not?"

"One's first sexual experience is very important, Sheala. You should take care to choose someone who is experienced, for only an experienced man can bring you to the height of pleasure your first time. That first experience will be the standard by which you will judge all others."

Sheala smiled mischievously. "Maybe a lack of experience would be better. What if I never meet anyone else as good as my first? My life will be filled with one sexual disappointment after another."

Both Jenneta and Fionilina laughed. "You minx," Fionilina said after she regained her composure, "we should just bundle you up and drop you in bed with the first unrelated man we can find."

"It's too bad you and Ban are cousins. He'd have been perfect for your first lover. I have yet to meet a woman he's had who doesn't long to be back in his bed," Jenneta said. "He's devilishly inventive from what I've heard."

"It's because he's half Medirian. He's trying to make up for his lack of a tail."

Both Sheala and Jenneta stared at Fionilina. "Oh?"

Fionilina smiled but said nothing.

"Better not tell Rodane," Sheala said with a laugh. "He's beginning to act more and more like Char. You'll soon find yourself buried in your suite like Brianna."

Jenneta shook her head bemusedly. "Don't underestimate Brianna, Shea. She initiates sex with Char as much as he does with her. Now aren't you supposed to meet Jami and Vani?"

Jenneta and Fionilina followed Sheala out of the room. "Any ideas as to who the man is she's been thinking about?" Jenneta whispered.

Fionilina shook her head. "No, but if I know you, Jenneta, you'll soon find out."

* * * * *

Sheala stared out her bedroom window. In just a few

short hours, the grounds of the estate would be filled with people celebrating Summer Solstice. She glanced back at the stack of notes on her dresser, all asking for an assignation. She chuckled. The Alalakan clan was rich and powerful, and many families were encouraging their sons and daughters to make themselves and their availability to be her first sexual liaison known. All of them were hoping for a lasting attachment that was often formed with a first lover. Every now and then, marriages did sometimes result from a young man or woman's first love affair. The possibility of an alliance with the Alalakan clan was not to be ignored.

"What kind of makeup and jewelry are you going to wear?"

Sheala looked back at Vani. "I don't know. At first I thought I wanted to look like everybody else, but now I think I want to look different."

"Well, Brianna is about as different as you can get, unless you want to ask Deni."

Jami giggled. "That would be different, dressing like a Gattan. Maybe Brianna will lend you her red diamonds."

Sheala shook her head. "No. They won't match my dress, but she'll probably have some ideas for me. Come on."

With both Medirian princesses in tow, Sheala led the way to Brianna's apartments. In a few short minutes, Sheala stood in the middle of Brianna's sitting room floor in her new dress as her sister-in-law circled her slowly.

"It certainly doesn't hide anything, Shea. That dress fits you like a second skin."

Sheala grinned. "Why would I want to hide anything?"

Her sister-in-law sighed and shook her head. "Never mind. I'll get used to it, I suppose. I guess you don't plan on wearing any underwear."

Vani and Jami both giggled as Sheala said, "Under what?"

Brianna just snorted. "Did you ever think of cutting your

hair, Shea?"

"I used to cut it all the time."

"No, I mean really short."

"How short? I don't want to look like Rodane," Sheala protested thinking of her brother's very short hair.

"No, not like that. I mean cut and styled. You have a lovely neck and should show it off."

"What do you have in mind?"

Half an hour later, with the help of Brianna's maid Verna, who was quite adept at styling hair, Sheala had a unique hairstyle for a Drakian. Most of her hair had been cut off. What was left was styled to frame her head—longer on the top and sides, tapered in the back.

She loved it.

Thick bangs stopped just short of her eyebrows and emphasized her brown eyes. Her ears were exposed, and thanks to her Medirian ancestry, she had earlobes, earlobes that now displayed a pair of blue Medirian pearls donated by Jenneta.

With her hair cropped short, her neck and shoulders were displayed to their best advantage. A man wouldn't have any trouble trailing kisses along either.

"Your grandmother's ear cuffs are lovely, and I have the perfect necklace and bracelet to match them," Brianna said as she walked into her bedroom. In a few minutes, she returned carrying a large box. Setting it on the table, she opened it to reveal row upon row of blue pearls.

Sheala gasped. "Brianna, they're beautiful."

Lifting them out of the box, Sheala draped them around her neck. Shimmering incandescently against the midnight blue of her dress, they fell below her waist.

Brianna gazed at her critically and said, "Let's try this."

Looping the necklace once around Sheala' neck, Brianna draped the necklace down Sheala's back like a cape. Clasping a silver bracelet studded with more pearls around Sheala's wrist, Brianna said, "Since this dress is backless, the pearls will seem to glow in soft light. A beautiful effect, I think. What do you think, Shea?"

Her reflection in the mirror had a stunned expression on her face. A stranger looked back at her. Brianna had applied small amounts of cosmetics earlier to highlight Sheala's eyes, high cheekbones and mouth. The haircut and pearls were the finishing touches.

Sheala swallowed. "I don't know myself."

The door connecting Brianna's sitting room with that of the guest quarters opened, and Ban sauntered in followed by Marljas. Both men stopped immediately upon seeing Sheala.

Smiling provocatively, Sheala glanced at the two men from under her lashes. "Well, Coz, what do you think?"

"Shea, if you weren't my cousin, I'd carry you to the nearest bed right now," Ban said in a very serious tone as he walked completely around her and examined her with a critical eye. "You're very beautiful, Coz. Men will ache to possess you. What do you think, Marljas?"

"It's a very nice dress," he managed to stammer, "but a Gattan maiden would not wear something so revealing."

Sheala snorted. There he went with that Gattan maiden nonsense again. "Well, I'm not a Gattan maiden, am I?" she quipped.

"Here, Sheala," Verna said with a mischievous twinkle in her eye. "Since you're all dressed, you may as well add perfume. You're an expert, Ban. What do you suggest?"

"Vedsissian musk, if you have it."

"There's some on my dresser," Brianna said.

Verna returned with an intricately carved bottle. Removing its stopper, she liberally applied the perfume to Sheala's wrists. Then she slowly drew the stopper down the deep valley between her breasts.

Marljas coughed, stammered something about Denieen, and fled the room.

"Don't forget that Jamiros wants to see us in the library in about an hour," Ban called out with a grin.

Char entered the room with a quizzical look on his face. "What's wrong with Marljas?" he asked. "He just passed me looking as if the ghosts of all seven hell were pursuing him."

Ban continued to grin and winked at Verna before he answered. "He forgot about something Deni wanted him to do."

Before Char could say anything else, Brianna said, "Don't just stand there, Char, tell your sister how beautiful she is."

Char turned his attention to Sheala. His eyes widened as he stared at her. "Is that really you, Shea? What did you do to your hair?" Then, with a grin, he lifted her into a huge hug. "You're absolutely beautiful. You're bound to receive offers tonight. Is there anyone you're interested in? Some of our business associates have unmarried sons."

"Leave her alone, Char," Brianna scolded with a smile. "Shea is going to have a good time tonight, and that's all that matters. There are other things in life beside possible business connections."

Sheala grinned as her brother winked at his wife. "There are a number of others things I find far more interesting than business, as you well know, love. Shall I start with your lovely breasts?"

Brianna blushed a fiery red. "Char!"

Grinning from ear to ear, Sheala said, "Come on, Vani, Jami. Let's go. You two still have to get dressed."

"Only if Verna comes," Vani said. "I want my hair cut like yours."

That remark silenced everyone.

"But Vani, you're a Medirian princess!" exclaimed her sister. "We never cut our hair."

Borrowing a comment from Brianna, Vani answered, "What does that have to do with the price of tea in China? I like that hairstyle, and I want it. I don't care what anyone says."

Verna shrugged. "I'll cut your hair, Princess. I'm too old to worry about your parents' possible anger."

With those words, Verna led the three girls from the room, Jami arguing vociferously with her sister.

Chapter Five

ဆ

Fingers laced together, Marljas rested his elbows on his knees and stared at the floor. For the last few days—and nights—he'd replayed his sexual encounter with Sheala over and over. If he'd done the same with a Gattan maiden, every male member of her family would want to gut him, along with many of the men in his own family. But this wasn't Gattan. Sheala wasn't Gattan—as she had so plainly demonstrated.

Straightening, he wiped his face with his hands. He'd never met a woman like her. Young as he was, he'd been captain of his own ship for the last three years. He'd been to many spaceports on all five known planets. Therefore, he had far more sexual experience that almost all other unmated male Gattans his age. But no woman had ever satisfied him the way Sheala had, and he hadn't even experienced true intercourse with her! She was intelligent and had a wonderful sense of humor which, in his opinion, was just as important as sexual desire. She was a woman a man could talk to and share his dreams with. And she had blooded him.

He wanted her. He would have her, no matter what anyone said. She was his.

He leaned his head back and closed his eyes. But what if she didn't want to mate him—mate in the sense it meant to truly mate with each other? She wanted sex, he had no doubt about that. But did she really understand what mating meant to a Gattan? Was it just casual sex to her? Drakians had many sexual partners before they mated or "married", as they called it.

Marljas shifted. More than a few Drakians had numerous sexual partners even after they married. Would Sheala be like that?

A low growl rumbled in his chest.

Sheala lying with another man! Anger surged. No man of any species would touch her. She was his!

Marljas didn't realize he'd snarled out loud until his brother sighed.

He glanced at Wendjas.

Wearing a resigned look on his face, his brother stared back. "As soon as I heard Sheala nicked your neck with that damned sword, I knew this would happen. You've become infatuated. You're still young, Brother, and impetuous. Take heed what happened last time you became obsessed with a woman."

Marljas' growl rumbled around the room. "Sosha was different."

"How so? You saw a beautiful woman. You wanted her. You thought you were in love. Where is the difference?"

"I was younger then."

"Oh? You're so old now?"

Snarling, Marljas leaped to his feet and paced back and forth, clasping and unclasping his fists. "You challenged and practically killed Chardadon over Denieen. Tell me, were you thinking rationally at the time?"

Wendjas started to reply, but his wife interrupted him as she entered the room. "Marljas is right, my love. You weren't thinking very rationally when you challenged Char. If you had been, you would have known he held no interest for me. And you know why."

Stopping his pacing, Marljas looked from Denieen to his brother and back again. Then began to grin. "So my straitlaced, by-the-rules brother dallied where he shouldn't have before he was properly mated."

Stiffening, Wendjas glared at his wife. "This is an unsuitable topic to discuss in mixed company, Wife. We've been among these morally loose Drakians too long. As soon as…"

Wendjas' voice trailed off as he stared at his wife.

Marljas looked back at Denieen and blinked.

Instead of wearing traditional Gattan clothing, she was dressed in a Drakian evening gown and, though it was much more modest than Sheala's, it was still the most provocative garment he'd ever seen her wear. "Wife of my brother, you are beautiful."

Denieen wore a vibrant scarlet gown of soft, silken material that fell lightly from her shoulders and hugged her breasts. The gown's neck was modestly cut, with only a hint of cleavage and the soft swell of her upper breasts revealed. Belted snugly beneath her breasts with golden ribbons, the gown's skirt fell in soft folds to the floor. Her graceful upper arms were bare, revealing to all that she too wore Gattan scars, though not nearly as many as her husband. Her abundant hair had been piled on top of her head and was held in place with three strategically placed hairpins that glittered with red diamonds. More of the jewels graced the golden necklace, earrings and bracelets she wore.

Marljas shook his head. Denieen had been spending a great deal of time with Brianna, and her choice of apparel underscored that fact.

Wendjas opened his mouth to speak, choked, cleared his throat, and growled, "Deni, what are you wearing?"

She twirled and the gown's skirt billowed provocatively about her. "It's beautiful, isn't it? Jenneta thought I should have the cleavage slit down to my navel, but I managed to talk her out of that."

"Wife!" Wendjas roared. "You can*not* wear such a dress. It is fit only for the bedroom!"

"Wait until you see what Sheala's wearing," Marljas muttered to himself.

Denieen stopped twirling and drew herself to her full

height. Crossing her arms, she said, "Do you question my morals, Husband?"

Marljas stepped back. A Gattan with an angry wife was not envied by anyone.

Swallowing, his brother held up his hands and shook his head. "Deni, I implied nothing like that. But none of our women have ever worn a dress like that—in public."

"It's about time one of us did," she answered with great dignity. "I ask you, Husband, does this dress reveal more of me than my training clothing, than my bathing costume?"

"No, but…"

Smiling, Deni walked to her husband and put her hand on his arm. "It's not a traditional Gattan dress, is it? But is that so terrible? We came here because our family decided that the old ways were not the best, that if we truly wanted to compete on a galactic scale, Gattan would have to change. This is a small change, Wendjas. One, I might add, that many Gattan women will enjoy, and you men will come to appreciate." Leaning closer, Deni whispered, "Wait until you see what I have to wear after the party, my love."

Marljas grinned at his brother. "What was it you argued about with Father? 'We cannot stay tied to past traditions which have little use in the future'?"

His brother shot him a disgruntled look but said nothing, obviously not stupid enough to argue against his own words.

Denieen patted his hand. "Go change. Marljas needs a woman's counsel. I've laid your 'traditional' clothing on the bed."

Mumbling something under his breath about wives in general, Wendjas disappeared into their bedroom.

Marljas' grin faded as Deni's thoughtful gaze locked with his. "Well?"

He glanced uneasily at his feet. "I don't know how to start."

"Let's start with the fact that Sheala blooded you."

Marljas looked up and nodded.

"Men!" Denieen muttered. "Why are you confused? Is Sheala a Gattan to realize what that cut meant? Do you expect her to understand the consequences of her actions?"

He shook his head. "No, she didn't realize the seriousness of what she did."

"Why, then, is this a problem?"

Marljas locked gazes with his sister-in-law once again. "I want her."

"Then take her, if she agrees."

Marljas' mouth dropped open. He snapped it shut. "But — she's a maiden, the daughter of our hostess. She cannot be treated in such a manner!"

Denieen sighed and rolled her eyes. "We have both just agreed that Sheala is not Gattan. She doesn't know our customs, and her own upbringing will make some of them seem ludicrous to her. Tonight she is acknowledged as a full woman in Drakian society, a society with much looser moral standards than ours. She is expected to take lovers."

A low growl rumbled in Marljas' chest. "I will not share her."

Denieen's eyebrows rose. "I have spoken a great deal with Sheala, Marljas. She doesn't impress me as the type of girl who will jump from the bed of one man immediately to that of another."

The growl deepened. "I don't want her in another man's bed — ever. I want to mate her."

Cupping his face in her hands, Denieen smiled gently. "Sheala is her own woman, Marljas. She'll make her own decisions. You've only known her a few weeks."

Marljas' shoulders slumped. "I don't understand, Deni. She's not even Gattan, yet something about her calls to me. I didn't feel this way with Sosha. I lusted after her body, but that was all. I want Sheala in my bed, but I also like talking with her."

Deni grinned. "When you're not arguing."

"Sheala does not understand Gattan values!"

"Maybe because they seem backward and unnecessary to her," she answered as she stepped back away from him. "Think. What exactly is it about Sheala that you truly want? Here on Drakan, you have the opportunity to discover that without being constrained by our society. Here you can bed Sheala without fearing the ramifications that would ensue if you were discovered on Gattan. If it is only her exoticness and sex that you want, you won't be long in discovering this."

"What if it is more?"

"That we will deal with if it arises. For now, take your place among the Drakian clan with which you have established a bloodbond. Learn their ways and adopt any which seem relevant."

"Including that of bedding willing women."

"Including that, Marljas. There is one thing you must take into consideration, though."

"What's that?"

"Sheala may not want you. Now go on. The Alalakans wish to speak to you in the library."

Fists clenched, Marljas strode from the room. Deni was wrong; Sheala wanted him as much as he wanted her. He just wished he knew for how long.

* * * * *

Standing in the shadows, Sheala watched as her father walk across the stage.

"My friends," Jamiros began, "welcome to my home on this Solstice evening. It is a time of momentous changes in the Alalakan clan, changes I will share with you tonight."

Listening to her father's voice but tuning out his words,

Sheala searched the crowd for her friends. Eventually, she spotted Vani and Jami standing close to the end of the stage amongst many of her other friends.

Her grandmother grabbed her and tugged her forward. "Pay attention, Sheala. It's your turn now."

When they reached her father, Jamiros pulled her into a tight hug then turned her to face the crowd. "I have saved the most important reason for tonight's celebration for last. My friends, today my daughter Sheala takes her place as an adult in our society. I ask that you celebrate this special occasion in her life with us."

Laughing, Sheala waved to her friends as the crowd burst into loud applause. Tonight was her night, and she planned to enjoy every minute of it.

Before she realized what was happening, Ban appeared at her side and swept her into his arms. Planting a huge kiss on her cheek, he took the few short steps to the edge of the stage and tossed her into the shadows to the side of the stage.

Shrieking, her dress billowing around her as her arms and legs windmilled, Sheala fell through the air. Squeezing her eyes closed, she sucked in her breath and braced herself to hit the ground. *Damn Ban and his practical jokes. I'm going to strangle him.*

She fell into a pair of strong arms, was hugged against a muscular chest.

A deep voice said, "I have you."

Throwing her arms around his neck, she held on for dear life.

Opening her eyes, she locked gazes with Marljas. Slowly, he loosened his arms and allowed her to slide down along the length of his muscular body.

Even more slowly, he slid his hands down her arms.

Goose bumps erupted on her arms.

He looked deeply into her eyes and smiled a slow smile.

He slid his right hand down her side and caressed her hip. "I will always catch you."

Before she could react, he released her and stepped back.

Yet another set of hands grabbed hers, and she was whirled away into the crowd — but not without craning her neck to search for the dark form hidden in the shadows.

Marljas had watched Jamiros' introductions from the shadows at the side of the stage. Those guests who noticed him stayed well away, none of them comfortable in the presence of a Gattan with his claws extended.

A teasing scent reached his nostrils, and he tensed as Jamiros hugged his daughter and turned her to face the crowd. He scowled at the thought of other men seeing how revealing her dress was. Her nipples pushed against the soft blue material and, when the breeze flattened her dress against her hips, the small tuft of springy hair at the juncture of her thighs was obvious.

Every man in the crowd who wasn't a relative had to be lusting after her.

From the corner of his eye, Marljas saw Ban's signal. Bracing himself, he caught Sheala as Ban tossed her down to him, grunting at the strain it put on his almost-healed ribs. Ignoring her shriek of surprise as she wrapped her arms around his neck, he dropped her legs and quickly wrapped his other arm around her, cupping her firm buttocks and pulling her hard against him.

Her eyes locked with his as she slowly slid down his firm body. When her feet touched the ground, he slid his hands down her arms, stroked her hip.

"I will always catch you," he murmured and stepped back.

His smiled faded as Sheala was pulled away from him.

Then his smile returned. The night had barely begun.

* * * * *

For the first time that evening, Sheala found herself alone. Her last dance partner had been dragged away by his unhappy betrothed, and she had no idea to whom she had promised the next dance.

"You haven't danced with me, Sheala."

Slowly, she turned around to face Marljas. "You haven't asked me."

"I couldn't get near you. You've been surrounded by men all evening."

She grinned. "You didn't try very hard then. Crowds have been parting before you all night."

His grin was feral. "You noticed?"

Glad she didn't blush like Brianna, Sheala dipped her head and changed the subject as she slipped out of her shoes. "Can we just find somewhere to sit down? My feet are, as Brianna says, killing me."

Marljas held out his arm. "I'd be happy to sit with you. There's a bench there, under that Chotton bush."

Placing her hand on Marljas' bare arm—he wore a sleeveless shirt that displayed the scars on his arms—Sheala walked towards the bench with him. She moved her fingers slightly, enjoying the soft feel of the hair on his arms against the pads of her fingers.

A bird called.

A muscle in his forearm flexed.

She looked up and batted her eyelashes. "Will you fetch me a drink, please?"

Marljas sighed. "Don't practice your flirting on me, Sheala. If you're thirsty, I'll be happy to fetch you a drink. All you need to do is ask."

Sheala began to pout but then broke into her more customary grin. "I keep forgetting when to stop. I'm sorry," she answered, rubbing her thumb against the tendons in his wrist. "I would like some punch, if you don't mind."

The muscles in his arm jumped again. "Sit and rest your feet. I'll get you a drink."

Smiling, Sheala sat down. "Thank you, Marljas. I'll be right here."

He has a remarkable ass, she thought as she watched him walk away.

Returning with two glasses of punch to where he had left Sheala, Marljas found himself alone. The rustle of leaves off to the left drew his attention, and he set the punch on the bench and followed the soft sounds through the shadows.

In a matter of minutes, he found Sheala in the grasp of a young Drakian.

"What are you doing, Histenc?" she spat as she tried to wrench her arm from the young man's grasp.

He jerked her forward and wrapped his other arm around her waist. "Just what you want me to. You've been teasing me for the last year. Tonight your teasing stops."

She struggled against him. "You must be deranged. Go away and leave me alone or I'll scream."

"No one will hear you," the young man snapped as he tried to kiss her.

Turning her face away, Sheala kicked his shin, gritting her teeth against the pain that shot through her bare toes.

Histenc cursed but didn't let her go.

In the shadows, Marljas lashed his tail. The fool had dared to lay a hand on Sheala! On Gattan, he'd be free to gut any man who tried to drag a woman away from her family. Here, though, there could be ramifications he didn't know about. Best to keep his temper under control. After one last deep breath, he stepped into the moonlight and crossed his arms over his chest. "Drop your hand, Drakian—or lose it."

Both Sheala and Histenc froze.

He glared at Marljas. "This is none of your business, Gattan. Leave while you still can. I have friends with me."

Marljas grinned, flexed his muscles as he uncrossed his arms, and unsheathed his claws. "Come then. You *and* your friends."

The tall young man looked back over his shoulder. "Rejis, Pazco, where are you?"

More leaves rustled, and the sound of running footsteps faded away.

His gaze locked on Histenc, Marljas drew a claw across his forearm. A fine line of blood appeared. "Your friends decided to leave. I suggest you do the same. Unless you wish to challenge me?"

As he watched a drop of Marljas' blood fall to the ground, Histenc swallowed nervously.

Sheala kicked him again and jerked free.

A full snarl erupted from Marljas when he saw the red marks on her arm. "Go, Drakian. Go now, if you wish to keep all of your blood."

After one more look at Marljas' claws, Histenc turned and ran.

Marljas' gaze never left Sheala. "Are you all right?"

Anger flashing in her eyes, she snapped, "I could have freed myself."

"I know," he answered with a grin, "but he found my claws far more intimidating."

For a moment she glared at him. Then she sighed heavily. "True. I wish I could get some for myself."

Marljas chuckled softly.

She continued to stare into the bushes where her assailant had disappeared as he stepped closer and gently clasped her upper arm.

"Sheala?"

"Why was he so mean? What did I ever do to him?"

Marljas slid his knuckles along her cheek. "He wants you."

She shook her head. "But why? No matter what he says, I never encouraged him."

Glancing up, she lost herself in his intense, golden gaze.

Marljas didn't answer. Lifting her wrist to his mouth, he kissed the angry red lines caused by Histenc's fingers. Then he slid his hands up her arms, over her shoulders and up the sides of her neck. Gently, he cupped her face. "You're very beautiful, Sheala. Few men can resist you. I know I can't." Lowering his head, he nuzzled her lips, then placed soft, quick kisses on the corners of her mouth.

She sighed and slid her hands up his forearms. He sucked her lower lip into his mouth. Moaning, she wrapped her fingers around his forearms.

Freeing her lip, Marljas pulled back slightly and gazed down into her face. He stroked her jaw with his thumb. "I have wanted you since the first moment I saw you."

A mischievous smile appeared on her face. "Oh? Why did you cut yourself when I was watching?"

His own chuckle answered hers. "To test your courage?"

"Like hell," she murmured as she placed her palms against his chest. "You wanted to scare me away. I don't scare that easily."

"For which I am eternally grateful." Marljas covered her mouth with his, moving his lips slowly.

Sheala leaned into his body and opened her mouth.

Dropping his hands from her face, Marljas wrapped his arms around her and pulled her against his chest. Slipping his tongue between her lips, he caressed the sides and top of her mouth, reveling in her taste. She was sweet and tart all at once, better than the finest Gattan wine. The silk dress she wore was a flimsy barrier, and her flesh quivered beneath his hand as he stroked her back and buttocks.

Her nipples stabbed his chest. Never had he wanted a woman so much! Then he slid his tongue against hers, groaning when she sucked it deeper into her mouth.

A shudder raced through Sheala's body.

Marljas' tongue was rougher than that of anyone she'd ever kissed. It circled the inside of her mouth, stroked teeth and palate, slid and twined about her own, its rough texture titillating and exciting.

Her nipples tightened more, and moisture seeped between her thighs as Sheala clung to his soft leather shirt, grateful that he was holding her so tightly because her legs were shaking. Inside her dress, her tail was twitching. If it were free, she'd have wrapped it around his thigh and tickled his balls with the tip.

He slid his hand down her back, cupped her buttock, and pulled her against his erection.

She rose on tiptoe and rubbed her hips against him.

His cock was a long, hard ridge in the front of his pants.

She wanted that cock, wanted it buried deep within her.

When he pulled his mouth from hers, she fisted her hands around the two braids of hair hanging in front of his ears and tried to tug his head back down to hers.

Sucking breath into his body with huge gasps, he resisted and stared down into her face. "Look at me."

When she did, he steadied her and then stepped back and held out his hand. "Come."

Her heart racing, Sheala looked at his outstretched hand. His voice both demanded obedience and cajoled at the same time. She hesitated only a moment. Silently she placed her hand in his and followed him into the darkness.

* * * * *

Ban picked up the blue slippers that still lay on the bench. Sheala would not have left them, and Marljas would not have left her alone. There could only be one reason for them not to be waiting here for him. The attraction between them had finally become too strong to resist.

He looked off into the darkness towards the landing pad where Marljas' ship sat. That's where he'd taken her, to a place where they wouldn't be interrupted.

Ban shook his head again, still amazed that no one else had noticed the growing attraction between them. How his grandmother had missed it, he'd never know. Sighing, he tucked Sheala's slippers under his arm. "I just hope the two of you know what kind of problems your actions might cause."

Chapter Six

ဢ

Fifteen minutes later, Marljas halted next to the *Scrathe*, his warbird. Taking a small controller from his belt, he entered the code that opened a small door in the side. A flexible ladder dropped to the ground.

Marljas turned to her, his voice low and intense. "Sheala, do you wish to come up?"

She looked up at the sleek ship and shivered in the gentle breeze. "Yes."

Marljas hadn't realized that he'd been holding his breath until he let it out. If she had asked, he'd have immediately taken her back to the house.

He grabbed hold of the ladder. "You had best go up first. I'll follow so I can catch you if you fall."

She punched him in the arm. "Fall! There's not a tree on the estate I haven't conquered." Grabbing the ladder, she climbed up.

Marljas admired the supple play of her buttocks against her thin, blue dress as he followed her up the ladder. The tip of her tail as it dipped below the hem of her dress was tantalizing.

Once they were inside the ship, dim lights flickered on. Marljas pulled the ladder up behind him then closed and locked the door. He took her hand and led her deeper into the ship.

Sheala looked about curiously. Gattan warbirds were deceptive in their size. She'd been in many types of interplanetary ships over the years, but no non-Gattan had ever been in a warbird. Fully capable of extensive interplanetary flight, they were also able to enter a planet's atmosphere, making a landing shuttle unnecessary. The *Scrathe* didn't seem that large yet was capable of carrying a full complement of ten warriors. Though cramped, there were sleeping quarters, a small mess and sanitary facilities that included a small shower. As captain, Marljas had private sleeping quarters. It was to those quarters that he led Sheala.

Before they entered, Marljas pulled her to him for a quick, hard kiss. "Wait for me here. A light was flashing in Communications, and I must see what it means."

Sheala nodded silently. That kiss had taken her breath away.

Marljas made his way back to Communications and pressed a button to save whatever message had been sent. His mind was completely on Sheala, or he would have realized that the message demanded immediate attention. Marljas and his brother had come to Drakan with the understanding that there would be a complete communications blackout with their family on Gattan. Only something very important would have caused their father to try to contact them.

Sheala glanced around Marljas' private quarters. There wasn't much to see. The bunk took up most of the space, and it was to the bunk she went. A mischievous smile appeared on her face. Pulling her dress over her head, she dropped it on the floor and arranged herself on the bed.

When Marljas returned to his quarters, Sheala was stretched out on his bunk. She'd removed her dress—he'd already known she wore nothing underneath. The pearls that had fallen so gracefully from her shoulders were now draped down her body, the strands parting around her pouting breasts and finally coming to rest between her legs, the luminescent pearls tangled amongst the dark tuft of curls on her almost completely shaved mons.

When he stopped next to the bunk, she snaked her tail around his calf.

He choked.

Lifting her hand, she smiled. "Not what you'd expect from the typical Gattan maiden?"

Falling to his knees, he took her hand, turned it over, and kissed her palm. His tongue followed his lips.

Sheala squirmed. What a tongue! The pearl necklace rolled across her body as her nipples hardened even more.

Dropping her hand, he rose to his feet and pulled off his vest. His belt thunked to the floor. He'd removed his boots before he came back into his quarters. When his hands slid to the waistband of his trousers, Sheala sucked in her breath, her gaze glued to the long, hard erection outlined against his leather pants.

Marljas had begun to ease his trousers down when he saw the eagerness flash in Sheala's eyes. He ached to possess her, but he forced himself to slow down. Sheala might technically be a virgin, but she was Drakian. From what she'd said about a sexual instructor—in his mind he snarled at the thought of another man touching her intimately—she probably had more sexual experience than he did. She'd quickly mastered him the day he and Ban had dueled. Her hot mouth had sucked all his self-control from him. Tonight, he wanted *her* mindless with passion.

Leaving his trousers hugging his hips, Marljas sat down on the bunk next to her.

Her gaze leaped to his face. "What's wrong...?"

"Shhhh. I don't want to rush, *Cheta*."

"But..."

Marljas didn't give her a chance to continue. Leaning over, he covered her mouth with his, his tongue thrusting and mating with hers.

Moving restlessly, she moaned low in her throat.

Lifting his head, he smiled. "Your skin is so soft." He trailed a finger over her collarbone then cupped her right breast, rubbing his thumb over her nipple. He laid his palm on her rib cage, slid it down over her abdomen and stomach. When he cupped his hand between her legs, she arched her back and rose up to meet it.

"Mmmmmmmm," she moaned when he pulled his hand away to caress her thigh, circle his thumb on her kneecap and trail his fingers down her calf muscle.

"Softer than the finest Deslossian wool, the rarest Varcian *guguntha* leather."

He slid his hand back up her body and looked into her eyes. His breathing became harsher. His voice was a growl. "I want you."

Her whisper embraced him. "I want you, too."

Sliding onto the bunk next to her, he propped himself up on one arm and plucked her nipple with his free hand. He rolled pearls against it.

Gasping, she arched again.

"Marljas, please…"

He ignored her entreaty. "You're so beautiful."

Again, he stroked his hand down over her chest, across her abdomen, and along her side to her hip. Then he stroked back up and cupped her breast.

"You belong in my bed." Lifting a strand of the necklace, he rolled the smooth pearls between her breasts.

She moaned then reached for him.

Marljas caught her hands and lifted them above her head. "Keep them there."

Her breasts bouncing with her rapid breathing, she nodded. "Don't just look at me! Please! Your tongue, Marljas. I want you tongue all over — and in — me."

He kissed her. Lifting his head, he stared into her eyes. "I could just look at you the rest of the night and die a happy man."

She opened her mouth to answer.

He laid one finger on her lips.

"I would die happy but unsatisfied, and I am not a man who leaves himself unsatisfied. Before I'm finished, I'll have tasted every inch of your body."

When he finally dragged his tongue across her right nipple, Sheala gritted her teeth.

When he lapped her left nipple, she moaned. When he stroked a long, slow line down the center of her chest and over quivering stomach, pausing for a quick dip in her navel, she sobbed. When he settled between her legs, pushed her thighs apart and lapped her moist, swollen lips, she screamed. Never had she considered or anticipated the possibility of such delicate roughness from a man's tongue. The exquisitely torturous abrasions tantalized every nerve in her body.

Sheala spread her legs wider.

He kissed the insides of her thighs, nibbled them, then followed his gentle nibbles with quick sweeps of his tongue.

Whimpering, she thrust her hips towards him. "More."

His chuckle was devilish. "How long can you hold back? How long shall I allow you to hold back?"

When she whipped her tail around his torso, he imprisoned it against the inside of her thigh then dragged his tongue up between her legs and over her clit. "That's too dangerous to remain free, I think."

Sheala wrapped the last eight inches of her tail around his wrist, squeezing and releasing pressure in time with the lapping of his tongue. He slipped first one, then two fingers into her and began to pump them.

When she groaned and thrust her hips up, he nipped her clit.

This second scream was louder. Arching completely off

the bed, she thrust her hips into his face and wrapped her legs around his head.

He sucked—harder and harder.

She jerked her hips once, twice, three times, then began to pump them rhythmically.

Marljas stabbed his tongue into her.

"Ahhhhhhh. More! More!" She fisted her hands in his thick hair, trying to pull his face closer to her body.

He resisted. "Easy, Sheala, easy." He nibbled the inside of her thigh.

She jerked his braids harder. "No! Now. I want to come now! Your tongue, gods, I love your tongue. Lick me—harder!"

Marljas tried to lift his head, but she clamped her thighs tighter.

Knowing when he was defeated, he buried his face between her thighs, sucked on her clit, and pushed the tip of his smallest finger into her anus.

Her scream echoed off the walls. Arching until only her head, neck, and shoulders remained on the bed, she rode Marljas' lips and tongue until the waves of her orgasm subsided. Then, loosening her legs from around his head, she sank weakly onto the damp sheets. She lay with her legs spread wide.

The sight of Sheala's sated body lying spread out before him on his bed was too much for Marljas. Rising, he unsheathed his claws and shredded the front of his pants, breathing a sigh of relief when his aching cock sprang free. Never had he been so hard.

Falling onto the bed, he settled himself on top of Sheala, nudging her thighs apart with his knees.

Claiming her mouth with his, he slid his fingers between her legs. Sheala moaned and rocked against them. She was hot, wet, eager.

Placing his hands on both sides of her head and resting his weight on his elbows, he settled his hips against her, sliding slid his aching cock up and down against her slippery lips—up, down, up, down. He kissed her once more, looked deep into her eyes, and said, "Tell me you want me, *Cheta.*"

Sheala spread her legs wider.

He could feel sweat beading on his forehead. His cock ached. He needed to bury himself deep inside her. "Tell me you want this!"

Sheala opened her eyes.

Dark fire danced in her eyes.

"Yes. I want you. Deep. Love me."

Marljas grinned at her words. "I will love you, Shea, until you are drowning in our passion."

Once more, he covered her mouth with his. His hands traveled down the side of her body to slide underneath and cupped her buttocks.

He positioned himself, slid the head of his cock against her. His stomach muscles tightened as he prepared to thrust.

She held him close, her hands traveling freely up and down his back, kneading and caressing his buttocks.

He pulled his mouth from hers and sucked a nipple into his mouth as he raised her hips.

She dug her nails into his ass cheeks.

When he thrust his cock in, her hot, wet muscles tightened around him, pulled him deeper.

She pushed her hips against his.

Fully embedded, Marljas lay perfectly still. Gods! She was tight!

She moaned.

He kissed her cheeks. "Hush. I'm sorry I hurt you. It will get better, I promise. The pain could not be helped."

She buried her hands in his hair and yanked his head up.

Staring into his eyes, she gasped, "Pain! I don't care about the damn pain. Move! I need you to move!" She wiggled her hips then thrust against him. "You feel good, damn it!" She wiggled beneath him.

Completely nonplussed, Marljas stared down into her face. The culture of Gattan didn't encourage promiscuity. Daughters were closely watched. None would have answered him as Sheala had. At least he didn't think so. Maybe all those tales about sex being painful for virgins were wrong. Or maybe Sheala was different because she was Drakian.

Sheala bucked against him again. "Move, damn it." A sharp crack echoed around the room when she slapped his ass.

That sharp pain caught Marljas by surprise. Burying his face in her neck, he nipped her — hard enough to draw blood — in approximately the spot identical to where she'd nicked his neck with her sword.

After a sharp intake of breath, Sheala bucked again, slipping her tail beneath her butt when she raised it. "If you want to play rough..." She whipped her tail between his thighs, wrapped it around his balls, and squeezed.

Again she bucked her hips against his, dug her nails into his buttocks. "Move your ass, Marljas, now!"

"Yes!" Dipping his head, Marljas lapped the blood from her neck and began to pump his hips, slowly at first, then faster.

Her thrusts matched his. Her squeezing tail matched his rhythm. Her slick, internal muscles gripped and pulled at his cock.

Sweat broke out on his brow. He snarled against her neck. "Mine."

She slapped his ass again. "Make me come again, Marljas. Swivel your hips. Make me come. Now!"

Hot lust pounded though Marljas' body as he gyrated his hips and thrust forward — harder and harder.

Sheala wrapped her legs around his waist and arched up

to meet every thrust. Her tail slipped from his balls. The tip probed his anus.

Roaring, Marljas slammed his cock into Sheala as far as he could, exploding like a volcano deep inside her body.

Beneath him, Sheala arched her hips against his. Her scream was muffled by his shoulder when she bit his shoulder. She raked her nails down his back and grabbed his ass. Deep inside her cunt, her internal muscles milked every last drop of cum from his cock.

He dropped his forehead against the pillow, brushing her shoulder with his lips as his hair fell forward to mix with hers.

She unwrapped her legs from around his waist and nuzzled his chest.

When he finally rolled from her body, the only sounds Marljas could hear were their combined breathing.

Finally, after a deep breath, Sheala rolled onto his chest and smiled a sleepy smile.

When she would have spoken, he placed a finger on her lips, then kissed her.

Yawning, she snuggled closer to his chest and wrapped her tail around his thigh. Her eyelids drooped. Soon, she slept.

His chest rumbling with contentment, Marljas pulled her closer and closed his eyes. His cock was still hard, but he'd let her rest a little. Then he'd put her on top of him and let her ride his cock as long as she wanted while he could stroke her soft skin until they both soared to the stars.

The message light blinking in Communications was completely forgotten.

* * * * *

Early the next morning before anyone in the Alalakan household woke, Marljas left Sheala at the door to her own room with a hard kiss and then made his way silently to the rooms he shared with Ban. Opening the door quietly, he slipped through the small sitting room and into his bedroom.

His chair leaning on two legs against the wall, Ban waited for him. "Sheala enjoyed the rest of her evening, I trust?"

Warily, Marljas eyed the man he had come to call friend. Being caught in a situation such as this on Gattan would result in a challenge from every male member of the girl's family. When they were finished with him, the girl would become his wife—if he lived.

Crossing his arms over his chest, he challenged, "What do you intend to do, Bandalardrac?"

Ban smiled. "I will neither do nor say anything. Shea's of age. It was her decision to spend the night in your bed. As long as she's content, I have no right to hold you accountable for anything."

Relaxing somewhat, Marljas pulled his tunic over his head and crossed the room. "Then why are you here?"

Ban's quick grin appeared. "If my sweet Coz were a Gattan, you'd be scarred for life."

Marljas looked over his shoulder into the mirror. "They aren't deep enough to scar, and she will be Gattan."

Ban's chair dropped to all four feet. His voice became hard. "Has she agreed to this?"

Marljas grinned ferally. "Relax, Alalakan don al' Bandalardrac. She's young, and I wouldn't force her into anything. I simply state a fact. She *will* be my wife, for I will have no other."

Muscles relaxing, the other man stared at Marljas and shook his head. "What if she doesn't want to become your wife?"

"She'll agree. She won't wish to do anything else."

Ban barked with laughter. "Don't think because you shared her first sexual experience, one that she probably enjoyed, that she'll come tamely to your hand. Sheala is an Alalakan and is just as strong-willed and opinionated as any other member of the clan. Be careful how you handle her, Marljas. She will not be led."

As he stripped off his breeches, Marljas said nothing but acknowledged Ban's words with a nod. Then he disappeared into the bathroom.

Soon Ban heard the water from the shower.

"Very well, my friend, think what you wish," Ban yelled over the sound of the water. "I'm going to find some breakfast."

Marljas walked out of the bathroom to an empty room. Naked, he stretched out on the bed. In minutes, he was asleep.

Not far away, Sheala hummed to herself as she stretched out on her bed. She too had taken the time for a quick rinse even though she'd used the shower facilities on Marljas' ship. Sheala closed her eyes and smiled as she ran the previous night's activities through her mind. She fell asleep remembering a pair of intense golden eyes gazing deeply into hers, a hard body moving over — and under — hers.

* * * * *

Early that afternoon, Sheala was awakened when Jami and Vani flopped onto her bed.

"Come on, Shea, wake up. You've been sleeping long enough, and this is our last day here," Vani said as she nudged her friend.

Sheala yawned and blinked. "Where are you going?"

"You're coming, too," answered Vani as Sheala sat up.

Sheala had been so tired when she and Marljas returned to the house, that she slipped into bed naked. When Sheala sat up, the light sheet that had covered her body slipped to her waist. Both Vani and Jami gasped.

"Shea! What happened to you?"

Looking in the mirror that hung across the room from her

bed, Sheala saw what her friends were talking about. Marljas was a thorough lover. Love bruises were evident on both her breasts, and there was a small scab on her neck where he'd nipped her.

Remembering, Sheala smiled.

"You did it, didn't you?" Vani choked out. "You made love with Marljas."

Nodding affirmatively, Sheala rose from the bed and disappeared into the bathroom. She returned wearing a silky robe wrapped tightly around her body. But before her friends were able to bombard her with more questions, the door opened and Jenneta walked in.

"So, you've finally awakened. I trust you enjoyed your birthday."

Both Jami and Vani giggled.

Sheala smiled widely. "It was wonderful, Grandmother."

A speculative expression appeared in Jenneta's eyes.

"We're leaving for Benishan tomorrow, and we've no idea how long we'll be there. You'll have to do your own packing since most of the staff is busy cleaning up. Can you be ready in time?"

"Of course."

Jenneta turned to the two Medirian princesses. "I expect you two to get busy immediately. I stopped in your rooms before I got here, and I know it's going to take the rest of the day for you to sort everything out. You won't have any maids to help you either. Now out with both of you."

Both girls groaned.

Sheala chuckled as her friends left. Neither one of them had to pick up after themselves at home.

"I promise to be ready on time, Grandmother."

Jenneta smiled at her granddaughter. "Marljas is a very handsome young man. The family would approve if you decided on him."

The door closed quietly behind Jenneta, and Sheala hugged herself and smiled. She'd already decided, though the family didn't need to know that just yet. She'd keep Marljas to herself for a while longer.

* * * * *

"We have plenty of room in the town house for you. Please feel free to accept our hospitality," Sheala heard her grandmother say as she hurried towards the transports waiting for them.

"We're honored by your invitation to stay with you while we're in your capital city, Jenneta," Denieen answered when they met on Benishan's landing pad next to the *Scrathe* and Ban's ship, the *Wanderer*. "However, it would be much wiser if we went on to the embassy. It would be extremely ill-bred of us to snub the ambassador and his wife. Marljas, however, will stay with you, if you don't mind."

Sheala smiled. She'd been disappointed that she had to fly to Benishan with Ban in the *Wanderer* rather than in the *Scrathe* with Marljas. True, if she'd revealed that she'd taken the Gattan as her first lover, she'd have been able to travel with him. And there was no reason not to tell her family. Still, part of her wanted to keep their relationship secret, at least for a while. What was more, though it was large, the town house was not as big as the estate. There were only a few possible rooms to which Marljas could be assigned.

"Take the first vehicle, Wendjas. I've instructed the driver to take you to the embassy," Char said as he rejoined the group.

As Brianna and Denieen were saying their farewells, Sheala hugged both Jami and Vani. They, along with Meri and her family, would be staying with the Medirian ambassador. Ambassador Prince Kavlalardrac was their uncle and he enjoyed whenever any members of his family could come to visit.

After exchanging quick hugs with Sheala, Jami and Vani disappeared into one of the cars. Shea waved as they drove off.

"Ban," Char called to his cousin. "I'm leaving you in charge. Make sure everything gets sorted out. I'm taking Brianna home."

Before Ban could answer, Char swept Brianna up into his arms and disappeared into one of the waiting transports.

Sheala looked around, but Marljas had disappeared.

"Posh," Jenneta said. "Come along, Fionilina, Sheala, Rodane."

Ban intercepted Sheala. "I'll keep Shea with me, if you don't mind, Grandmother.' I haven't had much of a chance to talk with her."

Jenneta smiled. "Of course, Ban. Just don't fill her mind with ridiculous ideas."

With a rakish grin on his face Ban said, "Nothing more ridiculous than asking for advice about a gift for Brianna's baby."

Jenneta smiled back but didn't answer. With a wave she and her companions were whisked away.

Ban pulled her towards one of the remaining transports. "Come on, Shea. I don't want to spend the rest of the day here at the landing pad."

"Relax, Ban," she answered, somewhat miffed. "It doesn't take that long to get home."

"It will today, Coz," he answered as he pushed her into the transport and slammed the door shut behind her. "Get out, Abas," he said to the Aradab sitting behind the controls, "I'll drive. You ride with Beti, Feni and Kahn."

* * * * *

Marljas grinned across the seat at Sheala. "Surprised to see me?"

Sheala glanced towards the driver, but opaque,

soundproof glass separated them.

He continued to grin. "Bandalardrac can be a very capable ally, yes?"

Sheala grinned back.

Before he could say another word, she scooted across the seat and plopped herself onto his lap. She wrapped one arm around his neck and freed his cock with her other hand.

"Kiss me. Now!"

Marljas needed no further encouragement.

In the front seat, Ban grinned and turned off the intercom.

Chapter Seven

ഇ

A day later, after a quick lunch, Sheala met Jami and Vani, who were accompanied by their Aradab guard Feni, at one of the more exclusive children's shops in Benishan. They were determined to pick out the best possible gifts for Brianna and Char's baby.

"I haven't seen anything I like better than the layette set we saw in the last shop," Jami said. "I'm going to go back and get that."

Sheala lifted a bright yellow suit. "I think I may buy the baby two gifts. These suits are just darling, but I also want to get some type of toy. If I'm not here when you return, I'll be in the toy shop across the street."

Feni frowned. "You should all stay together. I can't guard you adequately if you go to different stores."

Sheala grinned at her. "Relax, Feni. We're in Benishan, for goodness' sakes. What could happen to us here?"

"Princess Brianna should have been safe on our Medirian beach, but she was almost kidnapped."

Jami nudged the Aradab. "Oh come on, Feni. None of us are Brianna." She turned to Sheala. "We'll meet you in the toy store."

Grumbling, the Aradab glanced once more at Sheala, then followed her charges out the door.

After examining the infant clothing for another five minutes, Sheala chose a yellow suit and a green suit. "Just charge this to our account and have it delivered to the Alalakan town house."

"Of course, Alalakan dem al' Sheala. Your purchases will

be delivered within the hour."

Stepping outside, she sucked in a breath of fresh air and headed towards the toy store. A sharp pain in her shoulder caused her to swing around to face the stranger who had jabbed the needle into her. Before she could cry out, however, unconsciousness overpowered her.

"Pardon me, let me through," the tall man said as he carried Sheala down the street. "My cousin has fainted. I must get her to my transport."

"Should we call emergency personnel?" a helpful passerby asked.

He shook his head. "No. She suffers from a recurring medical condition. She just needs rest and that she can receive best at home."

Placing Sheala in the transport parked before him, the stranger shut the door and quickly jumped into the driver's side. In a few minutes, he had disappeared in the steady stream of traffic.

* * * * *

As Marljas grinned and laid down the winning hand in the card game he was playing with Brianna, Char and Ban, the door to the study burst open. Jami and her sister stomped into the room and dropped their packages on the floor. "Is Sheala here? It's not very funny of her to leave us waiting for her downtown."

Marljas froze. Sheala was missing? Where was she?

"A package from one of the infant shops was delivered about an hour ago, but we haven't seen her," Sheala's mother answered from across the room where she sat with Jenneta. "It's not like Shea to just leave you. I know she's got a playful streak, but she never purposefully causes undue worry. When did you last see her?"

"It has been over three hours, Alalakan dem al' Xdana," Feni answered from where she stood by the door.

Xdana turned to her mother-in-law. "Where do you think she could be?"

Jenneta shook her head. "I don't know. She said she was going shopping with Jami and Vani."

Marljas glanced around the room. Worried looks had appeared on everyone's face, except Ban's. The promise of death for someone swam in his eyes.

Marljas blinked and Ban looked as he always had—only just worried.

Marljas blinked again. He must have been seeing things.

Pushing his chair away from the table, Ban sauntered towards the Aradab woman in the doorway. "You all know what Sheala's like. She gets interested in something and loses track of time."

Marljas stared at Ban. His voice was calm and reassuring but something about the way he held his body...

Trepidation began to roll in Marljas' stomach.

"Are people kidnapped on your planet?" Brianna interjected in a worried tone.

Marljas jerked his attention away from Ban and concentrated on Brianna. *Kidnapped? Who would kidnap Sheala? Why?*

Char said only one word. "Bakom."

Xdana's scream drew everyone's attention from the vicious snarl that erupted from Marljas' throat as he tore the arm from his chair.

* * * * *

Eliana stared as her boss led her into the laboratory which was filled with various pieces of equipment resting on both the floor and tables scattered about the room. Until this day, she had been unaware that this place existed. Very quickly, she noticed the eight large cages against the back wall. Only two of them were occupied, one with an unconscious Drakian woman, the other with a Gattan female obviously in thrall to the drug mithrin. Both women were nude.

Bakom stopped before the Gattan woman's cage. "Interesting specimen," he said as he unfastened Eliana's shirt and absentmindedly stroked her bare breast.

Eliana hid her grimace.

"We've discovered that the Gattan can become addicted to mithrin," he continued. "Once addicted, they are subject to very painful withdrawal symptoms if the drug is not administered on a regular basis. According to her chart, she received her last injection two hours ago. From ongoing observations, we've learned that she'll be sexually insatiable for two more hours. Then, as the drug begins to wear off, she will regain control of her body. For approximately two hours, she will be as sane and levelheaded as you and I. Then her body will begin to demand the drug until she is mindless with pain. Only another injection will relieve her."

Biting the inside of her cheek, Eliana nodded. She'd become very adept at hiding her disgust. "Very thorough, Doctor. You must let me see the notes."

Bakom's breathing became harsher and his tail began to jerk as he watched the Gattan's writhing body. "She's quite safe now, my dear. She craves sexual satisfaction and is very receptive to anyone who cares to mount her. Odam has enjoyed her body quite often. Of course, we had to remove her claws. They made her too dangerous." He cupped Eliana's breast, kneaded it, then dipped his head and sucked on her nipple.

"Doctor, I didn't know you had arrived."

Raising his head from Eliana's breast, Bakom looked over his shoulder. "Eliana, meet Gothran, Odam's brother. You'll be happy to know he is as well-endowed as his brother is."

Gothran only grunted. His eyes were fastened on Eliana's

bare breasts.

As Bakom squeezed her breast again, Eliana heard another door open and shut. Soon a slender woman joined them. Smiling, she walked into Bakom's arms, her mouth seeking his.

"Eliana, this is Tetiras," Bakom said when the passionate kiss ended. "You must get to know her better."

Tetiras turned to Eliana and smiled.

Eliana smiled in return as Tetiras reached out and cupped her breast, very aware that ultimate objective was Bakom's downfall. She was ready to do almost anything to help bring that about, even have sex with his assistants, no matter how disgusting she found it.

Bakom patted Tetiras' ass and said, "Not now, my dear, we have other things to do." Turning to Gothran, he said, "What surprise do you have for me?"

Opening the door to the cage holding the unconscious Drakian woman, Gothran stepped inside, lifted her into his arms, and carried her to an examining table. "Alalakan dem al' Sheala," was all he said.

Luckily for Eliana, the other three were concentrating on Sheala, or her painstaking infiltration of Bakom's closest assistants would have been all for naught. As it was, she was barely able to cover the shock and disgust on her face before he smiled at her.

"A fitting revenge, is it not, my dear? The Alalakans have caused me enough trouble. They attempt to block me in the Ruling Council and their arrogant son Chardadon took the redheaded humanoid from me on his ship. Their daughter is a fair trade for her, don't you think?"

At that moment, Eliana knew Bakom was insane. No Drakian would countenance the kidnapping of another in retribution for the theft of a so-called specimen Eliana knew to be as human as she was.

"She only reached her majority a few days ago," Bakom

said as he prodded and caressed Sheala's body. "And her nose stud declares her virginity. It falls to us to introduce her to the joys of sexual intercourse. Gothran, wake her. But carefully. I want her to be able to feel and understand what is happening to her, but in no way is she to have control of her own body."

"Of course, Doctor," Gothran said as he walked away. He returned in a few minutes with a hypodermic needle that he jabbed into Sheala's thigh.

Sheala began to regain consciousness almost immediately.

Bakom began to strip. "Excellent, Gothran. Strap her down so she doesn't slip and then tilt the table. I prefer that her first sexual experience be upright."

Blinking as the room spun around her, Sheala regained consciousness quickly—but try as she might, she couldn't move.

The room tilted. Dizziness assailed her and she closed her eyes. She opened them again.

No, the room wasn't tilting. She was.

A naked hermaphrodite appeared before her.

At first she simply stared. Then she realized who he was. A cold dread surged through her veins, but she swallowed her fear and glared at him. "Rodak don al' Bakom, my father and brothers will break every bone in your body and hang what's left for the scavengers."

Laughing, he lifted his thick tail and began to stroke it. "You have spirit. Breaking you will be a joy indeed."

"Do you want mithrin, Doctor?" a huge, ugly hermaphrodite asked as he too began to remove his clothing.

Dropping his now jerking tail, Bakom stepped closer to Sheala and cruelly squeezed her breast. "I think not, Gothran. A virgin should experience the pain of her first sexual experience to truly appreciate it."

Sheala gathered as much moisture as she had in her

mouth and spit in his face.

He backhanded her.

Blinking back tears as her lip began to swell immediately, Sheala sneered, "You will live to regret this."

"I had thought to be gentle with you your first time, but I've changed my mind."

Before Sheala could reply, he jabbed his tail between her thighs.

She gasped but did not cry out. Raising her chin, she sneered into his face. "Not what you expected?"

He slapped her again. "Whore." Withdrawing, he pushed the now naked Tetiras over a table and finished on her what he'd begun with Sheala.

"Who?" he demanded from Sheala after he'd finished with Tetiras.

Sheala's refusal to answer earned her a third slap.

She blinked back tears.

Bakom grunted. "The high and mighty Alalakan daughter no longer a virgin. You didn't waste any time, did you? Or, perhaps, you lost your virginity long before you assumed your majority, and that nose stud you wear is nothing but a lie. An interesting tale to tell everyone, don't you think?"

Turning away from Sheala, he said to Gothran and Tetiras, "Enjoy yourselves with her and put her back in her cage when you finish. I'll return tomorrow. Eliana, you'll have to forego your pleasure for tonight. I wish to return to the Academy, and the shuttle must be returned to its owner. I leave that task to you."

As the door closed soundlessly behind her family's enemy, Sheala looked at the two naked hermaphrodites who stood before her. "My father will reward you handsomely if you return me to him."

Both Tetiras and Gothran ignored her. "Do you wish to

enjoy her first or shall I?" Gothran asked as he lowered the table to its usual horizontal position.

"You take her, my love," Tetiras said as Gothran untied Sheala and rolled her onto her stomach. "I will enjoy you while you enjoy her."

Only the Gattan woman writhing in sexual frustration heard Sheala's screams.

* * * * *

As Eliana maneuvered the shuttle down onto the roof of the building where her boss lived, Bakom snapped, "You know where to take the shuttle?"

"Yes," Eliana replied in a soft voice. Sheala's nonvirginal state had obviously soured his mood, and he'd brooded in silence for the entire time it had taken them to arrive here.

"Good," he grunted. "I'll see you in the morning."

Eliana sighed with relief as Bakom walked away from the shuttle. Now if only she could get to the Alalakans in time.

* * * * *

A single drop of blood rolled down over Marljas' elbow and dropped to the floor as he pushed a single claw into his arm. The pain kept him focused. His betrothed had been kidnapped. Whoever had committed this crime would die. Gattan honor demanded it.

Around him, Sheala's relatives argued.

"We have to do something," Ban snarled. "We can't just sit here."

"Bakom would never have taken Sheala if it weren't for me," Brianna said with tears in her eyes. "Perhaps it would be best if…"

Every gaze snapped to her.

"Don't think to complete that thought, Brianna," Jamiros snapped. "You're married to my son and carry my first grandchild. You're just as much a part of this family as Sheala, and you will go *nowhere* near Bakom. Do you understand?"

Brianna nodded, but she had a defiant look on her face.

"Char," Jamiros ordered, "keep an eye to your wife. Do *not* let her out of your sight. We don't need her to do anything stupid, we have enough problems."

Char nodded and sent a searing look to his wife. She didn't appear in the least intimidated.

"Don't even think about it," Ban added in a sharp tone. "Do you really think Bakom would give Sheala back if he got his hands on you?"

Before Marljas could add his opinion, a loud commotion in the street drew their attention.

Looking out the window, Char's brother Rodane said in an astonished voice, "Someone's landed a shuttle in the middle of the street!" He leaped away from the window and through the doorway into the hall.

Marljas joined Ban by the window. A slight figure left the shuttle and headed for the front door.

In what seemed only seconds, Rodane had returned, leading a panting woman.

"Come, quickly! I know where he has her!" she gasped.

Growling, Marljas stepped forward only to have Char lay a restraining hand on his arm. "Wait, she's one of Bakom's assistants. How do we know this isn't another trap?"

"You friend Dr. Sedenton," Eliana shouted. "I work for her. Cindar, one of the lieutenants on your ship, is my sister. Now hurry! There's no time!"

With those words, the woman ran back out the door.

Snarling, Marljas wrenched his arm free of Char's grasp. "Trap be damned! I go with the girl."

"So do I," Ban snapped.

"Char, Rodane," Jamiros ordered, "go with them. If this is a trap, I promise you, I'll pull the Academy down around Bakom's ears."

Chapter Eight

ℬ

Marljas pushed open the door and leaped from the shuttle before Eliana turned off the engine.

"Wait," she called as she locked the controls then slid out after him. "You don't even know where you are going. This way."

Snarling impatiently, Marljas waited for her to lead the way. The other three men followed after them. When she halted in front of an elevator door, Marljas held up his hand. "Someone might be inside."

The sight of five lethal claws emerging from his fingers precluded any arguments. After he made sure no one was waiting inside they all crowded in.

"I tell you this is not a trap!" Eliana said in frustration as she pushed a panel and the elevator began its descent. "Bakom has secret laboratories below this building that I only found out about tonight. He's never trusted me with this secret before."

"If you're lying..." Ban growled.

"...I will rip out your guts while you watch," Marljas finished with a snarl.

She did her best to ignore their threats. "The elevator will open onto a dimly lit corridor. I don't know what experiments Rodak is performing on the first two levels, but Sheala is being held on the third level. There's a stairway at the end of the corridor, follow it all the way to the bottom. There's only one door that I saw. Sheala will be in that laboratory."

Char's voice was as menacing as Ban's. "Laboratory?"

She swallowed and nodded. "You had best prepare

103

yourselves. I don't know exactly what her physical condition will be."

Rodane's voice was just as deadly. "Will there be anyone in there with her?"

A small voice in the back of Marljas' mind noted that having these three Alalakan men angry was far more dangerous than he'd originally thought.

"Two of Bakom's assistants were there when we left. Sheala has—she's been raped by now, more than once."

The blood ran cold in Marljas' body. Rape? Anyone who had touched Sheala was a dead man. As the door to the elevator opened, Marljas sprinted down the corridor, ignoring Rodane, who tried to stop him. No one was going to stop him from finding Sheala. He flexed his fingers and his claws emerged fully. Anyone who tried would lose a great deal of blood, and anyone who had hurt Sheala would die.

He exploded through the door of the laboratory as a hermaphrodite Drakian rolled off a table. Both he and another, more feminine hermaphrodite, whirled to face him.

Marljas' gaze leaped to the table.

Whimpering and moaning, an obviously bruised Sheala shuddered on the table.

"Sheala!" Rage pouring through his veins, Marljas attacked. Claws on both hands fully extended, he sliced the larger, male-looking hermaphrodite open from neck to groin. Ignoring the gushing blood and the running female, he kicked the screaming man out of his way, stepped to the table where Sheala lay, and gathered her into his arms.

"I'm here, my love," he whispered. "I promise, no one will ever hurt you again."

The sound of the door slamming into the wall jerked Sheala back to full consciousness—and pain.

Grunting, Gothran rolled off her. "What's going—"

Lifting her head, Sheala struggled to regain control of her body as the drug wore off. She blinked to clear her blurry vision.

When Gothran screamed, she turned her head to the left.

Blood splattered everywhere.

Sheala blinked again.

Fury radiating from his body, Marljas kicked Gothran out of his way.

His snarl echoing around the laboratory, he leaped to her side.

Tears rolling down her cheeks, Sheala began to cry as he pulled her into his arms. At last, she was safe. Marljas had found her.

She buried her face against his chest, her body shaking as she sobbed. "I knew you would come. I knew you would find me. Bakom, he…they…"

His voice cracking, he held her tight. "Hush, *Cheta*, I'm here. I'll never leave you again."

Sheala looked up into his face. Never? Did he mean it? Her body shaking, tears still streaming down her cheeks, she held up her left palm. "Forever?"

Marljas unsheathed the claws on his right hand. "I cannot do this for you. You must do it yourself."

As Sheala pulled her left hand over Marljas' unsheathed claws, Ban, Char, and Rodane stepped into the lab followed by the woman who'd been with Bakom earlier.

Char cried out and leaped towards them. "Sheala, no!"

Before he could reach them, Marljas ripped his vest open and sliced his claws down over his left breast. Taking Sheala's still-bleeding hand, he held it against his open cuts. "Blood to my blood, heart to my heart, we are one forever."

Relief surged through Sheala, and she stopped fighting the pain attacking her body. As her new husband placed a gentle kiss on her lips, she fainted.

Lifting his head, Marljas looked squarely into Char's eyes. "She's mine now, Alalakan Dragon. My wife. I will care for her."

Char looked to his older brother, who stared at the Gattan holding their bruised and battered sister in his arms.

Ban broke the heavy silence as he dropped an unconscious Tetiras on the floor. "No more than you're hers, Marljas. I hope you realize what you've done."

Marljas didn't reply.

"Help me," came a faint voice from one of the cages at the back of the room.

"Bakom treats people like animals," Rodane said with disgust as he looked at the other woman. "The cage is locked."

"Gothran has the keys," Eliana said in a helpful voice.

"Who? Oh," said Ban as he looked at the bloody body on the floor. "You definitely don't do anything halfway, do you, Marljas?"

His snarl rattled the jars on the shelves. "He raped her. What would you have done?"

"With your weapons, castrated him and shoved his balls down his throat," was Ban's terse answer.

Marljas said nothing but nodded with approval. Bandalardrac was becoming easier to like the longer he knew him.

As Marljas lifted Sheala's unconscious body into his arms, Ban lifted the ring of bloody keys from the floor next to the body then joined Char at the cages. He stopped short when he saw the naked woman imprisoned there.

"Sosha!"

Marljas looked up when he heard the name. Still cradling the unconscious Sosha in his arms, he joined Char and Ban.

Huddled on the floor of the cage, the naked Gattan wiped tears from her cheeks. "Please get me out of here. I only have an hour of so of coherent thought."

The anger that had begun to lessen now that Marljas held Sheala in his arms surged anew. "Sosha, what has been done to you?"

"I am addicted to mithrin," the young Gattan woman sobbed as they opened the door to her cage. "I've been the sexual plaything of Bakom and anyone else he brought here."

Ban lifted her into his arms and cuddled her to his chest. Sosha lay listlessly in his arms.

Eliana tugged at Char's sleeve. "We must get out of here. I don't think Bakom plans on coming back tonight, but you never know."

Hope leaped in Marljas' eyes. " Then he is a dead man."

Sosha struggled in Ban's arms. "The files. Bakom kept notes on everything. There are also videos."

An ugly smile appeared on Char's face. "Where are they?"

She pointed to a spot on the back wall. "In the wall safe, behind the cabinet. Be careful, it's set with a chemical dissolvent. The wrong number code will trigger it."

Char cursed fluently—in three languages. "Without the correct code those files may as well be on Gattan."

Sosha's voice was bitter. "Six, two, three, seven, four."

Char looked down at her. "Are you sure? If you're wrong..."

"I'm sure," she answered bitterly. "Bakom would often recite it in my ear when he mounted me. It was a game he played. He thought I wouldn't understand because of the mithrin."

Rodane shoved the cabinet out of the way. "There's only one way to find out." In a few short minutes, the safe was open.

"Hurry," Marljas snarled. "We must get the women to a doctor."

Char tossed a blanket to Ban for Sosha, then rummaged through the equipment and other items lying on the tables. "Just put everything in a case or sack or something. We can go through it at home. Marljas is right. We need to get the women home."

As Marljas and Ban left carrying Sheala and Sosha, Rodane found a large box and a sack and emptied Bakom's safe.

Char picked up the box. "The authorities have to be notified. Rodane, see if you can shake that other woman awake enough to walk to the shuttle. If you can't, you'll have to carry her. Eliana, can you get yourself home from here? We'll take care of the shuttle."

She handed him a slip of paper. "I'll manage. This is the name and address of the shuttle owner. Bakom never uses an Academy shuttle when he comes here."

* * * * *

Hours later, hands clenched together, Marljas stared into the darkness. The Alalakan household had finally become silent.

Dr. Sendenton dem al' Lorilana, a close friend of the family, had been waiting at the Alalakan town house when they'd returned with the two women. Now, both Sheala and Sosha were heavily sedated, and the doctor had promised to return early in the morning to give each young woman a more thorough examination. The Gattan ambassador, Mendas Teekeson, and his wife, Pikeen Sodasdotir, had been informed of their goddaughter's rescue and were upstairs with Sosha.

Restless and angry, incapable of sleep, Marljas sat in Sheala's darkened room. Earlier, only Brianna and Jenneta had had the courage to demand that he wash off the blood of the man he'd killed. Brianna he had ignored. Jenneta had proved to be more intimidating than any Gattan matriarch.

He glanced at his wife, his keen eyesight cutting through

108

the darkness. Even heavily sedated, Sheala moaned in her sleep. Frustrated, Marljas snarled again. He was completely helpless. Fury, barely held in check, coursed through his body with every beat of his heart. Instinct had taken control when he'd burst into the laboratory and seen Sheala sprawled naked on the table at the mercy of Bakom's assistant. Gothram had been easy to kill, but it was Bakom he wanted. On Gattan, his entire clan would have hunted Bakom down and made sure he died a very slow and painful death.

Unfortunately, Drakian customs were different from those of Gattan, and Bakom was a very powerful man here on his own planet.

Preoccupied with his anger, Marljas rubbed the already healing cuts above his left pectoral. Sheala, his wife, had been raped. Revenge would be paid in blood, no matter what planet he was on.

Chapter Nine

ഇ

When faint light appeared beneath the heavy drapes covering the windows, Marljas pushed himself out of the uncomfortable chair he had sat in all night. Sheala still slept. Though the room was still cloaked in shadows, he didn't have any trouble seeing the bruises that had appeared on her face overnight. A light blanket covered her to her neck. Just thinking about the additional bruises that undoubtedly covered her slender body had his rage ready to erupt. He couldn't remain still any longer.

Silently as only a Gattan could, he stepped into the hallway.

He was not alone.

Mendas Teekeson sat on a chair before the room where Sosha and his wife lay sleeping.

The older man glared at him. "Are they dead?"

"One," Marljas snarled. "Bakom was not there."

Mendas rose to his feet. "I will deal with him."

Marljas' snarl echoed down the hall. "His blood is mine!"

The older Gattan was not intimidated. "Sosha is neither your wife nor your betrothed, boy. Her honor is mine to defend in the absence of her father and brother."

"Alalakan dem al' Sheala is my wife, old man," Marljas snarled back. "I will avenge both her and Sosha."

"What the hell is going on out here?" Brianna snapped from the doorway of her bedroom.

Marljas glanced over his shoulder. Unlike the Alalakan estate, there were no separate suites at the Alalakan town house. All of the bedrooms opened into a common hallway.

110

Obviously, he and Mendas had awakened his bloodsister with their arguing.

Awakening a breeding woman was not something a smart Gattan wanted to do. At least Brianna didn't have any claws.

Mendas cleared his throat nervously.

Brianna, with her hair still mussed from sleep and clad in nothing more than a loose dressing gown, waddled into the hallway.

Clearing his throat, Mendas jerked to a bow. "I beg your pardon, Alalakan dem al' Brianna. I did not mean to disturb you."

She ignored him, grabbed Marljas' arm, and yanked it until he turned around. "Wife! What are you talking about?"

Chest bare, Marljas said nothing as he stood with his arms crossed and watched Brianna as she locked her gaze on the three new parallel scars on his left pectoral.

It was then that the fact that an Alalakan dragon flew on Marljas' right shoulder finally registered in Mendas' mind. His eyes widened. "You wear an Alalakan dragon, Marljas Drefeson. What does this mean?"

"He's my bloodbrother," Brianna snapped. "That makes him Alalakan, as far as I'm concerned." She turned her attention back to Marljas. "I want to know what this 'wife' business is."

"We thought it best not to mention it last night," Char said as he walked out of Rodane and Fionilina's room. "Emotions were already too volatile."

"Do your mother and father know?" Brianna asked Char.

"I go to tell them now, bloodsister," Marljas answered, his tone purposely belligerent. How he wanted to fight with someone. A slight insult to Brianna would bring Char to her defense. He wouldn't hurt Char—much. "Do you not approve?"

As Marljas had planned, Char's eyes narrowed and he took a step forward. One or two more comments directed at Brianna, and his bloodsister's husband would help him relieve some of the tension that made his muscles ache.

Unfortunately, his bloodsister didn't cooperate. Placing her palm in the middle of Char's chest, she stopped her husband in mid-stride then turned to Marljas. "How much sleep did you get last night? I've never seen eyes as bloodshot as yours."

"I guarded my wife."

Unintimidated, she placed herself as close to Marljas as her very obvious stomach would allow. "What good will you be to her if you collapse from exhaustion? Do you doubt my motives?"

Marljas gazed into the beautiful, worried face turned up to his, and some of his anger left him. Exhausted, he leaned against the wall, rubbing his face with his hand. "No, bloodsister, I don't doubt you. But you weren't there when we found Sheala. She was…"

Words failed him.

Marljas heard someone walking behind him, but ignored him or her. Who did he have to fear in the house of his wife?

Brianna placed her hand upon his shoulder. "I'm sorry, but your marriage is certainly a shock."

Opening his eyes, Marljas forced an exhausted smile. "I haven't been myself these last twelve hours."

The doctor stopped behind Marljas and quickly jabbed the hypodermic needle into his arm.

"What?" he snarled.

"It's just a sedative," she said gently. "You haven't slept."

"I…" was all he managed before the drug took effect.

Char caught him as he slid down the wall.

"Rodane," Char called as he braced himself, "come lend me a hand. This Gattan is a lot heavier than he looks."

"Allow me, Alalakan don al' Chardadon," Mendas said as he draped one of Marljas' arms over his powerful shoulders. "Where shall we put him?"

"Put him in Sheala's room," Brianna said. Continuing at three sets of raised eyebrows, "If he wakes up anywhere he can't see her, he'll tear the room apart."

"She is right, Alalakan," Mendas said as they struggled with Marljas' weight. "He is apt to react as she says."

Char scowled but nodded as Brianna led the way back into Sheala's room. The doctor followed them.

Brianna pointed to the left of the bed. "Put him in the chair there. The first thing he'll see when he wakes is Sheala."

After Char and the Gattan ambassador left, Brianna looked at the doctor. "How is Sheala?"

The doctor sighed. "She's been beaten and repeatedly raped, but there's no permanent damage to her body. It's her mind I'm worried about. Rape is almost unheard of on our planet, and I don't know what frame of mind she'll be in when the sedative wears off."

"How long will that be?"

"At least another eight hours. I wanted to make sure she slept as long as possible."

Brianna watched her sister-in-law sleep. "Bakom has much to answer for," she muttered more to herself than to Lorilana. "Denieen will know how to help." With those words, she left Sheala's room.

Chapter Ten

ೲ

Forty-five minutes later, Brianna joined the rest of the family downstairs.

"There's no doubt that Bakom will be held criminally responsible for his actions," Jamiros said as he steepled his fingers together. "We have only to decide how to go about revealing his crimes to the Council."

"Father," Char interjected after a moment of silence, "I believe Bakom's downfall will be much more effective if we let him believe he's in control when the hearing begins. Brianna's obvious pregnancy and her marital status will certainly cause him problems. I'd like to see just how he reacts."

Jamiros frowned. "Is that wise?"

Char nodded. "If we hadn't discovered his secret laboratories, that's the position we'd have found ourselves in. What's more, we might get an idea of who else is involved. Sosha said that Bakom would give her to others when she was under the influence of mithrin. If any Council member ever entered that laboratory, he or she is just as guilty and should be punished and censured accordingly."

Jamiros turned to Brianna. "What do you think?"

She shrugged as she ate her breakfast. "I'll go along with whatever plans you devise since the baby won't be in any danger."

A concerned Jenneta interrupted. "Will Sheala or Sosha have to be there?"

Char shook his head. "No, Grandmother. Sosha may be called upon another day to identify any other Council members who were in the lab, but the scientific records that

Bakom filmed will condemn him as far as their rapes are concerned."

Xdana winced and fresh tears began to flow at the word *rapes*.

Char sighed. "I'm sorry, Mother."

Xdana waved him off. "It is not your fault, Char. It's just that Sheala didn't deserve the treatment she received from that animal."

Jamiros rose and walked to his wife. Taking her hands, he lifted her from her chair and pulled her into his arms. "No one deserves what happened to Sheala and Sosha, but it has happened. Now, we must help her. As long as she has us to love her, she'll be all right."

Ban had remained silent up to this point. "Don't forget Marljas," he said. "We can be very sure that he intends to be part of any plans we devise for Sheala."

Jamiros frowned. "Yes, we are going to have to decide what to do about Marljas."

Brianna's eyebrows rose and her voice was icy. "What to do about Marljas?"

Most members of the family looked at her in surprise.

"We are discussing my brother," Brianna added meaningfully.

Xdana stared at her son's wife. "You can't believe that we will accept this marriage?"

Brianna stared back. "Yes. Mine and Char's marriage began under similar if less violent circumstances."

A slight smile on his lips, Ban turned to his aunt. "Brianna has you there. You're discussing Sheala as if she has no say in the matter."

Jamiros' voice was terse. "She was hysterical when she agreed to this so-called marriage. She didn't know what she was doing."

Ban shook his head. "I was there. Sheala's the one who

instigated the ceremony."

"Marljas would spirit her away to Gattan anyway," Brianna muttered.

The look on Char's face became thoughtful. "Brianna's right. We all know Marljas is impulsive. Right now he's convinced that he loves Sheala. Maybe he does. At this point, it won't harm anyone to agree with them. Later, if one or both believes there has been a mistake, well, there's been no formal marriage. It will be easier for them to walk away from each other."

Brianna looked at Char as if he'd grown another head but she kept her thoughts to herself. From Denieen, she had learned that nothing on Gattan was as binding as a bloodbond. Sheala's and Marljas' blood had mixed on his chest and her palm. To the Gattan, they were as married as married could be.

* * * * *

Snarling to himself, Marljas paced back and forth in the private box reserved for the Gattan ambassador. When the Alalakans, first Jamiros, then Chardadon and Rodane, entered the assembly room of Drakan's Ruling Council, he'd stepped to the railing but paid little attention to Chardadon as he answered the charges of treason brought against him by Bakom. Brianna and Denieen had had a long conversation with him earlier that afternoon. He knew exactly what he was expected to do.

Rodak don al' Bakom would pay for his crimes, and, with luck, he would also shed blood this day. Smiling, Marljas contemplated various ways to satisfy his longing for Bakom's blood—carve a map of the Gattan solar system into Bakom's naked flesh, castrate him and watch as he bled to death slowly, skin him alive...

Brianna's voice pulled Marljas from his fantasies. "I've had enough of this bullshit," she said in a voice that carried clearly.

Gripping the edge of the railing, Marljas leaned forward, waiting for his bloodsister's signal.

Brianna crossed the floor slowly, until she stood before Bakom. She drew the knife from the wrist sheath she wore and, very deliberately and slowly, slid the sharp blade across the fleshy part of her lower arm. As blood ran freely, she threw the knife so that it embedded itself in the wooden floor.

"I, Alalakan dem al' Brianna, call bloodfeud on Rodak don al' Bakom," she said in a clear voice that seethed with anger.

Pandemonium broke loose. Council members rose to their feet, shouting for explanations.

Council guards had rushed towards the platform, barring access by Ban and Char. Eventually, the pounding of the president's gavel and his shouts for order returned a semblance of order. "Alalakan dem al' Brianna, you aren't Gattan to call for bloodfeud."

That was the signal Marljas had waited for. Vaulting over the railing, he landed lightly at Brianna's side. Bare-chested, with his Alalakan dragon and leaping lion tattoo glowing in the bright light of the chamber, he answered Brianna's challenge. "I, Marljas Drefeson, answer my bloodsister's call for vengeance."

Unsheathing a claw on his right hand, he drew it across his left forearm, three separate times, reciting each accusation against Bakom clearly.

"I call bloodfeud on you, Rodak don al' Bakom," he snarled as the first rivulet of blood began to flow, "for your harassment of my bloodsister Alalakan dem al' Brianna and failure to honor her humanity.

"I call bloodfeud," he continued with the second cut, "for the kidnap and rape of my wife, Alalakan dem al' Sheala."

Audible gasps filled the Council chamber. A Gattan–Alalakan alliance of marriage could have profound interplanetary trade implications.

"Finally," Marljas finished with a roar, "I call bloodfeud for the kidnapping, rape, and inhuman scientific experiments on the Gattan woman Sosha Kanicsdotir!"

Again, loud voices demanded explanations as the third rivulet of blood joined the other two.

Only the light pressure of the hand Brianna placed on his arm kept Marljas, who stood on the balls of his feet sheathing and unsheathing his claws, from attacking the man who'd hurt Sheala.

"How do you answer these accusations, Rodak don al' Bakom," she demanded in a voice loud enough to be heard above the growing uproar. "Tell the members of your government how you kidnap women for sexual use by you and your friends."

"That is a lie!" Bakom screamed. "I know nothing of such women! How dare you accuse me, the First President of the Academy of Science!"

Brianna simply held her hand out to her husband. "Char?"

Angrily nodding his head to the guards, Chardadon picked up a sealed envelope from where it lay on the table and walked to stand in front of the Council president. "Mr. President, would you care to view the rape of my sister and the goddaughter of the Gattan ambassador by Bakom and his assistants now or later? We obtained enough evidence to support these and many other accusations when my family rescued my sister and the Gattan ambassador's goddaughter from a secret laboratory Bakom had for his private use. Even now, the police are combing through files and samples taken from three separate floors where he performed 'experiments'."

All eyes in the room returned to Bakom. The silence thickened.

"Well, Doctor...?"

The Council President never finished. Bakom leaped from the platform where he stood and fled the room much more rapidly than anyone had thought possible.

Snarling, Marljas leaped to the knife embedded in the floor and jerked it free. His catlike reflexes sent the blade flying after Bakom, who screamed and tumbled to the floor.

"Guards!" shouted the Council President, "arrest him!"

Council guards streamed into the chamber. Disgruntled — and panicked — Council members milled and darted about the room. Some returned to their seats. Others scuttled from one door to another, seeking escape. All were now guarded.

Ignoring the pandemonium that flowed around him, Marljas stepped to meet the guards that were hauling Bakom to the front of the room.

Brianna's voice was soft but the command in her voice cracked like a whip. "Let the guards have him now, Brother. We'll have our blood another day."

Still furious, Marljas grunted with approval. In that moment, Brianna was as much a Gattan as any inhabitant of his planet.

A furious Char halted any further conversation between the two. "Bandalardrac," he said in a tightly controlled voice, "take Brianna to the shuttle. I'll join you momentarily."

Brianna ignored Char. "Brother, I wish to go home now."

Snarling one last time at Bakom, Marljas extended his arm to Brianna. "Come, Sister. My wife has need of me."

Both Brianna and Marljas ignored everyone else as they left.

Once in Marljas' transport, Brianna sagged against the seat. "Get me home," she said with a grimace. "Then go get Deni."

Marljas' rage cooled considerably when he saw her drawn, white face. "What...?"

Brianna gasped and clutched her stomach. "Your nephew has decided to put in an appearance early."

* * * * *

Sheala opened her eyes to a room filled with shadows—and the antiseptic odor of medicine. She moved her legs, and aches exploded throughout her body. Then—she remembered.

Horror rolled through her mind as sobs exploded from her throat, and she wanted to bury herself under the blankets and never come out again. Then, slowly, she regained control.

Ignoring the pain coursing through her body, she shoved herself up and swung her head from side to side, straining to see through the darkness. As her hands clenched the sheets, she winced. In the dim light that filled her chamber, Sheala lifted her left hand and stared at the three parallel scratches on her palm.

It hadn't been a terrible nightmare. Bakom and his assistants had beaten and raped her—then Marljas had come. The events of her rescue were foggy, but Sheala remembered the blood rite she'd demanded. Marljas had not hesitated. He had married her and promised never to leave her again.

Where was he?

A dark shadow moved.

"Marljas?"

"No."

A light flashed on.

Tensing, she locked gazes with a man she had never seen before. Tall and completely white, he was without a doubt Deslossian. However, her initial fright vanished to be replaced with a feeling of deep empathy as she stared into brilliant blue eyes. Her aches intensified. Was he a doctor? "Who are you? Why are you here?"

"I am Bjin. Your clan has agreed to—shelter me for a while."

"Why?"

"My wife died, and the Elders fear I will seek a way to join her."

He stepped closer, away from the mirror he'd blocked. When he did, Sheala saw her reflection. Both of her eyes were black, and the left side of her mouth was cut and swollen.

"You were given something for the pain," Bjin said gently as tears began to run down her face.

Bjin held out his hand. "Please, come with me."

The entreaty in his eyes was so poignant, Sheala hesitated only a moment. Placing her left hand in his, she allowed him to help her up. Wiping the tears from her cheeks, she asked, "Where are we going?"

"To Sosha."

"Sosha?"

"A Gattan woman who was held captive by Bakom for almost a year. She endured far more than you."

Sheala followed Bjin through the door of the room next to hers. A slight Gattan woman with haunted eyes sat in the bed. What Sheala could see of her body was covered with new and partially healed bruises. Every now and then, she shook with a convulsion she couldn't suppress.

Aching as she was, Sheala was appalled.

"Bakom addicted her to mithrin," Bjin murmured quietly by way of explanation. "Help me with her."

The slender Gattan didn't fight them as Sheala gently wrapped a robe around her and Bjin lifted her in his arms.

"Where are we going?" Sheala repeated as they left Sosha's room.

"To save our souls," was his enigmatic answer.

Chapter Eleven

🔊

Char sat on the bed with Brianna lying back against his chest as Sheala followed Bjin into the room and stepped as unobtrusively as possible. Bjin sat Sosha on the settee before the heavy drapes covering the bedroom window. Slowly, Sheala lowered herself to sit next to the young Gattan woman. She felt terrible, but Sosha had obviously suffered far more than she. Grasping the Gattan's hand in hers, she smiled into her face then looked towards the bed.

Except for a quick glance from Denieen, everyone in the room ignored them.

Sosha's hand tightened around Sheala's. Sheala glanced towards her, but the young Gattan was staring intently at Brianna. Meri came over to them, and she and Sheala helped Sosha to the bottom of Brianna's bed. There, Sosha used Sheala and the bedpost for support. Both Sheala's and Sosha's expressions changed as they watched Brianna give birth. Pain they understood. Sosha, especially, had experienced much worse. But Brianna's pain brought joy, not suffering.

Brianna screamed, and her son slid into the world. Both girls watched with awe as Brianna's joy conquered her pain when her child was placed in her arms. Both perceived the deep and profound love Char and Brianna shared.

Turning to them, Denieen demanded,"What are you doing here with them?"

"We came because we were called," Bjin answered.

"Explain," Denieen snapped.

"The Flame of Mediria," Bjin answered, using the name the Nissian Patriarch of Mediria had given Brianna, "called to us." He nodded towards Sheala and Sosha. "We have all been damaged in mind or body or both. Now, life holds little or no joy for us. This is not what the Creator wants. Because she is bringing a new life into the world, she has the ability to help us heal. Alalakan dem al' Brianna O'Shea of Earth can help us relearn the meaning of life."

"Well, it's time to go back to your rooms. Brianna needs to rest and so do Sosha and Sheala."

After Meri placed Connor in the baby cot, she joined Deni. The two women guided Bjin, Sheala, and Sosha from the room.

As Sheala settled back into her bed, a cheer from downstairs slipped beneath the closed door. For the first time that day, she smiled slightly. Connor's relatives had been informed of his arrival.

Before she could close her eyes, though, the door opened and Char walked across her room and gathered her into his arms. Turning he walked back across the room.

Meri appeared in the doorway. Brianna's asleep, but the newest Alalakan should meet his family," she said and laid Char's son in Sheala's arms.

Sheala gazed at the sleeping child in her arms and then looked up at Char, who smiled fondly down at her. "Come along, Shea, it's time you said hello to the rest of the family, too."

With those words, he scooped her up into his arms, wincing at her shudder of pain. She was smiling at the child in her arms, however, and there was a new light in her eyes. Sheala was on the path to healing. Char left the room followed by Meri.

Marljas looked over his shoulder and nudged Wendjas out of the way when Char entered the room carrying Sheala.

"Char! What are you doing? Sheala should be in bed!" Xdana exclaimed. "And what about Brianna?"

Grinning, Char placed Sheala into Marljas' arms.

Shifting his weight to make Sheala as comfortable as possible, Marljas looked down and saw what she was holding. He laughed as Char carefully gathered his son into his arms.

"Brianna's resting," Char said as he turned back to his assembled family. "However, I thought you might like to meet our newest clan member, Alalakan don al' Connor."

Fully understanding the symbolism of Char's actions, Marljas had eagerly accepted Sheala. He'd glanced briefly at the child she held, but concentrated mostly on the woman in his arms. A few moments after Char had taken his son, Marljas backed out of the room and disappeared up the steps. In a matter of moments, they were in Sheala's room where Marljas placed her gently on the bed.

She didn't meet his intent gaze.

Placing his fingers under her chin, he lifted her head until she looked into his face. "I remember a brave woman who dared me to try her swords," he said quietly.

"Marljas, I…"

"Shhhh… You must sleep again. We'll talk tomorrow." He handed her the medication sitting on the nightstand.

Obediently, she swallowed the pills and closed her eyes. Soon, she slept.

Marljas was staring down at his sleeping wife when Denieen entered the room.

"You gave her the medication."

"Yes."

"And the other?"

Marljas shook his head negatively.

"You have doubts now? Do you still wish to give the abortifacient? It could still be done."

"If she carries a child, there's a good chance it is mine."

"And if she has a child, and it is obviously Drakian, what then? By Gattan law, she's your wife. Can you accept a child of rape? There are many on our planet who would not."

Marljas finally stopped staring at Sheala and turned to Denieen. Sighing he said, "I would raise a *chigian* swamp rat as my child if she asked it of me."

A warm smile lit Denieen's face. Gently placing her hand on his arm, she said, "You made the right choice. If Sheala is pregnant, it must be her decision to end it."

A long sigh escaped Marljas and his shoulders drooped.

She hugged him. "Don't worry. Drakians don't conceive readily so pregnancy is very unlikely. Besides, her mother and grandmother would certainly have explained exactly what was necessary for her to know about contraceptives in a permissive society such as this. However, I'll raise the subject with one of them when next we are alone, just to make sure."

Marljas stared at his sleeping wife. "Does she remember, Deni? Does she even realize that by Gattan law we are married?"

"She's alive, Marljas, and whole of body. You must take one day at a time. Tomorrow will be soon enough to talk to her. Now, you must sleep, too. What woman wants to claim a ragged, ungroomed Gattan as a husband?"

After a final hug, she left.

His heart heavy, Marljas stared at Sheala. Her body would heal, but would her mind? Blinking back the moisture in his eyes, he rolled his shoulders then stretched. He was tired. Silently, he stretched out on the bed next to Sheala, being careful not to touch her.

Soon he too had drifted off to sleep.

During the long hours of the night, Sheala snuggled closer until she slept wrapped tightly in Marljas' arms.

* * * * *

Muffled sounds from the hallway awoke Sheala. At first, she lay still, cocooned in warmth, smiling as she remembered the previous night and the birth of Brianna's child. She'd held him in her arms.

She shifted and froze. Someone was lying against her back.

"Nooo…!" she screamed and leaped out of the bed.

Marljas leaped from her bed, long, deadly claws unsheathed.

Shaking, Sheala stared at him from across the room.

The door opened and Denieen stepped in. Marljas snarled at her, and she backed out immediately.

Relaxing, he retracted his claws. "There's no one here but me, Sheala," he said softly after the door had been closed firmly, "and I'd never hurt you."

Tense, Sheala looked about the room. Marljas still wore his leather pants, but the robe Sheala had been wearing had slipped off during the night. She stared across the room at the reflection of her battered body in the mirror and burst into tears.

Bruises covered her upper arms and both breasts. Bruises were also very evident on both hips and buttocks, and there were scratches on her inner thighs.

Marljas leaped towards her. "Sheala, *Cheta*…"

Sobbing, Sheala lifted her hands to ward him off. "Don't call me that! Look at me! Look what they did to me."

He stopped.

Sheala wrapped her arms around herself and continued to sob.

His face betraying his distress, Marljas said, "Sheala, look at your left hand. Do you remember?"

Sniffing, Sheala turned her hand over and looked at her palm. Then she looked at his chest, at the matching cuts there. Slowly she nodded.

"Sheala, no Gattan would mark a woman so if he were not absolutely certain of his feelings."

She looked into his eyes, searching for a hint of how he felt.

He held out his hand. "I have mated with you. You're my wife."

Sniffing more, she dropped her gaze. "I'm no longer worthy to be your wife."

With a soft snarl, he closed the space between them and gently grasped her upper arms. "You're my wife because you are more worthy than any other woman I have ever met, *Cheta*. You didn't choose to be used so. What happened isn't your fault. And Gothran is dead."

She lifted her head and stared into his face. "Dead?"

"Gutted," Marljas answered in a self-satisfied tone of voice.

A ghost of a smile appeared on Sheala's face. "Bakom?"

"A prisoner, but not before my knife drew his blood."

"Thank you." She sagged against his chest. "I'm sorry. I feel so ugly."

"You're the most beautiful woman in the universe," he answered, wrapping his arms around her. At least she was accepting his embrace. He tightened his arms.

As his hands tightened, she tensed again and frantically pushed herself away.

He let her go.

With tears running down her cheeks, Sheala whispered, "I... I can't...be your wife, Marljas. I don't want you to...touch me. I—can't—love—you."

He felt the blood drain from his face as he stepped before her so that they were only inches apart. "Do you want to run from me now, *Cheta*?"

Sheala stared at him, at his naked chest and the Alalakan dragon that seemed to leap at her from his shoulder. Blinking, she trailed her gaze up the strong column of his neck and stared into his face.

His tawny hair was tangled. The braids he normally wore before his ears had loosened during the night, the leather cords dangled. When she looked up into his golden eyes, her heart constricted at the intensity and openness of his gaze, at the tenderness — and love — she saw there.

Her voice was low, barely a whisper. "Do you hate me?"

Shock appeared on his face. "Never!" Raising one hand slowly, he caressed her cheek with a single finger.

Sheala flinched slightly, but did not pull away.

"Do you wish to run from me now?"

She shook her head.

Trailing his finger along her jaw, he lifted her chin, and smiled. "I told you once before that I would not force you, *Cheta*. That hasn't changed. There's time enough for you to learn to trust again. I'm a patient man. I love you, Sheala."

Sheala sighed and closed her eyes. After looking into his eyes, into his soul, how could she doubt him?

Dropping his hand, he stepped back. "Go now, my love. Last night Deni said something about you soaking in a bath this morning. I'll be near if you need me. All you have to do is call me."

Marljas watched as Sheala walked through the doorway into the bathroom. When the door closed, he slumped down on a chair and buried his face in his hands. The fear in her eyes when she looked at him terrified him. He had fought more duels than he cared to count, had been seriously wounded twice and endured the pain those wounds entailed. But that paled in comparison to the pain in his heart at this moment.

What would he do if Sheala was unable to overcome her fear of him?

Growling a curse, Marljas jerked to his feet, extending and retracting his claws furiously. Somehow, someway, Rodak don al' Bakom would pay for what he'd done to her.

* * * * *

Later that day, as Sheala slept again, Marljas sat with Wendjas and Denieen in an empty conference room at the embassy.

"There's no reason not to expect her to recover fully," Deni said. "She's young, and we women are very resilient."

Marljas paced to the other side of the room. "You didn't see how she looked at me."

Denieen smiled gently. "She'll look at her father and brothers the same way if they startle her."

Wendjas rose to his feet. "Do you wish to end this marriage?"

Marljas whirled to face him. "No!"

Wendjas shrugged. "There's no doubting your feelings then. As Deni said, you must give Sheala time to heal. Patience. You will have to learn to use it."

Marljas snarled at his brother but said nothing. Both he and Deni were correct. Still, the look of fear on Sheala's face remained in his memory.

His brother interrupted his thoughts. "We must send a message to Father. News of Sosha's rescue is already on its way to Gattan. And we wouldn't want our parents to be the last to know they have a new daughter."

All thoughts of Sheala drained from Marljas' mind as his brother's words sank in. "Message," was all he said.

Wendjas frowned. "Message? What are you talking about?"

"Solstice Eve, when Sheala and I…" Marljas began. "The message signal was flashing on the *Scrathe*'s console. I forgot all about it."

"Father would not have broken our radio silence unless it were important. We need to get that message."

"The *Scrathe* is on Benishan's landing pad," Denieen said

in a vexed tone. "Security forces there would become very nervous if unaccompanied Gattan were wandering around." Then her face brightened. "Bandalardrac."

Marljas grunted. "Their security would be even more nervous if Bandalardrac were wandering around."

Deni smiled and cuffed her brother-in-law gently. "He'll be able to help us." With those words, she rose from her chair and disappeared out the door.

Fifteen minutes later, she reappeared dragging a mostly naked, disgruntled Ban by the arm.

"Damn it, Deni, ten more minutes, and I'll follow you anywhere," Ban complained. "I was almost ready to—"

"Be quiet, Ban," she answered calmly. "We need your help—now. That maid is supposed to be in the kitchen."

Even with all his troubles, Marljas couldn't keep a grin from sliding onto his face. Deni had interrupted Ban while he was making love to a woman.

Wendjas was aghast. "Wife! What have you done?"

"Pulled me off of a very willing woman," Ban snapped. "A woman with breasts like Medirian sweet melons and a tight, hot—"

"I didn't parade you through the hallway in all your rampant glory, did I?" Deni interrupted. "I allowed you to wrap yourself in a sheet."

"Deni!"

Choking back his laughter, Marljas had to turn away. Wendjas would want to leave for Gattan immediately after this.

Denieen shrugged and continued to stare at Ban. Eventually, the absurdity of the situation and Marljas' muffled laughter dissolved Ban's anger, and he began to chuckle.

"Wendjas, you must have led a very placid life before you married!" Ban said as he sat back in a chair tucking the sheet he wore more firmly about his waist. "What is it you need?"

Marljas swallowed his laughter. The situation was serious. "There's a message on the *Scrathe* from our father, and we're not sure how to go about retrieving it without causing a minor incident at the landing pad."

"I'll be glad to help you," Ban answered, "if you tell me exactly what's going on."

Marljas bit back a curse. Ban was far too intuitive to put off with a bad lie. They would need a good one.

Before he could think of one, Denieen said, "It's very simple, we're not supposed to be here."

Ban cocked an eyebrow.

"Deni…" Marljas began in a very low voice.

Denieen sighed. "Who else can we ask? Rodane and Chardadon are good friends, but will they truly understand and not overreact? Ban, on the other hand…"

"…is a disreputable rogue who is not always concerned with legalities," Marljas finished for her.

Ban grinned.

Wendjas frowned but nodded. "Our family believes that trade with other planets is best for Gattan. Not everyone agrees with us."

Ban leaned forward. "What do the others want?"

"War," Wendjas answered.

Muscles tensing, Ban stared.

"We could easily conqueror Varce and Deslossia," Marljas said. "Deslossia has no defenses and Varce's wouldn't be hard to overcome. Drakan and Mediria are in the same solar system and too closely allied. You would be impossible to defeat."

"We would come to the aid of one another," Ban finished for him quietly. "Singularly, our defenses aren't as good as they should be, but together—you can't attack two planets at the same time."

"Exactly what our initial ambassadors told us a hundred and fifty years ago," Wendjas answered.

Ban frowned. "Though you've kept it hidden from us, your government is a matriarchy. Are the women of your planet also so bloodthirsty then?"

Denieen waved her hand. "If all the women were against this ridiculous idea, nothing would come of it."

Ban cocked an eyebrow. "If all…?"

Marljas rose and began to pace. "The queen's sister favors conquest."

"How much influence does she have?"

"When we left, not that much. The young hotheads her son calls friends are most of her support."

Ban pursed his lips then said, "Hotheads with influential parents?"

Wendjas nodded affirmatively.

"Where are you supposed to be?"

"A seaside resort favored mostly by elderly Gattan," Deni answered. "My parents are there."

"What about the Gattan ambassadors already posted on other planets?" Ban continued.

"All of our ambassadors believe in trade," Marljas answered, "or they never would have agreed to leave Gattan. Ours can be a very prejudiced people, Ban. Many consider Gattan superior to all of the other races and prefer no contact at all with other species except to make them slaves."

Ban nodded. "What's in the message?"

"We don't know," Denieen answered with a grin. "Marljas was too occupied Solstice Eve to do more than save it in the computer banks."

Ban's bark of laughter echoed throughout the room.

Rising, he tossed the trailing edge of the sheet he wore over his shoulder and motioned them to follow. Leading them to the end of the corridor, he opened a doorway. A stairway led upward. At the top he opened another door, and the Gattan found themselves in a room full of state-of-the-art communications equipment.

"Gattan are not the only ones who keep secrets," Wendjas muttered.

Ban grinned over his shoulder as he sat down and motioned Marljas into the seat next to him. "If you could read Drakian, you'd have seen the sign on the door. It says 'Communications'."

He pushed a few buttons. "There, you can patch into the *Scrathe*'s computer banks. Just flip that switch."

Marljas flipped the switch Ban indicated and punched in his private code. In seconds, his father's voice filled the small room.

"Wendjas, Marljas, I hesitated to send this message, but your mother and I decided it was necessary. Don't worry, no great problem has risen. However, we have received a message from the queen's sister. With the blessing of the King and Queen, she has sent a formal proposal of marriage to Marljas on behalf of her daughter, Kadis. Kadis will be arriving at the spring equinox to further her proposal herself. My son, there was no way we could graciously decline the offer."

Thunderstruck expressions crossed the faces of all three Gattan.

"I will *not* accept," snarled Marljas.

Ban frowned. "What's the problem? You're already married to Sheala."

Denieen's voice was grim. "A Gattan male can have two wives."

Chapter Twelve

ಬಾ

Propping his feet up, Ban stared across the desk at his Uncle Kavlalardrac, Medirian Ambassador to Drakan, and sipped a very excellent Medirian brandy. "That's everything I know."

Kavlalardrac pursed his lips. "A delicate situation, indeed. There's no gracious way for Marljas to decline?"

Ban shrugged. "He should be able to. Gattans need not marry at all if he or she so chooses, but the queen's sister can be very adamant. She might attempt to have Marljas' marriage to Sheala annulled since she's not Gattan."

"And Marljas' reaction?"

"He wants nothing to do with the queen's niece."

Kavlalardrac smiled maliciously. "A power struggle on Gattan wouldn't harm us, Bandalardrac."

Ban nodded affirmatively, but his smile was sad. "This family of Gattan is part of us now, Uncle. I don't want to see them hurt."

Kavlalardrac sighed and shrugged. "Very well. As I understand it, Marljas' family has received a proposal of marriage from the queen's sister on behalf of her daughter. The message did not come from the Queen herself, therefore, it's not a royal command. I met Queen Mattis and her husband King Krondal. Neither is one to be browbeaten into anything by Jadis, who, by the way, rivals my dear mother in her plots to manipulate her family."

Ban grunted at that bit of news. He'd never liked his Hardan grandmother.

"In my opinion," Kavlalardrac continued, "the King and

Queen know nothing of how Jadis' proposal was worded. In all the years we have had diplomatic relations with Gattan, I can't remember hearing of any marriage forced on a family of the Drefesons' importance. It is more likely Jadis seeks to draw Marljas to her way of thinking by using her daughter. The girl is quite beautiful, I hear."

"Oh?"

Kavlalardrac jerked his bulky body up straight. "Don't even think about it, Bandalardrac. We had enough of a problem with you when that other girl disappeared."

"But I didn't do it!" Ban said innocently.

"She was found half-naked in your embrace. The Gattan are much more protective of their daughters' virtue than are we. They expect them to be virgins when they marry."

"If Kadis is caught with me…"

"No! We won't be able to save you. She is the Queen's niece. And she's not someone my dear brother would want in the family if the Gattan queen decided you should marry her."

Shrugging, Ban grinned. "If you say so, Uncle."

"Bah!" Kavlalardrac snorted. "Go talk to Denieen. She's a woman with a good head on her shoulders. The Queen's sister never has a contingency plan in place. Marljas is already married to the daughter of the most powerful clan on Drakan, a daughter, I might add, with connections to the Medirian royal family. I think I'll tell my dear brother to send a message to Gattan informing their king and queen how pleased he is that such a prominent Gattan has married into our family. I'll see if Findal will offer some trade concessions that Gattan's queen can regard as Sheala's wedding present."

Laughing, Ban rose and headed for the door. "I knew I could rely on you, Uncle."

* * * * *

In the nearby house of the Gattan ambassador, Pikeen

Sodasdotir, the wife of the Gattan ambassador, was discussing the queen's sister with Denieen, Wendjas and Marljas.

"Jadis, Mattis and I were girls together," she said to her three guests. "If Jadis wanted something, she devised a plan and went after it. If her plan didn't work, she became frustrated. Now she grasps at power through her relationship to the queen. You know, Jadis wanted to marry Krondal herself."

Denieen smiled at her hostess. "Mattis won though."

"Krondal is an intelligent man. It wasn't hard for him to see past Jadis' beauty to her cold heart. She thinks of nothing but her own ambitions. Krondal would never have been co-ruler married to her."

"So we should ignore the request?" Wendjas asked.

Pikeen shook her head. "No, the Queen is very fond of her niece, but she is also very fond of you and your family, Denieen. Mattis might see this as a way to make both families happy. Kadis is a very beautiful girl."

"But she has the temperament of her mother. I wouldn't marry her if she were the last woman in the universe," Marljas snarled.

Pikeen smiled at Marljas. His impetuousness had amused her since he was a child. Too bad he and Sosha hadn't been compatible.

Pikeen nodded as she sipped her tea. "I didn't think Kadis would fool you, Marljas. She's always meek and subservient around the Queen and King and their family. Kadis has always been very careful how others perceive her. There have been mistakes, however."

Grunting in agreement, Marljas bit into a bread square thickly spread with rich, red *kodala* meat. The Alalalakan chefs were excellent, but they didn't truly appreciate the Gattan love of raw meat. "I rode with her one day. She beat her mount when the mare wouldn't take a jump too high for her. Any woman who treats a beast in such a way will do the same to people."

The door opened and Mendas Teekeson, the Gattan ambassador, entered the room. "Your family has more allies than you realize, Denieen."

"How?"

"Kavlalardrac Hardan has just informed me that both he and his brother, King Findalardrac of Mediria, are sending messages to Gattan expressing their approval of the marriage between Marljas and Alalakan dem al' Sheala, who happens to be related to the Medirian royal family. In celebration of the event, starting three weeks from today, all import fees on Gattan goods to Mediria will be cut in half for thirty days."

Wendjas let out a long whistle, and Marljas' eyes brightened.

"Well, well, well," Pikeen murmured. "I wonder how that came about."

Denieen laughed merrily. "Ban."

Mendas shook his head and growled. "Bandalardrac Hardan, the bane of my family."

Pikeen laid a hand on her husband's arm. "Not Bandalardrac," she said in a gentle voice, "Bakom. Sosha told me that she never wanted Marljas, mainly because everyone in her family kept pushing her towards him. She arranged for Marljas to find Ban and her together. Marljas just didn't get there as quickly as she had planned."

Mendas sighed. "All this time he's been a convenient scapegoat."

Denieen smiled. "He hasn't changed his ways, Mendas. He is still the most notorious rake on five planets."

Marljas grinned a wicked grin. "Perhaps we should turn Ban loose on Kadis."

Wendjas and Mendas smiled at his suggestion, but both Denieen and Pikeen were shocked.

"Do you want him dead!" Deni exclaimed. "Jadis would

gut him herself, and that son of hers would help. And the Queen would be forced to look the other way!"

All three men looked at each other then nodded. With his womanizing reputation, Ban was as good as dead if he so much as touched Kadis.

"Well, that means you send a message home today," Mendas said. "As it is, the Queen and King will get the Medirian message first since it will go by way of diplomatic channels. They'll waste no time contacting your family."

Frowning, Denieen asked, "How long until the spring equinox on Gattan? It's past midsummer here."

Mendas consulted a calendar on his desk and then frowned. "It was last week."

Marljas looked at his sister-in-law. "Kadis is already at our holding."

She laid a hand on his arm. "Don't worry. Your mother can handle Kadis. And the Medirians have given us the perfect way to refuse the proposal."

Wendjas began to grin widely. "If the Medirians are going to give us thirty days of lower import fees as a wedding gift, imagine what the Alalakans will give us. It's time I spoke with Char."

"Just remember, Wendjas Drefeson, Marljas' bloodsister is Char's wife."

Wendjas' face brightened even more.

As Marljas grinned at his brother, Denieen's laughter rolled around the room. "Don't ever again complain of the Drakian ways Marljas and I adopt. You've been spending too much time with Chardadon. Soon, you'll be just as crafty as he when negotiating trade agreements."

Wendjas smiled broadly. "As ever, you're right, Wife. Defeat across the trading table can be so much more satisfactory than a kill. One can return to defeat the same enemy again and again."

"Just don't let Brianna hear you refer to Chardadon as the enemy," Marljas said with a wide grin, "or you'll find her knife at your neck."

* * * * *

Three days later, Bandalardrac slipped into Sheala's room. Denieen had told him she was worried about Sheala's emotional state. She needed something to occupy her mind, and he had exactly what she needed. Sosha.

"Shea, love, are you awake?"

Sheala pushed herself up. "Ban? Is that you?"

"It's me," he answered, "though I don't know how you can possibly see me. It's afternoon, let the sun in." Using the light from the hallway to guide him, he crossed the room and pulled open the drapes. Ignoring her gasp of protest, he opened the window to let in fresh air. Then he turned back to his cousin.

Sheala was hunched in the middle of the bed with the blankets pulled up around her neck.

Ban's voice was gentle. "Are you going to spend your days in here reliving your ordeal?"

Her head turned away so Ban couldn't see her face, she shook her head negatively.

"Then exactly what are you doing?"

"Please, Ban, I'd like to be alone."

Ban walked to the bed and clasped her shoulder. Pain wrung his heart when she cringed at his gentle touch, but he didn't let go. Marljas couldn't convince her to leave her room and was at his wits' end. If something wasn't done, she would become an emotionally crippled hermit, and she and Marljas would never find happiness.

"Come on, I want to introduce you to someone."

Sheala's protests fell on deaf ears as Ban swung her into his arms and carried her out of her room.

Pushing another door open with his shoulder, Ban walked into the room and placed Sheala on the bed next to Sosha.

"Hello, Sosha," he said gently. "I'd have liked to see you again under different circumstances."

"Hello, Bandalardrac," she answered in a weak voice. "Have you forgiven me my deception?"

Ban's ready grin appeared on his face. "A long time ago, love. I got off Gattan without a scratch."

A ghost of a smile appeared on Sosha's face.

"Sosha, this is my cousin Alalakan dem al' Sheala."

"We have met, somewhat. So it is the Alalakans I can thank for my rescue."

"The Alalakans," answered Ban, "and Marljas."

"Marljas?"

"He was there for Sheala."

"Yes," Sosha said slowly, searching her memory, "I remember."

As Ban turned Sheala's left hand so that her palm was visible, Sosha's eyes widened.

"Sheala is Marljas' wife, Sosha," Ban said. "Do you care?"

She shook her head. "I never wanted to marry him. That was my family's wish, not mine."

"Then I'll leave you two to get acquainted."

Turning, Ban turned and walked out of the room, leaving a flabbergasted Sheala sitting on Sosha's bed.

"Why did Marljas initiate the blood rite with you, Alalakan dem al Sheala?" Sosha asked while Sheala still stared dumbfounded at the closed door.

Sheala turned and got her first really good look at the woman Bakom had held captive for almost a year.

Involuntary tremors still shook Sosha's body, a side effect

of the drug she was taking to counteract the addiction to mithrin Bakom had fostered. Bruises, both new and faded, covered what parts of Sosha's arms Sheala could see. Ugly scars covered the ends of each finger where Bakom had ripped out her claws.

Sosha held up her hands and stared at them. "You were lucky, Alalakan dem al' Sheala. You spent only a few hours with that madman."

Sheala was appalled at Sosha's physical condition. "How did you survive?"

She smiled a sad smile. "I lived for revenge, as would any Gattan. One day, his blood will drip from my cl — knife."

Sheala shuddered. Sosha had been ready to say claws, but she didn't have them anymore. How would that affect her life once she got back to Gattan? Sheala blinked back tears. Sosha had suffered far more than she had.

"You didn't answer my question," Sosha continued after a moment. "Why did Marljas Drefeson initiate the marital blood rite?"

Sheala looked down at her hand. "He didn't. I demanded it."

"And he agreed? He must love you very much. Do you love him?"

Sheala nodded affirmatively, but tears began to fall.

"Why do you cry?"

"How can he love me when I look like this?"

The Gattan's voice grew stronger. "Gattans don't see only the physical body. One grows old. Physical beauty fades. Will you love him less when he is an old man?"

Sheala shook her head. "No. But I'm not worried about my feelings. I'm worried about his."

Sosha glared at her. "You're a fool. Your bruises will fade as mine have many times over."

"I can't bear to have him touch me," Sheala admitted in a

quiet voice.

Sheala watched as Sosha sank back against the pillows. Concern for someone other than herself stabbed her conscience for the first time in days. "Why are you able to understand me? Did you learn our language while you — were a captive?"

Sosha's voice was bitter. "Bakom inserted a Medirian translator, a *ghena*, into my ear shortly after I was delivered to him. He wanted to make sure I understood everything that was going to happen to me."

"I didn't think the Medirians sold their translators to the Academy of Science anymore. I have to remember to say something to Ban," Sheala said. "Do you need anything, Sosha?"

A weak smile answered her question. "Nothing you can give me. I envy you, Alalakan dem al' Sheala. Marljas accepts you. Even if he hadn't, you have your family."

Sheala was shocked. "You aren't alone, Sosha. I have heard your godparents as they walked through the hallway. They come every day."

"Yes," Sosha agreed, "but they remember me as I was. Look at me now."

With effort, Sosha threw back her blanket and lifted her nightshirt over her head. A tight bandage circled her torso to hold broken ribs in place. Bruises ranging in color from purple to yellow covered her body. On the insides of her thighs, scabs covered healing cuts. When Sosha laboriously rolled over, Sheala could see more bruises covering her back, and more healing cuts on her buttocks.

Sosha shook her head. "I am damaged beyond what any man on my planet would accept. The scars will be badges of honor, but these," she continued stretching out her fingers to display her lack of claws, "will prevent any man from offering marriage to me. My godparents know this and feel only pity. My parents will feel worse. They'll be forced to accept the comments and condolences of our friends and relatives. On

Gattan, I'll be a freak."

Sheala gazed at the sad girl next to her. Spying the scissors Lorilana had used to cut fresh bandages for Sosha's ribs on the dresser, she rose and fetched it. "I'm not exactly sure how to do this, but Brianna managed," Sheala said when she returned to stand by Sosha. Before she had more time to think, Sheala slashed the point across her right palm. Then she held out her bleeding hand. "I would be proud to call you sister, Sosha."

Sosha gazed at the blood dripping from Sheala's palm. After a moment, she held out her own right hand. Sheala slashed her palm as the door opened. Chardadon and Ban entered the room as Sheala and Sosha brought their hands together.

"One sex, one blood, sister to sister," Sosha said and Sheala turned to her brother. "I have a new sister, Char."

Shaking his head, Char mumbled, "What is it about this family and Gattans?"

Ban, on the other hand, stared at Sosha. He'd seen that she'd been badly treated by Bakom when they'd rescued her. However, he hadn't noticed the extent of her injuries that night. In the light of day, her bruised and battered body hid nothing.

Crossing the room, he gathered her into his arms before she could protest. "Oh, Sosha, how did you stand it, love?"

Sosha had tensed immediately, but Ban's embrace was gentle, and he did not release her. Loosening his grip, he held her out at arm's length. "Marry me, Sosha."

"Bandalardrac!" Deni exclaimed.

Failing to find Sheala in her own room, Denieen and Marljas had followed the sound of voices to Sosha's room. They entered to the sound of Ban's proposal.

Ban waited.

The amazement on Sosha's face was apparent to everyone. Slowly, her eyes filled with tears until they ran unchecked down her cheeks. "Bandalardrac Hardan," she whispered, "you are the most wonderful man I know, but I will not marry for pity."

A ghost of Ban's usual grin appeared. "But I would love you forever."

"Yes, you would — as much as you were able to." A small smile appeared on Sosha's face. "Somewhere in this universe is a woman who will truly love you. I'm not that woman."

"In that case..." Carefully, he set Sosha back down on the bed and pulled his shirt over his head. Picking up the scissors, he methodically cut three slits above his right pectoral muscle.

Sosha didn't hesitate to place her still-bleeding palm against his cuts.

Char groaned again.

Marljas began to chuckle. "We are tied by blood in so many ways, Char, the Gattan elders will have trouble deciphering our family ties."

Sheala helped pull the nightshirt back over Sosha's head.

"Let me see to those cuts," Denieen said. Pulling a small bottle from a pouch inside her belt, she cleaned each cut and then poured a small amount of liquid on each wound.

Sheala jerked her hand away. "That burns! What's it for?"

Marljas took his wife's hand in his, choosing to ignore the wary look in her eyes. He was encouraged by her being out of their room and helping Sosha. "The cuts were not made by Gattan claws. That liquid will make sure a scar remains."

Char mumbled a curse under his breath. "Somebody please inform Mendas Teekeson that his goddaughter is now part of the Alalakan family, and Ban is a member of his. Ban, you can tell King Findalardrac yourself that he now has a Gattan in the family."

"Well, Marljas," Ban chuckled, "Jadis may want to think

twice about marrying her daughter to you."

"What!" both Sheala and Char exclaimed together.

Ban's grin widened as he put his arm around Char's shoulder. "Wendjas is waiting downstairs with an interesting tale to tell."

Soon everyone had left Sosha's room but Denieen. "Ban's proposal was legitimate."

Sighing from where she lay against her pillows, Sosha nodded "I know. But he felt pity, not love, for me. I won't marry under those circumstances." *Or any other*, she added to herself silently.

Denieen helped Sosha get comfortable. "True, Ban loves all women. But for all his rakish ways, he would have remained faithful to you your entire lives."

Closing her eyes, Sosha sighed. "And he wouldn't have been completely happy. His is a true and noble heart, Denieen. How could I deny him the love and happiness he deserves?"

With a measuring gaze, the older woman stared at Sosha. "You're wise beyond your years, Sosha. Ban and Sheala did well to bind themselves to you."

Exhausted, Sosha closed her eyes. For the first time since she'd been rescued, she felt that she belonged somewhere. She drifted off to a dreamless sleep as Denieen left the room.

* * * * *

Down the hall in her room, Sheala sat stiffly in a chair and faced her husband.

"I have sent a message to my father telling him to inform Kadis that I decline her mother's proposal."

"Is that wise?" she asked weakly. "From what you say, this Jadis can be a vindictive woman, and she is your queen's sister."

Frowning, he shook his head. "It doesn't matter. You're

my wife, and I want no other."

Head bent sorrowfully, Sheala murmured, "I'll release you."

Leaping across the room and pulling Sheala from the chair where she sat, Marljas shouted, "You will not!" Then he lowered his head to hers.

Before she could protest or draw away, Marljas covered her mouth with his. She stiffened, but his kiss was gentle and undemanding. Slowly, she relaxed, and Marljas loosened his grip on her upper arms. Very slowly, he pulled her closer as his soft kisses and light nibbles on her lips began to draw a response.

Gently, Marljas pulled his wife completely into his arms.

Lost in her husband's tenderness, Sheala forgot Bakom and his assistants. None of them had ever kissed her, and Marljas' kisses teased and promised but did not demand.

Sheala lifted her hands rested lightly against his chest. As his kisses continued to tease, she gripped his shirt in her fists and pushed herself up onto her toes.

Then his hands slid lightly down her back to cup her buttocks.

"No!" Sheala gasped and pushed herself frantically away from Marljas.

He made no attempt to restrain her. "I won't force you, *Cheta*."

Sheala's head drooped. "I'm sorry. I can't help it."

"I know," he answered stepping close once again but making no move to pull her into his arms. He caressed her cheek gently. "Will you come down for dinner tonight? Deni and Wendjas will be returning to the consulate. Only your family will be there. They would be very pleased to see you up and about."

A weak smile appeared on Sheala's face. "I would like that."

"Good. I'll go tell them, and you can use this time to get ready."

Being careful not to touch her in any other way, he placed a light kiss on her forehead. Then he left the room.

Sheala stared as the door closed behind her husband. Then she sighed. Much as she'd like to crawl back in her bed and pull the covers over her head, she couldn't spend the rest of her life hiding. Besides, Sosha needed her help.

Out in the hallway, Marljas clenched his fists as he leaned his forehead against the wall striving to bring his body under control. Sheala's tentative response to his kisses had duped him into loosening the strict control he'd wrapped around himself. Memories of her moving under him, of her mouth on his body, of her tail and the deliciously wicked things it could do to him flashed through his memory.

Sheala's recovery was going to be hell—on both of them.

* * * * *

At the Medirian embassy, Kavlalardrac rose as the Aradab Kahn entered the room. "Who's the best woman with you?"

"Beti," was Kahn's abrupt answer.

"She'll accompany Sheala to Gattan."

Kahn waited unmoving.

Kavlalardrac sighed. "Aradabs," he muttered, mostly to himself.

Rapidly, he outlined the situation.

Kahn nodded. "Beti will agree to go. She's become very fond of Sheala, who shows as much promise as Prince Bandalardrac."

"She won't mind leaving Brianna?"

Kahn shrugged. "Beti can not be on two planets at one

time. She will see the necessity." With those words, he turned and left.

Kavlalardrac sat back down. "Aradabs," he muttered again.

Chapter Thirteen

ઝ

"What do you want, Mother?" Cadan drawled as he entered an opulent sitting room. "I'm ready for the hunt."

"Your sister Kadis has sent a message. It seems that Marljas has flown Denieen, Wendjas and the twins to visit Denieen's parents so he is not at their estate."

"Surely they didn't deny Kadis their hospitality," he said.

Jadis Franasdotir, sister to the Queen of Gattan, smiled maliciously. "One could only wish it were so, but Teena and Drefes are not so stupid as to offer insult to the Queen's favorite niece."

"The Queen's only niece," he interjected.

Jadis allowed a small frown to momentarily travel across her flawless countenance. "They have received our proposal and have given Kadis the best guest quarters. Once Marljas returns, she'll have no trouble trapping him into a compromising situation. Then we'll have him."

Cadan shrugged his shoulders. "Perhaps, but Marljas is no fool. He's eluded your traps for him before."

"It *will* work, fool. And once Kadis and Marljas are married, she'll guide him down the correct path. Where Marljas goes, his brother and father are sure to follow."

He rose and lightly kissed her cool cheek. "As you say, Mother. Now, if you'll excuse me, the hunt awaits."

"Of course, my son. Enjoy yourself. But remember, we dine with the Queen and her husband tonight," Jadis purred contentedly.

Cadan closed the door softly. His mother and sister were

fools. Marljas wanted nothing to do with Kadis, and he and his family would find a way around the proposed betrothal. It wasn't a royal command, even though his mother had dared hint that it was. However, there were other ways to bring the powerful families of Gattan to their way of thinking. He would see to it himself.

* * * * *

"I'll try to send you a full report when I return to Mediria," Ban said as he once again sat in Kavlalardrac's comfortable office. "Until then you'll have to be content with what I can send you. Once we get to Gattan, I'll have to be extremely careful. As far as I know, Rodane is the only Alalakan who knows I'm an assassin though I think Jenneta suspects. How many more assassins are already there?"

Kavlalardrac nodded. "I have fourteen assassins on Gattan and a few nonassassin spies. Ten of the assassins are in the Medirian ambassador's household and two have been insinuated with the Drakian ambassador's guards, without his knowledge. The other two are in the Gattan palace itself. The spies roam at large but answer to our ambassador."

Ban just snorted. As head of the Medirian secret police, Kavlalardrac probably had spies even he himself didn't know about.

"If any problems arise, I'll send a message through one of the others," the older man continued. "I don't foresee any reason to need the Monarch's Assassin for the next year or so. Since you eliminated the Gattan–Varcian half-breed who was attempting to unite all the pirates in this part of the galaxy, his subordinates have all been fighting for position. They've done a good job of eliminating each other."

Ban leaned forward. Eliminating that killer had been a satisfying assignment. The fool had, however, left a daughter. "Have you heard anything about Tali?"

Kavlalardrac shifted his intense gaze to his nephew. "His

daughter. She's remaining aloof from the infighting. Or so it seems."

Ban grinned. "She decided to listen to me then. The most dangerous men kill each other off and leave her to take command."

"Will we be dealing with a pirate queen?"

Ban shook his head. "There are too many Varcian pirates to allow that to happen. You know Varcians consider women second-class citizens. It's only within the last hundred years that widows have been allowed to own property. Just as well they follow Tali. She's much smarter than her father ever was." He started to rise. "If there's nothing else…"

Kavlalardrac's voice became serious. "One of our spy satellites picked up a strange signal from the fourth moon of Gattan. Our infrared scanning system recorded two ships—a pirate slave-trader. The other one was piloted by Hathnic."

Ban froze. "You're sure? I thought he died in that explosion on Varce."

"We never found his body."

Letting out a long breath, Ban laced his fingers together. "Slavers. Do you think he was involved in Sosha's kidnapping?"

His uncle nodded. "Probably, he was one of our most skilled assassins until he turned renegade. Disguising himself as a Gattan wouldn't be a hardship. Ban, I want him dead. We can't have rogue assassins roaming around the galaxy, especially one who's involved himself in the slave-trade."

"I'll take care of it." Ban rose. "I must leave. I'm supposed to be overhauling the *Wanderer*."

"No one saw you arrive?" Kavlalardrac asked quite unnecessarily.

"Uncle!" Bandalardrac exclaimed with a bark of laughter as he rose and walked to the door. "How could I be the longest-surviving Monarch's Assassin if I couldn't go where I wanted when I wanted without being detected?"

Kavlalardrac only grunted as his nephew left the room. It was amazing that Ban had survived as long as he had.

* * * * *

Marljas' mother and father looked up as the door opened after a short knock.

"Forgive me, Teena Seenasdotir, but there is a message from your sons," said the young woman as she hurried to the table where the pair was breakfasting.

"Thank you," Marljas' mother said. "Go back to your duties now."

After the servant left, Teena slowly opened the missive.

"What does it say, my love?" asked the handsome man who sat next to her.

Marljas' mother looked up once, reread the letter, and handed it to her husband without saying a word.

After reading quickly, he broke into loud laughter.

"What's so funny? Our son has married a Drakian— without my permission!"

"And taken a bloodsister from an entirely new planet. I can't wait to see the look on Jadis' face."

For a moment, Teena stared at her husband then chuckled. "Yes, an unknown Drakian is preferable to Kadis."

"Good. Tell her to go home."

Tapping her lips with her finger, Teena shook her head. "No, I think not. We don't want Kadis to discover what's in this message."

"Why not?"

"Too many people here have been talking about the honor done to our tribe by the Queen. Few realize that this is a plot of Jadis'."

"But Marljas wants us to tell Kadis about his marriage immediately."

152

"It will be better to wait and let Marljas tell Kadis himself. She's been here barely a week and is already angering people with her haughty manners. Let Kadis further alienate herself from our people."

Drefes nodded but rose from his chair. "A good idea, but I'll send a message to Marljas. It will be wise to warn him that Kadis will still be here when he arrives with his bride."

Teena clasped her husband's arm as he passed. "What do you think she's like, this new wife of his?"

Drefes shrugged. "She's an Alalakan. Her brother Chardadon conducted himself with honor when he was here."

"A noble man. Should we make a comparison?" Teena pursed her lips and frowned. "This message is not at all very informative. I'd very much like to talk to Deni."

"Well, they'll be home in a few weeks, my love. You can talk all you want then." With those words, Marljas' father left his wife to finish her breakfast and hurried to their communication center.

* * * * *

Sheala turned and waved as she and Sosha ascended the stairway that had been rolled next to the *Scrathe*. Brianna, holding Connor in one arm, waved back. Ban would be piloting all of the Alalakans except Jamiros and Xdana back to the country estate. Then in six to eight weeks' time, Brianna, Connor, Char and Ban would join Sheala on Gattan to finalize the Gattan marriage contract between Sheala and Marljas and introduce Brianna and Connor to their Gattan family.

Surprising everyone, Beti had asked to accompany Sheala and Sosha, and King Findalardrac had been more than happy to allow her to go for that was one less Aradab to bother him, he'd stated in the missive he'd sent granting Beti permission to go to Gattan.

Sheala was also grateful. She'd been uneasy about going to a planet full of people who thought nothing of declaring bloodfeud for imagined slights. Now not only would she now have Marljas and his family to protect her, she'd also have Beti. If some Gattan woman challenged her to a fight, there would be nothing Marljas could do about it because he couldn't fight a Gattan woman except in self-defense. But Beti could. She might be an Aradab instead of a Gattan, but she was female.

Then she glanced at the young woman at her side. Sosha had told her she was also glad of Beti's presence. She had been there the first time the Aradab had made a point of visiting Sosha as she recovered, casually discussing new fighting techniques since the Gattan no longer had claws. Beti had not once expressed any pity towards Sosha. She merely stated that life goes on, and Sosha must make the best of what she had. If she didn't wish to do that, she should take herself off and die. Or, Beti herself would be glad to aid in her suicide. Sosha had stared at the Aradab then declared that she did not wish to die.

Also, a Drakian plastic surgeon had also managed to devise very natural-looking fingernails and attach them. They weren't the claws she had grown up with, but they were certainly better than blunt fingertips. At least they made her look more "human".

As she entered the *Scrathe*, Sheala walked past the seats provided for passengers and continued to the control center, earning a wide smile from Denieen as she did so.

Once there, she slid into the seat usually occupied by the copilot. A few minutes later when Wendjas entered, he was startled to see Sheala where he had expected to sit. However, a slow grin spread across his face and he slid into the seat reserved for the navigator.

When Marljas stepped into the command center, he stopped for a few seconds then nodded. He said nothing as he slid into the captain's chair, but he did lift her hand and kiss her palm.

Swallowing the lump in her throat, Sheala smiled as she gently pulled her hand from his.

Marljas slid into his seat. In a short time, the *Scrathe* had risen from Benishan's landing pad. "We'll be out of Drakan's atmosphere in ten minutes, and as soon as the *Scrathe* clears the solar system, I'll engage the space drive. We'll be on Gattan inside of two weeks."

"There's a message from Father," Wendjas said as he monitored the computer.

Sheala started to rise. "I'll go back with the others."

Marljas reached out and gently clasped her wrist. "Stay. You're my wife, and I've nothing to hide from you."

Drefes Cardesson's voice filled the command center as his image appeared on the screen. "Greetings, my sons. Your mother and I have received your message. The information you sent was a great surprise, and we are looking forward to your return. Your mother and I, however, feel it is in the best interests of everyone if we wait to share the details of your message with the tribe until you arrive. Your mother also asks about her grandsons. They have been sorely missed. I hope the sea air was not too much for them."

A noise sounded behind him and he glanced over his shoulder. As soon as it was quiet again, their father turned his attention back to the monitor. "We are preparing for your return. Kadis Jadisdotir has arrived and waits with some impatience. Indeed Marljas, she would have liked to address you herself in this message. She was not aware of your sojourn with Denieen's parents."

Marljas grunted. That's what the noise behind his father had been. Good thing he locked the door to the communication center.

"He's told Kadis nothing," Wendjas stated.

"Enjoy the remainder of your sojourn. We look forward to your return with great anticipation."

With those final words, Drefes' image vanished.

The *Scrathe* left Drakan's gravitational pull and shot quickly past its sun's outer three planets. After thirty minutes,

Marljas punched in the navigational codes that would take his ship home to Gattan. Then he turned his chair so that he faced both his wife and brother.

"Ban said Findalardrac of Mediria would be sending messages to the Queen. Father made no mention of those, so they have probably not yet been received. Nor did Mother inform Kadis of my marriage to Sheala."

"Your mother is giving your tribe a chance to get to know Kadis," Denieen said as she joined them.

Marljas grinned nastily as Wendjas chuckled.

Confused, Sheala looked at the Gattan faces surrounding her. "Why? Won't your people prefer a Gattan princess to me?"

Denieen patted Sheala's shoulder. "Kadis Jadisdotir has the temperament of a wet desert rat, Sheala. She won't endear herself to our people. She'll be too busy trying to command them. She is what Brianna would call a 'bitch'."

"But she's a princess," Sheala began.

Denieen shook her head. "No, she isn't. Even though Gattan is a matriarchy, the royal line descended through our king. Mattis, the queen, only became royal after she married him. The queen's sister and niece are not princesses. What's more, you have more royal blood in you through your Medirian ancestors than Kadis has."

"And we don't need another bond with the royal family," Marljas snapped. It was his future they were discussing so nonchalantly.

"Another bond?" Sheala questioned.

"The *Leonine* tribe holds the royal title on Gattan," Marljas continued more gently. "Our father and Krondal's were brothers."

Sheala stared from one to the other. "You mean the King of Gattan is your cousin!"

The three Gattan watched Sheala with varying degrees of

amusement. Slowly the look of amazement on her face was replaced by mirth and she began to laugh.

Marljas began to grin. He didn't know why she was laughing, but this was the first time this emotion had gripped her since she was kidnapped.

Denieen and Wendjas were also pleased with Sheala's reaction, however, they were confused as well.

"Will you share the joke with us?" Wendjas asked.

Sheala gasped and slowly regained control. When she was able to talk once more she said, "Did anyone bother to tell Brianna that she is bloodcousin to the King of Gattan?"

Denieen allowed herself a short laugh and then countered. "Has anyone bothered to tell Krondal that he is bloodcousin to Brianna?"

* * * * *

The journey to Gattan passed quickly for Sheala. Though she shared his quarters, Marljas pressed no sexual demands upon her and made sure he was monitoring the controls of his ship whenever Sheala slept so that they weren't alone in each other's company. Denieen's sons, Hendjas and Charjas, also eased the sexual tension that was always threatening to envelop him. They were extremely active, and being forced to spend time confined to a spaceship required everyone to help keep them amused.

Beti took the time Sheala didn't spend with the twins. The Aradab made it very clear to both Sheala and Sosha that they needed to stop moping around and feeling sorry for themselves. Neither had claws so they needed to develop personal modes of self-defense, and there was no time like the present to begin. All in all, Sheala had no time to worry about her and Marljas' love life, and the two weeks it took to reach Gattan passed quickly.

* * * * *

In a private audience chamber in the royal palace, the Medirian ambassador, Princess Jessilindra Hardan, sister of Mediria's king, bowed low before Gattan's Queen and King.

"This is a very interesting tale you spin, Ambassador. How do we know you speak the truth?"

The Medirian grinned and presented a single sheet of paper to them. King Krondal accepted it and read the few sentences printed on it. When he finished, he handed it to his wife.

Her eyebrows rose as she quickly scanned it.

"Thirty days at half tariff," Queen Mattis said evenly. "This is unprecedented."

The ambassador's grin widened. "The girl is dear to our family, Your Highness."

Krondal leaned back in his chair and said, "So dear that you request a private audience instead of presenting this treaty in the usual manner."

Jessilindra acknowledged his comment with a slight nod. "King Findalardrac has no ulterior motives for himself. He simply did not wish to cause undue problems for Your Highnesses."

Queen Mattis laughed softly. "I wish I had your brother's spy system, Jessilindra."

The elder sister of the Medirian king smiled back. "The spies were unnecessary. This information came through family channels."

"A family to which," Queen Mattis countered, "I now belong."

"Only through marriage," Jessilindra demurred. "Technically, it is King Krondal who is now related to the Medirian royal family."

The Queen sighed. "At least we have that to hold out to the Council. There are more than a few of our people who will not be happy with this marriage."

Wisely, Jessilindra said nothing.

Queen Mattis stood. "Well, this will certainly require thought. Thank you for personally delivering the message from your brother, Princess Jessilindra. I'll have suitable replies drawn up and sent to you."

Jessilindra bowed deeply. "Thank you, Your Majesty — and may I add, welcome to the family."

A loud sigh of exasperation escaped Queen Mattis after the door closed behind the Medirian ambassador. "A pretty predicament, this."

"How so, my love?" Krondal asked as he rose and stretched.

"You know very well Jadis sent an offer of betrothal to your cousins' mother on Kadis' behalf."

Krondal poured himself a drink from a selection of wines available on the table next to his chair. "This marriage between Marljas and Alalakan dem al' Sheala is not a problem for us. I told you that Marljas was not interested in becoming Kadis' husband."

"But it is a logical arrangement."

Krondal chuckled and put his arms around his wife. "If logic were all that entered into marriages, my sweet, I'd have listened to my mother and married your sister."

Mattis smiled up into her husband's face. "She'd have made you miserable."

Krondal grinned wider. "So you would loose her on my poor cousin."

Mattis snorted. "Teena and Denieen would have kept both Jadis and her daughter in line."

Krondal threw back his head and roared with laughter. "So that's why you agreed to your sister's request, to let someone else manage her."

Mattis laughed with her husband but quickly gathered her composure. "Hush, you fool," she said playfully, "the servants will be coming soon. I think this marriage had best remain a secret until Marljas and his bride return."

Krondal nodded. "It will give us time to marshal our forces, but Teena and Drefes will expect to hear something from us."

"As with the rescue of Sosha Kanicsdotir, we will say nothing until the Medirian proposal is presented to the court. The tariff reduction does not go into effect for another week. Let's just watch and see how Marljas and his new wife handle Kadis."

"But we must inform Sosha's parents of her return. And Jadis could still cause trouble. Marljas married without his mother's consent."

Mattis snorted. "Humpf! Half of the men on this planet marry without their mother's permission, and we both agreed that it would have been cruel to keep the information about Sosha from her parents. That much I'll tell Jadis. Her family has incurred blooddebt to Cadan. My sister has them putting the estate of Cloudhaven in order. A request to come and fetch their daughter will be less likely to cause comment coming from her rather than us."

"From you, you mean. I'm only a mere male. As far as Jadis is concerned, the fact that I'm the king matters not at all. I am here only to sire a suitable daughter to take your place." Krondal sighed and dropped his arms from around his wife. "And you know as well as I that Jadis will make Marljas' lack of permission to marry an issue. She wants Kadis married to him, and she'll stop at nothing to accomplish her goal."

Mattis frowned. "We have had this discussion before, Krondal."

Krondal locked eyes with his wife. His fell first. "Very well, my love. Continue to believe that your sister is no more than stubborn and misguided, but I believe this time you will finally see Jadis for what she really is."

With those words, Krondal left the room. Mattis picked

up the glass of wine Krondal had not finished and drained the contents. This disagreement about Jadis was the only thorn in her otherwise happy marriage. Her sister could be haughty at times, but she truly didn't wish to harm anyone. Did she?

Chapter Fourteen

ക

"Sheala! Look out!"

Sheala turned, spied Denieen's sons barreling towards her and quickly stepped back. The two boys leaped through the doorway and disappeared down the stairs that had been rolled to the side of the *Scrathe*.

Denieen's defeated sigh rolled over Sheala's shoulder. "At least we're back on solid ground, and they can get outside to use up all the energy they have."

Smiling, Sheala nodded as she followed her sister-in-law out of the ship. For the last three days, Denieen's sons had constantly asked when they'd be home, when they could get out of the ship, when they could stop being careful how they played, the list went on and on.

"Now go on. Marljas is right behind me. He must introduce you to his parents."

Sheala swallowed the sudden lump in her throat and stepped out of the ship, stopping long enough to suck in a deep breath of fresh air. A warm breeze blew across the landing pad, carrying with it the smell of freshly mown grass and the spicy odor of—something. She inhaled again. Whatever it was, it smelled wonderful.

As she stood at the top of the staircase, she closed her eyes and let the hot afternoon sun warm her suddenly cold skin. How she'd love to disappear back inside the *Scrathe*! Hendjas and Charjas' yelling, though, caught her attention, and she opened her eyes in time to see them launch themselves into the arms of a tall Gattan who had to be Marljas' father, and the lovely blonde woman with the amused expression on her face at his side had to be his mother.

A firm hand slid onto the small of her back. "There's nothing to fear, *Cheta*. My parents will love you as much as I do."

"I just bet they will," she mumbled under her breath. But she acceded to Marljas' urging and started down the stairs.

The wind carried Hendjas and Charjas' excited, one-sided conversation with their grandparents back to her as she descended and walked across the landing pad.

"Sheala can spin her swords faster than anyone in the universe!" Hendjas shouted.

"She can kick as high as Marljas' head!" Charjas shouted equally loudly.

"She knocked him off his feet once."

"Beti is teaching both her and Sosha how to fight like an Aradab."

Both turned eager expressions towards their grandmother. "Can we learn how to fight like an Aradab?" both begged at the same time in their loudest voices. "Father said we had to ask you."

Before she had a chance to answer, Marljas said, "Mother, Father, this is my wife, Alalakan dem al' Sheala. Sheala, my mother and father, Teena Seenasdotir and Drefes Cardesson."

Marljas' father bowed. "Welcome to our holding, Alalakan dem al' Sheala, wife of my son. Our hearth is yours."

Before Sheala could answer, Teena pulled Marljas into her arms for a quick hug then stepped back. "You have ever been a source of surprises for us, Marljas. What of the proposed betrothal to the queen's niece?"

Reaching for Sheala's hand, Marljas laced his fingers through hers and pulled her closer to his side. "I do *not* wish to marry Kadis now, nor did I wish to marry her before I went to Drakan. Kadis is...a bitch."

A confused expression appeared on Teena's face. "A what?"

"A derogatory expression we learned on Drakan," Denieen said as she stepped to Sheala's other side. "Greetings, Teena Seenasdotir, mother of my husband."

Teena smiled and embraced Denieen. "Welcome home, wife to my son. Your presence was missed in our house."

As he joined them, Wendjas quipped, "You wouldn't greet Kadis in such a manner."

Teena sighed but smiled as she embraced Wendjas. "Still defending your younger brother, Wendjas."

"That's not a defense, Mother of my heart," Wendjas said with a grin as he lifted his mother into the air with his embrace, "merely an acknowledgment of the truth."

Sheala stepped back, watching her husband's affectionate reunion with his parents.

They were obviously as close-knit a family as hers was.

Beti appeared at her side. "Children who so love and revere their parents are a true blessing."

Both Teena and Drefes looked up at the sound of her voice.

Drefes didn't try to hide his amazement. "An Aradab? Here?"

Marljas grinned. "It's a long story, one better told in the comfort of the house rather than under the hot afternoon sun."

His mother ignored him, her attention concentrated on the lithe figure behind Beti. "Sosha Kanicsdotir, welcome to my home."

Sosha bowed her head. "Your welcome is a balm to my heart, Teena Seenasdotir."

"Your story is one we long to hear," was Teena's answer.

Grinning, Denieen nudged her mother-in-law. "As Marljas said, a story for the cool comfort of the house. The sun is warm."

Whooping with joy, Hendjas and Charjas spotted some other young Gattans standing in a nearby group and took off at a dead run. The other boys joined them, and the entire group headed towards a thick stand of trees.

"Well, we won't see them until mealtime," Teena said.

Sheala looked around. A large group of people stood not far away.

"Friends, family and servants who are eager to welcome Wendjas and his family home, Alalakan dem al' Sheala," Teena said.

Sheala inched closer to Marljas' side and slid her hand into his again. She could hear buzzing voices mentioning Drakian, Sosha Kanicsdotir, and Aradab.

Marljas squeezed her hand but looked at his mother. "What about Kadis?"

"She can wait," was her terse reply.

* * * * *

"Who are the women with them?" the elegantly clad young Gattan woman asked her maid.

"An Aradab, a Drakian, and Sosha Kanicsdotir," the girl answered timidly.

"Sosha Kanicsdotir?" Kadis questioned with a frown. "We thought she was somewhere with a Medirian prince. What did she say?"

"Nothing, Mistress."

Kadis' lip curled in a petulant sneer. "Her parents will probably beg Mother to take her into service also, the little slut. Who are the others?"

Kadis tilted her head and admired herself in the mirror. So what if Marljas had once wanted to marry Sosha. She was a nobody whose parents were the caretakers of her mother's country estate—mere servants—even if her godfather was the ambassador to Drakan.

She tilted her head the other way and admired the slim column of her neck. Marljas would never consider marrying the little upstart with her here proposing a betrothal at the queen's behest.

"They said nothing about the Aradab," the maid said swallowing nervously.

"And the Drakian?"

The maid swallowed again. "Alalakan dem al' Sheala."

Kadis sneered at her reflection. "Denieen must have brought them. The fool woman is convinced that trade rather than conquest is best. Mother and I will set her right after I've married Marljas. Where are they now?"

"They have all gathered in Teena Seenasdotir's private apartments," the maid answered with less tension. More persistent questioning by her mistress would have earned her a slap. As it was, she did not plan to be anywhere near Kadis Jadisdotir when she discovered Marljas had married the Drakian woman.

"Send a message that I am ready to join them."

"I will take it myself, Mistress."

"Good, you're finally beginning to learn your place."

"Yes, Mistress," the girl answered as she left the room. Tonight she would ask sanctuary from her mistress's hosts. From everything she'd heard from those who worked here, Drefes Cardesson would pay off her father's debt to Kadis' brother and would be much more understanding in their repayment of the debt to him.

Smugly, Kadis Jadisdotir watched her maid leave the room. It had taken only a few slaps and three days with no meals for the girl to learn her place.

Then Kadis frowned. With Denta gone, she'd have to brush her hair herself. Turning to face the full-length mirror, Kadis unbelted the robe she was wearing and let it drop to the floor so she could admire her nude body. Everyone said she was a younger version of her mother, and at forty-five Jadis Franasdotir was still considered one of the most beautiful women on Gattan.

Her mother, Kadis concluded, was correct. She was the great beauty of her generation. Unlike many other members of her tribe, she did not have stripes on her face or the front of her body. Instead, dark brown stripes began at her backbone and circled around her sides, fading into the warm tan skin of her breasts and belly. Black eyes hid beneath thick lashes, and full, red lips smiled beneath what was considered a dainty nose for a Gattan. Dark brown stripes began at the top of her forehead, snaking back through tawny, orange hair that fell to the middle of her back. Kadis was tall and lithe. She had firm, high breasts with pouting brown nipples and a slender waist. Long legs stretched upward to flaring hips, hips which carried the only stripes to completely circle her body. Those two dark stripes rode down over her hips to meet in the tangle of her pubic hair.

Kadis smiled. Once he saw her nude, Marljas wouldn't be able to resist her. This trap, with her as the bait, would work perfectly.

Kadis' musings were interrupted by a knock at the door.

She slipped on an exotic robe. "Enter."

An older Gattan woman entered.

Kadis preened. Teena had sent one of her personal servants. Finally, she was being honored as she deserved. "You are here to escort me to your mistress? You will have to wait until I dress. You may assist me."

Scowling, the old woman shook her head. "My mistress's apologies, but she is having a private reunion with her sons. She will be happy to receive you in the morning."

With those words the woman left the room, leaving Kadis momentarily speechless.

"A private reunion!" Kadis screeched, "with a Drakian, an Aradab, and Sosha Kanicsdotir, the daughter of a servant, present!"

Furiously, Kadis pushed the button that contacted the servant's quarters.

"Yes?" replied a disembodied voice.

"Where is my maid?"

"She is not here. Perhaps she is on an errand for you?"

"Bah!" snarled Kadis as she severed the connection. "How dare they treat me as a nobody!" Head held high, nostrils flaring, Kadis swept from her rooms towards those of her hostess not bothering to dress in more suitable clothing.

* * * * *

Sosha gripped Sheala's hand as she told the story of her kidnapping and captivity on Drakan. When she finished her story, Drefes Cardesson rose from where he was sitting, strode the fireplace, and jabbed the poker into the burning logs — three times.

Turning he said, "It is a most unsettling story you tell us, Sosha. Are you sure?"

"I have never been more sure of anything in my life," she answered from beside Sheala. "I may have been sold to the Drakian by Varcian pirates, but those who kidnapped me were Gattan."

Placing the poker gently back on its rack, Drefes sat down heavily. "I had never thought to hear of such perfidy on Gattan."

Marljas' mother had tears in her eyes. "You're welcome to stay with us as long as you like, my child. To think that—"

Before she could finish, the door burst open with such force that it bounced off the wall, and one of the most beautiful women Sheala had ever seen stomped into the room, visibly furious. "I demand to know why I was not included in this reunion. As Marljas' betrothed, I have more right to be here than do strangers and servants."

Complete silence blanketed the room. Then, before anyone else could say anything, Marljas rose from where he sat and growled, "I do not accept your offer of betrothal, Kadis

Jadisdotir. I wouldn't marry you if you were the last woman in the universe."

Gasping at Marljas' blunt rejection, Kadis turned to her hostess. "Teena Seenasdotir, I have never been so insulted in my life. You had better take your son in hand and explain his duty to him. I would have a docile husband."

Tugging Marljas' hand, Sheala pulled him back down beside her. Then she glanced over to his mother. On Drakan, any guest who behaved like this would be sent away immediately.

A smile tickled the corners of Sheala's mouth as Teena rose to her feet, her expression outraged. "You, Kadis Jadisdotir, are a guest in my house, you are not a family member. No betrothal contract between our families has been finalized. You have no right to tell me whom I can and cannot have as guests in my own private quarters. Even if you were married to my son, you would not have that right, nor the right to barge in here uninvited. I have never seen such a display of bad manners and ill breeding as you have just demonstrated. Be assured, your mother and the queen shall hear of this." Teena glanced down at Kadis' robe. "And to appear in such a manner of undress! I am disgusted."

Just great, Sheala thought, *guess I won't be walking around the halls naked here.*

A haughty sneer joined the anger on Kadis' face. "Who are you, Teena Seenasdotir, to deny *me!*"

That challenge brought Denieen to her feet, claws unsheathed. "Think, Kadis Jadisdotir, of where you are and what you say. I will *not* allow my family to be vilified."

Before things escalated, Beti stepped between Kadis and Denieen. "You, Kadis Jadisdotir, intrude where you were not invited. It is best that your return to your own rooms."

With no further ado, Beti spun Kadis around, locked her arms around her body, and walked out the door. The words "If you continue to struggle, I will knock you senseless" floated back through the open doorway.

Grinning, Marljas closed the door softly and locked it.

Drefes smiled at his youngest son. "Marljas, Aradabs are welcome in our home anytime."

Sheala looked around the room and uttered her first words since she'd been presented to Marljas' family. "Brianna's going to love it here."

Chapter Fifteen

ഇ

Much later Sheala sat propped up against the headboard of her husband's bed.

She had spoken little during the remainder of the evening with his parents, simply enjoying the delicious meal and listening to Denieen, Wendjas and Marljas telling and retelling the events, with some judicious deletions, that led up to her and Marljas' impetuous marriage. It was obvious that his parents hadn't completely accepted her, but Denieen's staunch support had won her at least grudging acceptance—that and the fact that neither of them wanted Kadis marrying Marljas.

"They *will* come to love you as I do, *Cheta*," Marljas said softly as he entered from the suite's bathroom and dimmed the lights.

Sheala tensed as Marljas lowered himself onto the bed next to her. Gently, he pushed the hair from her face. "I would never hurt you, Sheala," he said as his lips touched the side of her neck.

Struggling with her inner demons, Sheala stiffened. However, he didn't touch her anywhere else, and the delicate kisses and nibbles on her neck and face slowly relaxed her.

Then Marljas cupped her breast.

The memory of vicious pinches roared into her memory, and she scrambled from the bed.

Marljas didn't try to stop her.

"I can't," she sobbed softly.

Marljas closed his eyes and swallowed. He had so hoped that leaving Sheala to herself during their journey here would bring back the trust she had once had in him.

After a brief inner struggle, he opened his eyes and held out his hand. "Come to bed, *Cheta*. You've nothing to fear from me. I won't touch you again tonight."

Uncertainty evident on her face, Sheala nevertheless walked back to the bed and lowered herself onto the very edge, as far away from him as she could get.

Despair gripped Marljas' heart. Though he was encouraged by the fact that he had been able to kiss and nuzzle his wife, he was finally forced to admit to himself that her ability to trust had been damaged much more than he'd imagined, and simply bringing her home to Gattan wouldn't erase the memories of her rape or cause her to trust him not to hurt her.

* * * * *

Sighing, Denieen leaned back in the soft leather chair. "How I missed Gattan tea."

Her mother-in-law sat next to her in another chair. "How traumatized is she? I don't want Marljas wasting his life and love on a woman who won't accept a physical relationship."

Denieen sipped more tea. "Sheala sleeps in the same bed with Marljas, so it's only a matter of time. She is, after all, Drakian. Her sexual nature will manifest itself eventually."

Leaning against the fireplace, Drefes sipped a fine Gattan brandy. "What of this Brianna woman who is now bloodsister to Marljas?"

Denieen smiled broadly as Wendjas answered with a throaty chuckle. "A woman to set our planet on its ear. Marljas did the right thing when he chose to complete the ritual. Brianna is a woman who will enrich our family in many ways."

"Blooding herself even though she was pregnant. We can't find fault with her courage," Teena said with wonder in her voice.

Drefes' chuckle mimicked his son's. "Accepting the wife

of the Alalakan dragon as a bloodsister into the tribe is not such a bad thing. *Leonine* coffers will prosper with the trading contracts. Surely, family ties will lessen prices?"

Wendjas smiled broadly. "They already have, Father. Marljas' marriage into the Alalakan family has also strengthened those ties not to mention the ties to Mediria. And the Alalakans have many more ties to the Medirian royal family than anyone not of their clan realized. Sheala and her brothers carry Medirian blood, and Brianna is adopted daughter to the King and Queen."

"And the Aradab?" Teena asked. "You aren't going to tell me she's also a member of one of these families we find ourselves tied to."

Denieen chuckled. "No, the most obvious reason for her presence is for Sheala's protection."

Both Drefes and Teena bristled and interrupted before she could continue.

"They think I could not protect—"

"A woman who comes to me as a daughter…"

"Peace, second Mother, Father," Denieen said softly. "Char and his father have no doubts in your ability to protect Sheala while she's here in your house. They think ahead to possible challenges…"

Metal clanged against wood as Teena slapped her goblet down on the table. "If she cannot protect herself, she is not worthy to be wife to any Gattan, let alone my son."

"Mother," Wendjas said more sharply than he'd ever addressed her before, "let Deni finish!"

Both Drefes' and Teena's eyes widened at his tone, but they remained silent.

"Sheala is more than capable of answering any challenge, or, at least, she will be in a week or so. Beti is here to complete her training. No one on our planet could do an adequate job because we base our martial arts training around our claws. Sheala has none. Nor does Sosha," Deni continued. "Beti is here as much for Sosha as she is for Sheala. What's more, Beti will do more to ease both girls' minds about their captivity than anyone else could."

Drefes frowned. "Why is that?"

Denieen chuckled. "She's Aradab. She simply won't tolerate self-pity. If Sheala or Sosha cannot heal, she'll offer to help them end their misery."

Teena's eyebrows shot up. "Surely neither girl…"

Denieen's chuckle deepened as she shook her head negatively. "Sheala is too dear to her family and to Marljas, and too much effort was put into curing Sosha of her addiction to let either one of them die."

"But the Aradab will not tell them that," Drefes said, realization dawning. "Instead, she'll bully them into full health."

A thoughtful expression on her face, Teena lifted her goblet. "Will it work?"

"Sheala will most certainly recover. She spent only one night as a captive." Denieen paused and stared into her mother-in-law's face. "Sosha, on the other hand, was a sexual slave for almost a year. No one can be sure what emotional scars she carries. The physical ones are bad enough."

Teena shuddered. "Ripping out her claws…"

"She still almost tore the throat out of one with her teeth," Wendjas growled. "The scar on the throat of a Drakian senator implicated him quite clearly in her torture. He, at least, will spend the rest of his life in jail."

Drefes snarled, "He should be dead!"

Denieen leaned back again, a thoughtful expression on her face. "That's what Bandalardrac said. I wonder…" She looked up. "His uncle is the Medirian king, and they do have all those assassins…"

Teena waved her hand. "We're talking about Marljas and Sheala. What are we going to do about them?"

Drefes rose and sighed. "Let it be, Teena. They're young and will work things out for themselves. Come. It's late and I'm ready for bed."

Teena paused, opened her mouth to say something, then thought better of it.

"One more thing before you leave, Mother, Father," Wendjas said with a wide grin as he drew Denieen to her feet and put his arm around her.

His parents looked at them expectantly.

"You will become grandparents again in less than a year," Deni said with a smile. "Brianna assures me this one will be a girl."

Joy chased away the weariness on Teena's face as she embraced Denieen. "She's sure it's a girl? How does she know?"

Wendjas chuckled. "Brianna is a remarkable woman, Mother. I'm proud to have her in our family. However, she's no seer. It is only a 'feeling' she has that Deni carries a girl."

Drefes too embraced his daughter-in-law. "It matters not, Deni. Another grandchild will bring joy to our house whether it is a boy or a girl."

"But to have a girl…" Teena said breathlessly. "It's been three generations since a girl was born into our line of the *Leonine* tribe. Krondal's son is not yet betrothed."

"Mother!"

"Wife!"

Denieen's rich laughter broke out over the two men's simultaneous exclamations. "Peace," she laughed. "The child barely rests under my heart, and it will be many years before we need talk of any betrothal. Perhaps it will be another boy."

* * * * *

A few doors away Sosha slept fitfully. Though she had not cried while she was awake, tears stained her cheeks in her

175

sleep. Her parents had been informed of her return to Gattan, but no message waited for her from them or her brothers. She'd been correct, her family was ashamed of her.

* * * * *

Beti checked Kadis' door one more time. It was locked from the inside. That did not mean, however, that Kadis would not try to come out again. Beti settled on the floor across the hall from her door. One of the servants thoughtfully provided her with supper and a blanket. Many had witnessed the Aradab's humiliation of the queen's niece. All expected a challenge in the morning, and Kadis was a deadly fighter. The queen's niece wore her scars proudly.

Beti had heard the whispers and warnings but had nonchalantly shrugged them off.

She'd gotten a good idea of Kadis' strength when she'd carried her from Teena's apartment. She had no doubt that she could subdue Kadis without so much as a scratch.

* * * * *

From a house near the Gattan royal palace, a coded signal flashed towards its destination on an uninhabited planetoid. From there it was relayed to what was thought to be a deserted space on Varce. Eventually, it reached its destination on Drakan. There the Academy of Science computer that received the message buried it deep into data banks that could only be reached by secret code. Eventually, the message would reach the man for whom it was intended. There were angry people on Gattan who had questions they wanted answered.

Chapter Sixteen

ಬ

Shivers racing up her spine woke Sheala. Someone was watching her. Slowly, she opened her eyes.

Her gaze collided with a broad chest — her husband's broad chest.

Pushing herself back, she tilted her head and looked up into his face. Wincing inwardly from his steady gaze, she dropped hers, blinking back tears, cursing mentally at her reaction to the sexiest man she'd ever met, one who said he'd love her forever.

Sheala stared at the dragon and lion tattoo above his right pectoral.

The dragon and lion stared back.

She blinked again. Marljas' body was sex personified. Muscles bulged on his arms, like his chest, his shoulders were broad, his abdomen was well-developed — "six-pack abs", Brianna had called the muscles there. His stomach was flat, his hips lean, and his cock... She sighed. He had the most wonderful cock. She should slide across the bed onto his chest and kiss him senseless. Only a month ago that's exactly what she would have done. Now, though...

Now, she was nervous just because he was staring at her.

Why? Drakians didn't get nervous when someone stared at them. They liked it. *She* liked it. At least she had, especially when Marljas had stared at her. She'd spent a great deal of time on Drakan making him notice her. Now, she had his undivided attention, and she wasn't sure what to do with it.

She blinked again. Damn Bakom and his assistants! Every time Marljas touched her, one of their faces popped into her mind.

"You're very beautiful, *Cheta*," he murmured as he kissed her gently on the forehead.

Sheala moved restlessly, though not fearfully. His lips couldn't hurt her. He *wouldn't* hurt her. She knew that. If only she could convince her body...

Keeping firm control on his body, Marljas continued his gentle kisses. Knowing what would happen if he touched his wife in any other way, he used his lips to caress her face and neck, keeping the blanket fisted in his hands. He *would* keep his hands to himself—for now.

The contented sigh that escaped her lips and her stiff body relaxing told him his gentle approach was working.

Before he lost control, Marljas forced himself from his wife's side and rolled off the bed. He'd made progress this morning and didn't want to frighten her with an inopportune fumble.

"Where are you going?"

"Now that I'm home, I have responsibilities."

She pushed herself up until she sat leaning back against the tall headboard. "What do you do?" she called after him as he walked into the bathing room.

The question was music to Marljas' ears. Smiling at his reflection in the mirror, he splashed water on his face, cleaned his mouth, tied his hair back with a leather thong, and returned to the bedchamber. "I'm in charge of monitoring our herds—culling, breeding, and so forth." He shimmied out of the loose bed pants he was wearing.

After a quick gasp, Sheala jerked her gaze away from his naked hips.

Marljas turned to a large wardrobe, glancing back at his wife under his arm.

She was staring at his ass.

Chuckling quietly to himself, Marljas grabbed a clean tunic and pants and straightened. When he turned back to Sheala, she was staring at the ceiling.

Sliding into his pants, he adjusted his tail then shrugged his tunic over his head. After stamping into his boots, he settled a thick, leather belt around his waist. Then he leaned over and kissed the top of her head. "Go back to sleep if you want. Mother will give you a few days to adjust before she finds chores for you." After another kiss to the top of her head, Marljas spun on his heel and sauntered out of the room.

Sheala watched breathlessly as her husband left the room, whistling. She allowed her mind to wander back to his kisses and was surprised to feel her nipples tighten. Before she could dwell on her reaction, however, there was a knock at the door.

"Come in."

A young Gattan girl entered and smiled tentatively. "I'm Denta Grodanisdotir. Teena Seenasdotir has sent me to be your personal maid, if I am acceptable to you. If not, there are others she can send."

Sheala smiled back. "I'm sure you'll be fine, Denta, though I don't really need a maid."

A fearful look appeared on the girl's face to be followed almost instantly by one of determination. "Oh no, Alalakan dem al' Sheala, your husband is a son of the house. You must have a maid. Teena Seenasdotir would lose face with the other matriarchs if the wife of her son wasn't treated properly. Would you like me to draw you a bath?"

Sheala shook her head. "No. I had one last night. I'd like to have something to eat though."

"I'll order a tray. Is there anything specific you'd like?"

"I'd rather eat what everyone else eats and where everyone else eats if that's okay."

The young maid's smile broadened.

Sheala nodded to herself. Obviously, she'd said the right thing. Besides, if she was going to be part of Marljas' family, she'd better get to know them. And she couldn't do that hiding in her room.

Besides, Sosha needed her.

Denta's smile became even more relaxed. "Then if you will follow me, I'll show you to the dining room. Breakfast is about to be served. Normally, it's served earlier. However, the matriarch gave orders that it was to be delayed this morning."

Sheala followed the shorter girl out the door.

"You'd best pay close attention to where we're going," Denta said as she led Sheala down a flight of stairs. "The Drefeson home is a warren. Wings have been added haphazardly to the main edifice. The rooms you shared with Marljas are in what was considered the family wing, but the dining room, library, etc. are located in a newer wing of the house."

Sheala nodded then said, "May I ask you some questions? If you don't want to answer me, I will understand, but I am curious."

"Ask what you want, Alalakan dem al' Sheala, and I will answer as best I can."

"Most of the other people I've seen here in the house and out on the grounds look like Marljas, but you're different."

Slighter in build, Denta's skin was the color of rich cream. Both that and her shoulder-length hair were covered with brown ovals circled by black. Denta was also shorter than Sheala, well under six feet. Green eyes accented by black stripes that slid from her eyebrows down both sides of her very slender nose guilelessly met Sheala's. Denta was lithe and willowy and moved with an easy grace Sheala wished she could duplicate.

As she turned right into another corridor, Denta slowed her pace. "That's because I am not of the *Leonine* tribe. I am *Celet*."

"Then why are you here? Denieen told me that most families hired workers from their own tribes."

"My family owes blooddebt. To cancel it, I have agreed to serve as a personal maid for two years."

"What's bbooddebt?"

Denta led her down another flight of stairs. "Blooddebt came into existence about a thousand years ago. The queen of that time was visited by a delegation of *Snopards*, the tribe of the priesthood, and was told that Boodfeuds must stop. Too many Gattan were dying. So blooddebt was created. Instead of constant challenges to the death to satisfy honor, participants in quarrels were obligated to follow certain guidelines."

"Such as…?"

Denta laughed and turned left into a wider hallway. "The rules and consequences of blooddebt would take days to explain and we don't have that much time. However, my family borrowed money they were unable to repay on time. To settle the debt, one option for my family was for one of us to serve two years as a servant. I am the oldest child. Both Father and Mother are needed to raise my sister and brothers. I volunteered."

"So your family owed a debt to Marljas' family," Sheala concluded as they entered the main hall.

"No, our debt was to the queen's sister."

Sheala glanced at Denta in surprise. "Then how can you be my maid?"

"I was assigned to be Kadis Jadisdotir's personal maid and accompanied her here. Once here, I begged Teena Seenasdotir to accept my family's debt and pay the queen's nephew. I was willing to add a year to my service."

Sheala snorted. "I take it working for Kadis wasn't pleasant."

Denta ducked her head. "She starved and slapped me. I have never been treated so badly in my life, and I was willing to do anything to get away from her. Payment for the debt was sent to Kadis this morning. Teena Seenasdotir refused to add one more day to my service though my family will insist upon another blooddebt to repay the kindness I have experienced here." She stopped in front of a door. "Here is the dining room. I'll leave you with the family," Denta finished as she opened the door and led Sheala into the room.

Marljas' family was waiting for her. Sheala had no sooner smiled a thank-you to Denta when Kadis pushed her way into the room.

"There you are, you little slut," Kadis said when she saw Denta. "Who do you think you are to leave my service?"

Kadis' open palm swept towards Denta's face.

It never connected.

Sheala grasped Kadis' wrist. The force of her grip kept Kadis' lethal claws in their protective sheaths.

Kadis glared at the Drakian who held her wrist. Cognizant of where she was and the audience that was watching, she struggled to keep her temper under control. Slapping a servant was one thing, but lashing out at a guest in the house of the man she wished to marry would not endear her to his family. She'd erred last night. After she and Marljas were married, she would be able to take her rightful place as matriarch of this house. The fact that Teena Seenasdotir was still a relatively young woman and would probably live many more years didn't matter. Nor did the fact that when she did eventually die, Denieen would head this household because she was wife of the oldest son. Kadis ignored those facts. She was the queen's niece. Her position in Gattan society was higher. Both Teena and Denieen would be brought to understand that. First, though, she would get rid of this Drakian interloper.

Glaring into Sheala's face, Kadis snapped, "Since you are a stranger to our planet and a guest in the house of my betrothed, I will attempt to forgive your rash actions. Know, however, that you have committed a grave offense against the niece of Queen Mattis of Gattan, one that would normally demand bloodfeud. You are not Gattan, so you do not understand this. Release me, and I will let this incident pass."

From the corner of her eye, Sheala saw Marljas push his chair back to rise. She also saw his father place a hand on his arm.

She nodded to herself. This was definitely her battle to fight. She had to prove herself if she wanted to be wife to a *Leonine* Gattan.

She tightened her grip on the other woman's wrist. "Have you finished, Kadis Jadisdotir? Because if you have, I have a few things to say to you."

Kadis glared at her with hate-filled eyes.

Sheala ignored the hate. "I have never in all my life witnessed such callous treatment of a servant. As for being the niece of the queen, your behavior is deplorable. One in a position of authority does not mistreat those under her."

Kadis' voice dripped with sarcasm. "What could you possibly know of servants, Drakian?"

Sheala grinned. "I carry royal blood, Medirian royal blood, though it is somewhat diluted, from my grandmother Alalakan dem al' Jenneta whose grandmother was a Medirian princess. I am first cousin to Alalakan don al' Bandalardrac, Prince Hardan, nephew to the King of Mediria. I am sister-in-law through my brother Chardadon to Alalakan dem al' Brianna of Earth, adopted daughter to the King and Queen of Mediria and bloodsister to Marljas Drefeson."

The widening of Kadis' eyes told Sheala that Marljas' having taken a non-Gattan bloodsister was not widely known on Gattan.

Sheala smiled at that. Kadis was in for more surprises. "What's more, the Alalakan clan could buy and sell you, your mother, and your brother ten times over."

Kadis' indignant gasp followed that comment. She tried to jerk her wrist free.

She failed.

When Sheala finally did release her wrist, Kadis rubbed it, rose to her full height, and threw back her shoulders. Her voice was haughty. "That matters not. All of those connections are inferior, you are not Gattan."

Sheala smiled. "Marljas doesn't see non-Gattans as inferior. He married me."

Kadis' mouth dropped open. "He what?"

A chair scraped against the floor and Marljas appeared at Sheala's side, where he placed his arm around her. "Alalakan dem al' Sheala is my wife. I married her on Drakan."

Kadis snarled. "This is not acceptable! We are to be betrothed!" Her voice became calculating. "You did not have your mother's permission to marry."

Denieen moved across the room to stand next to Marljas. "As Teena Seenasdotir's acknowledged representative on Drakan and the next matriarch of this family, I approved the marriage of Marljas and Sheala. Alalakan dem al' Brianna became Marljas' bloodsister when the blood from her hand mixed with that from his chest. She is now Gattan by virtue of Marljas' blood running through her veins, and she, too, approved the marriage between Sheala and him."

Marljas' mother joined the group standing before Kadis. Wendjas and Drefes joined the rest of the family to present a united front against Kadis. Only Beti and Sosha remained on the other side of the room.

"As I said last night, Kadis Jadisdotir," Teena said firmly, "the betrothal contract was never finalized. Marljas has already married, and I find his wife to be most satisfactory. Our family declines the betrothal proposed by your mother."

She glared at them. "It's acceptable for a Gattan male to have two wives. Surely the *Leonine* tribe would enjoy the added honor of being related to the Gattan royal family?"

Marljas looked at Kadis in amazement. "Wendjas and I are already Krondal's cousins, my father is his uncle. How can we possibly become more related than that?"

Sosha chose that moment to speak. Rising, she joined the group before Kadis and said, "The proposed betrothal between Marljas and me was never cancelled. If he takes another wife, I have first claim, Kadis Jadisdotir. That is the law."

Marljas smiled broadly at Sosha's defense. The possibility of the second wife was the only thing he, his parents and Denieen had worried about. Though there was no law against a Gattan taking an alien wife, the queen's sister could demand that he take a second, Gattan wife, citing their family's closeness to the throne. He and his family would have fought it, but the outcome would have been uncertain. Many on Gattan, even those who believed in trade rather than war, would have agreed that having a Gattan wife was necessary for a man tied by blood to the royal family.

However, he'd forgotten about the contract for Sosha. Her parents, his parents, and he had signed. It had only been Sosha who'd refused. If she now agreed, Kadis and her mother would have to bow to Sosha's prior claim. Also, with Sheala's connections on Drakan and Mediria, not even the most warlike Gattans would want to anger the governments of Drakan and Mediria simultaneously—especially not the Medirians. The skill of Medirian assassins, especially the Monarch's Assassin, was acknowledged throughout the galaxy. No intelligent person on Gattan doubted that an assassin could reach him or her even here.

Hugging Sheala more tightly against his side, Marljas watched as Kadis fumed. At this moment, there was nothing she could do about his marriage. Still, he didn't trust her. She was almost as devious and crafty as her mother. She would try to get even somehow.

Her gaze leaped from face to face. "Very well. I will return to my mother's house, but before I go," she said, holding up her arm and drawing one claw across its inside until blood flowed, "I call bloodfeud on the Aradab woman you call guest. She handled me in a manner unacceptable to any Gattan."

Before Marljas or anyone else could protest, Beti crossed the room far more rapidly than anyone could have imagined possible and stood before Kadis. Placing her palms together, she bowed slightly. "Your challenge is accepted, Kadis Jadisdotir."

Kadis smiled haughtily. "This is a fight to the death, Aradab."

Beti shrugged unemotionally and said, "I will not kill you but will leave that to someone else. You need not fear for your life nor try to intimidate me with false bravado. I am challenged. I will meet you in four hours' time before the stables."

With those words, Beti turned away from Kadis and went to the table where she sat and proceeded to finish her meal.

Kadis' jaw dropped at Beti's nonchalance. "I will rip your guts out!" she sputtered. She stepped towards Beti.

"Hold, Kadis," Teena warned. "The challenge has been given and accepted. You must now depart."

"But I have not yet eaten! You would favor an alien Aradab over me, a Gattan!"

Marljas' mother crossed her arms over her chest. "Justly so. Ever since you arrived, you have acted as if you were the queen, ordering servants not yours to perform menial tasks because you were too lazy to do things for yourself. The Aradab Beti has not reviled guests or mistreated servants in our home. She is far better company than you, Kadis Jadisdotir. I will have a tray sent to your room."

Kadis stamped her foot. "How dare you speak to me so!"

Marljas squeezed Sheala's arm as his mother unsheathed her claws. He couldn't remember when he'd seen her so angry. "You act like a spoiled child, Kadis. Leave now before I'm forced to do something you will regret."

Kadis turned her angry glare to Sheala. "You'll be sorry for the way you've treated me."

She cocked an eyebrow. "Me? What did I do? Why don't you just get the hell out of here before your hostess claws your eyes out? She looks pretty angry to me."

After stamping her foot one final time, Kadis whirled and stomped from the room.

Teena looked confused. "Get 'the hell' out?"

"You'll get used to it, Mother." Marljas pulled Sheala in his arms and hugged her tightly. Sheala's set-down of Kadis had definitely impressed Teena and Drefes, as had her obvious strength and lack of fear of Kadis' claws. "I told you she was a fit wife for a Gattan."

Teena sighed and took her husband's arm. "Shall we eat? Our meal is becoming cold."

Chapter Seventeen

ဆာ

Leaning against the top rail of the corral next to Marljas, Sheala watched Beti teaching Sosha how to fight with a pair of knives.

"The knife is to be an extension of your arm, Sosha. Do not flail about with it," the Aradab said critically as Sosha moved through a set of complicated patterns.

Turning too quickly, Sosha lost her balance. Disgusted, she threw down the daggers. "It will never work, Beti. I am too used to having claws."

Face completely impassive, Beti stared at the dejected Gattan. "Do you dance?"

Sheala brightened at that question. "You should see her, Beti. She flows like water around rocks. Marljas told me Sosha could have joined a professional company if she so wished."

Turning to an idle farmhand who'd been watching the practice session, Beti said, "You, bring music." She gave the man no time to refuse. She simply turned away and went back to her instruction.

In a few minutes, the man returned with the Gattan equivalent of a portable disc player. Soon strains of Gattan martial music boomed across the stable yard.

"Now," Beti said as she handed Sosha her knives, "dance."

At first, Sosha moved stiffly, obviously self-conscious. Soon, however, she lost herself in the music. Her dancing became smoother, more controlled. The knives in her hands flashed in the sunlight.

Beti watched critically and, as soon as it seemed that

Sosha was totally engrossed, she attacked.

Without pause, Sosha flowed into one defensive stance after another, adequately parrying Beti's calculated attacks. Then, almost without a thought, she flowed into an attack.

Beti's grunt was all that revealed she had been taken by surprise.

An abrupt cessation of the music caused both women to stop suddenly.

"Enough," Marljas said. "You're bleeding, Beti, and still have another fight."

Both Beti and Sosha looked down at the thin ribbon of red on Beti's biceps. The joyful expression and tone of Beti's voice took them all by surprise.

"Very good, Sosha! You have done well! From now on, listen to the music of your soul."

Sosha stared at Beti. "I blooded you."

Slipping between the rails, Sheala sprinted across the corral and hugged her friend. "No one, I mean no one, except Kahn has been able to land any blow on Beti for the longest time, Sosha."

After blinking a few times, Sosha began to smile.

The girls' celebrations were soon interrupted.

"Have you finished with your playing?" Kadis asked in snide tone. "There's much I must do before I leave in the morning. I would have this duel concluded."

Beti wiped the blood from her biceps and crossed her arms over her chest. "I am ready."

"Wait," Marljas' mother commanded as she and her husband entered the corral. "The proper rituals will be observed."

Her face twisted with hate, Kadis sneered. "She is *not* Gattan."

Dressed in a white robe, Denieen joined them in the corral. Her husband accompanied her, carrying an elaborately carved chest.

Kadis stared at Denieen. "Why are you dressed in such a manner?"

Sheala glanced at Marljas. Denieen's robe made Kadis nervous. Why?

"Just watch," he whispered to her.

Denieen stopped directly in front of Kadis, smiled serenely, and bowed first to Beti and then to Kadis. "You are well aware of the fact that I was schooled among the *Snopards* for five years, Kadis. As a level four priestess, I can witness and approve the outcome of any bloodfeud challenge."

Sheala turned to Sosha who now stood on her other side. "Denieen is a priestess?"

Sosha looked just as surprised. "She must be. No one would dare make such a claim if it weren't true."

Sheala tucked that information into her memory. She'd heard the *Snopards* mentioned more than once, and it was about time she learned more about them — and the other tribes of Gattan.

Denieen fixed her gaze on Beti's arm. "You're bleeding from a prior fight. You may take time to have the wound bound."

"It was made by a Gattan knife," Beti answered with a grin. "The bleeding has already stopped thanks to the potion you dip them in."

Denieen nodded. "So be it then. Kadis Jadisdotir claims bloodfeud on you, Beti, Aradab of Mediria, for bodily insult against her person. Do you concur?"

Beti nodded once. "Yes."

Denieen motioned Wendjas forward.

He placed the chest on the ground and opened the lid.

Denieen gestured towards its contents. "As the challenged, Beti of Mediria, you have the right to choose weapons."

Beti never so much as glanced towards it. "I have need of none."

Sheala looked around. Every member of Marljas' family was frowning, except for her husband. But then, he'd fought Ban.

"You aren't Gattan, Beti. You put yourself at great disadvantage," Deni added.

"Wouldn't it be better if she'd at least use a knife?" Sosha asked Sheala in a low voice. "Kadis is a very good fighter."

Sheala shook her head. "In the last four years, only Kahn has beaten Beti in a fight, fair or foul. He trained her himself, and I've been working with her off and on for the last three years. You're the first I've ever seen touch her with a weapon."

Sosha shook her head. "She was careless. She never expected me to flow with the music like I did."

Smiling, Sheala nodded. "You're right, but no Aradab ever makes the same mistake twice."

Sosha turned her gaze back to the combatants. "I hope you're right, Sheala."

"Stop trying to influence the duel, Denieen," Kadis demanded in a superior tone, "or I will call foul here and now."

After once last glance at Beti, Denieen nodded. "Very well. Kadis Jadisdotir has called bloodfeud on Beti, an Aradab of Mediria. As an acknowledged fourth-level priestess, I demand here and now that this fight be to first blood only."

Kadis' smile was more of a sneer. "I refuse. Nor can you make such a demand when my opponent has already agreed to a fight to the death."

Denieen stared at Kadis. "Think carefully, Kadis. The political ramifications from this duel could be profound. The queen will not be pleased."

Kadis' smile became superior. "But my mother will. Nothing else matters. You would do well to remember that,

Denieen."

"What a bitch," Sheala murmured.

Marljas shook his head. "A statement like hers could be construed as treason. She and her mother must be watched."

Sheala nudged him with her elbow. "Shhhh. They're about to start. Just wait until you see Beti in action."

As soon as Denieen stepped out of the way, Kadis launched an immediate attack.

Sidestepping, Beti retreated.

"She was hiding in the barn while Beti worked with you and Sosha, watching and planning her attack," Marljas said.

Sheala shook her head. "She won't defeat Beti."

A particularly vicious slash caused Beti to fall to the ground and roll away from her opponent.

"I wish I had your confidence," Sosha murmured.

For five or so minutes, a seemingly one-sided fight progressed.

Sheala leaned her arms on the top rail of the fence and concentrated on Beti. "Pay attention, Sosha, she's teaching us a lesson about retreat."

Eyes wide, Sosha tore her gaze from the combatants and stared at Sheala. "Teaching us a lesson?"

Sheala nodded. "Aradabs turn every fight into a lesson."

"But Kadis is trying to kill her."

Sheala smiled. "She won't."

"She must attack," Marljas muttered from her other side as Kadis barely missed slicing open Beti's stomach.

"Beti is just playing with her, my love," Sheala answered absentmindedly. "There, that move. That's the second time she's done that. She'll end the fight any minute."

Marljas shook his head.

Sosha snorted.

Sheala sighed. "Look. Beti had used Kadis' initial charge to gauge and weigh her attack and teach Sosha and me different ways to retreat from a particularly lethal move. Look at Kadis. As close as she's been to slashing Beti, she's hasn't touched her. She's frustrated and will soon make a mistake."

Sheala had barely finished speaking when Beti attacked. In a series of feints and lightning moves, she had Kadis flat on her stomach in less than a minute. Both arms were bent at the elbows with Kadis' wrists drawn up towards her shoulders. Beti's knee was in the small of her back. "I told you I would not kill you, but if you do not yield, I will dislocate both of your shoulders."

Silence enveloped the two women. Every member of the household who could had made his or her way to this fight. All of them had heard of the hand-to-hand fighting prowess of the Aradabs of Mediria. Many had not believed the stories, thinking that they had surely been exaggerated. The stories had not been exaggerated.

Kadis groaned but refused to yield.

Beti sighed. "Stupid is the warrior who refuses to acknowledge she's been beaten."

Kadis screamed as her right shoulder popped out of its socket.

"Do not mistake my promise not to kill you for weakness, Kadis Jadisdotir," Beti said grimly. "Like you, I am a guest in this house. A guest does not spill blood on her host's floor."

"I suggest you listen to her, Kadis. The queen will not be impressed by your stupidity," boomed a voice from behind Sheala.

"I yield!" Kadis screamed as Beti began to apply pressure to her left arm.

"Colonel Radris Nardinson of the royal guard," Marljas whispered to Sheala as his mother and father greeted their newest guest.

Sheala kept her concentration on the corral.

Denieen went to where Kadis lay. Running her fingers gently over Kadis' shoulder, she said, "Let me help you to your feet. Once you're standing, I'll put your shoulder back into its socket."

Kadis pushed herself to her knees. "Get away from me, you traitor. You will all pay for this outrage."

The colonel dismounted his riding beast and walked into the corral to stand before Kadis. "Still acting like the spoiled brat you are. I'd have thought you'd have grown up by now." Reaching down, he gripped her waist and lifted her to her feet. Before she could move away, he grasped her upper arm and jerked her shoulder into place.

Her scream seemed to reverberate off the distant mountains.

Radris grinned at her. "Spite won't heal that shoulder, and the longer you would have waited to have it set, the more painful it would have been."

"The queen shall hear of this, you fool," Kadis snarled as she stomped away.

"I know. I'll be giving her a full report. By the way, I witnessed the entire duel."

Screeching with frustration, Kadis cradled her arm against her chest and stomped towards the house.

Teena signaled two stout women servants to follow her. "Make sure her belongings are packed. She will be returning to her mother's house in the morning."

The older of the two women smiled and nodded her head. Both of them followed Kadis into the house.

"Those two won't be intimidated by the niece of a queen, I don't think," Radris said from where he stood with his hands on his hips.

Teena smiled a wide smile. "Sarti was nursemaid to both Wendjas and Marljas. She's wanted to put Kadis over her knee since the day she arrived."

Smiling broadly, Radris turned to where Marljas stood with Sheala. "So, you are the Drakian wife. You're pretty enough, I'll give you that."

At her side, Marljas stiffened and his gaze became decidedly cold.

Radris laughed. "Ease yourself, cub. I can still defeat you in hand-to-hand combat."

Marljas wasn't intimidated. "I've learned a few things since the last time we sparred, Colonel."

Denieen stepped between them. "Wife? Who told you that Marljas had married?"

Chuckling, Radris answered, "The King and Queen, who else?"

Sheala stared at the huge black man before her. Both his skin and his close-cropped hair were black, as were his eyes. At least three inches taller than Marljas, who was taller than any other Gattan Sheala had ever seen, Radris was also much more muscular. If anything, he reminded Sheala of a rather tall Aradab. He certainly had as many muscles as any Aradab man she'd ever met. He wasn't *Leonine* either. Just how many tribes of Gattan were there? And why did he appear on a riding beast? Didn't Gattans travel in sky ships or land vehicles like everyone else?

Sheala frowned. No. Kadis was taking a shuttle home. "Do you always choose to travel on the back of a beast? Surely you're a modern enough man to appreciate flying?"

Radris laughed. "Of course I fly. However, my mare prefers to use her own four feet."

Sheala blinks. "Your mare?"

He stepped back, glared at Marljas then looked back to Sheala. "Has no one told you of *pholola* mares?"

Marljas put a protective arm around Sheala. "There's much she hasn't had time to learn yet."

The colonel burst into loud laughter. "You have been too

busy to talk, yes?"

Sheala was not one to be intimidated or bested in a game of wits.

"And you, Sir, would stand here and crow like a barnyard fowl while a *pholola* mare stands in the afternoon sun still saddled, unbrushed, and unwatered, virtually ignored by her rider?" she countered.

Amazement sweeping across his countenance, Radris was struck dumb. Then he laughed louder. In two strides he was before Sheala. Before she could even think what he'd done, he engulfed her in a huge hug and tossed her into her husband's arms. Still laughing, he walked to his mare and proceeded to lead her into the barn.

Sheala watched with a decidedly smug expression on her face—until the mare turned her head and winked at her.

Her mouth dropped open.

Marljas just grinned. He had Sheala right where he wanted her, in his arms. And he knew exactly what he wanted to do with her.

Chapter Eighteen

ஐ

Spinning on his heel, Marljas headed in the opposite direction towards another barn.

To steady herself, Sheala wrapped her arms around his neck, recognizing the grunt that escaped his throat as pure satisfaction. The memory of her birthday celebration flashed into her mind. Marljas had caught her in his arms that night— and she'd been disappointed when he let her go. A shiver danced up her spine.

"Where are we going? Put me down. I can walk."

He grinned at her. "You haven't seen the foaling barn, and I don't mind carrying you."

"But…"

Before she could finish, he reached the barn and kicked the door open.

The two men working there looked up, surprise quite evident on their faces.

"Out," Marljas growled.

After quick smiles, both men disappeared.

Striding into a large stall, he kicked the door shut and dropped his arm from beneath her legs.

He let her body slide down against his—slowly—until her feet finally settled on the wooden floor. Wrapping his arm around her waist, he pulled her tight against his body.

Again, the memory of that night of her birthday celebration surged. She'd slid down his hard body that night too. And much later in the evening, she'd savored every inch of it.

This time the shiver danced down her spine—all the way to the tip of her tail. It twitched, and she wrapped it around her own ankle to control it.

Swallowing, Sheala placed her hands flat against his chest to push herself away from the erect cock pushing against her belly.

His voice was low, urgent, compelling. "Sheala, I need you."

Blinking, she looked up into his face. "Marljas… I…"

When he dropped his arm, she stepped back. He caught her face with his hands, caressing first the corners of her mouth and then her cheeks with his thumbs. "I love you, Alalakan dem al' Sheala, my wife and the keeper of my heart. I honor you above all women. For you, I would leave my mother's hearth. I would leave Gattan. Just ask it of me."

Her heart swelled in her chest as a tear rolled down her cheek. "Marljas, I…"

A finger over her lips stopped her from finishing what she had to say.

"Do you love me?"

Sheala looked up into his intense, golden gaze. Butterflies fluttered in her stomach. Gods but he was handsome.

His face blurred.

Did she love him? How could she help but love him? "Yes, I love you."

When he pulled her back into his arms and hugged her close, Sheala buried her face against his chest. She did love him, more than she'd ever thought it was possible to love anyone else. How could she not love him, a man who had killed for her, one who would sleep with her, hold her close, comfort her, yet not demand sexual satisfaction because of her fears? She would always love him.

She shivered as the hard ridge of his cock rubbed against her belly. Memories of how good his cock tasted surfaced in her mind.

Sheala wiped her face against his shirt. Just because her sexual desire had been ruined by Bakom didn't mean she couldn't satisfy him. It wouldn't take long. And he would be so happy.

Dropping her arms from around his waist, she pushed herself free of his arms.

The hurt look that appeared in his eyes had her blinking back tears again, but she held her voice steady. "There was a day on Drakan that I remember very well. Do you?" That day, she'd almost given in to temptation, stripped off her clothing, and mounted him then and there. But she'd conquered that urge and pleasured him instead. She could do that again.

Dropping to her knees in the thick bed of straw, she freed his cock from his pants, kissed its tip, and sucked it into her mouth.

Sighing, her husband leaned back against the wall and spread his legs.

Grasping his cock, she wrapped her fingers around its thick base and slowly slid them up its length. Then, just as slowly, she slid them back down.

Above her, Marljas moaned and thrust his hips forward.

The contentment in that moan excited the butterflies in her stomach even more as Sheala leaned forward and dragged her tongue down the length of his cock then back up again, tickling the base of the head with her tongue.

His moan became a groan.

Reaching up, she jerked his pants down over his hips. They fell to his knees, where the tops of his boots caught them.

Above her, he jerked his tunic over his head.

Sheala sighed with satisfaction. He had such a beautiful body. Flat stomach, ridged abdomen, broad chest. All hers. Turning her head, she nibbled the inside of his hard thigh. Then, lifting his cock out of her way, she sucked his balls into her mouth.

As his tail jerked and tried to untangle itself from his pants, Marljas dug his claws into the hard wood of the wall behind him.

She wrapped her own tail around her thigh. Its tip rested close to her crotch.

"Hmmmm. You taste like sweat."

Splinters of wood fell to the floor as he dug his claws deeper. "I will soon taste like more."

She licked his cock again, kissed its tip.

A drop of silvery liquid seeped onto her lips.

"You taste like love." She sucked him into her mouth.

His breathing became harsher. Claws sheathed, he dropped his hands onto her shoulders and pushed her away from his cock.

Sheala released it slowly and looked up.

"Take off your shirt. I want to come on your breasts. Like that day back on Drakan."

Hesitating only a moment, Sheala pulled her shirt over her head. She wouldn't mind him touching her breasts.

Cupping them, she pinched her nipples and looked up. "These breasts?"

His answer was mostly choked out. "Yes. Rub my cock against them—please."

When she leaned her breast against his cock and rubbed herself back and forth against it, he pounded the wall with his fists then dug his claws in once more. "Yes, like that. Gods, Sheala, you make me ache."

Chuckling, she pushed his cock down and squeezed it between her breasts. Leaning forward, she buried her nose in the wiry hairs at the base of his cock and inhaled. After a quick kiss, she leaned back, freeing his cock—momentarily. Almost immediately, she wrapped the fingers of both hands around it and began to pump. "Come for me, love."

The tip of her tail began to caress the inside of her thigh.

His hips jerked then he matched the rhythm of her hands. "Yesssssssss. Pump me. Squeeze me—harder."

After licking the head of his cock once more, Sheala complied. "Are you ready to come?"

"Lean back—now!"

Spreading her knees, Sheala arched her back.

In her hands, Marljas' cock jerked.

Warm cum spurted onto her breasts—and spurted and spurted.

Finally, she loosened her grip and Marljas slumped back against the wall.

Straightening, Sheala looked down at her breasts then at her hands. His silvery-white cum covered her.

"You're wet."

Sheala looked at him and smiled. "You got me that way."

He shook his head. "No, between your legs. Your cunt is wet—for me."

She sucked in a breath but didn't deny what he said. It was true. She'd tried to ignore it, but she was wet—and throbbing. "Marljas, I…"

Smiling, he shook his head. "I won't touch you, *Cheta*, not if you don't want me to, but you can't remain unsatisfied. You need to come too. Touch yourself."

"But…"

"You won't hurt yourself, and I would die before I allowed anyone to hurt you. Help yourself heal."

Her crotch still throbbing, she looked at her hands.

His voice was low, hypnotic. "Just touch your breasts then. Proof of my love is all over them."

Slowly, she lifted her hands and cupped her slippery breasts. She slid her hands around, over and under them. Closing her eyes, she pinched her nipples.

Her own moan surprised her, as did the stab of desire between her thighs when she pressed her tail against her cunt.

His voice was no longer above her. "Yes, Sheala, please yourself. Begin the healing process."

"Hmmmmmmmmmmmm." Arching, she leaned back.

A strong arm slid beneath her back and she stiffened and opened her eyes. Marljas was behind her, supporting her body with his. She turned her head against his chest and looked up at him.

He stared down at her with a love-filled gaze. "I'm only supporting you so you don't fall. I won't touch you, *Cheta*. Close your eyes again. Relax. Love yourself."

Minutes passed, but when he made no other move to touch her, Sheala relaxed, sliding her hands though Marljas' cum, spreading it over her torso.

She stopped when the waistband of her pants prevented her from moving her hands lower.

A ripping sound reached her ears, and her pants fell down over her hips.

Again she stiffened and opened her eyes. "Marljas…"

The arm beneath her never moved. "I'm only helping you to help yourself. You're so wet, so needy. I can smell your desire. Touch yourself, *Cheta*."

Sheala stared up into his face. He was hiding nothing, not his concern, not his love, not his desire. But—she trusted him—more than she trusted even her own family. Sighing, she closed her eyes and let her hands drift down over her stomach and into the soft hair of her mons. Then lower to her wet, swollen lips. When her finger touched her aching clit, she jerked and shuddered. A long moan escaped from her throat.

As she rubbed her clit, her tail slid between the lips of her cunt and her hips jerked involuntarily.

With her other hand, she pinched a nipple.

More heat stabbed her groin. Prickly straw tickled her ass.

The tip of Marljas' cock nudged her back. Centering all her concentration on the wonderful, powerful ache between her legs, she ignored it. She rubbed harder, her fingers and tail sliding between her slippery lips. The tip of her tail slid into her cunt.

"That's it, my beautiful *Cheta*, love yourself."

Sheala swallowed, gulped down a mouthful of air, and groaned. Pressure built rapidly, and she didn't try to hold on to it. Hips jerking, she arched her back even more and stiffened as her orgasm rolled through her body. Her cunt sucked at her tail as heat engulfed her, spreading outward and upward from her groin.

Dimly, she noted that warm cum spurted beneath her and onto her shoulder blades.

When the bright motes of light disappeared from behind her closed eyelids, she opened her eyes and stared into Marljas' face.

Sheala lowered her eyes and straightened, lifting her weight from his arm. She looked at her husband from under her eyelashes. He was still kneeling on the floor of the stall, naked from the knees up, his cock slowly relaxing. A piece of straw dangled from its tip.

Sheala smiled then started to giggle.

He cocked an eyebrow.

"What's so funny?"

She jerked her chin towards his hips. "Your cock has a beard."

He grinned back. "And you, my love, now have gold growing between your lovely thighs."

"What!" Leaping to her feet, Sheala pushed her pants midway down her thighs and slid her hand between her thighs. Straw was stuck to her. Her shoulder blades itched.

"There was a lot of straw on the floor." Rising, he pulled up and fastened his pants.

Muttering, Sheala pulled as much straw loose as she could.

"Want some help?"

His voice was entirely too jovial.

Her tone was exasperated. "No!"

Finally she tried to pull up her pants, but stared down at them in dismay. With the cut Marljas had made in them, no way would they stay up. "How am I supposed to get back to the house? My blouse won't cover this."

Still grinning, her husband lifted his tunic from the floor and dropped it over her head. "Here. This will cover you, and I'll carry you." He slid the stall door open and swept her into his arms before she had a chance to protest.

"Marljas! Put me down. I can walk."

He chuckled. "And have your pants fall down around your ankles. You'd trip and fall. Then everyone would see far too much of your lovely body, and I'd have to challenge every man out there to defend your honor."

"I can defend myself!"

Amusement still swam in his voice as he kicked the barn door open. "Not on Gattan, *Cheta*. Just as a woman is expected to defend the honor of her husband against other woman, a man isn't a man if he doesn't defend the honor of his wife against other men. His mother, especially, would never forgive him. Of course, if any of the women comment on your lovely ass, there's not a thing I can do. You, however, are free to defend your honor against them all you want."

She stopped struggling. "Fine! Carry me if you want— half naked the way you are. Everybody will know what we were doing. I thought Gattans were more circumspect."

He grinned down at her. "But this Gattan is married to a Drakian. And everybody knows Drakians don't care who knows they've been making love. You're corrupting me. And—I like it."

Chapter Nineteen

♱

Two hours later, after a long soak in warm, scented bathwater, Sheala sat before the huge fireplace staring at the dancing fire, one that was always lit no matter what season of the year because tradition said it was bad luck for it to go out. As she stared into it, she mulled over the time she'd spent in the barn with her husband, time she'd spent making love. That's what they'd done even though there hadn't been any true sexual intercourse between them, and Marljas hadn't touched her except with his arm.

Drawing her knees up, Sheala rested her chin on them and continued to watch the flames flicker and leap. Could she do it? Could she let Marljas touch her intimately, slide his cock into her? The memory of their night on his ship slipped to the forefront of her mind. Smiling, she sighed. It had been a wonderful night.

Closing her eyes, she slid deeper into the memory. Marljas kissed her, nibbled his way down over her stomach, and looked up into her face. But as she lifted her hips in invitation, Marljas' face was replaced by Bakom's.

Gasping, Sheala yanked her eyes open. Shivering, she stared blindly at the fire, shoving her attacker from her mind, struggling to replace him with happy memories. Her brain returned to that afternoon as Marljas had carried her from the barns to the house. Anyone who'd seen them had called a greeting and then chuckled. Her husband had grinned and told them he had the most passionate wife on Gattan.

Not to be outdone, she'd smiled and told them Marljas was a fantastic lover.

Instead of embarrassing him like she thought it would,

he'd roared with laughter and thanked her for the compliment. When they'd finally reached the house and encountered his mother talking with some of the household's women, he'd repeated what she'd said — much to her mortification.

All the women — except Teena — had gaped at them. Marljas' mother had smiled, nodded, and gone on talking.

According to Deni, Gattans, especially Gattan men, didn't talk of such things in mixed company. Was Marljas different from other Gattan men? Or was she changing him?

"Did you have a nice bath?"

Sheala wrenched her thoughts away from her husband.

Blinking, she turned her head from the fire and stared at her mother-in-law. "What?"

The older woman smiled at her. "We'll eat our last meal of the day within the hour. Now, how much do you know about Gattan history?"

Sheala gathered her scattered wits and focused on her mother-in-law. "Umm, history?

Teena laughed. "The history of Gattan? You're a member of the family now. You should know our history."

Sheala blinked again. "Oh! History, yes. Gattans are as technologically advanced as Drakians and Medirians. Your small interplanetary battle cruisers are superior to any Drakian or Medirian ships, but our larger ships are better than yours." Sheala smiled. "And though you've kept it hidden, even from other planet's ambassadors since you first made contact with us, Gattan is a matriarchal society. Your queen, not your king, is in charge."

Teena smiled. "All true, but that isn't our history." She handed one of the mugs she carried to Sheala. "Tea. Sit back and relax, and I'll give you a very quick summary. Yes, we're as technologically advanced, but we also still cling to as many of our traditions as possible. Naturally, our homes have every modern convenience, but we disguise them with traditional packaging."

Sheala nodded. "I noticed that in the bathroom. At first I thought I'd have to ask to have hot water sent up."

Teena chuckled then sipped her tea. "Centuries ago, we Gattan were nomadic herdsmen. Our lives revolved around our huge horse and cattle herds."

"Horse?"

"That's what we call our riding beasts. Anyway, technology has made the Gattan nomadic way of life obsolete. However, there are some Gattan who cling to the old ways, and every tribe still had its traditional herd of horses. The *Leonine* tribe, especially, still takes pride in its horse herds. No matter how technologically advanced we become, we will always retain those. But I think it might be better if you asked questions, and I answered them."

Sheala nodded. There were things she wanted to know. "How many different tribes of Gattan are there?"

"Seven. Our tribe, *Leonine*, is the largest, followed closely by the *Tigre* tribe. Radris is of the *Pantra* tribe. Though a small tribe, they have some of the finest warriors and have traditionally provided much of the king's guard. The *Snopards* are our tribe of priests, seers, and sages. No major decisions are made without their advice and, in most cases, approval. They also provide warrior priestesses who are the queen's guard. The final are the *Jagar*, the *Lynex*, and the *Celet*."

Sheala sipped more tea. "And you all look different?"

Teena nodded. "Superficially. The *Lynex*, of which Sosha is a member, look a great deal like the *Leonine*, except they're smaller and are the only tribe without tails."

"I noticed Sosha didn't have one. At first I thought Bakom cut it off until she told me all members of her tribe are born like that."

Teena nodded again. "*Tigres* have striped skins, and *Celet* and *Jagar* have spotted skins though the *Celet* are smaller in stature, about the same as the *Lynex*. The *Pantra* usually have black skins and the *Snopard* are mostly white with ivory or cream-colored spots."

"Do you intermarry?"

"Generations ago, raiding and warring among the tribes was the norm until the *Snopards* demanded a halt. If we didn't stop fighting, they said, we'd exterminate ourselves within ten generations. We had no reason to doubt their pronouncement. Everything they'd ever told us before had come true."

Sheala sipped her tea. *Snopards*. All conversations about Gattan came back to them. She'd have to learn more about them. They seemed to have more power than the queen.

"They also told us we had to choose a queen. All tribes but the *Snopards* were to choose a champion from among their female warriors, not just one who was brave and skilled in battle, but one who also excelled in riddle games and debate, among other things. The women would be tested seven different ways. She who had the highest score would become queen."

Sheala smiled. "And the *Leonine* won."

Teena nodded. "Yes, and was immediately challenged for the position by the *Tigre*."

"But she was defeated."

"Yes, and claimed the contests were unfair. The *Snopards* allowed the challenge since it was the only way to bring harmony. The *Tigre* lost. The royal line has descended from our tribe ever since."

"Don't the tribes intermarry?" she asked again.

Teena sipped more tea. "As the years passed, there was more and more intermarriage. Our current queen is *Tigre*. However, like I said, the royal line passes through the *Leonine* tribe. She had to marry into our tribe in order to become queen."

Sheala snorted. "I'll bet there were some angry *Leonines* when that happened."

Teena laughed. "You have no idea. But she's a good

woman and a good queen."

Sheala's mind leaped to another question. "What about that riding beast—the horse—of the colonel's? She winked at me. At first I thought I was seeing things, but then she winked at me again." She stared at her mother-in-law. "That mare wasn't just blinking, was she?"

Chuckling, Teena set her empty cup down. "No. She is a *pholola* mare, very rare, very special. *Phololas* are as intelligent as humans. Most are mares. If *pholola* manifests in a stallion, he is sterile."

Sheala also set her cup down. "You can't breed them?"

Teena shook her head. "No. *Pholola* mares do not necessarily birth *pholola* foals. Once we had the technology to understand DNA, our scientists tried to study *pholola*."

"Tried?"

"The scientists were unable to learn anything. The five mares they studied submitted willingly to all of their tests, watched with amusement in their eyes, then walked away after twenty days. No one on Gattan understands how or why *pholola* are born. They just are. And now, with the advent of technology and the lessening of horses' importance to our lifestyles, fewer and fewer *pholola* foals are born into the herds of the tribes—except for the herds of the *Snopards*. They have at least several born every generation."

"*Pholola* are important then?"

"When one is born, it's treated with more reverence than the queen herself. Ancient myths and legends speak of the consequences of ignoring the importance of *pholola* or hurting them in any way. In our more warlike past, when tribe fought with tribe, *pholola* foals were exempt from the many raiding parties that swept through the herds. To steal one was a sure death sentence—from the *pholola* mares themselves. Every foal is born in a specific place and time with a specific purpose."

"How do you know if a horse is *pholola*?"

"*Pholola*s are always completely white with velvety brown

eyes. No other white horses exist on Gattan. *Pholas* choose their riders, not necessarily from within the tribe where they are born."

"So the Colonel was chosen by that mare."

Teena nodded.

"Who exactly is he?"

"Colonel Radris Nardinson is head of the King's personal bodyguard and the acknowledged hand-to-hand combat champion on Gattan. Surprisingly, he was not a member of the *Leonine* tribe since the King's champion usually was. However, Radris and Krondal have been best friends since they were boys. Besides, no one on the planet could defeat him in any type of personal combat. He is the best one to protect the king."

A knock sounded at the door, and an older woman servant walked in. "The evening meal is ready to be served. The family only awaits you and your daughter-by-marriage."

"We'll be right there. Come along, Sheala. The men become grumpy if their evening meal is late."

Smiling, Sheala followed Teena from the room. Men were the same everywhere.

* * * * *

When Sheala hid her third yawn with her hand, Deni kicked Marljas under the table. "Someone should have warned her that the Gattan evening meal lasted four hours," she murmured.

"I had my mind on other things."

Deni laughed softly. "So I heard."

"Go to bed, Sheala," Teena commanded gently. "You still aren't used to the time change."

"Or our long meals," Deni interjected with a grin. "You'll get used to it. Go on. Sosha has already gone to bed."

Sheala didn't try to hide her next yawn. "I am tired.

Please excuse me." A bit tipsy from the potent Gattan wine she'd drunk at dinner, Sheala smiled at her husband and said, "Stay and talk with your family, Marljas. I can find my way to our rooms without you." With those words, she kissed his forehead and left the room.

Radris chuckled. "You should show her the way. I can remember getting lost in this warren you call a house."

A contemplative look on his face, Marljas nodded and rose. "You could be right, Colonel. If you will excuse me," he said. Nodding first to his mother and father and then to the others, he disappeared after his wife.

"I too shall bid you good night. My deepest thanks for the invitation to your table," Beti said with a short, formal bow.

Radris broadened his smile. "Good night, lovely Aradab flower of Mediria. May your sleep be blessed with dreams of strong and virile warriors."

Beti eyed him speculatively and then did a rare thing for an Aradab, she chuckled. "All those strong and virile warriors, no doubt, being black of skin and hair with pointy ears, claws, and tails. Tread carefully, Gattan. I may be too much woman for you." With those words, Beti left the room.

Radris roared with laughter.

"I'll be damned," Wendjas said as he pulled Deni to her feet. "I think you were just propositioned, Colonel."

His laughter dying to a slow chuckle, Radris said, "I believe you are right, Wendjas. I will have to do something about this."

"Such as?" Deni teased, raising one eyebrow.

"Why, defeat her in hand-to-hand combat, of course," was his answer.

His laughter followed them out of the room.

After he left the library, Marljas didn't follow Sheala to their room. She had relaxed more and more during their long

211

evening meal, and he wanted to give her time to get to their room and get comfortable. So, he took a more circular route, stopping once to check with the guards who had been placed in a strategic position to watch Kadis' door. He didn't trust her not to try and murder Sheala in their bed.

After a few brief words with the guards, he turned left down another corridor, stopped and knocked softly on another door.

"Come in," said a soft voice.

Opening the door, Marljas found Sosha propped up in her bed reading.

"How did you know I would still be awake?"

"I remembered that once you told me you like to read at night," he answered from just inside the door. "I stopped to see if you need anything."

Soshas smiled. "Four maids, Denieen, and your mother have already asked the same question. Why are you really here, Marljas?"

He shifted his weight from one foot to the other, swallowed, then said, "I want to thank you for what you said to Kadis today. If it is what you truly wish, I will talk to Sheala, and we will work something out. Sosha, I will marry you if that is what you want."

For the first time in what seemed like years to her, Sosha laughed—laughed until tears ran down her cheeks.

She laughed so hard, Marljas became disgruntled. "I'm not joking."

Hiccupping as she regained control, Sosha smiled through her tears. "I know. Thank you, Marljas Drefeson. First Bandalardrac and now you, these proposals will go to my head. But as with Ban, I am not the woman for you. Sheala is as much wife as you will ever want or need."

Marljas smiled and bowed gracefully. "You will always have a home with me and mine, Sosha Kanicsdotir, bloodsister to my wife."

With those words, Marljas left the room.

Staring at the closed door, Sosha sighed softly. It had felt good to laugh.

Chapter Twenty

ဢ

Sheala awoke slowly. Warm breath caressed her neck, and the firm arms around her waist held her close to a hard body. Sighing, Sheala snuggled closer.

Soon, soft kisses meandered their way down her neck and onto the shoulder her nightgown no longer covered. Humming softly, she turned her head towards her pillow so that there was greater access to her neck. Simultaneously, Marljas slid his hand along her side to her breast, and Sheala moved back against her husband. The combination of him cupping her breast and rubbing his hard cock against her ass brought her fully awake.

Gasping, she tried to pull away. Unfortunately, both she and Marljas were tangled in a sheet and light blanket, and he still had one arm wrapped around her.

Bakom's face appeared before her. She couldn't get away! She was a prisoner! She reacted violently.

"No!" she screamed, trying to turn in his arms and shove the flat of her hand against his windpipe. "Don't touch me!"

Luckily, Marljas held Sheala too closely for her to do any real physical damage, but she did deliver a glancing blow beneath his eye, and he immediately released her. Propping himself up on his elbow, he watched as she rolled away. The panic and terror on her face were genuine. His heart clenched as he gritted his teeth and growled with frustration. "I will *not* hurt you!"

Sheala burst into tears. "I am so…so…sorry, Marljas. I can't help it. I thought you were…"

Throwing the blanket aside, Marljas rose from the bed, strode across the room, and gripped his wife's upper arms. In

214

the back of his mind, he noted the fact that she did not cower away from him. It seemed as if his cock was the only part of his body she feared. Unfortunately, yesterday's oral stimulation in the barn notwithstanding, his sexual frustration was beginning to override his common sense.

"I *am* not Bakom, and I *will* not harm you. Didn't I prove that yesterday? Sheala, you must get over this fear of me. You enjoyed my body before."

Standing limply in his arms, Sheala dropped her gaze from his. "I'm sorry," she whispered. "I'll free you to take another wife. Don't waste your time with me."

Anger flared in his eyes. "No! I don't want another wife! I want you." Releasing her, Marljas turned and disappeared into the bathroom.

Sobbing quietly, Sheala stumbled back to the bed and collapsed.

When he left the bathroom, Marljas paused momentarily when he saw the dejected picture his wife made. However, he did not go to her. Instead he left the room without saying a word.

Sheala was sure she heard her heart break.

Sosha watched as Marljas closed the door firmly behind him. Shoulders slumped, he leaned his head against the closed door.

After a minute or so, he straightened and stared at her.

Sosha knew he'd been aware of her presence. The fact that he let her see just how dejected he was spoke volumes for his mental state.

"Please, Sosha, help me. You're her bloodsister. Talk to her. Convince her I won't hurt her."

Sosha gave Marljas a wry smile. Since her ordeal, she had made great strides towards healing, both mentally and physically. Sheala had spent far less time in Bakom's clutches than Sosha herself had. She was of the opinion that Sheala would also have come to terms with her own rape sooner if she hadn't been married. Marljas' masculine presence and obvious sexual needs put too much of a strain on her.

"I'll try, husband to my bloodsister," she said to the distraught man, "but perhaps your mother would be a better one to talk with her."

"Thank you, Sosha. I am in your debt."

Around the corner, Kadis smiled maliciously. She had been passing by Marljas and Sheala's room when she heard Marljas give voice to his frustration. She hadn't been able to hear Sheala's reply, but Marljas' side of the argument had been quite clear. His new Drakian wife was refusing his sexual advances. Such a refusal was enough to dissolve a marriage. Her mother would know what to do. Then she, Kadis, would marry Marljas and teach this family of upstarts what it meant to antagonize the sister and niece of the queen.

Flinging the door open, Marljas burst into his mother's sitting room.

"Marljas! Surely I have taught you better manners than that?"

He began to pace. "Forgive me, Mother. My behavior is inexcusable, but I don't know what else to do. I've been patient. I haven't forced myself upon her, but she isn't getting better. She still won't trust me."

"Sheala? I thought yesterday in the barn..."

Marljas braced his hands against the mantel and stared into the empty fireplace. "Yesterday was—a small relief. But we didn't make love, not completely. I didn't touch her."

Rising, Teena walked to her son, turned him to face her, and embraced him. "Denieen told me everything that happened with Rodak don al' Bakom. I'll talk to Sheala. Perhaps I'll be able to ease her mind. My advice to you, though, my son, is that you might be too understanding. I saw the kiss she gave you last night, and I know she sleeps in your bed."

"And my arms," Marljas muttered.

Teena ignored the interruption. "Sheala obviously trusts you. Push her a little. Maybe she needs only to be reminded of the joys of physical love. But," she cautioned, "do not push too hard. You don't want her to start fearing you."

He curled his hands into fists and growled. "Push but don't push. That makes no sense!"

Smiling, Teena stepped away from him. "Go to your father and brother. They're in the barn getting ready for the herd. The mares will be foaling soon."

After a deep breath, Marljas unfisted his hands. Nodding, he kissed his mother's cheek and left the room.

Teena sighed. Marljas was easy to console. Now, however, she had a much harder task ahead of her.

Lower lip clenched between her teeth, Sheala slumped on the bed while Sosha held her hand. Sheala had cried herself dry while her friend sat in silent support. Both girls looked up when the door opened.

Sosha rose when Teena entered.

"Excuse me, Teena Seenasdotir," she began.

"Sit back down, Sosha. What I have to say applies to both of you."

With those words, Teena locked the door behind her and began disrobing. Both girls watched in amazement as each piece of clothing fell to the floor until Teena stood naked before them. Both girls' eyes widened when they saw the scars that covered her body, especially those on her thighs.

"Look closely, girls. These aren't all battle scars."

Sheala swallowed. "What happened to you?"

"You aren't the only women to suffer rape at the hands of a madman."

Sosha stared into her hostess's face. "Who did this to you, Teena Seenasdotir?"

Teena began to redon her clothing. "His name was Fordrin Hodresson, and he wanted to marry me, but I chose Drefes."

"He kidnapped you?" Sheala interjected.

"Patience, wife of my son, it's my story to tell."

Sheala dipped her head. If she were capable of blushing, she would have.

"Wendjas was eight and Marljas five when Fordrin struck. Drefes and I were in the capital celebrating our tenth year of marriage when Fordrin seemingly met us by accident. He was gracious and lulled away our wariness. Leaving us in a restaurant, he concealed himself outside until we finished our meal. It was late by the time we left, and there were few people on the streets.

"We were only a few feet from the door of the restaurant when Drefes was struck on the back of the head and knocked unconscious. I learned later that Fordrin's intent had been to kill, but he'd misjudged his blow. I tried to defend Drefes, but an accomplice sprayed something into my face, and I also lost consciousness. When I awoke, I was Fordrin's prisoner. The scars tell you how he treated me."

Sheala gripped Sosha's hand harder. "What happened to him?"

Sitting in the chair next to the bed, Teena continued. "Fordrin wasn't a very intelligent man. He'd taken me to the home he'd recently inherited from his grandmother. Drefes rescued me three days later. Fordrin died very slowly."

Sheala stared into her mother-in-law's face. "How did you…"

"Accept Drefes' physical love after the way I'd been treated? I was very much like you, Sheala. I had a husband who loved me very much, one who did not hold me responsible for the horror I'd been through. But I could not stand to have him touch me."

"What did you do?"

Leaning forward, Teena smiled and cupped Sheala's cheek. "I healed. First in body then in mind. Eventually, I was able to accept that Drefes loved me, and his love would never harm me in any way."

"How long did it take before…?"

"I could make love with him?" asked Teena, slightly amused. "For a Drakian, you seem to have a great deal of trouble talking about sex, Sheala."

Sheala's temper flared, but before she could comment, Teena said, "Good, you can become angry. I think there is little for you to worry about. Rape is not pleasant, but Sosha endured far worse than you, far worse than I."

"But Sosha doesn't have a husband."

"Neither did you. Who was it that demanded Marljas marry her?" Teena asked sternly. "You had firsthand knowledge, from what I was told, about how virile a man my son is. Did you expect him to change? To live platonically for the rest of your lives? You? A Drakian?"

Sheala lost her stubborn look. "No. Teena Seenasdotir, I didn't. I could only remember how safe I felt with him."

"Then how can you doubt your safety with him now?"

"I don't," Sheala whispered, "but every time I feel his—erection, I remember. Bakom's assistants hurt me. They enjoyed hurting me. They got excited from the pain they inflicted. I have to block it out."

"With the unpleasantness, you block out Marljas' love," Teena stated. "Stop blocking it out. Let the memory continue. Then you will be able to compare my son's behavior with that of your captors. The difference will be obvious."

Sosha stared into her hostess's face. "Is that what you did, Teena Seenasdotir?"

"Yes, Sosha, and please don't be so formal. You're

bloodsister to my daughter-by-marriage, a member of my family. Call me Teena. Now," she continued as she rose to her feet. "The herd comes in today. It's a sight neither of you will want to miss. Sheala, you must shower and dress. Sosha, go down to the kitchens and get the two of you something to eat. Tell Cook I said she was to accommodate you this once."

Both girls nodded and hurried to do her bidding.

"I hope," Teena muttered to herself as she exited the room and made her way to the lower floors, "this past half hour proves to be productive."

A loud crash and an angry voice hurried Teena along. Once she got Kadis and her things loaded onto a shuttle and on the way back to her mother's house, things would become much more peaceful around here.

* * * * *

An hour later, Sosha and Sheala walked down to the corral.

Raking his hair back off his forehead, Marljas strode across the corral to join them. "The herd's been sighted and will be here within the hour."

Before he could say anything else, Radris' *pholola* mare ambled over and pushed him out of the way.

"Beautiful, isn't she," Marljas said as he rested his arms nonchalantly on the top rail of the fence. "She was foaled here. She likes to return to view each year's foaling when she can."

"Her name is Jota," Radris added, coming to stand on the other side of his mare.

Ignoring her rider, Jota stuck her head between the top two rails of the fence and nuzzled Sheala's chest.

A genuinely happy smile spread across Sheala's face as she stroked the mare's soft neck.

"Traitor," Radris mumbled in an amused tone. "Very well, I leave you with your new friends." With those words, he turned and disappeared into a stable.

At Sheala and Sosha's curious looks, Marljas shrugged, "She hasn't had her sugar yet today. She won't have anything to do with him until he gives her some. Jota's been spoiled horribly."

Sheala continued to stroke the mare's neck. Even with the rails of the fence and the mare between them, she could still feel Marljas' overwhelming masculine presence. He was big and strong, more than capable of throwing her over his shoulder, carrying her off, and forcing himself on her. And he hadn't done it. Closing her eyes, she leaned her forehead against the mare's. What was she going to do? Would this fear ever leave her?

Trust yourself and your mate, Drakian.

Jerking her head up, Sheala stared at the mare.

Warm, dark eyes stared into hers.

A rumbling sound like thunder rolled over the hill.

Marljas stopped staring at her and turned. "The herd's here." He pointed to a not-so-distant ridge, and soon the first of the herd appeared. Heads held high and nostrils flaring, the heavily pregnant mares and last year's foals galloped over the crest of the hill and down towards the corrals in a rainbow of green, blue, yellow, and pink.

"This year there are ninety-five mares in foal," Marljas said proudly as the mares headed for the grain spread for them in long troughs. "The yearlings will be separated from their mothers today," he continued, "and each family will decide what to do with the horses they own. Some will be sold, and others will be transferred to the nonbreeding herd."

Sheala stared at all the horses. "What do you do with all of them? With technology, there can't be much need for them."

Chuckling, Marljas watched the stragglers come down over the hill. "There's a great deal of truth in your words, my love. Except for racing, our horses have become mostly an expensive hobby. Many will never know the weight of a saddle on their backs."

Sheala shook her head. She'd always enjoyed riding and was considered quite accomplished on her planet. But riding on Drakan was nothing more than a hobby, and there were far fewer riding beasts. However, if their mounts looked like Gattan horses, perhaps more Drakians would ride. They were truly magnificent animals.

"Something's wrong," Marljas mumbled, turning to where his father and brother talked with the outriders who had accompanied the herd. "The herd stallion has not come."

At that moment, a galloping rider crested the hill and made a beeline towards the barn. Close behind him followed an obviously irate stallion. He stopped on the crest of the hill, reared, and turned to face the direction from which he'd come. In a few moments, one last mare slowly crested the hill. She took only a few steps before she sank to the ground.

"It's the renegade mare," yelled the galloping rider as he pulled his lathered horse to a quick halt. "She went into labor on the trail and is having complications. The stallion won't let anyone near her."

Along with his father and brother, Marljas ran towards the barn where their mounts were stabled.

Jota's head came up and she scented the wind. Her neigh vibrated off the hills, and she used her nose to push the gate open. A swing of her head and neck pushed both Sheala and Sosha towards her side.

"I think she wants us to get on, Sosha."

The mare's commanding neigh confirmed Sheala's statement.

They were barely settled on her back when the mare exploded into movement and shot up the hill towards the downed mare.

Far faster than Sheala had imagined possible, Jota reached the laboring mare's side. As both girls slid off, the high-strung stallion bugled a challenge and started towards them.

One snort from Jota stilled him.

"Will he try to come after us?" Sheala asked cautiously as she and Sosha knelt beside the laboring mare.

"No." Sosha gasped as she jumped back when the laboring mare tried to bite her. "But this mare might. Everyone on Gattan has heard of her," she continued. "She's a complete throwback to the horses that ran wild across our planet's grasslands centuries ago. She won't allow anyone near her."

"Why not just turn her loose, then?" Sheala asked. "Marljas said there are still wild horses in very remote parts of your planet."

Sosha walked around the young mare. "Jota is her mother. There are only three *pholola* mares on Gattan that are not part of the *Snowpards'* herds, and Jota is the only one who has had a foal. Ah, here's the problem."

Sheala joined Sosha behind the mare and saw what Sosha meant. The unborn foal had one hoof and foreleg protruding from the birth canal.

Sheala squatted down for a closer look. "The other leg must be bent at the knee."

The laboring mare screamed and attempted to rise. Both girls jumped back.

Sheala glared at the recalcitrant mare. "How can anyone help her if she won't cooperate!"

Jota had watched the two girls closely. Taking a few steps forward, she brought her head down to her daughter and whickered. Then she turned her head and looked at the girls.

A strong female voice popped into their heads. *Help her.*

Sheala looked at Sosha. "Well, if that's not an order nothing is. Let's see what we can do."

Once again squatting behind the laboring mare, Sheala motioned Sosha down beside her. "If we can push this leg back in, maybe the other one will straighten out and the foal will just slide out."

Sosha knelt beside Sheala. "Do you think it will work?"

"Well, I read about it in a book, and I watched Rodane do this with one of our riding beasts that had the same problem. I don't see that there's much else we can do unless there's a veterinarian near here somewhere."

Sosha shook her head.

"Let's try then."

Grasping the part of the leg that was visible, Sheala tried to push the foal back into its mother.

The mare screamed again, but Jota's nose on her neck kept her still.

"I need your help, Sosha. This is harder than it looks."

Both girls wrapped their hands around the foal's leg and pushed. Slowly, it went back into the mare.

When they let go, the hoof began to reappear again.

Sosha shook her head. "I think you'll have to push it all the way back into the womb to get it aligned with the other leg."

Sheala swallowed. "Why me?"

"Because it was your idea. I'll sit behind you and brace you."

"I hope you know what I'm doing," Sheala muttered.

With Jota nickering what sounded like encouragement, Sheala pushed her hand into the mare's birth canal. Grasping the single ankle she felt, with Sosha's help, she pushed until her entire arm was within the mare.

"I think I found the other leg."

Sosha wiped the sweat from her forehead on the back of Sheala's shirt. "Make sure you have both legs. I don't think she could go through this again."

"I...have...it."

Sheala pulled her arm out and leaned back against Sosha.

Two small hooves appeared. Soon both forelegs were

visible.

The laboring mare groaned.

"She's exhausted," Sosha mumbled. "Grab a leg and pull when she has another contraction."

Another contraction gripped the mare's body. With a rush that knocked both girls flat on their backs, the foal slid into their laps followed almost immediately by the afterbirth.

Jota backed away, and the mare scrambled to her feet. Whirling, she turned towards her foal and the two girls.

"Get a rope on her," someone shouted. "She's going after them."

Neither girl had heard the party of riders that had come upon them as they delivered the foal. Nor had they paid any attention to the angry stallion, trusting Jota to keep him away from them.

Contrary to what everyone expected, the mother of the new foal did not attack the girls. Instead she began to lick them all dry. Unsteadily, the foal tried to climb to its feet.

"It's white," said a hushed voice.

"A *pholola*," said another.

The mare turned a wild eye towards the men on their horses and bared her teeth.

"Well, I never thought to see anything like this," Drefes said as he dismounted slowly. "Sosha, Sheala, can you come here?"

Both girls rose slowly to their feet, but the mare continued to swipe both her foal and them with her tongue. She snorted in Sosha's face, but rubbed her head against Sheala.

The stallion screamed again as another horse joined those on the hill. This one was a heavily pregnant mare, and she carried Denieen.

Wendjas frowned. "Should you be riding her, Deni?"

Both Deni and Jota snorted. "She won't foal for another week, this little ride won't hurt her. She's the lead mare.

Between Jota and her, they'll get that foolish stud down with the herd where he belongs."

Sliding off the mare, Denieen unsnapped the bridle, and slapped her on the rump.

The sight of the mare loping away and the sharp nip Jota gave him convinced the restless stallion to rejoin the rest of his mares at the feeding troughs.

"You two have had a busy day," Deni said to Sosha and Sheala as she bent to examine first the foal, then the mare. A bit leery of Denieen at first, the mare settled when Jota whickered softly. "They're both fine, considering the circumstances. It's amazing that she was able to come this far. But then this mare has been nothing if not contrary all of her life," she added as she straightened.

The foal sighed and lay down.

"We'll have to carry it down," Drefes said as he walked closer and bent to pick up the foal.

He was met by wickedly bared teeth.

"Now what?" he asked in an exasperated tone.

Jota let out a very human sigh and shook her head. Walking over to the foal, she lay down carefully. With Sheala's help, Sosha was able to drape the foal across Jota's withers and climb on herself. Carefully, Jota rose to her feet. With the mother pacing nervously next to her, she headed down the hill towards the stables.

"She did it again," Radris said with wonder in his voice as he stared at his mare and the girl riding her. "Keep Sheala and Sosha close, Drefes, my friend. There's much about them we don't understand."

"Now he's getting mystical on us," Wendjas mumbled as he boosted Deni up onto his horse then swung up behind her.

Radris swiftly mounted his borrowed horse and turned to follow Wendjas and Drefes.

Chapter Twenty-One

∞

Marljas bent over his horse's withers and held his hand out to Sheala.

She glanced down at herself. "I'm not exactly in the best condition to ride double. I'm covered with mud, blood and afterbirth."

Marljas shrugged. "I have helped at many a foaling. A little dirt and blood don't bother me."

Shrugging, Sheala gave him her hand. However, instead of swinging her up behind him he boosted her up before him and tucked against his chest.

"I am very proud of you, *Cheta*. You saved the life of a *pholola* foal. You've brought much honor to our family."

Sheala attempted to hold herself upright. "I didn't do anything anyone else wouldn't have done."

Marljas had reined his horse in the opposite direction of the barns.

"Where are we going?"

"I thought you might like to clean yourself off," he answered into her hair. "I know of a pool."

"I could just as easily take a bath at the house—in a bathtub with nice *hot* water."

"The pool has a hot spring."

Sheala didn't answer and, after ten minutes of riding, their horse pushed his way through some bushes and stopped on the bank of a small, secluded pool.

Marljas lowered Sheala to the ground and swung off after her. Turning, he kicked off the soft leather boots he wore, stripped off his thigh-length tunic, knelt beside the stream that emptied into the pool, and began wash the garment.

Sheala leaned back against the horse and admired his broad shoulders and strong back, watching the play of his muscles under his brown skin.

In a few minutes, he shook the tunic out and spread it in the sun to dry. Turning, he looked at his wife.

"Are you going to wear those dirty clothes all day?"

Looking down at herself, Sheala grimaced. Without a word she walked past Marljas and into the water and began scrubbing her clothing — without removing them.

She glanced back over her shoulder.

Grinning, Marljas stood on the bank of the pool, feet planted slightly apart with his arms crossed over his bare chest. The afternoon sun turned his hair into burnished gold. The muscles on his arms bulged, and his tight leather pants clung to sculpted thighs. The dragon and lion on his shoulder glowed like red gold.

"Are you going to finish washing, *Cheta*, or do you just prefer to admire me?"

Sheala abruptly ducked her head. Then she heard a splash, and Marljas was soon at her side.

"What are you doing!" she gasped as he pulled her shirt over her head.

"You'll never get all the filth off your shirt this way," he said as he walked away from her and up onto the bank. Kneeling, he began to scrub.

Sheala was standing waist-deep in the water with her arms crossed over her breasts.

Without looking back, Marljas said, "Those leggings need to be washed, too. Throw them to me."

"Then I won't have anything to wear."

"Put on my tunic. It will reach to your knees."

Sheala didn't answer, but Marljas heard a wet thud as her

leggings landed on the bank and her splashing as she made her way from the pool to where he'd laid his tunic to dry. It was a thin garment and had dried completely the short time it had lain in the sun. Even though it covered her from knees to neck, it was very revealing.

When Marljas stood to lay out her garments, he smiled.

A slight breeze had come up, pebbling her nipples against the soft material.

His cock responded immediately.

Dropping her soaking garments Marljas stepped towards his wife and said, "Have I told you, my love, how beautiful you are."

Nervously shaking her head, she stepped back.

Marljas stopped then decided to take his mother's advice. Two more steps, and he was holding Sheala by the upper arms.

"Look at me," he said, not trying to hide the desperation in his voice. "Look at my chest."

Sheala stared at the three parallel scars riding high on his left breast.

"Those scars pledge my love to you, just as the scar on your hand pledges yours to me."

Lifting her head, her face shouting her misery to the world, she looked into Marljas' eyes.

Her voice was miserable. "I'm so scared."

Marljas pulled her into a tight embrace. "I will never hurt you." Placing his fingers beneath her chin, he lifted her head until her eyes once again met his. Slowly, he lowered his mouth to hers and placed a gentle kiss against her lips. The soft sigh Sheala released as she closed her eyes encouraged him to continue.

Sheala stopped thinking and let her body enjoy the sensation of the gentle kisses Marljas rained on her face and neck. Soon, his hand had cupped the back of her head. Ever so gently, he nuzzled her mouth with kisses. He circled her lips with his tongue.

After another sigh, she parted her lips.

As his rough tongue mated with hers, his kisses became more passionate and waves of pleasure washed over her. When he cupped and squeezed her breast, however, her eyes flew open and she pushed her hands against his chest.

He refused to release her. "Look at me," he demanded. "Have I ever hurt you? Do you think I will ever hurt you?"

Sheala closed her eyes, but shook her head.

"Then trust me. Let me love you."

Leaning her forehead against his chest, Sheala blinked back tears. What kind of Drakian was she? How could she let someone as loathsome as Bakom keep her from enjoying sex with the man she loved more than anything? No! She would not let that evil man ruin her marriage, not now and never again.

Eyes snapping open, she met her husband's golden gaze. "Help me, please."

"I will, *Cheta*," he answered, his mouth again sweeping down on hers. "Just trust me." Then her mouth was prisoner to his once more.

He kissed her—and kissed her and kissed her, one deep passionate kiss following another until she was breathless.

"I love you," he murmured against her lips. "I need you. I want you. Do you love me?"

"More than anything," she gasped between kisses.

Clinging helplessly to his shoulders, Sheala answered his kisses with her own, lost in his gentle passion. She was unaware she had been laid on the ground until he stopped kissing her long enough to strip off the tunic she wore.

She opened her eyes to see his pants fall to the ground.

When he lowered himself on top of her, she felt as if a

bucket of cold water had been tossed over her head.

"No!"

Marljas held her immobile with his body. "Look at me, *Cheta*. Look at *me*! I am *not* Bakom."

Staring into her husband's face, she saw only concern, love, and passion.

He slid his cock against her. "You're slippery and wet, love. Your body wants me. Do you?"

She stiffened but didn't struggle.

As she stared into his eyes, he spread her thighs with his knees and slid his cock into her. Then he lay perfectly still.

His voice held a tinge of desperation. "Am I hurting you?"

Blinking, Sheala shook her head.

"I'm not going to hurt you, *Cheta*. I'm going to love you." He ground his hips against hers, pushing his cock deeper. "Am I hurting you?"

Again, Sheala shook her head.

"Let me love you," he whispered against her mouth. "Let me love those memories away and give you new ones."

Blinking back tears, Sheala nodded. "Yes," she whispered, "oh yes."

Marljas covered her mouth with his. Caressing her tongue with his, he began to pump his hips slowly.

At first, Sheala remained stiff and unresponsive, but as waves of heat began to radiate from her groin, she slowly relaxed her muscles.

He cupped her left breast, trailing a line of kisses down her throat to the firm mound he kneaded gently. Then he sucked her nipple into his mouth.

She arched her back. "Ahhhhhhhhh."

"Do you like that? Like the way it feels?" he whispered

between her breasts.

"Oh gods, yes."

She wrapped her arms around his neck — and her legs around his waist. Her tail curled around his calf muscle and squeezed gently, matching the rhythm of his slow thrusts.

"You're so tight, so hot, *Cheta*. You feel so good, you make my cock even harder."

Marljas began to thrust deeper, twisting his hips as he did so, grinding into her.

Moisture surrounded his cock, and her internal muscles squeezed.

Sweat beaded on his forehead. He twisted his hips into a long, grinding thrust.

As he nipped her nipple then sucked on it, she threaded her fingers through his hair and pulled his head up. "Keep looking at me, please. Let me see your eyes."

Gritting his teeth as her slippery cunt muscles sucked at his cock, he asked, "What do you see?"

He felt a shiver race through her body.

She arched again then looked into his face. "Fire," she whispered. "I see fire. And I see love."

"I will always love you, Sheala. Only you."

The tip of her tail began to stroke his balls, and he groaned, unsure how much longer he'd be able to last.

Her muscles tightened around his cock, and she stiffened.

"Marljas! Now!"

Covering her mouth with his, he surged into her one final time, as deeply as he could. His balls tightened and hot fire erupted from his cock.

The muscles of her thighs quivered as she tightened her legs around his waist, Sheala ground her hips against him and screamed into his mouth.

When cum finally stopped spurting from his cock, with

what seemed to be the last of his strength, Marljas rolled onto his back pulling Sheala with him. Not taking any chances, he kept her pinioned to his chest with tightly clasped arms.

Sighing contentedly, Sheala kissed the three scars on her husband's chest and propped herself up on her elbows.

His arms tightened.

Sheala met his worried gaze and smiled. "I've been a fool."

His tense body relaxed and his tight grip loosened. "No, *Cheta*, never a fool." He grinned. "Misguided, perhaps."

She grinned back. "Misguided?" Her tail slid up the inside of his thigh and wrapped around his still semierect cock.

It hardened again immediately.

Elbows on Marljas' chest, her chin propped in her hands, Sheala looked down into his face. "Misguided?"

Her tail began to pump his cock.

His eyes narrowed. He cupped her ass cheeks and began to knead them.

At first, Sheala stiffened, but then she relaxed as his fingers drew small whorls on each cheek.

Her nipples pebbled.

There was a catch in his voice. "Mis—guided."

She tightened her tail around his cock.

"Tease me, will you!" Flipping her over on her back, Marljas thrust his cock between her spread legs, into her hot, wet pussy.

Her laughter quickly turned into moans of ecstasy.

Night was falling by the time Sheala and Marljas rode back to his parents' house.

"Do you think they saved us anything to eat?"

Marljas slid his fingers between her spread thighs. "You can think about food now?"

Chuckling, Sheala leaned back against his chest. "Play all you want, but I know your cock won't rise before tomorrow morning."

He nuzzled her neck. "I swear, I'll be between your thighs before midnight."

"You were between my thighs all afternoon."

"I'd still be there if the horse had left us alone."

Sheala grinned. "He's hungry."

Laughter rumbled in his chest. "Like you."

"Like me."

He cupped her with his free hand. "You should have put your own clothing on instead of wearing my tunic. You wouldn't be so much of a temptation then."

Sheala looked down at the still-wet clothing draped over the horse's withers. "They're wet and filthy. Your tunic was a much better alternative." She stroked the forearm holding the reins. "The hair on your arms is so soft."

Marljas snorted. "I'd rather hear you praising my cock."

She chuckled. "Your cock is not soft, love. At least it wasn't."

Horses in the corral whickered as they rode by.

A grinning farmhand took the reins of the horse after they'd both dismounted.

Hand in hand, they strolled towards the house. When they reached the wide veranda facing the barns, Denieen's smile and Wendjas' raised eyebrow and wide grin elicited a comment from Sheala.

"Well, you really didn't expect me to wear those filthy clothes back, did you?"

Totally unconcerned with the fact that Marljas' tunic, which she had belted tightly around her waist, revealed more of her body than it hid, Sheala perched on the arm of an overstuffed chair.

"Is there anything left to eat, Mother?" Marljas asked with a grin as he draped an arm around Sheala's shoulders and pulled her close. "We're starved. I'm sorry we are late, but we were—sidetracked."

That comment prompted laughter from everyone.

"Cook kept something warm for you, but I wouldn't complain about whatever it is, my son," Teena said with a laugh. "You know she doesn't like her schedule disrupted."

"How's the foal?" Sheala asked contentedly from Marljas' arms.

"Sleeping with a full belly," Drefes answered, "and the mare is down beside her. Sheala, our tribe owes you a debt that cannot be repaid. I speak for both Teena and myself when I say anything we have is yours."

Sheala grinned. "But I already have your most valuable possession," she countered, sliding her arm around Marljas' waist.

"Bah," Beti snorted from a dark corner. "I'm going to bed. I have no wish to listen to a Drakian spouting about the joys of sex."

As Beti rose to leave, Radris bolted out of the chair where he sat. His attempt to intercept Beti was wasted, however, for she neatly sidestepped and tripped him into another chair. "You will have to do better than that, Gattan," she said as she disappeared into the house.

"Radris has become infatuated with Beti," said a grinning Sosha by way of explanation. "That's the third attempt he's made to capture her."

Her laughter echoing across the yard, Sheala crowed, "I must send a message to Jami and Vani, and I wish I could see the look on Uncle Findal's face when they tell him one of his Aradabs is being courted by the head of the Gattan royal guard."

"You call the King of Mediria uncle?" Teena asked.

"I told you the Alalakan clan was close to the Medirian royal family," Deni interjected.

"The wife of my youngest son calls the King of Mediria uncle," Drefes mused.

Wendjas grinned at his father. "I told you that this business of trading can be more rewarding than war."

Sheala laughed. "Don't ask for my help. I intend to stay neutral in any trading battles between you."

Laughing, Marljas lifted a giggling Sheala into his arms and strode into the house. "Come, Wife, I'm hungry."

Everyone heard the comment that drifted back through the still open door. "For food or for me?"

"Both!" was the emphatic answer.

A look of consternation crossed Teena's face. "I have a Drakian daughter-in-law," she said in a slightly worried tone. "She won't insist upon running through the house naked, will she?"

Denieen burst into laughter. "She has better manners than that, Teena. But I would find Marljas and her a larger suite of rooms. I don't think there's a Drakian alive who could even conceive of being able to make love in only one room. And I would certainly knock before I entered any room they were in at the same time."

Unbelieving looks on both their faces, Drefes and Teena gaped at Deni. But Wendjas and Sosha nodded in agreement, Wendjas ruefully and Sosha with some amusement.

"You can't possibly begin to believe how many couples I interrupted when we were on Drakan," Wendjas muttered.

"Don't forget the threesome behind the bushes in the herb garden," Deni interjected with a grin.

A beseeching look on her face, Teena looked to Deni.

Continuing to grin, Deni only shook her head. "I am sorry, Teena, but Sheala is Drakian. It's her nature and upbringing to be open about her own and everyone else's sexuality. However, as I said before, she is a well brought up young woman. Both her mother and grandmother were quite thorough with their training, and Sheala has spent many hours with me seeking to learn about Gattan. Have no fear, she will shame neither the family nor the tribe, but we will have to become a bit more flexible in our treatment and traditions about sexual relations."

Radris stretched and rose to his feet. Smiling he said, "I for one won't be averse to beautiful young women with few sexual inhibitions wandering around."

Completely surprising his parents, Wendjas rose, held out his hand to his wife, and said, "I, too, am hungry, Deni. Shall we go to our bed?"

Denieen chuckled as she put her hand into Wendjas', and he led her into the house.

Teena and Drefes looked at each other.

"I told you that trip to Drakan might not be a good idea," Drefes mumbled. "Who knows what ideas Hendjas and Charjas picked up."

Mentally agreeing with her husband, Teena sighed but said, "We all agreed that they should go, that the future of our planet depended on trade not war. It's too late for recriminations now, my love. It is late." She turned to Sosha. "Are you coming?"

"I'd like to sit here a bit longer, if you do not mind."

After her hosts left, Sosha turned off the light. Sheala had overcome her fear of Marljas' almost overpowering sexuality and was obviously very happy.

"Will I ever be so lucky to experience such joy?" she muttered into the darkness.

Chapter Twenty-Two

ɛɔ

Jadis Franasdotir paced back and forth in her luxurious sitting room. "Are you sure it wasn't a Drakian ceremony?"

"I saw his scars myself, Mother," answered a pouting Kadis from where she perched primly on an uncomfortable chair, "and he's got a matching set on the right side for that alien bloodsister of his."

Sprawled in a comfortable chair, Kadis' elder brother Cadan said nothing. He wasn't about to remind his mother and sister that he'd told them their plan to have Kadis marry Marljas and take control of that particular branch *Leonine* tribe wouldn't work.

Jadis stopped pacing in front of her daughter. "But you're sure she's refusing him sexually?"

Kadis preened. "I heard him say it myself."

Stomping over to her seemingly bored son, Jadis kicked at his foot and snapped, "Don't just sit there, say something!"

Slowly, he sat up. "What would you have me say, Mother? That your plan will still work?" Then throwing discretion to the winds, he continued. "I told you that Marljas wouldn't marry Kadis, but you insisted that he would. Well, that marriage won't happen now, and we have squandered three other viable plans in favor of this farce."

Jadis swung unsheathed claws at her son. "Get out, you puling male!"

As always, quick on his feet and knowing his mother's explosive temper, Cadan ducked and leaped at his opportunity to escape the room.

"And don't return until I summon you," his mother

shrieked at the closing door.

Still fuming, Jadis disemboweled two pillows and slashed the jacket her son had left to shreds. "Why weren't you born first?" she snarled at her daughter. "Then I wouldn't have a weakling son to tolerate."

"Mother, control yourself," Kadis said cautiously. "You know how servants gossip. Do you want some menial whispering in Krondal's ear that you can't control yourself? Aunt Mattis listens to him entirely too much."

Fantasizing that the pillow she was currently ripping to shreds was her son, Jadis dropped the tattered remains as her daughter's words penetrated.

"Krondal," Jadis spat, "another male with far too much influence. If he'd married me, he'd have been put in his place years ago."

Nodding in agreement, Kadis said, "But first we have to do something about this Drakian woman."

An evil smile appeared on Jadis' face. "We could push for a second wife."

Kadis shook her head. "Sosha Kanicsdotir will then push her claim, and she and her parents have a signed betrothal contract. If the Council insists on a second, Gattan wife for Marljas, she has first claim. Before I left, I heard Teena's maids gossiping that Marljas had already offered Sosha the position of second wife."

Muttering to herself, Jadis resumed her pacing. "Bah! How did that upstart escape? That damned pirate guaranteed that he had the perfect buyer, and we'd never see that little slut again. I'm glad I didn't inform her parents of her return."

Kadis frowned at her mother. "Pirate? Who are you talking about?"

Realizing that she'd said too much, Jadis turned to face her daughter. "Never mind. Do you think you could win a personal challenge?"

Warily, Kadis looked at her mother. "As long as the

Aradab can't take the Drakian's place."

Shock dropped over Jadis' face. "The Aradab is that good?"

Kadis rose and began pacing. "Mother, you know my skills. Of the young women my age, none are better. However, I am absolutely positive that there is not a woman on this planet who could best the Aradab, not even Jenia Drostindotir. I even think the Aradab woman could defeat many of the men."

Dropping to the chair nearest her, Jadis nodded silently. She did not doubt her daughter's word. If Kadis said the Aradab could defeat Jenia, sixth-level *Snopard* priestess and personal bodyguard to the queen, then she could. The thought was sobering.

Shaking herself out of her reverie, Jadis gathered her composure. "We can find something which will allow you to challenge the girl. If she is afraid of sex, her fighting skills will be lacking. And she has no claws."

"The Aradab is training her," Kadis interjected uneasily.

Jadis understood her daughter's fear. She too had lost once to an enemy she thought to defeat easily.

"This wife of Marljas is Drakian, my love," Jadis said stroking her daughter's cheek. "From what you learned, the Aradab woman had been on Drakan only a month or so before coming here with them. Even if they trained every hour of the day, there is no way even an Aradab could make a fighter out of an indolent Drakian."

Kadis relaxed and began to smile. "You're correct, of course, Mother. Even Sosha, who has been trained since birth, is no longer an effective fighter since she lost her claws. A Drakian couldn't possibly defeat me in a fair fight." She chose not to tell her mother how strong Sheala's grip had been on her wrist.

Or one not so fair, Jadis mused silently. Then she continued. "I'll consult with the *Tigre* lore masters, but I'm sure we'll be able to challenge on the grounds that we were led to believe that the betrothal was agreed upon, and Marljas is the one who reneged on the agreement. Teena wasn't on Drakan with Marljas, and I doubt Denieen ever gave him permission to marry even though she had the right to do so."

Her lips curled, Kadis sneered, "Denieen is one Gattan I will enjoy seeing humbled. When I'm married to Marljas, I will put her in her place."

"And that condescending Teena, also, my love," Jadis added as the fantasy she had developed and refined since her daughter was a girl took over. "We'll teach the people what it means to be truly Gattan, and they will bow down to me in gratitude. That stupid Mattis will be pulled from the throne, and I'll take her place. Then she'll learn what it means to deny and humiliate me!"

* * * * *

Some two weeks later, snuggled comfortably beneath the blankets on her bed—Gattan spring nights were cold—Sheala dreamed about her husband. Considering their newlywed state, the other men in the family had been willing to overlook the fact that Marljas was shirking some of his duties to spend time with his wife. However, it had been diplomatically pointed out to him that he had not yet taken a night watch in the foaling barn, and a full half of the mares had not yet foaled. It was only fair that he take his turn at night watch in the foaling barn.

Sheala had laughed and told him to go. And so, she'd spent last night alone in their bed for the first time since they'd arrived on Gattan.

Smiling, Sheala willed herself deeper into sleep, for she was enjoying the eroticism of what she thought was a dream.

Nuzzling her neck and breasts, Marljas lay beside her. One hand caressed her hip and back while the other roamed every other curve and crevice of her body. Finally, he dipped his hand between her thighs and gently divided her moist lips in search of the hard little bud hidden there. Sighing, Sheala rolled onto her back and spread her legs as soft chuckles and whispers of endearment nagged her from sleep. Opening her eyes, she watched her husband's head slide down her torso until he reached the juncture of her thighs. Once there, his mouth replaced his fingers.

When Marljas' open mouth and tongue parted the moist lips of her vulva, Sheala almost arched completely off the bed. Using both hands to keep a firm grip on her thighs, Marljas continued to suck and prod and lave until she was mindless with ecstasy. Her orgasm seemed to shatter her into a million pieces.

When she finally regained control of her body, Sheala gazed levelly at her husband and said, "You can't keep your mouth from me. That's supposed to be the first gift a Drakian gives to his wife when he learns she carries their first child. I'm not pregnant."

"And I," Marljas murmured with a grin as he slid up to lie beside her, "am not Drakian. Why wait for something we both enjoy so much."

Rolling over and straddling her husband, Sheala pressed both hands against his chest. His hard arousal pressed intimately against her buttocks. "You're very forward for a male, my love. I have been studying Gattan history, and males historically are submissive to the female members of their families."

Marljas' hands moved swiftly. Grasping Sheala's hips, he lifted her up and impaled her on his throbbing erection. "Dominate me then, *Cheta*. Ride me to the stars and back."

She needed no further encouragement. Sliding up and down, matching her rhythm to his thrusts, she rode him, gripping and clasping his straining cock with her pelvic muscles until he bucked wildly against her. They rode farther than the stars.

* * * * *

"Has the message been sent?" Brianna asked.

Nodding, Chardadon watched contentedly as his fiery-haired, strong-willed wife nursed their eight-week-old son. The evening before the Alalakan clan had celebrated the birth of its heir, and he and Brianna had resumed their more than satisfactory sexual relationship.

Grinning fondly, he leaned over and placed a light kiss on his wife's forehead. "An hour ago. I am sure Sheala is expecting us to arrive any day now. I merely confirmed the arrival date with the message."

Brianna nodded and switched her son from one breast to the other, a move not as easy as one would think considering he had his very flexible tail wrapped around her arm.

"Now I know what else you Drakians use these tails for," Brianna muttered, more to herself than to Char.

"But you prefer the uses I put my tail to, don't you, love?" Char whispered against her neck. His chuckle followed the flush of red that traveled up her neck to her face.

"Stop it. You kept me up most of last night."

"You seemed to be enjoying yourself."

"Char!" Brianna gasped when he cupped the breast Connor had finished with.

"Stop fondling your wife," Bandalardrac interjected as he sauntered into Brianna's private sitting room. "A message from Sheala arrived half an hour after you sent yours."

"How is everyone?" Brianna asked, eagerly forgetting that her bared breasts were fully exposed to Ban's appreciative gaze.

Ban grinned at her. "Ah sweet Coz, two more beautiful globes of pleasure surely exist nowhere else in the universe."

"Oh!" Brianna blushed again and quickly covered herself as best she could.

Char roared with laughter.

Sighing, Brianna finally snuggled her son against her shoulder and rubbed his back until he burped. Drakian sexuality could be frustrating at times. She simply could not adjust to the Drakian nonchalance towards public nudity, especially when Ban kept composing bad poetry about various portions of her anatomy.

It didn't help that everyone else in the family found Ban's compliments utterly amusing.

Patting her son, Brianna muttered, "You better not be listening to this, Connor."

Still chuckling, Ban crossed the room and kissed Brianna lightly on the head. "But you bring so much joy to my life, Coz. What other woman on this planet becomes so embarrassed by a simple compliment?"

Brianna snorted, but before she could say anything, Ban handed a sheet of paper to Char. "It's from Sheala," he said.

Seating himself next to his wife, Char read the missive to her.

"Hello everybody. I'm sorry this isn't video, but there simply isn't time. The mares are foaling and everything is more hectic than you can imagine! I've even taken my turn on night watch, though it proves to be rather boring. Teena and Drefes have absolutely refused to allow Marljas and me to take another watch together. The one night we did, we got...diverted, and two of the mares foaled without any supervision. The mares and foals are fine, but Drefes was somewhat disturbed. Both mares belonged to him."

Brianna smiled. "Sheala seems to have gotten over her problems with intimacy."

"She's Drakian, Coz," Ban answered in an amused voice. "What did you expect?"

"Oh, be quiet. What else does she say, Char?"

"The head of the Gattan Royal Guard is visiting and has developed an interest in Beti. She's encouraging him."

An amazed look crossed Ban's face. "You have got to be kidding!"

Char shook his head. "No. Sheala is quite specific. Beti says that, if he's hung half as well as he's built, he could prove to be an interesting diversion."

Ban barked with laughter. "That's Beti, direct to a fault."

"Every Aradab I've ever met is direct to a fault," Brianna mumbled.

Char glanced down over the sheet and finished. "Everyone is looking forward to our arrival, and when will we get there?"

"The message you sent will be there in two days, so she'll have her answer," Ban said. "Now if you will excuse me, I have packing to do, and flight checks to complete. I'll see you at dinner."

After gently lifting Connor from his wife's arms and placing him in the cradle next to Brianna's chair, Char turned his attention back to his wife.

Leaning down he placed a passionate kiss on her slightly open mouth. "I find that I am sleepy, too. Perhaps you would care to join me in a nap?"

Brianna wrapped her arms around his neck. It was all the answer Char needed.

* * * * *

In the Alalakan communication center, Ban entered a code known only to him. In a few minutes, an answering light blinked. Message was received and confirmed. If Beti began a liaison with the man in charge of Gattan security, they might just finally be able to infiltrate that very secretive organization.

Chapter Twenty-Three

ॐ

"A message from Drakan has arrived for you."

Smiling, Sheala dropped the book she was reading and grabbed the message from Deni. Now that Marljas had helped her overcome her fears of intimacy, her marriage was wonderful, but she had always been close to her family and missed them.

After perusing the message in silence, she quickly outlined its content. "Connor's introduction to the rest of the Alalakans was a huge success. He even managed to smile at Great-Aunt Bettleinia thereby assuring her undying affection. Char will be taking a few more days to settle some business affairs, and then they'll come over to introduce Connor to his Gattan relatives here. Rodane and Fionilina are staying home with Mother and Father because of Fio's unsettled stomach. Brianna calls it morning sickness even though Fio is usually sick in the evening."

Marljas smiled. "Then she should call it evening sickness, don't you think?"

Still smiling Sheala shrugged. "You know Brianna. It's one of her Earth expressions." She looked back down at the message. "If everything goes according to plan, they should be here in two to three weeks. Ban will be flying Brianna, Char and Connor over on the *Wanderer*. Since Beti is already here, Brianna was able to convince all the other Aradabs but Kahn and Feni to go back to Mediria. That's strange," she finished.

"What?" Deni asked.

"Bjin has asked to accompany them."

Teena looked up from the baby blanket she was weaving. "Who?"

"A Deslossian. Right after we arrived in Benishan, their ambassador brought him to our house saying we were the only ones who could help him. He'd just lost his wife in childbirth."

Deni frowned. "But why would he want to come here?"

Sheala shook her head. "He didn't tell them. He just said he had to come, and they saw no reason to deny his request."

Teena set her hand loom on the floor. "We'll need to decide how to house them properly. As bloodsister to Marljas and sister-in-law to you, Brianna is considered one of the family. Char is your brother, and their child is your and Marljas' nephew by Drakian bloodline and Gattan blood rite. Bandalardrac, nephew to the King of Mediria, is not only cousin to Sheala, but also bloodbrother to Sosha who is also bloodsister to you. Two more Aradabs? And what does one do with a Deslossian?" She shook her head. "Complicated relationships you have managed to form for us, my son."

Grinning, he shrugged. "I don't think the Deslossian is related in any way."

Before Teena could reply to his gibe, Drefes appeared in the doorway. "Marljas, that mare you bought last fall is ready to foal."

Marljas rose to his feet, kissed Sheala's forehead, and followed his father.

Smiling, Sheala watched her husband leave the room. Teena and Deni smiled to each other when she stretched complacently. Their knowing smiles in no way embarrassed her.

"I never really did understand what Mother and Grandmother meant to be sexually content until now," she purred.

Both Deni and Sheala laughed at the flustered look on Teena's face. She still wasn't used to Sheala's open attitude towards her and Marljas' sexual relationship, but she was learning. Teena was extremely grateful that Sheala was very circumspect around other Gattans not of the immediate family. Even though he was coming to love his daughter-in-law, Drefes would flee the room when a certain smile appeared on Sheala's face.

"You gave Marljas and me that entire tower to ourselves, Teena," Sheala said. "There are more than enough rooms there."

Deni nodded her head. "A good idea, Teena. I think our people would be much more comfortable with all of you staying together."

Sheala burst out with laughter. "You mean you'll be more comfortable knowing exactly where Ban is, don't you?"

Deni's answering grin confirmed Shea's suspicions.

Teena frowned. "Bandalardrac Hardan, the most notorious rake on five planets. More than a few men and women on this planet still believe he kidnapped Sosha and want to castrate him, at the least. But I don't want him to think we're segregating him."

Shaking her head negatively, Sheala swallowed her giggles. "Teena, if you put Ban in any other wing, an inability to find my rooms will be his reason to wander about in every other room in this house. Your maids are going to be distracted enough by him as it is."

Teena didn't try to hide her dismay. "His reputation is warranted then?"

Deni grinned as widely as Sheala. "More than warranted. He could charm the birds from the trees."

Sighing, Teena closed her eyes. "And I have invited him to my house. The queen's council may never forgive me."

Both younger women laughed louder at their mother-in-law's discomfort.

Sosha wandered into the room. "What's the joke I missed?"

"Bandalardrac," Sheala and Denieen answered in unison.

Joining in their laughter, Sosha commented, "He's coming then. The maids will be shirking their work, and will Marljas, Wendjas, and Drefes be able to control all of the jealous men?"

"I'll make sure Ban knows which maids are married. Challenges from irate husbands couldn't be shrugged off," Deni said. "As for the others…"

"I won't have my maids bothered by the most notorious rake in the universe!" Teena stated emphatically. "The parents of the younger maids will castrate him if their daughters are compromised in any way."

Still chuckling, Deni patted Teena's arm. "I spent a great deal of time in Ban's company while we were on Drakan. You needn't worry about his behavior."

"He can be quite courteous and proper when necessary," Sheala added with a giggle.

"Don't forget discreet, Shea," a grinning Sosha added. "Ban can be very discreet."

Teena gazed from one girl to the next, horror spreading across her countenance.

Sighing, Deni said, "Enough teasing, you two. Don't worry, Teena. Ban won't do anything to bring shame or dishonor upon his family or this one. While he may flirt outrageously, he will not compromise any of the maids. You can be assured that Ban won't do anything to jeopardize the acceptance of Sheala and Brianna by our tribe. I do recommend, however, that you invite two or three lonely widows to visit."

Teena pursed her lips speculatively as she gazed into her daughter-in-law's eyes then nodded slowly. "I have some friends who are not interested in finding new husbands, but who do enjoy masculine company now and again. It's been a while since I spent any time with them. Perhaps a visit would be in order."

Giggling, Sheala nodded. "Lonely widows are a specialty of Ban's."

A resigned expression settled on Teena's face. "I think that for the duration of their visit, I'll be assigning the older maids to the tower rooms."

Sosha began to giggle, but Teena raised her hand to forestall any comments. "I know, Ban loves all women. However, I don't think he'll be able to sweet-talk his way around Auctia and Sarti."

Chuckling, Denieen agreed. "Marti won't tolerate any foolishness. If Ban doesn't behave, she'll put him over her knee."

Still giggling, Sheala interjected, "But Ban may enjoy the spanking."

Throwing her hands up in frustration, Teena rose to leave. "Then I expect you to keep him under control. You too, Sosha. Deni told me he asked you to marry him. If you'd agreed, I wouldn't have these worries."

With those final words, Teena exited the room, the three young women she left behind laughing uproariously.

* * * * *

Two and one half weeks later, late in the afternoon, Ban guided the *Wanderer* down on the landing pad adjacent to the *Leonine* compound. As soon as the stairway was rolled to the side of the ship, Sheala sprinted up the stairs, flinging herself into her brother's arms when he appeared in the doorway. Chatting gaily, she grabbed his hand and pulled him down the steps. They were closely followed by Brianna, who carried her son, and Kahn, Feni and Bjin. Ban was the last one out of his ship, carefully closing the door and setting the ship on defense mode. One could never be too careful, and there were certainly those on Gattan who did not agree with this visit.

"Welcome to my hold, Dragon of the Alalakans," Drefes said formally as he clasped Char's forearm.

Grinning, Char returned his host's grasp.

Wendjas slapped Char on the back, knocking him

forward two steps. "Brianna," he said with a twinkle in his eye, "perhaps you're tired of this weak, indolent Drakian and would be interested in a strong Gattan for a husband."

Shifting her son to her other shoulder, Brianna laughed then shook her head. "Somehow, Wendjas, I can't see Deni agreeing to share you. And a Gattan with an angry wife…"

"…is not envied by his friends," Wendjas finished with a bark of laughter. "You're right. If I so much as looked at another woman, Deni would castrate me."

"A good thing for you to remember, Husband," Deni said as she took Connor from Brianna's arms. "He's grown so much since I last saw him. Does he sleep well at night?"

As Deni led Brianna towards the ground transports waiting for them, Ban grabbed Sheala, tossed her into the air, then hugged her tightly when he caught her. "Married life seems to agree with you, Coz."

Laughing, Sheala threw her arms around Ban's neck and hugged him back. "Oh, it does, Ban. Marljas has the most amazing tongue."

Marljas made a grab for his wife. "Sheala!"

Ban swung her away. "Oh?"

Sheala nodded. "Oh, yes. All Gattan have tongues with all these wonderful bumps on them. And when Marljas starts licking my—"

Marljas yanked Sheala out of Ban's arms and into his own. He kissed her to shut her up, then threw her over his shoulder. Ignoring her screech, the sharp smacks on his ass, and the tail wrapped around his neck, he trotted towards the house.

Ban glanced at Char. "I'd say that marriage is working just fine." Rubbing his hands together, he looked at Wendjas. "I don't want to be impolite, but—have you got anything to eat? I'm starved."

As Wendjas led Ban and Char away, Drefes turned to Bjin, Kahn and Feni. "Welcome to my hold. My wife has prepared a light repast since our evening meal is served late. Please, join us."

Bjin bowed. "Your courtesy is much appreciated, Drefes of Gattan. I will be honored to join you."

Kahn just grunted and nodded his head. Feni remained stoically silent.

Wondering what his youngest son had gotten the family into, Drefes led them to the last transport.

When they reached the house, Marljas was introducing everyone to his mother. "Mother, I would make known to you my bloodsister, Alalakan dem al' Brianna, her husband Alalakan don al' Chardadon and my nephew by bloodbond, Connor. I would also make known to you Alalakan don al' Bandalardrac, Prince Hardan. Just coming in with Father are Kahn and Feni of Mediria and Bjin of Deslossia."

Teena curtsied formally. "Welcome to my hearth, Dragon of the Alalakans, Prince Hardan, Brianna bloodsister to my son, everyone else. Your arrival is greeted with joy."

Char bowed his head in greeting and answered just as formally. "Well met, Teena Seenasdotir. We accept your hospitality with delight and honor."

Smiling warmly, Teena opened her arms and gave Brianna a firm hug. "My eldest son and his wife tell me that Marljas chose well when he blooded you."

Returning Teena's embrace, Brianna answered, "I blooded myself, Teena Seenasdotir. I didn't give your son much choice in the matter."

Chuckling, Drefes replaced his wife and also hugged Brianna warmly. "Welcome to our family. I didn't think there was anyone in the universe more impetuous than Marljas."

Tilting her head back, Brianna looked up into the face that looked so much like Marljas'. "I know a good thing when I see it."

He frowned. "Know a good thing when you see it?"

Laughing, Marljas swung Brianna out of his father's arms, and folded her into a huge hug. "Never mind, Father, you'll get used to it."

Sosha, who had been standing quietly next to Teena, stepped forward, locked arms with Ban and pulled him before her host and hostess. "Brother by blood, say hello to your host and hostess."

His usual devilish grin on his face, Ban bowed low, raising Teena's hand to his lips.

"A truly beautiful woman, these younger buds pale in comparison next to you."

Drefes stiffened, but Teena gently disengaged her hand. "I see your reputation is well warranted, Bandalardrac Hardan," she answered with a sigh.

Wendjas clapped his hand on his father's shoulder while Marljas laughed outright.

"Ban," Brianna warned, "you promised to be good."

Turning back to Sosha, Ban hugged her again and innocently answered Brianna. "But, Coz, what have I done?"

Chuckling, Deni laid Connor into Teena's arms. "Here, Teena, your newest grandson. I'll deal with Bandalardrac."

Linking her arm in Ban's she led him towards the veranda. "There are some friends of Teena's here who may interest you, Ban. All are widows."

A glint appeared in Ban's eye. "Widows?"

"Widows," she stated firmly.

"Deni, I think I'm going to like Gattan. Sheala was saying something about Gattan tongues…"

"How am I ever going to keep my eye on him," Brianna muttered as Wendjas linked his arm through hers.

"Don't worry, Bri," Sheala called after her. "You haven't met the widows yet."

Teena was enjoying herself cuddling Connor in her arms. With a fond grin, Drefes gently admonished her. "Wife, our guests are hungry."

With a smile, Teena handed Connor back to Brianna. "He's a fine son. Forgive me. Please, join us. There are refreshments on the veranda. Now, how sure are you that Deni's child will be a girl?"

Chuckling, everyone followed Teena outside.

* * * * *

"Well, Marljas," Brianna asked in a somewhat worried tone later that evening. They were relaxing in the sitting room of the suite she and Char had been given. "Did I pass muster?"

Marljas looked at Brianna with a confused expression on his face.

Giving her husband a punch on the shoulder, Sheala answered for him. "The minute Deni put Connor into Teena's arms, you won her over. Deni said that babies are her weakness. You gave her another grandchild. She'd fight tooth and claw for you."

Marljas nodded affirmatively all the while his wife was speaking. "Truly, bloodsister, you are one of us, a *Leonine*. You will always be welcome here."

"What about me, Coz?" asked Ban with a grin.

Marljas grinned widely. "Judging from what Sheala heard my mother's friends whispering to her, you may not be able to leave."

Ban's grin grew wider, but he wisely refrained from comment.

Char, however, had more serious thought on his mind. "What of this summons by Queen Mattis?"

Marljas shrugged. "It was to be expected. Father is uncle to the king, and his son has married a woman from another planet. They also want to meet the alien woman I took as bloodsister." He grinned. "As Brianna says, I've rocked their world."

Ban rose and headed for the decanter of wine. "And everybody says I cause trouble. You've managed to defy two old traditions in less than a month."

"He didn't exactly defy tradition, Ban," Sosha said from where she sat. "It just that no one else from such a high-ranking family has ever married or bloodbonded with an alien."

Ban's grin grew wider. "I knew there was something about him I always liked."

"Nevertheless," Char interjected. "What kind of reception will we get?"

"The family has been invited to a formal reception," Denieen said from the open door. "The atmosphere will be — cordial. And Brianna and Sheala will be presented to the entire court."

"Another formal presentation," Brianna muttered. "Findal of Mediria jumped off his throne and hugged me. What in the world will the Gattan queen do?"

Chuckling, Char stroked his wife's shoulder and said, "I doubt very much if Mattis will come down off her throne to hug you, my love."

"Yeah, more she'll more likely want to kick my ass for bonding myself to a cousin of her husband."

Deni sighed. "She is much too dignified to 'kick your ass'."

"Don't worry," Deni interjected with a chuckle. "The thirty days at half tariff the King of Mediria granted Gattan to celebrate Sheala's marriage has gone a long way to smoothing your acceptance."

"Not to mention the Alalakan concessions we'll be adding," Char added.

"And Mattis has an eye for beauty," Deni continued.

"She'll simply adore that dress you brought her. I can guarantee that she has nothing like it in her wardrobe. You can be sure she'll wear it to the reception which will be held later that night."

"Once women start talking about dresses, it's time for me to leave," Ban said as he rose and stretched. "It has been a long day, and I'm ready for bed."

"Alone?" asked every female voice in the room.

His devilish grin stretching across his face, Ban winked as he exited the room.

Chapter Twenty-Four

໖

"They've arrived?"

Kadis nodded. "The queen had them shown to apartments in the visitors' wing. She's not going to meet them until the formal presentation."

Settling into her chair, Jadis pursed her lips. "What's my dear sister up to now? Why didn't she meet them immediately?"

Cadan sauntered into the room and flopped onto the settee. "She wants the entire court assembled when she grants her approval for Marljas' marriage to the Drakian woman, of course."

Jadis looked from her daughter to her son. He was handsome, the masculine version of Kadis, but then, with her as his mother, why wouldn't he be? She smiled. She'd had many advantageous marriage offers for him. All she had to do was determine which would most advance her political plans.

He smirked at her.

A ripple of discontent tripped up her spine, and her smile disappeared.

Arrogant—male! Looks should have been enough for him! He should have had a malleable personality and just enough intelligence to follow her orders. Instead, he'd been born with a sharp wit and the quick intelligence Kadis should have gotten. A smart son! What had she ever done to deserve one such as he!

"Yes, Mother?"

The look he bestowed upon her was entirely too knowing. She should never have divulged her entire plan to him.

"Everything is ready?"

He inclined his head. "Of course."

A small flutter of unease swam through Jadis' stomach. Cadan wouldn't go against her orders, would he?

Rising from his chair, he walked across the room and poured a glass of wine. Turning, he returned to her side. "You look thirsty, Mother."

Sighing, she squashed her unease and accepted the goblet he proffered. He was only a male. He wouldn't dare defy her. "I am. Thank you."

Leaning over he kissed her cheek. "I'm off then to check on final preparations. I'll see you later."

"Don't forget to wear your black vest. It sets off the stripes in your hair, and you do want to look your best."

He inclined his head. "Of course, Mother. Everything will be as you wish." After a last smile, he left the room.

Kadis sniffed. "He could have gotten me some wine too. I'm his sister, after all."

After draining the wine from her goblet, Jadis set it down and rose. "Never mind about him. He's male and understands his place." She turned to face her daughter. "You know what you must do?"

Kadis preened. "As soon as Marljas introduces his Drakian wife, I challenge her for Marljas on the grounds of a previous betrothal."

Biting off a curse — why couldn't Kadis have at least *some* of her brother's intelligence — Jadis shook her head. "No! Not a previous betrothal. We agreed that wouldn't work because Teena didn't accept our offer. You must remember that! You must challenge on the grounds that Marljas is too close to the royal line to marry an alien. Any daughters he sires could become heirs to the throne."

Kadis began to pout. "Even if something would happen to the queen and her daughters, Denieen's daughter would be next in line."

Her temper already rising, Jadis made no attempt to hide the anger in her voice. "Silly twit. Denieen has sons! If Marljas sires a daughter, she would become queen. Don't you want to be the mother of the queen?"

"But Denieen's pregnant, and she said it was a girl."

Jadis stopped her pacing. "Denieen's pregnant? Why didn't you tell me?"

Swallowing, Kadis shrugged. "I was so angry at Marljas and his mother and..." She swallowed again. "I forgot."

Kadis began to pace again. "So she's pregnant. There's no guarantee the child will be a daughter."

"Marljas' alien bloodsister told Denieen it would be a girl."

Fixing her stare on her daughter, Jadis snapped, "How can she know this? Was she tested?"

Her daughter shrank farther into her chair. "I don't know. That's what I heard Denieen tell Teena."

Grabbing a small figurine from a table, Jadis threw it against the wall. "Impossible! No one can just look at a pregnant woman and tell if an unborn child will be a boy or girl."

"I'm just telling you what I heard."

Glaring at the smashed figurine, Jadis ignored her daughter. The right potion in her drink, and Denieen wouldn't have another baby. Enough of the potion, and Denieen wouldn't be around to interfere with her plans.

She glanced back to where her daughter was hunched in her chair. "How many times have I told you to sit up straight? Proper posture is important. Now go get dressed. Your new orange gown is ready. I want you looking your best so everyone can see how much more attractive you are than a washed-out Drakian slut."

Smile returning to her face, Kadis rose to her feet. "Yes,

Mother. I *am* much more attractive than she is."

In the back room of a tavern on the other side of the city from the palace, Cadan accepted the goblet the hooded Gattan offered to him. "Everything is ready?"

The man nodded once.

Cadan sipped his wine. "Good. I'll see you later then."

"The secret door?"

"The bolt is already thrown. The men will have no trouble entering the palace."

As the other man left, Cadan gulped his wine. Treason was thirsty work. He refilled his goblet and drank that. Deceiving his mother made him even thirstier.

* * * * *

"I don't know why I came," Sosha mumbled as she glared at herself in the mirror. "I'm not important. Nobody wants to see me."

Sheala chuckled and pulled Sosha's bodice down.

Sosha grabbed it with both hands and pulled it back up again.

Sheala stomped her foot. "Sosha! You have great breasts. Why do you keep trying to hide them?

"They're my breasts! If I want to hide them, I will." She yanked her bodice up farther. "I'm not a Drakian who's happy to show off her breasts to anyone who wants to look, you know. Besides, they're full of scars."

Sheala grinned. "You're bloodsister to a Drakian, and those scars are barely noticeable."

Sosha scowled back. "Then *you* show off *your* breasts. Go topless if you want."

"Your queen and her court would really love that."

"The men would, Coz," Ban quipped as he sauntered into

the room. "I thought you decided to be circumspect and dress conservatively."

Sheala glanced over her shoulder at him. "Me, yes. But Sosha's a heroine. She could get away with showing a little cleavage."

Chuckling, Ban nodded to Sosha. "Sheala's right, love."

Sosha shook her head. "I'm not a heroine. I'm an object to be pitied. I've not even heard from my mother and father, I'm so pathetic."

Pulling her against his chest, he tsked. "You aren't pathetic. You are the bravest and most desirable woman I know."

Sniffing, Sosha pushed herself out of his arms. "Obstinate, inflexible Medirian! But you'll see. Just wait."

Before Ban could reply, there was a knock on the door and a servant entered. "A message for Prince Hardan."

As Ban read it, Sheala glanced at the servant, looked away, then stared at her more closely. Something about her piqued Sheala's curiosity. Perfectly coiffed dark hair, black skin, immaculate uniform. She looked like all the other servants Sheala had seen, though they did have different skin tones depending on their tribes.

"Something wrong, Sheala?"

Blinking, Sheala turned her attention to Ban.

He had his usual smile on his face.

She blinked.

What was that strange look in his eyes?

Sheala blinked again.

He was grinning at her. "Something in your eye, Coz?"

"What?" She shook her head. "No. I..."

"Finish helping Sosha with her dress. And if she wants her breasts completely covered, that's her decision. Once we get her off of Gattan again, we'll work on her inhibitions. Now,

I have to go. I'll see you later at the reception."

"But..."

Before she could finish, both Ban and the servant were gone.

Sheala frowned at the door then glanced over to Sosha. "Did you think there was something strange about that servant?"

The Gattan met Sheala's gaze in the mirror. "No. I didn't really notice."

A strong grip on the servant's upper arm, Ban pulled her down the hallway and into a small alcove. No one was around. "Do you know what's in this message?"

"Of course."

"Send it to Kavlalardrac—top priority."

She nodded.

Ban stared at her. Her disguise was excellent. Anyone looking at her would be sure she was a member of the *Pantra* tribe. "Does anyone here know who you are?"

The disguised Medirian stared back. Her answer was an emphatic "No!"

"I want you off Gattan by tomorrow. Something about your disguise alerted my cousin. If she noticed, the Gattan will. We don't want any more dead assassins."

The servant bowed her head. "I'll be gone by morning, Sir."

Cursing silently as the woman walked away, Ban tore the messages into small pieces and placed them in a small pocket sewn into the waistband of his pants. It was damned hard to place spies on Gattan. But if Sheala looked twice at her, then a Gattan would too, if one already hadn't. Kavlalardrac would not be happy to lose this woman.

Then he smiled. With the story Sosha had to tell about her kidnapping, the servant's disappearance from the palace could be turned into an advantage. Everyone would assume she'd been kidnapped too, especially after a few well-placed rumors about more girls disappearing were spread on Gattan. Someone in league with the slaver-pirates was sure to slip up. With any luck, he'd soon be able to let Kavlalardrac know who the pirates' contact on Gattan was.

He slid his finger along his waistband. First, though, he had to make sure the Gattan queen survived the night. And there was no way to warn her or anyone else of the plot without revealing his identity as the Monarch's Assassin. Luckily, the Medirian ambassador knew exactly who he was. Time to pay a visit to Aunt Jessilindra. Between them, they should be able to come up with a plan.

"Trouble follows you like a jealous lover, Bandalardrac."

Chuckling, Ban kissed the ambassador on the cheek. "It's nice to see you, too, Aunt Jess."

Snorting, she waved him to a chair.

He glanced around the room. They seemed to be alone. "The room's secure?"

She pressed a button on a console next to her chair. A soft Medirian lullaby began to play softly. "It is now."

Ban cocked an eyebrow.

She smiled. "Electronic scrambling waves embedded in the music which interferes with their listening devices. The Gattan remain frustrated on how to counter it. Now, what do you want?"

"There's a plot to murder the queen and her family at tonight's reception."

She stared at him over steepled fingers.

"Her sister is behind it."

Jessilindra shook her head. "We knew Jadis was envious of her sister. She feels Krondal's mother should have ordered him to marry her, because she was his mother's first choice.

But Krondal preferred the younger sister Mattis, and his mother agreed with his choice. Jadis is a bitter woman, but I never thought she'd physically harm her sister and niece." She looked up at Ban. "They'll never be able to get weapons into the reception room. Every door is monitored by listening and tracking devices."

Ban laced his fingers behind his head and stretched his legs out before him. "They're going to use traditional weapons."

She cocked an eyebrow. "Traditional weapons?"

"Bows, arrows, swords. They'll kill someone just as dead as a laser."

She shook her head. "This can't be. This just doesn't sound like Jadis. The queen dying now is completely at odds with the plan she's been formulating over the last year."

"Oh?"

She nodded. "Her plan was to marry her daughter to Marljas and have Kadis produce a daughter."

Ban snorted. "That girl would be pretty far down the line of succession."

"Not if something happened to the royal family. Krondal and Marljas are cousins."

"But Wendjas is older. Denieen's daughter would be queen."

She stared into her nephew's eyes. "Do you think she'd stop at killing Denieen if she'd already killed the queen?"

Ban nodded. "Good point."

Jessilindra rose. "But her entire plan revolves around Kadis marrying Marljas. She can't dispose of the queen until that part of her plan bears fruit. Why would she decide on assassination now? If the queen and her daughters die, the line of succession passes to Drefes. Teena would be declared queen."

Ban shrugged. "I'd show you the message if I hadn't

destroyed it."

"Was it the original?"

Ban shook his head. "A copy. Sent from her son Cadan to a compatriot here in the palace."

Her head snapped up. "Cadan? I'll be damned. The little bastard has balls after all."

Ban stared at her. "He's acting without his mother's knowledge?"

Tapping her chin with a finger, she shook her head. "No, but I'd say he's modifying whatever plan she had for tonight." She smiled at Ban. "He's as good an actor as you are. Instead of playing a rake, however, he plays the spoiled young male Gattan very well, interested only in clothing, hunting, and drinking. We started watching him more closely when the last girl disappeared. He bought a new hunter and paid off outstanding debts to his tailor."

"He's involved with slavers?"

She nodded. "We don't have definite proof, or I'd have given it to Mattis."

Ban pursed his lips. "Hathnic has been seen with the slavers."

His aunt's curse was impressive. "That explains the hooded Gattan my people can't identify then." She leveled a stare at Ban. "You will take care of him?"

Ban nodded. "When I find him. Do you think he'll be involved tonight?"

Jessilindra pursed her lips and stared blankly. Then she shook her head. "Not directly. His price would be far higher than Jadis would be willing to pay, especially to someone she thinks is a Gattan."

Again, Ban nodded. "What about the daughter? Is she involved?"

His aunt shook her head. "No. She's completely self-centered and interested only in her own wants and needs.

What's more, she has a habit of bragging to her sycophants about everything she thinks she'll get. Marljas Drefeson was one of them. Her return to the palace was not pleasant." His aunt grinned. "Jadis would not convey all of her plans to her daughter. Everyone would know them in twenty-four hours."

"Okay, she's stupid. That doesn't change the facts, though." Leaning forward, Ban rested his elbows on his knees and laced his fingers together. "So, how do we stop the queen's nephew from murdering her tonight? My identity must remain secret."

She sighed. "I know."

Ban waited, absolutely sure that Jessilindra had a plan. Kavlalardrac was smart and devious. Aunt Jessilindra was even smarter and more devious.

"I must go pay my respects to Bjin."

Ban frowned. "The Deslossian? How can he help?"

Her lips twitched with a secretive smile. "There are things even you don't know, Bandalardrac."

Chapter Twenty-Five

so

The doors opened, and Sheala gripped Marljas' hand tighter as she walked with him into the reception room. "Are you sure I look all right?" Her shimmery pink gown was conservative by Drakian standards—her entire bosom was covered. However, the lightly boned, corseted bandeau top left her shoulders and arms completely bare. Traditional Gattan gowns, while usually leaving the wearer's arms bare, had high necks.

He lifted their joined hands and kissed the back of hers. "You're the most beautiful woman here."

"Even though I'm not Gattan?"

Halting, he looked down into her eyes. "Especially because you're not Gattan."

The usual shiver whirled up Sheala's spine. Squeezing his hand, she stepped closer to his side.

Stopping just inside the door at the top of a short stairway, he tilted his head and motioned his chin forward. "What do you think?"

The half-dozen steps allowed Sheala to see the entire room, a room far larger than she'd imagined, larger than the throne room of the Medirian king. To her left, a huge set of double doors was closed. A single guard holding a long spear stood on each side. A waist-high, white shield with a red flame in the center rested on the floor before each guard. At the opposite end of the long room from the doors was a raised dais. A long row of tables lined two sides of the hall. A single table with six chairs was on the dais.

Two tables sat on angles on each side of the dais. Whoever sat there would be seen by the entire assembly.

Sheala looked up. A balcony at least fifteen feet from the ground hugged the walls on three sides. At measured intervals, torches flickered from its railing. She stared. "Torches? In this day and age?"

At her side, Marljas chuckled. "They're holograms. Fiberoptic lighting is embedded in the walls. You must admit they add atmosphere, though."

She snorted. Atmosphere. Like the people milling about the hall needed any reminders of Gattan's violent past. All of the men—and most of the women—wore sleeveless tunics, vests, or dresses so their arms were bare. Sparkling jewels were as obvious as challenge scars, flashing from ears, necks, arms, wrists, rings, and belts.

"Well, now I know why you dressed like you did for my birthday party," she muttered more to herself than to Marljas as she glanced at the open, sleeveless vest he wore. The vest was heavily embroidered with gold and jewel-toned threads, but he wore it hanging open. The white scars on his brown arms and chest were visible to everyone. Depending on how he moved, the vest gaped, and the Drakian lion and dragon tattoo he wore appeared. Already, a few Gattans they'd passed in the hallway had wrenched their heads around for a second look.

Red diamonds glittered from his belt and wrist sheaths. The bands around his upper arms, however, held rarer jewels, jewels that matched her own.

Sheala glanced down at her wrists. She too wore red diamonds, but hers were far more precious than most, being so pale they looked pink. Marljas had presented her with matching wrist sheaths, thick mating bands for her upper arms, a ring, earrings, and a choker necklace containing the rare gems a week after they'd arrived on Gattan.

Another woman stared at her jewels.

"Um, how rare are these pink diamonds?" Sheala murmured.

He chuckled again. "I will not have anyone doubt my commitment to you. No other woman will wear as many as you do. These are from a small cache I discovered a few years ago in our mine. We kept all of them."

"You have a diamond mine?"

"Only one. But it's very productive," he answered with a grin. "The *Jagar* control most of the diamond mines. *Leonine* has most of the gold mines."

Sheala shook her head. "There's still so much I don't know. Do all the tribes have mines of some kind?"

"No, but I don't have time to tell you about it now. Mother and Father are already seated, and Deni and Wendjas are joining them. We must go."

"I don't see Brianna and Char."

"That's because we're standing behind you," her sister-in-law said with a chuckle as she and Char stopped beside them. "Damn, but this looks like a scene out of a trashy medieval romance novel," she added as she looked out over the crowd.

"A what?" Sheala asked as she looked back out over the crowd.

"It's a—" Brianna began, but Char sighed, cupped his hand under her elbow, and led her down the short staircase before she could finish.

"So what happens now?" Sheala asked as she watched her brother and sister-in-law meander through the crowd. They caused quite a stir since both displayed their Alalakan dragons blatantly. Wearing traditional Drakian clothing, Char was bare-chested, and Brianna's dress left her right shoulder bare.

"We eat first," her husband answered. "Then Mother will present you all to the queen. Are you ready?"

"As long as the meat's cooked."

Marljas chuckled. "The look on your face the first time you saw *alathan* was priceless."

She snorted. "Spicy raw meat isn't exactly a delicacy to me, and I don't care what you Gattan think."

As her husband chuckled and squeezed her hand, she looked out over the crowd again. Striped, spotted, brown, tan and black Gattans milled about the room, singly, in pairs, or small groups. Others already sat at the tables. She even noticed Drakians, Medirians and Varcians, part of their ambassadorial parties, no doubt, but there were no white Gattans anywhere to be seen.

"Why aren't there any *Snopards* here?"

Tucking her hand under his arm, Marljas guided her down the stairway. "With the exception of the twenty-four priestess-warriors who guard the queen and her children and a few of their elders who sit on her council, the *Snopards* prefer to remain on their lands."

As they meandered across the room, more than a few people looked askance at them. A few men nodded to Marljas, but none attempted to talk to him.

Most women stared at Sheala.

Straightening her shoulders, she held her head high. "You'd think they'd never seen a Drakian before."

"None wearing so many of our rarest jewels." Marljas patted her hand. "Most Gattans have never left our planet and don't associate or socialize with ambassadors from other planets. They all know Kadis boasted she would wed me, yet here I am with you close to my side, and you wear a pink diamond armband, as do I, a declaration of our marriage. They're confused. Few want to dare the wrath of the queen's sister until they know how the queen feels."

"I'll probably say something stupid when I'm introduced."

He kissed her hand again, which caused more conversations to stop and more Gattans to gape. Gattans normally didn't show affection to members of the opposite sex in public. "I think Deni is far more worried about what

Brianna might say. You're used to socializing with royalty."

"Royalty that's almost family. I don't think your queen plans on hugging me."

His laughter had even more heads turning towards them. "She'll love you just as I do."

"Yeah, that's what everybody keeps saying. Why don't I believe you?"

Before he could answer, a plainly dressed man standing on a landing on the opposite side of the room pounded a staff against the floor. "Her Majesty, Queen Mattis and her consort King Krondal."

"This way," Marljas murmured after they bowed and curtsied with everyone else. "The meal will be served now that the queen and king are here."

She sighed when she saw the table he led her to. "Naturally we have to sit way up here where everyone can see us."

Marljas bent and whispered in her ear. "Krondal is my cousin, *Cheta*. We're family."

As Sheala and Marljas seated themselves, whispers and mutters of surprise about the queen's apparel drifted to her ears. She smiled. The queen had obviously received Brianna's gift and decided to wear it.

Seated between her brother and husband, Sheala leaned forward, caught Brianna's gaze and murmured, "She likes the dress."

Brianna smiled. "Deni said she would."

"That means she'll support my marriage, right?"

Sliding his arm around his sister's shoulders, Char hugged her. "Don't worry, Shea. The queen is a smart woman. I don't think it matters to her that you're not Gattan. However, the trade concessions from Mediria and the Alalakans will go a long way in convincing those who might object to your marriage."

Sheala sniffed. Char always considered the business angle.

Her sister-in-law looked directly into her face. Her voice was a soft murmur. "This isn't like you. Why are you so nervous? Marljas loves you. He'd leave Gattan to keep you."

Sheala sighed. "I know. But he shouldn't have to."

With a low chuckle, Brianna shook her head. "You worry too much. Now be quiet and eat your meal. It smells delicious."

For the next two hours, conversation was light as everyone enjoyed the meal. Finally, after the final course, fresh Gattan pears in a tangy yet sweet sauce, Denieen nudged Sheala from her other side. "Hush, Teena is ready to introduce everyone."

Taking a deep breath, Sheala again laced her fingers through Marljas'.

Rising from the end of the table closest to the queen, Teena stepped to the center of the floor before the dais and curtsied to the queen and king. "Your Majesties, thank you for your cordial invitation. My guests, family and I were more than pleased to accept."

As Teena continued, Sheala gazed at the woman who would decide the fate of her marriage.

The resemblance between Queen Mattis and her niece Kadis was obvious though the queen's facial stripes dipped down over her forehead. She was also plumper. And instead of the pouting expression Kadis had worn every time Sheala had seen her, Mattis was smiling—widely. The shimmery blue dress she wore looked lovely on her, even if it did have loose sleeves that completely covered her arms and a lower neckline that showed more skin than any other woman's in the room, except Denieen's. Still, the square neck completely covered her bosom. Brianna had said it was even conservative by her own planet's standards.

Teena herself was a sight to behold with her still-golden

hair swept on top of her head held in place with red diamond-studded pins. Her traditional yellow dress was sleeveless and had the usual high neck. The bodice was ornate. Bright threads and precious jewels glittered when ever she moved. The full skirt was long and brushed the floor. Her marriage bands flashed with red fire.

Sheala turned her attention to the king. Typically *Leonine*, Krondal's resemblance to his cousins was obvious. His long golden hair was brushed back behind tufted ears. His eyes were golden, his nose flat, his smile wide. He had a neatly trimmed golden beard. His ornate tunic was sleeveless, and his muscular arms bore a multitude of white scars. His smile was open and welcoming.

Sheala smiled to herself. He looked like a man she could like.

A hiss and snort drew her attention to the other angled table. Kadis sat there, next to an older *Tigre* woman, obviously her mother. Next to her, dressed in black, sat a young *Tigre* man, probably Kadis' brother. Other members of the *Tigre* tribe sat with them.

Sheala concentrated on Kadis and her mother. Both women were dressed traditionally, Kadis in orange, her mother in red. Both women displayed numerous challenge scars on their arms. Both women looked at Sheala with hate in their eyes.

Lifting her chin, Sheala straightened even more and stared back at them. Smiling slightly, she nodded her head.

Kadis' hiss was almost audible.

Marljas squeezed her hand again.

Sheala turned her attention back to the queen.

"You have guests with you, Teena."

Smiling, her mother-in-law nodded. "Kahn and Beti, Aradabs from Mediria. A third, Feni, stays in the apartments you so thoughtfully provided as nurse to an infant that also accompanies us."

Seated at the end of the table, both Kahn and Beti stood, bowed their heads and sat back down without uttering a word.

Queen Mattis smiled at them. "Welcome. The ambassador from Mediria has often boasted of Aradab fighting skills. Does she speak truly?"

Beti looked first at Kahn then at Teena. Then she shrugged, rose, and bowed again. "We have some small skill. As to how our fighting style compares to Gattans', you'd do better to ask your niece." Bowing once more, Beti sat back down.

The queen turned to her niece. "Kadis?"

Anger flashed across the younger woman's features, and she clenched her hands before her.

Whispers floated around the room.

Her mother rose and quickly stepped forward. "When Kadis visited with Teena and her family, she and the female Aradab—sparred. Kadis found her to be—skilled."

"Why that hateful—bitch!" Sheala hissed, using one of Brianna's favorite words.

Marljas squeezed her hand. "Nothing will be accomplished by shaming her," he murmured. "Besides, it's for Beti to say something."

Muttering under her breath, Sheala pulled her hand from Marljas' and clasped her hands in her lap. Just let that bitch say something to or about her.

"A story I want to hear later," Queen Mattis was saying as she stared at her sister and niece. She turned back to Teena. "Your other guests?"

"Bjin of Deslossia," Sheala's mother-in-law said.

Hand over his heart, Bjin rose from where he sat next to Beti and bowed.

A white-skinned woman with white hair completely dressed in white rose from her seat next to the queen and stepped around the table and down off the dais. Gliding across the floor, she bowed to Bjin. "I am Jenia Drostinsdotir, *Snopard* priestess of the sixth level, leader of the queen's guards. Welcome, Bjin of Deslossia, favored of the All-Knowing Creator, Elder Brother to all *Snopards*."

Bjin shook his head. "I am no Elder, Jenia Drostinsdotir. I am just a guest."

"Elder brother of the *Snopards*? What does she mean?" Sheala whispered to her husband.

He shook his head. "I don't know. The queen and king look just as confused. We'll ask Deni later. She trained with the *Snopards*. Maybe she knows what he's talking about."

As the priestess reseated herself, Sheala started listening to the crowd. Questions meandered down tables as they had throughout the meal. Aradabs here? A Deslossian? Some voices were eager, some curious. Others were angry.

Sheala chuckled to herself. *Wait until she introduces Ban.*

"You bring unusual guests to us, Teena," the queen commented.

Sheala's mother-in-law nodded. "And one who had been lost to us. Your Majesties, Sosha Kanicsdotir returns to us, with her Brother by blood, Alalakan don al' Bandalardrac, Prince Hardan."

Uproar ensued as Ban pulled out Sosha's chair and led her around the table to stand at Teena's side. Grinning, he bowed to the queen as Sosha curtsied unsteadily.

Angry shouts exploded—some demanding Ban's death.

Across the room, the queen's sister smiled with delight.

Standing with his back to the room, Ban stared at the queen and continued to grin rakishly.

A slight smile on her face, Mattis held up her hand.

After a few minutes, the crowd quieted.

Sheala looked from the queen to Teena. She glanced at Deni. All three women looked extremely satisfied with themselves.

"Deni and Teena orchestrated this entire introduction," Sheala murmured.

Marljas chuckled then answered in a low voice. "Of course they did. You already know how sly Deni is. Don't ever underestimate the queen — or my mother either."

Mattis leaned forward. "Bandalardrac Hardan. More than a few of my subjects would see you gutted and hanged for the scavengers. Why did you kidnap the woman who now calls you bloodbrother?"

Crossing his arms over his chest, he continued to grin.

Sosha placed her hand on Ban's forearm. "Bandalardrac didn't kidnap me, Your Majesty."

"You went willingly? Even so, he broke many of our laws. Your mother did not give you permission to leave her home. What's more, I didn't give you permission to leave Gattan."

Mutters of satisfaction reached Sheala. Anticipation swirled through the crowd.

Sheala glanced across the room again.

Kadis was smiling gleefully, but her mother's expression was worried. Her gaze darted around the room.

Sosha shook her head. "I did *not* leave willingly, Your Majesty. I was kidnapped and sold into slavery, but not by my bloodbrother."

Expressions of shock and unease replaced those of anticipation coming from the crowd.

After swallowing once, Sosha continued, "I was drugged, tied and blindfolded. I didn't see my kidnapper."

"You have no idea who it was?" Krondal asked. The anger on his face was plain for everyone to see. So were indentations on his biceps from his claws.

Mutters drifted from the crowd.

One man, braver — or angrier — than the others shouted. "Then we have only the word of the Medirian bastard that he did not kidnap her."

Cocking an eyebrow, Ban tilted his head and continued to grin at the queen.

Sheala bit her lip. *Damn it, Ban*, she thought, *sometimes you're too arrogant for your own good.*

The queen again raised her hand for silence. "Sosha?"

Taking a deep breath, Sosha blinked, looked into the queen's eyes, and said, "I didn't see my kidnapper, but I did hear his voice, one that I will never forget. He was Gattan."

Shouts of denial and outrage raced through the crowd. Both the queen's and king's guards stepped forward. The queen signaled her chamberlain, who pounded his staff on the floor. Loud accusations and denials still rolled around the hall.

Marljas eased his chair back. His claws were fully extended.

Rising, Krondal flattened his palms on the table, leaned forward, and roared, "Silence!"

Slowly, the hall quieted.

No sooner had order been restored, though, than the door through which the queen and king had entered burst open, and a Gattan rushed into and through the crowd.

The guards on the dais drew their weapons.

The man ran straight for Sosha. Ban grabbed her and thrust her behind him. Pushing Ban out of the way, Sosha stepped towards the intruder. "Talon?"

His yell echoed from the ceiling. "Sosha!" When he reached her, he pulled her into his arms.

Sheala looked up at Marljas. "Who's that?"

Grinning, he sheathed his claws and relaxed. "Talon, her brother."

"Sosha has a brother?"

"Two, as a matter of fact," her husband answered.

Talon was shorter than many Gattan, a few inches short of six feet. Like the other members of the *Lynex* tribe, he didn't have a tail. His hair was brown like Sosha's, cut short. And he wore the uniform of the Gattan space fleet.

Sosha didn't bother to hide the tears rolling down her cheeks as she clung to him.

His arm around her waist, his brother turned to face the queen. His voice cracked like a whip. "Why wasn't my family informed Sosha was found?"

His tone shocked many in the crowd. Irate mutters about his lack of manners reached Sheala.

The queen's eyes widened for a moment then narrowed. She turned to her sister. "Jadis, you were instructed to inform Sosha's parents of her rescue and return."

A haughty expression on her face, the queen's sister shrugged. "They're unimportant servants. Her brother now knows she's back. It's enough."

"What a bitch," Brianna said loud enough for Sheala to hear.

Talon growled. Ban and Sosha each grabbed one of his arms. He wrenched free from Ban but tolerated his sister's grasp.

Rising, the queen paced to the edge of the dais and stared down at her sister. Anger colored her tone. "Enough?" She turned her attention to her subjects.

Wrapping herself in the royal authority of her office, she continued. "Enough? Everyone heard Sosha. She was kidnapped by a *Gattan*, sold to pirate slave-traders, then resold into slavery." She looked straight at Sosha and her brother. "Sosha, for the pain and degradation you suffered because of another Gattan's greed, all blooddebts owed by your family are acknowledged complete. Furthermore, because of Gattan laxness, I myself am partly responsible for your suffering. I owe blooddebt to you. In payment, I deed to you and your family the royal residence of Cloudhaven."

Gasps of surprise echoed around the room.

Jadis' voice drowned them out. Her chair rocked and clattered as she surged to her feet. "Cloudhaven is mine!"

Ire obvious on her face, Mattis turned to her sister. "Yours? A royal residence? I think not! Cloudhaven belonged to the royal family. You were permitted to use it and its tenants' rents. Now, however, I am giving it to one who truly deserves it. A message will be sent instructing its servants to pack whatever personal items you have there and send them to our family estate."

Her voice became strident. "*I* am the queen's sister!"

Mattis' voice drowned out Jadis'. "And *I* am the queen. Do you challenge *my* authority?"

Fists clenched, body tense, Jadis glared at her sister.

"And I thought Findal had problems with his relatives," Brianna murmured to anyone listening.

Sheala shushed her. The queen's public rebuke of her sister was too entertaining to miss.

Finally, Jadis swallowed. Nostrils flaring, she bowed her head. "Forgive me, Sister, but an entire estate? For only a year working perhaps a little harder than she would have here on Gattan?"

Her tone was terse, dismissive.

Sheala gasped.

Everyone else with her stiffened or muttered under their breaths.

Fists clenched, Ban stepped towards Jadis.

Sosha let go of her brother's arm, grabbed Ban's, and jerked him back. Stepping in front of him, she raised her chin and glared at the queen's sister. Her entire body shook as she lifted her hands to the neck of her dress. "Working a little harder than I would have worked here on Gattan? Working? Let me show you how hard I worked!"

Ripping her dress open, she let it fall to her waist. Sliding a knife from her wrist sheath, she sliced the silk chemise she wore in two. Standing half-naked before Jadis, she snarled. "Look, you arrogant, condescending woman, at what I endured." Using her knife, she ripped a gash in the dress's waistband. The dress pooled at her feet.

For long seconds silence reigned as everyone else in the room gaped at Sosha's body, at the white scars that crisscrossed her back, hips, thighs, breasts, and arms.

Gasps and moans filled the air. Women shrieked in anger and agony. Blood ran from more than one masculine arm.

Disgust obvious on her face, Jadis flopped back down into her chair.

Burying his face in his hands, Talon sank to his knees.

Holding herself erect, Sosha spat, "Tell me, Sister of the Queen, does normal work here on Gattan give a woman scars such as these? Does it rip her claws from her hands as she screams in agony? Does it mean constant rape by so many I stopped counting?" Tears began to stream down her face. "You have not answered me, Jadis Franasdotir. Do you think every servant should wear scars such as these for *work*?"

"That fucking bitch!" Dragging his shirt over his head, Ban leaped forward, dropped it over Sosha's, and hugged her to his side.

Blinking back her tears, she leaned against him.

Even without Medirian translators, many of the Gattans in the room understood Ban's tone perfectly. It quieted the crowd more quickly than anything else would have. Everyone wanted to see Jadis' reaction to the slur.

Anger replacing the disgust on her face, Jadis grabbed her son's arm and pushed him to his feet. "I have been insulted by this mewling Medirian fop, Cadan. Challenge him."

Stepping to Ban's side, Talon crossed his arms over his chest and glared at Cadan.

The blue-green dragon on Ban's shoulder glittered incandescently in the hall's bright light. The white scar on his shoulder also gleamed.

"You wear a Gattan scar, Bandalardrac," interjected the queen. "How did you come by it?"

Never taking his lazy gaze from the queen's nephew, he said, "Marljas and I had a—disagreement."

"Bloodfeud?"

Ban nodded.

Comments and exclamations ran like wildfire around the tables. Marljas was a very skilled warrior. If the Medirian fought him and was still alive...

"The outcome?" she asked.

"A draw."

The queen glanced at Marljas. "Is this true?"

Sheala winked at him.

Grinning, Marljas nodded. "The Medirian half-blood fought me to a draw—and cracked three of my ribs."

Mattis smiled at her nephew. "Interesting. Why didn't you finish the duel?"

"Both Denieen and my new bloodsister declared the feud satisfied."

As whispers about "new bloodsister" swirled around the tables, sweat began to bead on Cadan's brow. He stared at Ban.

"You little..." His mother raised her hand to slap her son.

"There will be no challenge to Bandalardrac Hardan, nephew to the King of Mediria," Queen Mattis stated. "Too many Gattan cuts on a Medirian prince would raise too many questions. I do not wish my hall overrun with assassins. What say you, Cadan?"

He bowed his head. "So be it, Aunt." His relief evident on his face at the way his aunt allowed him to save face, he sank back into his chair.

"She should've let Ban kick the shit out of him," Brianna

muttered.

Sheala nodded in agreement. Better yet, Jadis was the one who needed "the shit kicked" out of her.

Mattis stared at her sister until the other woman dropped her eyes. Then the queen turned to face the assembly. "Bandalardrac Hardan, I absolve you from all blame for Sosha Kanicsdotir's disappearance and recognize your bloodbond to her. Talon," she continued, "go fetch your parents. You have my permission to use your battle cruiser."

After a final snarl in Jadis' direction Talon bowed then took a step forward. "A boon, Your Majesty. When the Gattan who caused Sosha's suffering is found, he's mine."

Mattis nodded. "Your boon is granted."

After a quick bow, Talon gently grasped Sosha's hand and led her from the room.

After they were gone, the queen turned to her subjects. "I have learned that other girls have gone missing from their families. A full investigation has been launched. We will discover how many are responsible. And when they are found, their blood will run red." ·

Silence reverberated around the large room—except for Brianna's murmur, "Gattans are almost as bad as Klingons."

"Who?" Sheala whispered, her eyes on Ban.

He still stood before the queen, chest bare, arms crossed.

Settling herself back into her chair, the queen cocked an eyebrow at him. "Something else?"

For a moment he stared at her. Then his normal cocky grin appeared on his face. "Not yet." Bowing, he stepped back.

Sheala closed her eyes and shook her head. *One of these days, Ban will go too far.*

Chapter Twenty-Six

"Well," Mattis said as she leaned back in her chair. "This is becoming an interesting evening. What other surprises do you have for us, Teena?"

Gowns rustled as the women in the crowd shifted. Whispers danced from one to another. Rumors of Marljas' refusal of Kadis had been circulating as had his subsequent marriage to a Drakian since they'd arrived at the palace earlier that day.

Both the king's and queen's guards stepped back, still tense, more alert than they had been before.

Teena bowed her head and smiled. "Just a few, Your Majesty. As you know, with your permission, my sons and daughter-by-marriage have recently visited Drakan."

More whispers and rumbles rolled through the crowd. The queen had granted permission for a family to visit Drakan!

The queen nodded. "Your trading negotiations with the Alalakans went well?"

The whispers became louder. "Trading negotiations!" leaped from one mouth to another.

Glancing at the crowd, Teena smiled. "Far better than we had hoped, in a strange roundabout way."

"Oh?" The queen chuckled. "Then you do have more surprises?"

Again, Teena glanced about the room, making eye contact with as many people as she could. "Most of you know my son Marljas and his…impetuousness…"

More than a few of the men and women chuckled.

Sheala snorted. Marljas was *not* impetuous.

Teena continued. "As he mentioned, he's returned with a new bloodsister, Alalakan dem al' Brianna, wife to the Alalakan Dragon and mother of the Alalakan heir, adopted daughter of King Findalalardrac of Mediria." Holding out her hand, she motioned Brianna forward.

Ignoring the mutters, whispers, and exclamations that surged around the room, Brianna accepted Char's hand and allowed him to lead her to the dais. She stood with head held high, wearing the white-gold gown that bared her right shoulder, displaying the leaping, fire-breathing dragon tattoo. Red diamonds glittered in her hair and on her body—Gattan red diamonds. Necklace, rings, earrings, bracelets, a wrist sheath on her left wrist and, of course, her Medirian bridal net. She wore more red diamonds than any other woman in the room.

Queen Mattis inclined her head slightly. "Welcome, Alalakan dem al' Brianna. For a woman who's never been on our planet before, you display a great wealth of our red diamonds."

Brianna curtsied, her white gown billowing around her as she sank to the floor. Rising, she threw her long, auburn hair over her shoulder. The diamonds of her bridal net glittered with red fire. "Gifts from my husband, who has visited your planet before."

"Yes, earlier trade negotiations with the *Leonine*." The queen ignored the outraged hisses from some in the crowd and smiled a challenge. "Alalakan don al' Chardadon found our planet quite interesting."

Smiling in return, Char stepped forward and bowed his head. "Gattan is a fair planet with even fairer flowers."

Brianna placed her hand on his arm. "Fair flowers indeed. Wendjas Drefeson tried to gut him."

Mattis' smile never left her face. "Because he courted Denieen, I believe."

A wider smile appeared on Brianna's. "But he married

me."

Krondal stopped trying to hold back his laughter. "We'll be here all night while you two trade quips," he finally said.

Brianna crossed her arms over her chest. The diamonds on her wrist sheath sparkled.

The queen stroked the sleeve of her dress. "I thank you for your gift."

Brianna dipped another slight curtsy. "You're most welcome, Your Majesty."

Mattis leaned back. "Tell me, Alalakan dem al' Brianna, is your knife sharp?"

Brianna's smile widened. "Sharp enough to gut a man or woman."

Krondal chuckled again.

Mutters of approval about Brianna's conduct drifted from the crowd.

Mattis finally looked at Marljas. "You chose your bloodsister well, Marljas Drefeson."

Marljas bowed his head. Rising, he tightened his grip on Sheala's hand, pulled her up behind him, and led her forward to stand next to Brianna. "Not just a bloodsister, Your Majesty."

Teena raised an eyebrow at him then shook her head. "Your Majesty, my impetuous son also returned from Drakan with a wife, Alalakan dem al Sheala, sister of the Alalakan Dragon."

The whispers among the crowd were louder.

"He chose the Drakian over Kadis."

"He's married an alien."

"Why did his mother allow this?"

Ignoring the whispers, Sheala curtsied to the queen.

Then another voice rang out. "I, Kadis Jadisdotir, challenge this marriage."

"Stupid bitch," Sheala hissed mostly to herself as she rose to her feet.

As Kadis stepped around her table, she drew a claw across her arm. Blood trickled down over her wrist and dripped slowly to the floor.

"Blood challenge!" echoed through the crowd.

The queen eyed her niece. "Why?"

"My mother requested that Marljas become betrothed to me."

Behind her Jadis hissed with anger.

Her brother smirked, ducked when his mother tried to slap him, glared at her, then slipped away from the table, his face contorted with anger.

"Your Majesty," Teena stated in a flat voice. "Kadis speaks the truth. Her mother did propose a betrothal between my youngest son and her daughter. However, my family has never had any interest in a marriage between Marljas and Kadis. No betrothal was ever encouraged. I deny Kadis Jadisdotir's challenge as nothing more than wishful thinking on the part of her and her mother."

Jadis leaped to her feet again. "And what of the danger to the throne of Gattan!"

That comment shocked the crowd into silence.

Mattis stared at her sister, shock evident on her face. "Danger to Gattan? Because Marljas married a woman from another planet?" Nostrils flaring with obvious irritation, she leaned forward and stared at her sister. "Explain this danger to me, *Sister*."

"Why, if something happened to the royal family, the line of ascension would revert to Drefes' sons. Marljas' daughter could conceivably take the throne. Gattan does not want someone with alien blood to be her queen." Jadis crossed her arms over her breasts, a smug look on her face.

More whispers circulated around the room. More than a

few saw merit in Jadis' argument.

The queen stared at her sister thoughtfully. "Let me clarify your train of thought. If I die, and both my daughters die before they have daughters of their own, Gattan will turn to the cadet branch of the royal line for its queen. So, if Marljas had a daughter, she would be in line for the throne. But he is the younger brother. Wendjas and Denieen are certainly young enough to have female children. They too would have to die before any daughter of Marljas could ascend the throne." The queen paused. "That is assuming, of course, that Teena would not give birth to a daughter."

Chuckling, Teena shook her head. "I'm fairly certain I will not give birth to any daughter, Your Majesty."

The tension eased as many in the crowd chuckled with her.

Mattis smiled briefly at Teena then turned back to her sister. "A rather long and convoluted train of reasoning." She held up her hand when her sister would have spoken. "However, to give credence to your...worries, you fear a non-Gattan queen."

Jadis nodded. "As do many others in this hall."

The queen looked around.

So did Sheala.

Many in the assembly had risen, scowls on their faces.

Others were angry.

Some leaned back in their chairs, obviously amused.

Satisfaction evident on her face, Jadis continued. "If Marljas remains married to this—alien—Gattan could possibly have a queen with unacceptable blood."

"I see," Mattis said. "And what would you suggest?"

Sheala's blood ran cold, and she gripped Marljas' hand.

He squeezed it. Looking down at her, he mouthed, "Don't worry."

She blinked back a tear. *Don't worry? What else am I*

supposed to do? The queen is listening to her sister.

Jadis voice was triumphant. "The marriage should be dissolved, and Marljas should be married to Kadis."

The queen looked at Teena. "And what do you think of my sister's reasoning?"

Teena looked directly into Jadis' face. "If Your Majesty orders the dissolution of my son's marriage to a girl I find completely acceptable, well then, I remind you that my family holds a signed betrothal contract between Sosha Kanicsdotir and Marljas. Sosha would become Marljas' wife."

The queen waved her hands. "There you have it, Jadis. Marljas is contracted to marry Sosha. A marriage to Kadis is unnecessary."

Uncrossing her arms, Jadis snapped, "A man can have two wives."

Teena unsheathed a claw on her right hand and ran her left index finger over it. "And why does my son need two wives, Jadis? Why is it necessary for him to marry *your* daughter?"

Jadis straightened to her full height. "She is the queen's niece."

"But if the queen and her daughters were dead," gasps at her bluntness followed that comment from Teena, "Kadis would no longer be the queen's niece. Our previous queen and Krondal's father didn't have any daughters, which is why the royal line descends through him to his daughters. Jadis, neither you nor your daughter have any royal blood. Until she married Krondal, Mattis was not royal." It was unnecessary for Teena to continue because everyone in the room knew if Mattis and her daughters were dead, Teena herself would be queen with Denieen as her heir apparent because Drefes was the younger brother of Krondal's father.

"Of course," Teena continued after her short pause, "if Krondal survives the deaths of his current wife and daughters, he could always remarry. Then his new wife would become queen." Teena's voice grew stern. "However, nothing is going to happen to the queen or her children, Jadis, and I would sooner marry my son to a Varcian sand snake than to your spoiled daughter. What's more, I would rather see the royal line of Gattan pass to another family than to see either you or your daughter influencing a child that could become our next queen." Teena transferred her stare to the queen. "Your Majesty, never in all the history of Gattan has the royal family interfered in a mother's right to marry her son to whom she wants. I can't believe that it will do so now."

Chin quivering, fists clenched, Kadis stomped forward. "You would have your son married to a woman who won't share his bed!"

A look of amazement on her face, Teena allowed herself to gape at Kadis. Then she said, "A Drakian not share her husband's bed?"

Drefes, Wendjas, and Denieen smiled.

Brianna and Char chuckled.

Ban's laughter crashed against the walls of the hall.

Most in the crowd snickered. Every Gattan there knew about the Drakians' hedonistic proclivities.

Teena turned to Sheala. "Do you share my son's bed?"

Sheala grinned. "Of course." Looking over at Kadis, she added, "Watch and learn, idiot." Stepping in front of Marljas, she grabbed his braids and pulled his head down to hers. "Cooperate, or I'll ride your cock until you can't walk for a week," she murmured against his mouth.

"Promise?" was his answer.

Cupping her ass in his big hands, he pulled her close.

Letting go of his left braid long enough to reach down and hike her dress almost to her waist, Sheala wrapped her bare leg around his and snaked her tail up around his thigh.

He shifted, spreading his legs.

As she concentrated all her senses on Marljas, the sounds

around her became more and more muted until they finally disappeared. There was only him—his scent, his taste, his touch.

His lips slid across hers, soft at first, then more demanding.

She opened her mouth.

Their tongues parried with each other, danced apart, then mated.

"Mmmmmmmmmmm," escaped from her throat.

"Ahemmm."

An elbow from Brianna in her ribs got Sheala's attention, while a slap on the back of his head from his mother got Marljas'.

Slowly, Sheala uncurled her tail and slid her foot to the ground.

After one last squeeze of her buttocks, Marljas slid his hands up to her waist.

She let go of his braids and rested her head against his chest. After a long shaky breath, she turned, leaned back against him. After another shaky breath, she looked at the queen. "You wouldn't happen to have an empty bedroom close by, would you?" She glanced over at Kadis. "If she still doesn't believe that Marljas and I have a great sex life, she can come watch. She might learn a few things."

Krondal's bellow of laughter drowned out every comment, outraged and otherwise, that erupted from the crowd.

Mattis placed her hand on her husband's arm. When he stopped laughing, she said, "I think, Kadis, you are mistaken." Holding up her hand, she said, "Enough. Teena, your guests are welcome, and Brianna and Sheala are acknowledged as Marljas' bloodsister and wife. All treaties negotiated with the Alalakans are acceptable to me." She looked out over the crowd. "I suggest the rest of your tribes and families follow the *Leonine* lead. Gattan *will* learn to live with its neighbors—

peacefully."

"You fool!" Jadis screeched. "They are all beneath us. It is Gattan's destiny to conquer and rule. You are too softhearted to be queen. Krondal should have married me. Men would know their places, and we would rule the galaxy."

"Treason!" gasped some in the crowd.

Others murmured their agreement.

Only a few cheered.

As Mattis surged to her feet and leaned across the table, a thrumming noise reverberated around the hall, and two arrows thunked into the back of the chair where she'd been sitting.

"Assassins!" Krondal bellowed as he overturned the table, tackled his wife behind it, and covered her body with his.

More arrows buried themselves in the table.

Pandemonium ensued as more tables were flipped over. Stray plates rolled across the floor. Cutlery clattered.

Some of the queen's guests leaped across the tables.

Shouts and screams reverberated around the room.

"Get down!" Marljas commanded as he pushed Sheala to the floor and fell on top of her.

"This is not how I want to be underneath you!" Sheala yelled.

But Marljas was far stronger than she and kept her pinned to the floor.

She tried to wiggle free. "We have to help."

"Don't move," he snarled in her ear, "or I swear you will not sit for a week!"

Beneath him, Sheala froze. Were Gattan males allowed to talk like that to females?

An arrow thunked into the floor.

She looked out from under his arm. The shaft quivered

not two inches from his shoulder.

"Chardadon," Drefes yelled as he scrambled over the table towards his wife. "Get Brianna out of here. Wendjas, Deni must go too."

Both men hurried their wives out. Brianna led the way at a dead run, yelling for her son.

"Where's Bjin?" Char yelled as he shouldered past a Gattan who'd stepped in front of him.

"Gone!" Ban yelled back. He stood with Kahn and Beti. All three were using their bodies to block any arrows that might fly after the retreating couples.

Char stopped at the door and looked back. "Sheala!"

"Marljas has her," Ban yelled. "I'll make sure she stays safe."

"The nursery," Sheala heard Krondal roar.

Four of the men who'd been guarding him rolled, zigzagged across the floor, and disappeared out the door through which the queen and king had entered earlier.

Almost immediately, Marljas pushed himself off her.

More arrows whirred. Most flew towards the dais. One of the priestess-warriors fell. Sheala ducked as an arrow flew past her head as she spun around on her knees. Marljas cursed as blood trickled from his arm.

"Marljas!"

"It's only a scratch!" Another arrow whizzed by. "By all that's holy, Sheala, get behind that table. Now!" he snarled as he jumped up on the dais to help defend the queen and king.

Rising to her hands and knees, she crawled towards the barricade.

Off to her left, a man fell, an arrow through his thigh. Cursing, he broke off the end, grabbed the part sticking out the back of his leg, and pulled it through.

Blood spurted.

Ripping a long strip of cloth from her hem as she ran, a woman sprinted from behind the table where the queen's sister had sat and knelt next to him.

Changing direction, Sheala scrambled to her, wadded up the hem of her own gown and pressed it against the bleeding wound. As she kept pressure on it, the other woman tied the strip of cloth above the wound and tightened it.

Slowly, Sheala pulled her hands away.

The wound stopped spurting.

The woman nodded to her. "My thanks, wife of Marljas Drefeson." After the man struggled to his feet, both he and the woman staggered towards safety.

Still crouching on the floor, Sheala looked around. She expected to see people panicking, running in all directions. Some were. Some ran towards the king and queen—to help or hinder, she didn't know. Others stood with unsheathed claws, watching, waiting.

All of the arrows were raining down on and about the royal dais.

"Up there," Ban shouted, "on the balcony. There are at least two dozen."

He and the two Aradabs leaped over the table and stood before the dais in a loose semicircle, deftly sidestepping any arrows that came near them.

Kahn caught one in midair, flipped it, and threw it at the closest archer.

A loud curse told Sheala he'd found his mark.

"Damn it, Sheala, get out of there!" Ban bellowed when he saw her still kneeling on the floor.

She rolled towards the table, but a dagger whizzed past her ear and sprouted in front of her face.

She blinked and looked around.

Kadis crouched next to a table, a satisfied smirk on her face.

"Damn it, Sheala," Ban yelled again. "Get under this." An ornamental shield slid towards her, and she pulled it over her back. An arrow careened off it and slid across the floor. Sheala shivered then awkwardly crawled towards the table.

On the dais, Marljas felt relief surge through his body when Ban slid the shield across the floor to Sheala. Stopping to help the wounded man was honorable but stupid. She could have been killed!

An arrow sliced the air next to his ear and he ducked.

Next to him, Krondal still hovered over his wife. Guards crouched around them.

"Are you both all right?"

"For now, but we need to get those archers off the balcony," he snarled. "And how did they get into the palace in the first place?"

The queen's muffled voice drifted from beneath her husband. "The children. Did the guards make it out?"

"I wouldn't worry too much about them," Marljas muttered. "Brianna's son is with them. That means Feni is there. She will die before anyone gets past her, as will your *Snopard* guards."

"Where is Radris!" Krondal snarled.

"It's a six-day ride by horseback from my father's hold. He didn't fly in with us because he didn't think he had to hurry," Marljas answered. Rising to his knees, he looked over the top of the table in time to see Kahn and Beti reach into the wide belts they wore around their waists. Almost immediately, the four-pronged silver stars that were the favored weapons of Medirian assassins flew into the balcony. Few missed their targets. Archers started to fall, a few over the balcony railing.

Then, with a boom like thunder, the huge double doors at the opposite end of the room crashed open, and a magnificent white stallion thundered into the hall, his trumpeting neigh both demanding and challenging as he galloped towards the king and queen. Leaping onto the dais, he spun around and reared up onto his hind legs.

Surprise flooded Marljas. "A *pholola* stallion!"

"There are no *pholola* stallions on Gattan right now!" the queen snapped.

Arrows flew into the ceiling as archers jerked their aims away from the stallion.

One skidded across his withers.

Red blood rolled down his white shoulders as the stallion trumpeted and reared again.

Up on the balcony, an archer cried with fear and misery as he gaped at the wound he'd caused.

A star thudded into his chest and he fell over the railing.

Another neigh reverberated around the hall.

Sheala jerked her attention back to the other end of the room. On the back of his *pholola* mare, Radris galloped into the hall, lasers drawn. Anyone who stepped into their path was trampled by the mare. Few challenged them, and he concentrated his fire on the remaining archers in the balcony.

One, dressed and masked completely in black, stopped firing and looked around. Most of the other archers were down. He called something to the archer on his right. A shrill whistle pierced the din, and those that were left slipped back through open doors.

He remained, drawing back his bow, aiming directly for Sheala where she crouched next a table.

"No!" Vaulting past the still-rearing stallion, Marljas leaped from the dais and tackled Sheala to the floor, covering her body with his. He looked up.

Instantly, the archer changed his aim and released his arrow. A female scream behind him told everyone he'd found his mark.

"Not the queen, please don't let it be the queen," he

prayed as he rolled over, his wife in his arms.

On the other side of the room, Kadis slumped over a table as she clenched the arrow protruding from her breast.

"Bastard," Marljas hissed. He didn't like Kadis, but she didn't deserve to be murdered.

He rolled back over in time to see the archer topple over the balcony's railing as a silver star implanted in his chest. He landed on the floor with a thud.

Troops began to pour into the hall, weapons drawn.

"The balcony. After them!" Radris shouted as he slid off his mare and leaped onto the dais. "Your Majesties! Are you hurt?"

Some of the troops left. Others stayed, rounding up everyone in the room and herding them together.

On the dais, the *pholola* stallion stepped aside, the guards moved back and Krondal rose to his feet and wiped blood from a small gash on his forehead. Reaching down, he helped his wife rise.

"We're fine, Colonel," she answered as she looked around. Her gaze fell on the stallion and her eyes widened. Nickering, he bowed his head, leaped from the dais and galloped from the hall.

"How many wounded and dead?" she demanded.

"Five wounded here, Your Majesty," the same guard answered. "None of the wounds are life-threatening. But— your *Snopard* guard, Eliha, is dead."

Mattis' snarl reached Sheala where she now stood in Marljas' arms. "I will personally gut the man responsible for this."

"Noooooooooo!"

Everyone whirled.

Jadis was on her knees next to her daughter's body.

"No! No! No!" With each denial, she cut a bloody line across her right arm.

Marljas stepped forward, drawing Sheala with him. "One of the assassins purposely shot her. I witnessed it."

"Which one?" the queen snapped.

Marljas pointed. "Him."

"Get him," she commanded.

Two of the guards leaped from the dais. "He's still alive," one of them shouted when they reached his side.

Mattis' claws slid from their sheaths. "Bring him to me."

Each guard hooked a hand in one of his armpits and dragged him to her. His groan of pain was audible as they dropped him. Blood seeped around the silver star protruding from his chest.

The queen stood at the edge of the dais and looked down. "Get that hood off him."

Blood dripping from her arms, Jadis pushed the guards out of her way. "His blood is mine!" she snarled. Reaching down, she ripped the hood from his head.

Deathly pale, Cadan smiled up at her. "Hello, Mother."

Chapter Twenty-Seven

ဢ

Gasping, Jadis stared at her son. "You!"

Stunned, everyone else remained quiet.

Cadan coughed and blood trickled from his lips. He tried to suck in a breath, coughed and swallowed. His labored breathing was deafening in the now silent hall.

The queen stepped down off the dais and knelt next to him. "Cadan…"

His smile remained on his face. His voice was faint. "It…was…nothing personal…Aunt, but Mother wanted…to be queen." He shifted and gritted his teeth.

"Shut up, you worthless male!" Jadis spat. Claws extended, she bent towards her son.

"Hold her!" Krondal ordered.

Two guards grabbed her arms.

The queen kept her attention on Cadan. "Why Kadis?"

He coughed again. "Mother…only…tolerates me. She always…regretted…I wasn't female. I…couldn't please…her." His voice was weaker. "Kadis was…her angel. I…was tired of…being compared to her. Now, Mother…will suffer."

He closed his eyes.

"Cadan!" Radris snapped in a sharp voice. "Who else was involved in this plot?"

His eyes fluttered open. "Mother, of course… Who else?"

"You lie!" Jadis shrieked as she struggled in the guards' grasps.

"Do I?" His chest fell one last time as his head slid to the side and he stared unseeing at his kneeling queen.

Jadis screamed. Then suddenly, she stopped struggling. "Kadis, my daughter...gone." Moaning, she collapsed in the guards' iron grips. Only they kept her upright.

"Take her to her rooms and lock her in. I want two guards at the door of her apartments and two more at the bedchamber door," the queen ordered. "Are any of the other assassins alive?"

Kahn's voice was flat. "No."

"They're all dead," confirmed Radris as he pulled the hood off the last assassin his men had dragged to the center of the floor. "And they are all Gattan, sons of *Tigre* families."

"*Tigre!*" she spat. "My tribe." Face stern she motioned to Radris. "I want their families brought to the palace, if they aren't already here, and kept under heavy guard. Have the bodies of their sons tossed into the rooms with them and make sure they all know what happened to them. And use *Leonine* and *Pantra* troops—those you know you can trust."

Radris bowed. "It will be done."

Then she drew herself up to her full height and turned to Kahn. "Without you, many more, including my husband and myself, could have died. We owe you blooddebt."

Crossing his arms over his chest, Kahn grunted and looked around the room. His gaze settled on the *Snopard* warrior-priestesses who guarded the queen. "When they learned I would be journeying to Gattan, both the Patriarch of the Nissians and Matriarch of the Aradabs commanded that I ask for a boon of you. This boon would settle all blooddebt between us, Queen of the Gattan."

She didn't hesitate. "What do you ask?"

"That you grant permission for *Snopard* elders to travel to Mediria to meet with the Patriarch and Matriarch."

Mattis blinked. "I cannot command them," she admitted.

Kahn nodded. "The Patriarch and Matriarch assured me they would come."

"How can you be so sure?"

Kahn bowed again. "It is not for one such as I to question the commands of the Patriarch and Matriarch."

Still a bit nonplused, the queen nodded. "Very well, if they wish to go to Mediria, I'll have one of my fastest ships take them. Blooddebt will be satisfied."

Kahn and Beti bowed.

The queen shook her head then gazed around the shambles that had once been her reception hall. Medics were caring for wounded Gattan. A small group of *Tigre* was still guarded.

"Would you like me to question them, my love?" Krondal asked with a gleam in his eye.

A slow smile meandered across her lips. "I would like that very much." She motioned to the guards. "Take them away."

Amid a chorus of protests, the guards herded everyone but those who were wounded and Teena's family from the room.

As soon as arrows started flying, the guards of both the Drakian and Varcian ambassadors had hustled them from the hall.

The Medirian ambassador, however, had remained. Smiling, Jessilindra nodded her head to the queen. "I've said all along you know how to throw a party, Your Majesty. With your permission, my people and I shall retire."

"Of course, Jessilindra. Please, inform me of anything you need." When the Medirians were halfway across the room, she muttered to those around her, "Not a hair out of place. Not a wrinkle in any of their clothing. Not a drop of blood." She looked at one of her guards. "How many dead attackers lay where they were standing?"

"Five," he answered.

"Only Medirian assassins can kill with so little effort," she hissed.

"You don't expect Uncle Findal to send his youngest sister to Gattan without protection, do you?" Ban asked dryly.

An eyebrow cocked, the queen turned to face him. "Not a scratch on you, either."

Shrugging, he grinned. "I had two Aradabs guarding me."

A guard hurried across the room and bowed. "The children are safe. From what we can determine, this was the only attack."

"Kill us first, then the children," the queen muttered. She nodded towards Cadan's body. "Get this carrion out of here." She looked over at her niece and sighed. "Have Kadis' body carried to her rooms and prepared for burial. She'll be interred in the family vault. Allow Jadis to see her, but don't let her interfere with funeral preparations." She looked once more at her nephew's body. "Put him in an unmarked grave as he is."

Radris' mare whinnied. Nostrils flaring, she gazed at the open doors.

More whinnies answered hers.

Still in Marljas' arms, Sheala followed the mare's gaze.

Pacing sedately through the huge door were nine more white mares. Each carried a white-haired *Snopard* on her back.

Marljas' arms tightened around Sheala. "All *nine* elders!"

Sheala glanced at the queen. She'd drawn herself up to her full height. Consternation was evident on her brow.

When the mares halted before her in a loose semicircle, the queen bowed to the elderly man who sat on the back of the mare directly in front of her. "Elders. Be welcome."

"He's male!" Sheala gasped. "The queen of Gattan is bowing to a man?"

Marljas clapped his hand over her mouth.

Shifting his gaze, the old man smiled at Sheala, then winked.

The queen couldn't keep the confusion from her voice. "Elders, as always, you are most welcome, but why have you come?"

The leader of the group looked around the shambles that was the reception hall. Broken dishes and bent cutlery littered the floor. Here and there, a wounded Gattan was still being tended.

The body of the dead warrior-priestess lay off to the side.

"Our seers told us you would have need of us." He looked directly at her. "We are the keeper of the law. It is for us to judge guilt and innocence. We shall question the families of the dead in three days' time. Keep them guarded until then. Bury their sons with your nephew, in one grave. The *Snopards* will mark it."

Behind her, Sheala heard Krondal mutter a curse.

The elder glanced over the queen's shoulder at him. "Unrest and dissatisfaction would come from your questioning, Krondal of the *Leonine*. And," he added with a twinkle in his eye, "they fear us far more than they fear you." He nodded to the queen. "We will camp outside the city. Send word if you have need of us before we come for your prisoners."

All nine mares wheeled smoothly and loped from the room.

No sooner had they disappeared out the door, than a rumpled *Tigre* woman stepped before the queen.

Mattis sighed. "What is it, Aunt?"

The older woman crossed her arms over her chest and turned to Sheala. "I owe blooddebt to the wife of Marljas Drefeson. Without thought for her own safety, she aided me as I bound my husband's wound. I wish to settle the amount."

The queen shook her head. "It can wait."

The woman frowned. "Settling a blooddebt is serious business, Niece."

The queen's temper flared. "My own nephew just tried to murder me, Aunt. Settling your blooddebt can wait a few days. Now, go care for your husband."

Stiffly, the woman curtsied, spun about, and stomped from the room.

Mattis sagged against her husband. "Krondal, get me out of here before some other poor fool comes to me with something stupid. I'm likely to declare bloodfeud myself."

Chuckling, he swept her up into his arms. Followed by their guards, he carried his wife from the room.

Sheala looked around the room. What a mess.

At her side, her mother-in-law still stood grasping one of her hairpins in each hand. Blood dried on both of them. Her husband stood behind her, unwounded but disheveled.

Sheala looked down at her dress. Dried blood was caked on the hem. A large ribbon of fabric trailed off to her left side. She raked her fingers back through her hair and dislodged a piece of fruit. She leaned back against Marljas' broad chest. "I think I'd like to go back to our rooms now, too."

* * * * *

"There, all finished. The cut was shallow enough, but it was a Gattan arrow. You will have a scar, though it won't be too obvious against your white skin."

Picking up his shirt, Bjin nodded to Jessilindra. "Thank you."

She stared at him. "You looked exactly like a *pholola*. Nobody doubted you were really a horse."

Bjin grimaced as his shirt settled on the jagged wound that stretched from one shoulder blade to the other. "Anyone observant enough would have seen I wasn't big enough—and I have blue eyes."

"Everyone was too busy ducking arrows to look that closely." She pursed her lips. "Why did you do it?"

"Last year, our eldest seer had a vision in which the Gattan queen was assassinated. War erupted and spread throughout the galaxy. I was sent here to prevent that assassination. All Gattan would rather commit suicide than hurt a *pholola*. By morphing into one and placing myself in front of the queen and king, I protected them. Also, everyone who saw me cannot deny that the *pholola* support Mattis' rule. Very, very few will now conspire against her."

Jessilindra snorted. "You could have been killed."

Smiling sadly, Bjin nodded once. "Since my wife died, death would be welcome to me. But my planet's elders believe the Creator still has uses for me. After today, I believe they may be correct." He bowed formally. "May the blessing of the Creator bring you happy dreams." After one last nod, he left the room.

Jessilindra glanced over to the woman holding the basin of bloody water. "You will not tell anyone else Deslossians are metamorphs."

The assassin assigned to be Jessilindra's personal bodyguard bowed her head. "Of course, Princess."

* * * * *

The door creaked open slowly. The musty odors of a room long sealed combined with unwashed bodies wafted out.

"Where have you been?" a young *Tigre* hissed. "We've been here for two days with no food and only a little water."

The hooded Gattan stepped into the room. "I was making arrangements to get you off the planet. There are troops everywhere and all transports are being searched."

Four other men stepped through the doorway.

"Varcian pirates!" snarled the first man who'd spoken.

"Who else do you think can get you off Gattan? Or would you rather turn yourselves in to the queen's guards? The *Snopard* elders are here too."

The five young *Tigres* stopped muttering. The scent of fear permeated the air. "What do we have to do?" the youngest asked.

"Gladic here will hide you in a secret compartment of his ship and take you to a safe house on another planet. From there, you'll be able to contact your families for whatever help they can get to you."

"We must go," another stated. "If we stay, we'll be executed—and our families will suffer huge blooddebts."

Mutters of agreement circled the room, and the five *Tigres* followed the pirates out.

The pirate called Gladic remained behind.

The hooded Gattan smiled. "Take them to the asteroid belt in the Darlin quadrant. Your people are always looking for more slaves for the borium mines."

The pirate snorted. "They won't last a month."

White teeth flashed inside the Gattan's hood. "Do you care?"

Laughing, Gladic followed his men.

The Gattan waited a few minutes left. Walking steadily but not quickly enough to cause undue notice, he navigated through back alleys and narrow streets until he reached the tavern where he had a room.

Pausing long enough to make sure the traps he'd set for intruders hadn't been disturbed, he slipped through the door and bolted it behind him.

"Hello, Hathnic."

Whirling, his hand dipped into his belt. A silver star whirled across the room. It thunked into the wall. The lights flashed on.

Four feet to the right of the star, Ban leaned against the wall, arms folded across his chest.

Hathnic shrugged out of his hood and cape and tossed it over the back of a chair. "Bandalardrac Hardan. Your fortunes have improved lately. I hear the Alalakans have taken you back into the family. Back on hedonistic Drakan. All your dreams have been fulfilled."

Ban nodded. "You seem to have come down in the world. This — luxury — is not what you're used to."

His eyes never left Ban's face. "Actually, it's much like the room I lived in the first nine years of my life."

"You have forsworn your oaths."

The other man shrugged. "Not my oaths. My life of poverty."

"Assassins don't live in poverty."

"They do not live like Medirian princes, either."

Shaking his head, Ban straightened. "You always were too greedy. How much did you charge Jadis to assassinate her sister?"

"Enough," Hathnic said as he stepped to his right. "Why did Kavlalardrac send you? I can't believe he wants you dead like the others he sent after me. I always defeated you when we sparred."

Ban smiled. "Times change."

"There's not an assassin who can defeat me, not even the Monarch's Assassin."

Ban's smile slid into a grin.

Hathnic stopped moving. "You?"

Ban uncrossed his arms. Two stars flew towards Hathnic.

He fell to the floor and rolled left to his feet.

"Is that the best you can do, Monarch's Assassin?"

His voice dripped with contempt.

"Good disguise," Ban commented as he shifted his weight to the balls of his feet. "If one doesn't look closely, you easily pass for a *Tigre*." A knife slid out of his sleeve.

Hathnic grinned as he stepped to the left again, keeping Ban in front of him. "Another stupid throw, Bandalardrac.

Your style is so obvious to one with my skills. And this is an excellent disguise. No one thinks I am anything other than Gattan."

"I do," Kahn said as he stepped from the shadows and slipped a cord around Hathnic's neck. He died almost instantly. The rogue's body fell to the floor.

Kahn looked at Ban. "You talk too much."

Ban chuckled. "And you, my friend, don't talk enough." He stared at the body. "Hathnic was very skilled. He should have realized there was a third person in the room."

"He was always overconfident," Kahn answered in a flat voice. "Besides, assassins always work alone. He never expected two of us."

Hands on his hips, Ban stared at the body. "A fatal error on his part, to think we wouldn't break with tradition." Bending down, he searched the body. "Nothing. If someone other than Jadis was involved, we won't find out from him."

"Kavlalardrac will be disappointed but not surprised. We'll have to find how the pirates are linked to Gattan some other way."

Ban wiped his hands on the dead man's shirt. "Our main priority was to neutralize Hathnic. Mediria can't afford to have rogue assassins wandering about the galaxy."

Kahn's grunt was affirmative. He added, "What will we do with the body?"

"The river next to the city is deep." The gills on the side of Ban's neck fluttered. "I am half Medirian, you know. Breathing underwater is easy enough, and it's a nice night for a swim, don't you think?"

* * * * *

Arm in arm, Sheala and Sosha walked to Sheala's suite. "Do you have everything packed?" Sheala asked.

Sosha nodded.

"Are you sure you want to come with us? The queen gave you that estate. You're the daughter of a landed family, now. Didn't your mother say something about finding you a husband?"

Sosha smiled a sad smile. "Even with the estate, no man will want me." She held out her hands. "No man would take a clawless, scarred woman such as I for a mate. No mother would want me for her son."

Sheala sighed. Gattans could be so stubborn! "I still say you're wrong. You need to give the men here a chance."

Sosha's voice was sharp. "No! I have accepted Teena's invitation to stay there. I will return with you to visit Drakan and then go on to visit Brianna's planet, too." Then she smiled. "Or I could go with Ban to Mediria. He says he can't wait to introduce me to his grandmother."

Sheala's laughter echoed around the hallway.

"Has Teena settled the blooddebt the queen's aunt owes you?"

Her laughter changing to a snort, Sheala nodded. "Five breeding mares, all in foal to their herd stallion. What am I supposed to do with ten horses?"

Both were still laughing as they rounded a corner and stopped short.

Radris had Beti pinned against the wall and was kissing her as if there were no tomorrow.

Minutes passed — slowly.

Finally, Beti worked a hand free and slapped him along the side of his head.

He staggered and she slipped free. "You are becoming more devious, Radris. There is hope for you yet." Nodding to Sheala and Sosha, she disappeared around the corner.

After shaking his head, Radris grinned at the two girls. "I waited until she was finished training with the priestesses. I figured three hours of working with them would slow her reflexes. I was right."

Sosha clamped her hands over her mouth.

Sheala didn't bother to stifle her laughter. When she finally caught her breath and stopped hiccupping, she said, "To satisfy your Gattan—sensibilities—Colonel, Feni is Beti's sister, her older sister. I'm sure she will give you permission to court Beti."

Grinning from ear to ear, Radris bowed. "My thanks, wife of Marljas Drefeson." He followed Beti around the corner.

Sheala blew her hair up off her forehead. "Why do you Gattan have to be so formal! Why can't everyone just call me Sheala?"

Chuckling, Sosha linked her arm through Sheala's again. "Only close family and friends may call you Sheala. Ask Deni and Teena to tell everyone your mother's name. Then at least, you'll be Sheala Xdanasdotir."

Still grumbling, Sheala sauntered into her suite with Sosha. She was barely inside the door when Marljas appeared out of the bedroom, lifted her, and pinned her against the wall.

"You *will* control your Drakian impulses in public!"

Laughing, Sosha retreated the way she had come, closing the door behind her.

"I didn't do anything!"

"Silence, Wife! Today, I had five separate men stop me and ask if they could watch when you make love to me. Since the day in the reception room when you offered to let Kadis watch, they wondered if the invitation was open to everyone. What's more, my mother has informed me that at least six of the older women have asked her the same thing."

Flat against the wall, her feet dangling a good foot above the ground, Sheala stared into her husband's face and began to giggle. "Do you think we should?"

His roar reverberated around the room. "No! This is not Drakan. My wife will not make love to me while other men or women are watching! And when we are on Drakan, we will not make love with others watching, nor will you make love with any other man." He stared into her eyes. "Or woman," he added, obviously as an afterthought. "You may be Drakian, but you are mated to a Gattan and will remain faithful to me."

Sheala tilted her head.

He continued to glare at her.

Behind the anger glittering in his golden eyes, she spied something else—fear. Of what? Realization dawned. She was Drakian and many Drakians were promiscuous after marriage. "Oh my love," she whispered as she lifted her hands and cupped his face. "You fascinated me from the first day I first saw you standing half naked in my mother's house. Yes, I learned about sex from instructors, but you—you're the one who introduced me to love. You're the only one I completely trust with my body—and soul. I love you, Marljas. I will never want anyone else."

"Sheala," he sighed as he pulled her into his arms, "my wife." He covered her mouth with his.

Sheala answered his kiss by sucking his tongue into her mouth. She lifted her legs and wrapped them around his waist.

She kissed him until she had no breath left, then pulled her mouth from his.

Gasping for breath, he rested his forehead against hers.

Sliding her hands down his cheeks and neck, she flattened them against his muscular chest and rubbed her nose against his. "So, are we going to make love standing against the wall or are you taking me to bed?"

Shouting with laughter, Marljas tossed her into the air and caught her in his arms. "The wall can wait until next time." Spinning on his heel, he carried her towards the bedroom.

Chuckling, Sheala wrapped her arms around his neck and nuzzled his chest. Loving this Gattan was the smartest thing she'd ever done.

Why an electronic book?

We live in the Information Age—an exciting time in the history of human civilization, in which technology rules supreme and continues to progress in leaps and bounds every minute of every day. For a multitude of reasons, more and more avid literary fans are opting to purchase e-books instead of paper books. The question from those not yet initiated into the world of electronic reading is simply: *Why?*

1. *Price.* An electronic title at Ellora's Cave Publishing and Cerridwen Press runs anywhere from 40% to 75% less than the cover price of the exact same title in paperback format. Why? Basic mathematics and cost. It is less expensive to publish an e-book (no paper and printing, no warehousing and shipping) than it is to publish a paperback, so the savings are passed along to the consumer.

2. *Space.* Running out of room in your house for your books? That is one worry you will never have with electronic books. For a low one-time cost, you can purchase a handheld device specifically designed for e-reading. Many e-readers have large, convenient screens for viewing. Better yet, hundreds of titles can be stored within your new library—on a single microchip. There are a variety of e-readers from different manufacturers. You can also read e-books on your PC or laptop computer. (Please note that Ellora's Cave does not endorse any specific brands.

You can check our websites at www.ellorascave.com or www.cerridwenpress.com for information we make available to new consumers.)

3. *Mobility.* Because your new e-library consists of only a microchip within a small, easily transportable e-reader, your entire cache of books can be taken with you wherever you go.

4. *Personal Viewing Preferences.* Are the words you are currently reading too small? Too large? Too… ANNOYING? Paperback books cannot be modified according to personal preferences, but e-books can.

5. *Instant Gratification.* Is it the middle of the night and all the bookstores near you are closed? Are you tired of waiting days, sometimes weeks, for bookstores to ship the novels you bought? Ellora's Cave Publishing sells instantaneous downloads twenty-four hours a day, seven days a week, every day of the year. Our webstore is never closed. Our e-book delivery system is 100% automated, meaning your order is filled as soon as you pay for it.

Those are a few of the top reasons why electronic books are replacing paperbacks for many avid readers.

As always, Ellora's Cave and Cerridwen Press welcome your questions and comments. We invite you to email us at Comments@ellorascave.com or write to us directly at Ellora's Cave Publishing Inc., 1056 Home Avenue, Akron, OH 44310-3502.

Cerridwen, the Celtic Goddess of wisdom, was the muse who brought inspiration to storytellers and those in the creative arts. Cerridwen Press encompasses the best and most innovative stories in all genres of today's fiction. Visit our site and discover the newest titles by talented authors who still get inspired - much like the ancient storytellers did, once upon a time.

CERRIDWEN PRESS

www.cerridwenpress.com

Discover for yourself why readers can't get enough
of the multiple award-winning publisher

Ellora's Cave.

Whether you prefer e-books or paperbacks,

be sure to visit EC on the web at
www.ellorascave.com

for an erotic reading experience that will leave you
breathless.